PROUD WATERS

Ewart Brookes

PROUD WATERS

THE SHERIDAN
BOOK COMPANY

This edition published in 1995 by
The Sheridan Book Company

Arrow edition 1969
Random House, 20 Vauxhall Bridge Road, London SW1V 2SA

Printed and bound in Great Britain by
Cox & Wyman Ltd, Reading, Berkshire

ISBN 1–85501–710–5

'We found trouble and heaviness: we were even at
death's door.
The waters of the sea had well nigh covered us: the
proud waters had well nigh gone over our soul.'

Hymn of praise and thanksgiving from
Forms of Prayer to be Used at Sea.

Author's Note

This is the story of two ships and two men, minesweeping, an unglamorous job at its best, requiring, as one character states, 'the mentality of an intelligent ploughman.'

And it is fiction.

Some of the details, by the very nature of the story, inevitably have to be biographical, but I have not consciously drawn a picture of any senior officer under whom I served. I remember several of them with affection and deep respect, and possibly their unfailing patience and tolerance with the liberties we Wavy Navy officers took with naval usages and traditions have helped me to draw some characters with fairly certain lines.

They, at least, knew minesweeping was not, as one Senior Officer remarked to me at a dinner recently, 'a nice quiet job, out in the morning, back for tea and every night in your cart.'

Figures can be made to prove anything. If they help me to prove that it was anything but a 'nice quiet job' I will rest content, so let the figures speak.

At the outbreak of war Great Britain had in service 76 minesweeping ships, of which 40 were converted trawlers.

By the end of the war there were 1,464 minesweepers. Of their officer total 63 per cent were R.N.V.R., 34 per cent were R.N.R., and 3 per cent R.N. So minesweeping was largely a job for 'Temporary Actings' and 'Hostilities Only'.

A much larger and more factual book than this should be written on the work they did.

Right round these islands was an unbroken track, the Swept Channel along which shipping moved in convoy. From that main channel branched innumerable other tracks leading to every port in the country. ALL THOSE TRACKS HAD TO BE SWEPT EVERY DAY, not only to find mines, but, as the late King George VI once remarked: 'You have to keep on sweeping, even if there are no mines, to find that out.'

Thoughout 1940–41–42 the enemy kept up his mining offensive in the channels and at port entrances with the dual object of sinking ships and closing the ports, and it has been estimated that one in three of German aircraft operating over this country in that period was minelaying. On several occasions mines were laid simultaneously from the Firth of Forth round the coast, south about, and north to the Clyde. Look at a map and see what that involves.

Tyne, Humber, Thames, Dover Straits, Portsmouth, Southampton, Solent, Bristol Channel, Mersey, Liverpool Bay, Belfast, Clyde and one or two other smaller areas temporarily useless . . . until chunky little ships sailed on the order: 'Sweepers will sail 0500 hours and will sweep. . . .'

No flamboyant, blood-stirring 'to-the-last-man' battle call. Just '. . . and will sweep . . .' Dogmatic and definite.

Their success can be measured by the counter-offensive the Germans mounted in 1943. They adjusted the settings of their magnetic and acoustic mines, so that they exploded under the small sweepers. In 1943, of 67 ships lost by mines 29 were minesweepers.

One detailed example will serve. Dover's small minesweeping force, working in atrocious weather, laboriously cleared a field reaching from the harbour mouth to beyond Folkestone. Scarcely had the last mine been cleared when a combined air and E-boat attack laid another and larger field from Folkestone to Dungeness and two important convoys were scheduled to sail through in a few hours.

8

Working under Lieutenant-Commander Richard Hawes, R.N.V.R., in *Waterfly* (he died when she was blown up later) the sweepers went into action, located the approximate limits of the field—WORKING IN DARKNESS—cut a vital gap through it in a few hours and guarded the gap as the dim shapes of the convoys steamed through, in safety. It took nine nights of hard work, the loss of two ships and valuable men before that field was cleared. The Germans never succeeded in filling that hole again.

The Germans laid 126,000 mines in European waters; sweeping them cost us 327 minesweepers, 4,600 men and officers.

Not bad for a 'nice quiet job'.

January 1953

1

Lieutenant William Haley, R.N.V.R., threw his brass dividers on to the chart table, stubbed out a cigarette and turned to follow the messenger.

Probably the Old Man wanted to discuss routeing, or some navigational point involved in his report. As Haley's hand sought the handrail he subconsciously absorbed the peacefulness of the afternoon. The full heat of the sun had gone but it was still strong enough to wrap the shore in a fine haze. Around him was the atmosphere of quiet but poised readiness. From below decks there came a faint hum which transmuted itself into an even fainter tremble which could be felt through the decks. H.M. destroyer *Culver*, a somewhat aged lady, *circa* 1922, brought out from retirement, was momentarily moored to a buoy in Dover Harbour after four of the busiest days in her not uneventful life.

For four days, and large parts of a similar number of nights, she had been engaged in that glorious failure elevated to the status of an epic—the Dunkirk evacuation. Time stood still, incidents had merged one into the other: decks thronged with dead-weary soldiers; long—far too long—periods in and around the flame-framed French port; as the soldiers clambered on board, hideously screaming Stukas bringing death at the crescendo moment of their howl; the incessant chatter of the multiple pom-pom and the ear-cracking bark of the 4-inch anti-aircraft gun; these had all merged into an exhausting whole which was framed in an indescribable feeling of exhaustion.

Haley had lost accurate count of the number of trips they had done to and from Dunkirk. Eight? Ten? Maybe more. From that feeling of exhaustion he had to drag out a shredded remnant of energy sufficient to enable him to correct charts according to latest signals . . . God, the number of wrecks he had inserted! Must be dozens. Then: 'The Commanding Officer would like to see you in his room, sir.'

Haley tapped the door and entered.

Commander Payne, R. N., *Culver's* Commanding Officer, was sprawled, legs wide apart, in a deep, worn leather chair. Haley had seen him an hour ago on the bridge, unshaven, eyes red-rimmed, shoulders hunched, apparently on his last legs after an almost unbroken spell on the bridge of three days and nights, together with the acute tension of being under fire some of the time.

Now, shaven, bathed and wearing feet-easing slippers, an open-necked shirt, a pair of none-too-clean flannel trousers, and a huge pipe hanging contentedly from the corner of his mouth, he looked as if weariness was beyond the next horizon.

'Come in, Haley. Sit down. Cigarette?'

Haley accepted a seat on a long settee which ran two-thirds the length of the Day Room.

Commander Payne lifted a bunch of signal sheets from his lap, touched them with his pipe-stem, and went on: 'We've got six hours' rest, then back to Harwich. Apparently the job is finished over there.' He looked up at Haley with a faint smile playing round his mouth. 'Six hours of sleep— imagine it! I expect you can do with some.'

'Yes, sir. It seems years since I closed my eyes.'

'Hm, hm. Charts all touched up and beautiful?'

'I don't know about the "beautiful", sir. I've almost completed the corrections on the "immediate use" charts. Wrecks all over the show, buoys moved, swept channels shifted. But I've nearly finished.'

12

And why the social invitation? Haley pondered. It was not Payne's habit to invite a junior officer down for a cigarette and a sit down, especially when he knew that officer was busy.

'I'm afraid a whole lot of things are going to be altered now we have lost . . .' Payne completed the sentence with a faint jerk of his head, presuming France to be in that direction. 'My grandmother on the maternal side, who scrubs the front step at the Admiralty, thinks things are going to be tough round the coast now.'

Haley smiled. He had heard on previous occasions of the mythical maternal grandmother behind whose identity Payne would elaborate some extremely shrewd observations, sometimes tinged with almost uncanny prophecy.

'She says that with half the Northern French ports in German hands, plus their airfields, it will give scope to the Hun's inborn sense of naughtiness. Convoying will be tough —aircraft, submarines, motor torpedo-boats . . . all operating from their doorsteps, so to speak.'

Haley nodded as he visualised the possibilities.

'Minelaying, too. They will be able to step up the rate of minelaying to an alarming degree,' Payne continued. He rested the weight of his pipe-stem on a signal, flicked the sheet of paper once, then said levelly: 'You've done a mine-sweeping course, haven't you?'

'Yes, sir, before the war started. It was a sort of holiday. Two weeks, on pay, working from Plymouth on a grubby little trawler. Out after breakfast and back for tea.'

Payne chewed his bottom lip for a moment, settled his shoulders comfortably in the chair. 'The Navy is going to expand to enormous proportions before this war is over. Sub-lieutenants will eventually get to command, and,' he paused a moment, 'so will R.N.V.R. officers of any ability.'

Haley searched that innocuous statement for a moment, then his train of thought was interrupted as Payne went on :

'We Commanding Officers have been asked to report on

13

R.N.V.R. officers in our commands with just that'—he pointed with his pipe-stem—'just that in view.'

Haley offered a non-committal 'Yes, sir.'

'Read that.' Payne sat up with a jerk and handed Haley a single sheet of signal pad. Haley read:

'From SL 2 to Adl Cmdg Destroyers, Harwich, Captain D 40, Commanding Officer *Culver* (R) M/S Training Base. Lieutenant Wm Haley RNVR will report forthwith to M/S Training Base, South Queensferry, for refresher course on M/S, subsequently to HMS *Palisade* additional to command M/S trawler.'

'I don't understand, sir, I don't want . . .'

Payne's face hardened slightly. 'A lot of us don't want to do the things we are doing. I wanted Fleet Air Arm. I've got destroyers. You have trained for minesweeping. You have qualities which, I think, will fit you for command of a small ship as a minesweeper . . .'—he smiled momentarily —'to begin with, at least. And that's all there is to it.'

'But on a grubby little trawler, sir. I . . .'

'It will be up to you to see that she ceases to be grubby, in double-quick time, Haley.' Payne stood up and leaned against the ledge below a port-hole.

'Minesweeping is going to be no soft job. Without it nothing will move, either in and out of port, or round the coast. There will be losses . . . but when a convoy moves, when a ship comes out of harbour, it will do so because'— he turned back to Haley—'because some of your "grubby little trawlers" will have first done their jobs.'

Haley stood up. He felt a surge of resentment. Why could they not have left him alone? As far as it was possible to enjoy his duties—he did enjoy his job as Navigating Officer and, so far as he knew, did it efficiently.

Payne watched him closely for a moment, then pursued

14

his theme. 'Even greyhounds of the seas, like destroyers, will be immobilised unless somebody clears the mines . . and if they don't, or can't, because there is not enough of them, then . . . it will be just too bad.'

The interview was at an end and Haley stood up, still holding the signal. Payne took it and read it again.

'You will return to Harwich with us, where your relief is waiting for you, then hey ho for the Firth of Forth for you. *Palisade?*' He pondered for a moment. 'Why, you will be just round the corner from here. We'll see a lot of you as we go on our lawful occasions. Don't be careless and miss one or two, will you?'

As Haley moved towards the door Payne picked up another signal. 'Like to see this?' he said.

'From Vice Admiral Dover to *Culver* [it read]. Sail 2200 hrs for Harwich. Operation Dynamo is now completed. Matthew 25, verse 23 applies.'

'It's the one about the Parables, you know. The servants to whom were given talents. That verse is: "Well done, thou good and faithful servant." I've never felt much sympathy for the bloke who buried his because he thought it was of little value. Have you?'

Haley felt Payne's ice-blue eyes boring into his. 'I've never given it . . . no, sir,' he amended quickly.

Payne's arm dropped lightly over his shoulder for a moment. 'Good man! Tell Number One I would like to see him—if he is awake, that is.'

In the wardroom the feeling of relaxed peace was accentuated. Propped in a corner, mouth slightly open, a middle-aged Warrant Gunner snored softly, catching up on arrears of sleep. From the bathroom outside came sounds of somebody singing discordantly, 'Roll out the barrel, umpity um tum . . . barrel of fun.' That was the Engineer Lieutenant. Engrossed by copies of *Men Only*, from which they were cutting extremely daring art studies of the opposite sex, were a sub-lieutenant, R.N.R., and a midshipman, R.N.R.— Benson. The mid's tongue was slowly following the scissors as he trimmed carefully. As he finished he leaned back.

'Look at those blue eyes and fair hair. Luverly grub. Her, a week-end leave and ten quid, and I wouldn't mind calling Adolf my uncle.'

The Sub-lieutenant looked up. 'Oh, Pilot, glad you came. You can buy me a drink.' He raised his voice. 'Steward.' The Warrant Gunner stirred slightly. 'Count me in. Mine's a pink,' he muttered drowsily.

'I'll buy you all a drink,' Haley said. 'It will be very nearly the last.'

'You going to be shot at dawn?' queried the midshipman. 'Wonder if the editor would forward a letter to her from a lonely sailor?'—shifting his tack to the picture in front of him.

'I'm going on a course—minesweeping—when we get back to Harwich.'

The others absorbed this in silence. The steward served the drinks, then the Sub-lieutenant asked: 'And then?'

'Command of a minesweeping trawler.'

'Command!' the Sub whistled. 'What pull have you got?'

'You can have it, for my part.'

Haley had lived in comparative intimacy inside this steel-walled box with the men in the wardroom for more than nine months, yet he knew that in a couple of weeks he would be, 'Haley, remember? That R.N.V.R. Pilot we had,' until time blotted all but the haziest memories of him.

'Good luck, old chap. When we meet we'll send you a respectful signal.'

A week later Haley casually picked up a morning news-paper from the table of the ante-room of the Officers' Quarters at the Minesweeping Training Base lying in the shadow of the spidery Forth Bridge. It wanted a few

16

minutes to breakfast but something caught his eye and all thoughts of food departed.

In a flash he absorbed the headlines and flew on to read what lay beneath.

NAVAL LOSS

Destroyer 'Culver' Mined: Casualties

The Admiralty regrets to announce the loss of the destroyer H.M.S. *Culver,* Commanding Officer, Commander R. G. L. Payne, R.N., in the North Sea through enemy action. There were some casualties. It is believed *Culver* was mined.

Just that; the barest of bare details. Haley read it two or three times. Finally it broke through his façade of disbelief. *Culver* was gone. 'There were some casualties.' He slowly read the last line in the comparatively insignificant story tucked away at the bottom of a page: 'The next of kin have been advised.'

Bill Haley let the paper slide through his fingers. Then got up, went to his room and sat on his bed for a time.

For a while he was unable to take it in. *Culver* gone. The C.O., Number One, Benson's nudes . . . a whole series of disconnected pictures flitted rapidly through his mind, eventually slowing down until he focused them sharply on two points.

She had been mined. When?

He knew the Admiralty practice of delaying announcements for a few days so that the next of kin could receive thse bald telegrams before reading the news in the newspapers, and also for some obscure security reasons.

He worked it out. She must have got it within a day or so of his departure.

There came a sharp knock at the door and a Lieutenant, R.N.R., poked his head round.

'Come on, cock, breakfast. We're due on board in fifteen minutes. What's up? Binge last night? Sleep in, or something?'

Bill shrugged, then stood up and reached for his hat.

'I don't want any. I've just read that . . . that my old ship, the *Culver,* was sunk by a mine.' His tone was flat, invited no comment.

'That's tough. That's the way it goes. But your bloody luck was in, wasn't it? Did she lose many?'

'I don't know. There's just a bit in the paper this morning.' Bill made his way wearily through the door. 'I wonder if I can find out more.'

'We'll ask Staff here. C'mon, we've just got time.'

A few minutes later a sympathetic Lieutenant-Commander R.N.R. of the training staff promised Bill that he would contact a pal at the Admiralty and would find out all he could.

'I'll have it all laid on by the time you are back this evening. What's her name again? *Culver*? Leave it to me. Mined, was she? That's one we didn't sweep up in time.'

He looked at Bill shrewdly.

'This will make it sort of personal, won't it, Haley?'

At that moment Bill realised the first simple lesson of minesweeping. Every mine swept is a ship less blown up. Pursue the lesson a stage further and every channel swept and searched means a greater degree of safety for every ship which sails along it.

The rest of the day, out in the Firth of Forth Bill, listening to lectures by Instructor Officers, watched sweeps going in and out as if he was listening to some idle chatter and watching movements of people in whom he had no interest.

Try as he might his mind kept slipping back to the *Culver*. Was it night-time? Who was on the bridge? What happened? And after each question he tried to visualise the scene.

'. . . we don't know an awful lot about this latest bit of frightfulness. It is set very fine, and from all reports has a nasty habit of going off right under the bridge.'

From a long way off Bill's attention was focused on the speaker, a Lieutenant, R.N.V.R., who had the green piping of the special branch between his two wavy gold rings.

'So far as we know it is still a magnetic job, but our magnetic sweeps don't seem to have complete control . . .' The words grew clearer, nearer, and Bill concentrated. 'That is why it is so important that every scrap of information about any mine blown up MUST—I repeat MUST—be noted and sent to D.M.S.'

The young officer leaned against the rail of the trawler, crossed his legs and put his hands in his monkey-jacket pocket with the thumbs outside.

'Sooner or later we will recover one and get the answer, and when we get the answer . . .'

'We've got the answer,' said a Sub-lieutenant brightly, amid laughter.

The Lieutenant eyed him soberly for a moment then said:

'Where are your next of kin?—the Zoo? We'll send 'em a nut with the telegram. Now,' his voice changed, 'at this moment every port round the East and South coast is one hell of a gamble. Ships go in and out, but . . .' he lit a cigarette, flicked the match over the side into the glassy water . . . 'quite a lot succeed in doing neither. Far too many. Which is why we are putting pressure on you fellows to do this course in a week instead of the usual sixteen days.'

The bright young Sub-lieutenant asked with deceiving innocence: 'What happens to the minesweepers which go in . . . and . . . out?' He did a weaving motion with his hand.

The Instructor looked at him briefly, drew heavily on his cigarette, exhaled, then replied:

'Some go,' he weaved with his hand; 'but others go . . .' he described an unmistakable motion upwards with the palms of both hands turned up. Before anybody could add anything he went on: 'Tyne lost four, Humber eleven, Yarmouth and Lowestoft ten between them, another dozen in

19

the Thames, and Dover lost five . . .'

An elderly R.N.R. Lieutenant with a small array of ribbons across his chest asked flatly: 'Since the war started?'

The Instructor shook his head. 'Since Dunkirk. The Hun is stepping it up.'

Another officer inquired: 'When you say lost, you mean . . .?' He repeated the palm upwards gesture.

'Some . . . a few damaged, but all out of play. Trawlers are not built for withstanding explosions either under the stern or the bridge.'

The Instructor threw his cigarette away.

'All of you blokes are going to command or as Jimmys on minesweeping trawlers. It is no longer a haphazard game first cousin to trawling, like it was in the last war, or even in the beginning of this war. It is precision work with fifty yards being the difference between you blowing up a mine in safety, and the mine blowing you up.'

The young Sub-lieutenant broke the ensuing silence with a bleak comment: 'And I gave up a refined, quiet job on an armed merchant cruiser for this.' He looked at the Instructor then raised a chuckle. 'I'll take the nut now, if I may.'

From then onwards Bill found himself taking a more technical interest in the talks and in the practical sweeping that made up the remainder of the day. He found that even in the comparatively small tideway of the Forth it required neat navigation to take the trawler all along the theoretical channel laid out for instruction.

'Fifty yards means the difference between blowing it up and being blown up,' a voice said in his ear as he completed a run in command. 'Nice going, Haley. But for that last alteration you might have escaped, but the ship astern would have bought it.' Bill turned to find a Lieutenant-Commander standing behind him. He was the Senior Instructor. 'Does this mean anything to you? It was signalled to us from Inch Keith.'

It was from the Staff Officer ashore. Bill read it. And knew.

The Commanding Officer, First Lieutenant and Benson the midshipman, were lost; others picked up, but some were wounded. Total loss of lives, forty-eight.

'Thanks, yes. It's about *Culver*, my last ship. She—she ...'

'I know. I saw it in the paper this morning,' the officer returned gently. 'Hard luck.'

He changed his tone after letting his hand rest on Bill's shoulder for a moment. 'Now, I want a run across tide. It's a three-mile channel, maximum six cables wide, and the drill is: aircraft were suspected of laying mines down it last night.'

For the next few hours Bill was too busy to allow the dull ache somewhere in his chest to become too obvious, and it was only when reaching for his cigarettes that he found the crumpled signal and remembered again.

'If some silly swine had been more careful with that fifty yards *Culver* would have ... Payne, Mid, Number One, all of those forty-eight might have been alive ... just that few yards.'

William Haley, Lieutenant R.N.V.R., had learned the first hard lesson of minesweeping.

2

Haley dropped his magazine and sat up in his corner seat as the train steamed slowly out of a cutting and gave him a view of the sea.

From one window he had rolling green fields with here and there darker patches of wood with an occasional cluster of farm-houses and their attendant buildings. From the other he could see the lazy rolling surf only a couple of hundred yards from the railway line.

The sea was like glass. Above it the blue sky was flecked with occasional white cloud. Four or five miles out, their outlines softened slightly by the haze, four trawlers steamed in line ahead.

'Nice station keeping,' Haley reflected professionally, then his mouth tightened as a plume of water climbed slowly upwards astern of the second trawler.

It brought back to him with some force the job he might be doing in a couple of days.

He stood up as the train crawled past a few low sand dunes which partially blocked his view of the sea, and his eyes were still on the trawlers when the train swung away from the sea front, turned inwards through rows of houses and clanked to a stop in a station.

The station was strangely deserted as he climbed from his compartment. With the exception of two seamen he could see no other passengers alighting. As soon as the seamen were out of the train they ducked swiftly through an opening marked 'Way Out'. Beneath the direction was a newer white-painted stencil sign which read, 'To the Shelter.'

Haley started to make his way towards the doorway when a porter came to meet him.

'Two cases in the van and this,' Haley said, indicating a smaller case which had travelled in the compartment. Then he noticed that the porter was wearing a tin hat well down over his eyes.

He watched the porter shuffle towards an upturned barrow, push it alongside the van and climb inside.

As he waited Haley became conscious of a feeling of tension which he could not quite pin-point. It was a composite of lack of sounds of traffic, lack of voices; generally missing was that subdued hum one could always hear even in a small town on a hot afternoon.

Threaded through the silence came the thin snarl of aircraft flying high, and this was punctuated by a series of sharp barks from anti-aircraft guns. Bill tried to locate the aeroplane but failed until there came a series of woolly plops high up in the blue sky. He followed their line and eventually picked up the 'plane.

The reason for the hush was obvious to Bill. There was a raid in progress. And, although he had seen a fair amount of war with its attendant shooting and general nastiness, he felt his heart give a jump and set to on its task of pumping in an extra supply of adrenalin.

It was only his second air-raid ashore; it brought a new and rather frightening emotion.

His first raid had been no further back than the previous afternoon in London. Haley had called at the Admiralty, searching for more details of the loss of the *Culver*, and had met an infuriating character, an exquisite Lieutenant, R.N., long hair curling up at the back, perfectly tailored uniform, with the buttons grouped closely together.

Bill had lost heavily in the engagement. The Lieutenant quite obviously couldn't care less, a point he made in mincing accents at least four times in their short argument, and his parting shot as the visitor went out had twisted Haley's lips into a silent snarl.

'Try writing in, old boy. After all, we have other things to do. There is a war on, y'know.'

Bill walked to the lake in St. James's Park seething and had just realised that he was scowling fiercely at a quiet, inoffensive and attractive Wren when he heard, for the first time, the heart-quailing wail of an air-raid warning.

He looked about him quickly for a moment, then saw that the Wren went on feeding the ducks.

'Don't we dodge for cover?' he asked.

'We don't. Those 'planes are just having a quick look-see. Probably down Tilbury way, or somewhere,' the Wren answered. 'Go away. I don't like you. You are too greedy,' she went on with no change of tone.

'I beg your pardon.'

'Oh, dear. Not you. I mean that fat drake with all the colours. He reminds me of the Commander in my office. All the glamour and colour, and as greedy as a pig.' She looked up at Bill and smiled. 'You looked fierce enough to frighten away ducks, German 'planes and . . . Wrens having an after-noon break,' she continued.

Bill apologised and told her briefly of his losing encounter with the exquisite in the Admiralty.

'They are not all like that. Anyway, you have come right to headquarters. I can find out for you all about . . . what was her name again? *Culver* . . . oh, yes, I know. A destroyer.'

Bill thanked her, then added: 'You have a grandmother at the Admiralty, too, eh?'

That made more explanations necessary about Lieuten-ant-Commander Payne's famous grandmother who scrub-bed the steps.

By this time they were walking towards Horse Guards Parade and the 'All Clear' went as they left the park.

'Told you! Just peeping. They are doing it three or four times a day now,' she said.

The girl found out some details for Bill and joined him for tea. She had to go on duty that night, so he said good-bye and it was only after they had parted that he realised that he had neither asked her name nor given his.

They were, he reflected as he sat in a cinema that evening, just ships that passed. That was naval life. He found that the first pain of the shock of realising that *Culver* and some of her officers were gone was no longer acute. Already, after only a few days, it required a slight mental effort to bring himself to think at any length about them.

'I should put your tin hat on, if I were you.' A husky voice broke in on Bill's reverie and he found the porter standing near him with his luggage on a truck. 'All sorts of things are dropping these days.'

The porter moved towards the entrance, pushing the truck before him.

'Going to the Base? Best thing you can do is to bob into the shelter for a while. The naval car meets the train and will be up soon.'

Bill surrendered his warrant to a collector sitting snugly in a sandbagged office near the doorway and followed the porter across the yard to where a large arrow continued the legend 'Shelter', pointing to the basement of a half-demolished house.

He tipped the porter, who had put his luggage near the steps, and watched him scuttle back into the station no doubt to share the snug sandbagged shelter with the ticket collector.

Leaning against the doorway was a large notice which read, 'Raid in Progress'. Above it, hanging slightly askew, was a roughly printed notice which ran: 'Shelling taking place'.

'What the devil? Shelling?' Haley puzzled.

'They send a wagon to the station to meet the train,' said a quiet voice at his side. 'Even in the raids the Wrens drive up. But I don't think they like the shelling much and wait a bit. Usually lasts about an hour.'

'Shelling?' Haley turned to the seaman standing at his elbow.

'Started in the last few days. I've heard the Jerries have set up a gun the other side which can reach here,' the seaman continued. 'You can't hear them coming. They just arrive and . . .'

His explanation was cut short by the wailing note of the 'All Clear', which, although it climbed steadily and remained on its high key, still sent tingles down Haley's back.

'That's it,' the seaman said, turning to his friend. 'C'mon, Lofty, that's the lot.'

As he spoke a station wagon driven by a Wren swung neatly into the station yard and the girl leaned out of the window.

'Haven't kept you waiting, have I?' she asked with a smile.

'No, ducks, not more'n a minute or two,' the tall seaman replied. 'Bin hiding, have you? Shells got you scared?'

The girl chuckled. 'Anything that goes "boomp" has got me scared to death. But really I went out of my way to give a lift to a woman. She was caught out with a small boy.'

She looked at Haley and treated him to a dazzling smile. 'I came to meet you, sir,' she said. 'Do you mind if these two children ride with us?' She flickered her eyebrows towards the two seamen waiting with confident expectancy.

Bill agreed and the two seamen climbed into the back seats after lifting Bill's luggage in.

'You are Lieutenant Haley and you are the new Commanding Officer for *Arandite*,' the girl said as she straightened up after leaving the station yard. 'She's a nice ship. Nearly as nice as *Pearl*.'

Haley looked sideways at her. Her chin was slightly tilted as she looked over the driving-wheel. She was not more than twenty and her grotesque Girl Guide's hat was perched precariously on a mop of unruly fair hair.

'You are not the Number One? No, of course not,' Bill added regretfully. 'But—purely professional curiosity—why is *Pearl* better than *Arandite*, and how do you know, anyway?'

The girl chuckled.

'Andy—that's my friend— commands *Pearl*.' It seemed sufficient.

The girl slowed down and threaded her way through some debris which overflowed from a pile of rubble, the pathetic remnants of a house. From the ruins faint wisps of smoke ascended. Firemen were playing one jet on the rubble and rescue workers heaved at ragged timbers.

'Nobody in there, so I'm told,' the girl said as she accelerated. 'One of the first shells did that an hour ago.'

Haley digested this information. Shelling brought the war close and intimate, almost like being under rifle fire. A thought occurred to him.

'Do the gentlemen across the way drop these shells on the ships while they are sweeping?'

The Wren's eyes flickered towards him momentarily.

'Not up to now. The town is a bigger target. Andy—my friend—says they are doing quite well with the bombs.' She bit her bottom lip. 'Far too well, I'm afraid.'

Bill pursed his lips.

'An untidy way to run a naval war, don't you think?'

'. . . any war which includes children is untidy—and dirty,' the girl replied quietly.

They pulled up in front of the heavily sandbagged building. Across the front was a sign which read: 'Bay View Hotel. Open to Non-boarders.' The porch, which formed the foundation for the sandbags, was converted into a tunnel with a blanking-off section of bags round which peered a naval sentry.

The two seamen climbed out, thanked the girl and hurried

into a side door above which was the legend, 'R.P.O.'. The sentry, seeing an officer follow them from the car, stepped out and prepared for the ceremonial of a salute.

'I'll back the car in the side,' the girl said. 'I expect you'll be going on board in a few minutes. I'll nip and have a cuppa while you are talking to the Commander.' She looked at Bill with a steadfast gaze for a moment then went on: 'You'll like him. I hope you'll like *Arandite*. She could be a really smart ship.'

This statement of possibility interested Haley. He digested it for a few moments, then decided not to explore it further for the time being.

As he hitched his gas-mask haversack and tin hat round to a comfortable angle in preparation to entering the tunnel he replied: 'I see I am to have much competition with—with *Pearl*, was it?—in the future. Lots of competition. Your name doesn't happen to be Pearl, does it?' he added ingenuously.

The girl laughed merrily as she slipped into gear and started the car moving. 'No, it's Heather. Competition will be fierce . . .' Bill lost the last few words as the car moved away to the side entrance.

He returned the smart salute from the sentry, asked him the way and walked along a polished hall, on which had been laid two strips of coconut matting, and knocked at a door which had painted on it, 'C M S P'. As Bill knocked he could see the barely obliterated word, 'Manager' under the letters.

He entered in response to the shouted invitation.

The room was roughly fourteen or fifteen feet square. Across the corner facing the door was a large table. Behind this, just climbing to his feet, was a naval Commander, well past middle-age.

'Lieutenant Haley, to join *Arandite*, sir,' Bill said, then accepted the proffered hand.

'Glad to see you, Haley. Take a seat.' And Bill sat down

28

on a bentwood chair on the opposite side of the table. 'Had a good journey? I'm afraid the people on the other side did not put on much of a welcome for you.'

As Haley replied the door opened behind him and a Wren entered with a tray bearing two cups of tea, one of which she put down before the Commander and the other before Bill.

'Good! First-class hotel, this,' the Commander smiled. 'I'm thinking of opening the bar again and putting my secretary in as barmaid.'

The girl smiled at the pleasantry and withdrew.

One of the three telephones on the desk rang and for a couple of minutes the Commander was busy, which gave Haley a chance to look at the room and to study the man who was more or less to control his destiny for some immeasurable time ahead.

Covering half of one wall was a large graph with thick red and blue lines chasing each other in valleys and on peaks. Bill leaned forward and read the words at the root of each line. At the beginning of the red one was 'Moored mines,' and on the blue line was 'Magnetic.' Half-way across the graph a pencil line climbed steadily, an acute climb, and Bill saw that at its root it had a large '?'.

On the other wall was an equally large board divided into strips. A list of names ran from top to bottom while across, from each name, were squares marked in with red and blue pencil shading. Alongside each ship hung a small square card with 'At sea' or 'In harbour' or 'Boiler clean', and in three or four instances just a black cross.

Completing the decidedly utilitarian decorative scheme was a large chart which Bill scrutinised with professional interest. He recognised it as a section of the channel immediately outside the port.

Half a dozen long, narrow, shaded portions he saw were marked with the QZ sign which showed that they were British minefields. Smaller strips, running into the channel herring-bone fashion, were marked with the swastika. Bill studied them and saw that they provided a formidable threat to the safe passage along the channel, overlapping as they did. At one point, where the channel narrowed to a gap between two long stretches of sand-banks, he saw that the enemy strips were concentrated in greater numbers than elsewhere.

From the charts and graphs Haley turned to look at the Commander, who was having a heated conversation. Bill saw a squarish face topped by thinning fair hair which threatened to turn white, if the wisps above each ear were any indication. The face was ruddy, but it was a clean sun-sponsored ruddiness gathered over many years, not the purple-tinged gin-born colour which so many people mistake for 'naval tan'. Bushy, sandy eyebrows were now drawn in a frown over blue-grey eyes which at the moment were staring out from under the lowered brows with a hard glint about them. Bill could imagine them become really frosty.

'Might be late fifties, not more than sixty and has seen lots of service,' Haley decided and his opinion was backed by the coloured ribbons of the D.S.O. and D.S.C. on the Commander's jacket, together with several other ribbons.

'Well, that's the position,' the Commander growled into the telephone. 'Ships and men are doing their maximum and cannot do more.'

He listened for a moment, then went on: 'The answer is, give me more ships. I've thirteen doing the work of twenty at the moment, besides other odd jobs you people think up.' Once again he paused, then concluded: 'The same old story —no ships and you want four times the work. . . . I know. . . . I know. . . . I know whose damned fault it is. . . . Well, we'll do our best. G'bye.'

He hung up, drained the last of his cup of tea then turned to Haley.

'Staff want us to work forty-eight hours a day. Do this, do that, sweep here, sweep there. Such is life.' He pressed a

30

bell-push at his elbow and when the Wren entered he said:
'Nobody is to see me for fifteen minutes. Take all calls first
and let me know before putting them through.'

He leaned back in his chair and surveyed Haley.

'Now we can talk. Cigarette?' Haley accepted it and a
light, then he too leaned back with one arm over the back of
the chair. 'You had a good course?' the Commander went
on, more as a statement than a query. 'You'll need it.'

He slewed round in his chair and looked towards the chart
and graphs on the wall.

'I saw you admiring my frescos.' He smiled and Bill
thought: 'I'm damned! I imagined he was busy on the
'phone.'

'That gives you the field of play. I have roughly forty
miles of channel to watch. It gives me the Main Channel.
Then I have eight short channels leading in to the ports
along the coast. Call it a hundred miles altogether.'

The Commander heaved himself up from his chair and
walked towards the wall chart. Haley noticed that he had a
slight limp.

'In parts of it we can get by with two or three searches a
week, and I use detached ships to clear the channels from the
other harbours. My main headache is here.' He covered the
narrow gap leading between the sand-banks with his hand
for a moment, then continued: 'And a first-class headache it
is, too.'

With a wide, sweeping motion he traversed the whole
chart.

'Eight convoys go through here each week, four each way,
besides other stuff going through at night. If the Hun can
close that gap with mines and keep it closed for a week you
can imagine the trouble it would cause. And he is having a
damned good try. In two hours' darkness he can lay enough
by aircraft to keep us busy for days.' He sat on the edge of
the table with one leg swinging. 'He doesn't allow us to
sweep them up in peace.'

After a moment or two of silence the Commander went on, with a wave towards the large graph:

'Up to quite recently he mixed them up fairly impartially. Moored mines, magnetics, with variations, and we've managed to cope. It was bad enough before Dunkirk. We had to sweep out and search before destroyers went out on patrol. Now we have to do the sweeping all day and do the patrols at night.'

He detected Haley's eyebrows going up and chuckled.

'Shakes you, does it? Well, it is so. We have nothing at the base now only trawlers and drifters, a couple of M.L.s. and a few M.T.B.s. Those laddies do not come inside my orbit. So the patrols—four of them, once done by destroyers—are now made by trawlers. With the Hun setting up bases just across the way it should become extremely busy very soon. I hope you don't strike any Rhône class destroyers on your patrols,' the Commander concluded grimly.

He clicked his fingers. 'Your dunnage? Outside in the car? We'll send it down on board and you can follow. There is a lot I want to talk about.'

Suiting his actions to his words he gave orders to the Wren to have Haley's luggage sent on board.

'Give 'em a chance to get tidied up before you join,' he said. 'I have a young Sub looking after her for a while.'

Right then Haley started piling up a list of things which puzzled him. Why a sub looking after her? Why not Number One? He did not raise the point immediately. Later it wasn't necessary, after the Commander had talked at length.

At the end of the talk he knew that minelaying had, for the Germans, become extremely simplified by the collapse of France. From airfields not more than thirty miles away German aircraft were able to make repeated runs and lay many more mines than when they had to operate from fields inside their own country.

Added to this, *E*-boats operating from French and Belgian

ports, with only a short distance to steam, could supplement the mines laid from the air.

From the masterly, concise talk the Commander gave him he soon gleaned that minesweeping, far from being a Cinderella side of the Service, was a grim, relentless struggle which never slowed down its tempo.

Convoy work could be tough, almost beyond endurance at times, but there came a time when pressure was relaxed, when the convoy and its escort could travel in peace with the last attack 10,000 years behind and the next yet to come.

'But,' the Commander said grimly, 'here, especially, the devils are watching us from their front lawns. They can, and are, doing their damnedest to keep us on the jump every hour of the day. If only we had the ships,' he went on wearily, running his hand through his scanty hair, 'but we haven't . . . and we won't have for some time to come, so in the meantime we have to do with what we have.'

Haley learned that nearly every port on the East and South coasts were being subjected to continued, relentless minelaying pressure. Not only merchant shipping, but also naval craft were being locked in for days at a time until the minesweepers could hammer through a clear passage.

The Commander paused, lit another cigarette and looked at Bill through the faint haze rising from his fingers. He screwed up one eye reflectively.

'And my bet is that we have not yet suffered the peak of his effort. If he can once close this little corner he can clutter up every harbour from Falmouth to—to—Newcastle until we get it clear. It is the most deadly bottleneck on the coast. Stop this gap, fill up the harbours and anchorages, seal them with mining, then start air-raiding them. . . . Nice prospect, eh? Now you see that, come what may, however many ships we lose, WE MUST KEEP THAT GAP OPEN. WE MUST.'

Bill glanced at the chart. He knew that stretch of water very well from his pre-war yachting days. To him it had always been the most flat and uninteresting part of his

33

annual sail down channel. Flat, uninteresting but with an underlying threat for anybody who was careless in the simple navigation necessary to cope with the rapid cross-tides which whipped the sand-banks.

'Fifty yards out in your estimate and you blow up the ship astern,' a voice whispered and Bill started.

'Did you say something?' the Commander asked as he moved towards the ship graph on the wall.

'I . . . I . . .' Haley hesitated. Had he whispered it himself or had a voice prompted him? 'I was thinking . . . an error of fifty yards would be too bad in those tides, sir.'

The Commander looked at him with interest. 'You know that neck of the woods, eh? Fifty yards would mean missing an estimated position of a suspected stick of mines and when the convoy came through . . .' He concluded with a familiar gesture—the upturned, upwards motion of the hands.

'The Hun has got a new type . . . did you hear much about it at Port Edgar? No? We don't know a lot about it. We only know the damned thing goes off with monotonous and expensive regularity. Magnetic, maybe a new type; we suspect it is a ticker. Each ship passing over it ticks it over once and then it goes off when the twentieth or thirtieth goes over it. But it keeps getting my ships. I'm inclined to suspect a new sort. D.M.S. tells me they think it is worked by sound, set off by the acoustic properties of a ship's propeller. Diabolical swine, aren't they? And bloody efficient. *Culver*, weren't you? Hm, hm. It was one of that sort which got her. The Channel had been swept twice, yet up she went.'

A shadow flickered across Bill's face as he recalled *Culver*, but the Commander went on without pause.

'Minesweeping is no longer a question of trawling tactics, dragging a wire between two ships and calling it a day. That is the reason for the changes we are making in the system of unit and groups.'

He explained that the Admiralty had introduced before the war a system of training for trawler skippers, paying

34

them a bounty and training them. At the outbreak of war they came in with the rank of skipper, R.N.R., and commanded trawlers with Sub-lieutenants and Lieutenants, R.N.V.R., as sweeping officers in charge of two ships.

The skippers did the disciplining and ran the ships, the R.N.V.R. officers were responsible for the sweeping. In theory it was good. In practice it did not work out. With few exceptions there was constant friction between the R.N.V.R. officers and the skippers, who considered themselves, in lordly fashion, to be superior professionals.

Accuracy went by the board in far too many instances because skippers would not, or could not, enforce discipline.

Eventually a modification was arrived at which showed an improvement. The more intelligent skippers were given complete command and their ships were embodied in a group of four, of which an R.N.V.R. Commanding Officer was Senior Officer.

'A good skipper is a pearl beyond price. A bad one is a damned liability. I've no bad ones left, so far as I know,' the Commander said grimly. 'The good ones you'll meet. Accept any advice they offer.'

He ran his finger-tip down the list of ships, then turned to Haley. 'I've had one or two dud R.N.V.R. officers, also,' he said flatly. 'They, too, have gone their way. The job was too tough for them.'

Bill made no answer, but a feeling of resentment surged up inside him. He chose to read it as a warning and his resentment was hot within him. He had not asked for the damned job of minesweeping. What did the Commander want? A terrific outburst of enthusiasm for a job one did not seek?

The Commander did not pursue the theme.

'Odd names here,' he said, and Bill followed his finger. '*Almarina, Red Wing, Morning Glory, Pearl, Jacinth, Ivy, Sheila, Honeybell, Dog Rose, Solan, Golfitt, Yoshmite, Amalekite.* . . . This last pair belong to a Scottish firm, very religious directors. All their ships have biblical names. We hope to scrounge one called *Tishbite* . . . you shall have her if we do.'

Bill shuddered and the thought of calling from a quay wall one wet night, '*Tishbite* ahoy!' or, worse still, hearing a ribald hail from some humorous destroyer.

The Commander chuckled. 'Lends itself to possibilities, doesn't it?'

'Damn him, he reads my mind,' Haley thought and the idea was strengthened by the Commander's next remark.

'Now, your ship. You have *Arandite*. She is a good ship. One of the newest in the base, and the fastest. She can do a good eleven and a half. Built for Iceland fishing. Good accommodation. She was intended for Asdic patrol work but there was a switch. She is an Oropesa sweeper, so much of your work will involve patrols as the L.L. sweepers chug away trying to put the penny in the slot.'

He moved back to his table and picked up a sheaf of papers, glanced at them, then went on.

The man you relieve has gone to hospital. He was a sick man. Did good work, ran himself ragged at Dunkirk and was shot up and bombed too many times since. He was slightly wounded in the last attack and . . . it more than tipped the beam. He broke down. People will tell you that Carter . . . you are taking over from him . . . ratted because of a slight scratch. I know different. I should have given his ship a . . . a little more attention. The signs were there.' He tossed a sheaf of papers over to Bill. 'These are requests from the crew, up to Number One, for transfers to other ships . . . nearly every man on the ship is due to come before me for petty offences.'

'Fine prospect,' thought Bill as he glanced at the sheaf. 'Taking over a shipload of malcontents to do an exacting job of minesweeping.'

He could see the time, a not-far-distant date, when his request for a transfer would join the others.

'I'm holding these up for a while until you have sounded her out,' the Commander went on. 'You may have noticed that the requests—and the punishments—have all accumulated in the past couple of weeks. I've made allowance for everybody being on edge. It doesn't explain it all. I want your views.'

He moved to a wire basket and picked up three pieces of cardboard. He glanced keenly at Bill, then spread the cards out face up. *Lilla, Tokay, Moss Rose*, Bill read.

'We lost those last week,' the Commander said softly. '*Golfitt* is badly damaged in dock, *Jacinth* is limping along waiting for you to take her place and she comes in. I'll give you two days to take over, then be ready for sea. You'll be second Senior Officer to Regan in *Solan*—he's a tip-top man and you'll . . .'

The 'phone rang. The Commander picked it up, spoke briefly, listened for a moment or two, then put the 'phone back slowly. He moved to the basket, shuffled the cards, took *Pearl* from the graph, held it for a moment and tossed it into the basket with the others.

He looked at Bill for a second or two.

'*Pearl*. Hit and run Jerry 'plane got her just outside the harbour. Some casualties.' He turned decisively to Haley.

'Belay that two days. Be ready for sea at midday tomorrow.'

'Aye, aye, sir,' Bill answered, preparing to go. 'I'll make my way on board and start Number One on whipping things up.'

The Commander stared at him bleakly for a while. 'Oh, yes, Number One. You've got a new one. Joins you tomorrow morning. The last one was killed by a machine-gun burst from a 'plane in the last raid made on her. He had practically got the ship in after his C.O. collapsed.'

Bill felt himself sagging mentally. New ship, full of defaulters, a new Number One, and be ready for sea in twenty hours for a job which seemed to have no future. A job in which one was apparently just a target for German 'planes and big guns. He found himself shaking hands with the Commander in almost a daze.

As he passed through the hall he muttered to himself, 'Grave, where is thy victory,' then he saw the Wren driver of the car waiting for him.

'You've been having quite a party, haven't you?' she said brightly. 'Learn anything?'

Bill followed her to the car without speaking.

As she moved off Bill said: 'What was the name of the ship you said your . . . you said would be my competitor?'

'*Pearl*,' the girl replied. 'Has that been worrying you? You'll have *Arandite* back on a top note in quick time. But you'll have to step lively to follow in *Pearl*'s footsteps.' She laughed merrily.

Haley glanced at her from the corners of his eyes. Why should he tell her? Why should it fall to him to blot out the laughter from her voice, the light from her eyes?

'Yes,' he murmured. 'I imagine so.'

He stayed silent at her side as she drove swiftly through the small town to the short piers alongside which several ships were moored.

'This is *Arandite*,' she said, pulling on her brakes. 'There is a young officer on board. A Sub. Is he to be your Number One? If so, tell him off for me. He is far too fresh,' she chatted. 'He has had your luggage put on board.'

Bill climbed out and thanked her.

As she swung the car round she laughed again. 'Keep at it. You'll soon catch *Pearl* up. But I warn you Andy likes things to go with a bang.' And she drove away still laughing.

'Likes things to go with a bang,' Bill muttered dully. 'You poor child.'

And he turned to inspect his new command.

As the tide was high the ship's main deck was almost on a level with the stone quay. There was no sign of life on board as Haley allowed his eyes to travel from one end of her to the other in one all-embracing survey.

She was painted dark grey; round the funnel Haley noticed one thin white line showing that in the Base designation she was commanded by second Senior Officer of her group.

There was nothing beautiful or sleek about her. After the pencil-slim lines of a destroyer and its bare decks the trawler seemed to be cluttered up with an enormous amount of additional gear.

His eyes swept up from the wooden deck, which he noticed had been recently scrubbed white, upwards past the small wheelhouse to 'Mount Misery', the small, square, canvas-surrounded top bridge.

Fastened to the front of the bridge was a small crest-board upon which he dwelt for a few moments. A faint smile adorned his face. Against a background of sea and cliffs a craggy fist was depicted landing smack in the middle of a face remarkably like Hitler's. Beneath, on a scroll, were the words 'Keep plugging'.

Haley wondered what the reactions of the austere, correct Civil Servants at the Admiralty were when that design for a crest was submitted. If it ever was, which he doubted.

Then he saw a number of starred scars round the wheel-house, now dabbed with new paint. Above them, in a roughly defined line climbing upwards, were more scars in the top bridge, patched and painted over. He followed the line of marks and saw them ending in a diagonal series of ragged holes in the top of the funnel. ·

'All the earmarks of a successful machine-gun attack coming in from the port bow,' he concluded, and found that reflection far from pleasant. There had been too many bullets whizzing in that confined space.

'Liable to hurt somebody if . . .' He remembered that the First Lieutenant of the ship had been hurt, hurt to death in probably the attack which made the scars he was surveying.

'Wonder if they got anything back.' He pursued the line of reflection to embrace a canvas-covered machine-gun on the lower bridge, then looked aft to see if the machine-gun placed there could have been brought to bear and concluded that it could not.

'One machine-gun and an antiquated 12-pounder against a Jerry using a cannon,' he mused. 'A hell of a reply!'

A quick glance included the lifeboat, a chunky job compared to a whaler, resting in its chocks. A faint oil smudge on the crown of the davits and on the blocks earned approval from Haley. Then he saw the rather dingy ensign hanging from the short gaff fixed to the after side of the funnel. It was by no means close up; in fact more than six inches of gap showed between the peak of the gaff and the hoïst of the ensign, and Haley frowned.

He heard footsteps somewhere on board and from under the boat deck came a young seaman. He was dressed in a rough blue jersey and rather greasy seaman's trousers tucked into a pair of rubber knee boots, the tops of which were turned down about four inches.

Round his waist the sailor wore a broad webbing belt from which hung a revolver holster out of which peeped the butt of a pistol. The seaman—he was scarcely more than a boy about twenty, Haley hazarded—squinted up towards the quay, but said nothing.

Haley stepped across the rail, jumped down on deck and looked levelly at the youngster.

'There is an officer on board,' Haley said, after executing a slick salute which sent the boy's eyebrows up a few degrees. 'Where is he? I'm the new Commanding Officer.'

The seaman made no reply but briefly scratched the back of his head and pushed a woollen monkey cap over his eyes.

Then a hazy recollection of his duties and some dimly assimilated instructions came to him.

He described a sketchy sort of salute, with his fingers bent, just reaching his forehead above his eyebrow.

'He's on board,' he replied in a curious twanging voice. 'I'll get him . . .' Then hazy recollections expanded slightly and he recalled another stern admonition. His hand dropped lightly to the butt of the revolver and he said with a greater show of confidence: 'Gotta card?'

Haley breathed explosively through his nose. 'A card? CARD? What sort of card? What in hell are you burbling about?'

The youth stood his ground and his thumb loosened the press stud on the holster and his fingers closed round the butt of the revolver.

'Identity card,' he replied sturdily. 'Nobody comes on board unless they got one.'

Bill recognised the legitimacy of part of the ritual but his temper was rising rapidly and he gave no time to vivisection of the claim into rightful and wrongful sections.

'You mean everybody has to show one on coming on board? Here it is. And Now,' he laid heavy emphasis on each word, 'I AM THE NEW COMMANDING OFFICER. WHERE IS THE OFFICER WHO IS ON BOARD?'

The young seaman had run his gamut. Somebody had come on board, had been challenged to the best of his ability and had produced a card which he now held upside down, in his grubby hand. Beyond that he was lost, but the situation was saved.

'Anything wrong?' queried a pleasant voice behind them. Haley spun round to face a young Sub-lieutenant who was standing near a doorway leading to a hatch. 'Somebody seems to be kicking up a hell of a row.'

'This officer . . . the Officer . . . Commanding . . .'

'I'm the new Commanding Officer . . .'

Haley and the seaman spoke simultaneously and stopped together, then Haley went on with slow emphasis—'. . . of this ship, from now.'

He glanced at the seaman, who had surrendered the initiative rather gladly.

'I seem to have some difficulty in making that clear to this . . . this,' he eyed the youth up and down, then continued,

41

'this Pirate from Penzance. Perhaps if we go below I can satisfy you.'

'Surely.' The self-possessed young Sub-lieutenant turned and indicated the hatch from which he had emerged. 'The wardroom is down there, sir.'

Bill disappeared below. Before the Sub-lieutenant followed him he turned and looked at the seaman. It was more a warming of the eyes than a smile, involving no movement of face, which he gave the seaman and the youngster answered with a wide grin, then busied himself adjusting his holster.

'Fair enough,' the officer said, then his face split in a grin. 'You'd better give me that,' and he took Haley's identity card from the seaman and followed on below.

They each took a seat in the small but snug wardroom and Haley felt an immediate pleasant reaction to the room. His only experience of a trawler's wardroom had been in an over-crowded one used more as an office by the Instructor Officers on the instructing minesweepers as they lived ashore, sailing only on day-to-day trips.

'Drink, sir?' the young officer asked and Haley nodded as the Sub held up a bottle of gin for approval. In silence he poured out two and Haley noticed that they were generous, topped with only a little water.

'Cheerio!'

After the drinks had been sampled the two men faced each other for a moment, neither speaking, as two fencers face each other each waiting for the other to move.

'You are not the Number One. You are holding a watching brief, so I understand.' Haley broke the silence eventually.

'Correct. My name is Booth. I'm Number One of *Golfitt*. She was caned the other day and is being patched up. I'm standing by her and . . . and . . .' He finished his drink. 'I act as general dogsbody. I might have to ship with you if your Number One doesn't arrive in time.'

42

Haley nodded.

'He's due tomorrow. Don't know anything about him. And I have to be ready for sea by midday tomorrow,' he added with studied casualness. He expected reactions from the young officer—either surprise of shocked disbelief.

Instead, the youth reached for the bottle again, questing an eye towards Haley's glass still half full. Haley shook his head, thinking meanwhile: 'If you were my Number One you would have a longer interval between drinks, me lad.'

Booth poured out a generous measure and as he did so Haley studied him.

Slim, fair-haired with almost a schoolgirl face now slightly tanned. There was a distinct wave in his hair although it was cut fairly short. The eyes had a curiously sooty look about them caused, Bill realised, by the extremely long and thick eyelashes which threw deep shadows.

At the moment, even in repose, the oval face had a trace of tightness about the corners of the mouth and the whole face carried a picture of subdued tenseness.

The Sub-lieutenant drank half his measure, replaced his glass on the table, looked at Bill for a moment, then a cheerful, boyish smile broke up the tightness.

'You'll be ready all right. In fact you could go to sea right now ... with me as Number One.'

Bill searched for a trace of conceit but failed to detect any.

'Anyway, if Commander Mahoney says midday at 1200 hours precisely'—he pronounced each syllable with emphasis so that it became 'pree ... cise ... lee'—'then at 1200 hours precisely you'll sail through the harbour entrance, being in all respects ready for sea and to meet the enemy.' He intoned the last part as if reading from a signal.

'Mahoney? Is that Commander Minesweepers?'

'Commander Minesweepers and Patrols. Godfather, buffer State between us and the straight-striped higher hierarchy of dug-outs and Hell on two feet if you fail by as much

43

as a hair's-breadth on any job he gives you. He's a great bloke,' the Sub wound up enthusiastically. 'You've met him, of course? Had a signal that you were with him and would be aboard shortly.' He used 'signal' in the accepted sense as a substitute for 'message'.

' "See that the ship is tidied up", his message said. "this new Commanding Officer comes from real ships and is a Tartar." '

Haley glowed slightly for a moment, then wondered if the Sub-lieutenant was pulling his leg or was elaborating a plain, straight message. Afterwards he found out that it was Mahoney's trick to write notes while interviewing people, send for his secretary on some pretext and palm the note to her. She, being well used to his little foible, would play along. The message to the Sub-lieutenant on *Arandite* had been worded roughly as the Sub had related; it had been scribbled as Mahoney argued with the Staff Officer on the telephone and had been slipped, folded, on to the tea-tray for the girl to collect and act upon.

'So we tidied her up a bit. Not that she wanted it. She's in good shape,' he went on, tacitly defending his temporary residency.

Haley decided it was time he lived up to the picture of being a Tartar.

'Is that rig-out of the laddie on deck the usual thing for quartermasters on these ships?' he asked grimly. 'He looked like a cross between a Balkan brigand and . . . and . . .' he swiftly decided that his previous simile was good enough for repetition, 'and a Pirate of Penzance.'

The Sub looked at him levelly. 'Some do, some don't. Depends on the Number One and Commanding Officer.'

'This one will not in future,' Haley said flatly. 'And'— he employed a poor weapon, sarcasm—'is there somebody dead on board?'

The Sub-lieutenant paused with a lighted match half-way to a cigarette and looked at Bill.

44

'No.' It was a sharp, monosyllablic answer.

'Then why the devil is the ensign hanging half mast?'

Haley knew, of course. At Colours that morning the halliards had been damp and pulled tight. As the warm day wore on they had dried and slacked off. Inattention had left them hanging with the long gap between full hoist. It was a little trap so often set for slack officers and quartermasters and signalmen whose duty it was to see that the colours were close up.

Booth pressed a bell-push as he replied softly: 'I'll turn the Quartermaster to it at once.' He gave the order as the young seaman came to the top of the hatch. Then he turned back to Haley and delivered his devastating broadside which made Bill squirm.

'The dead were taken off three days ago . . . five of them.'

The very softness, almost a whisper, of the answer made Bill clench his fists and wish that he had used anything but that cheap, sarcastic comment.

He busied himself with a cigarette before trusting himself to speak.

'I heard about it. Outside the harbour, wasn't it?'

Booth nodded. 'Right on the doorstep.'

He drummed on the table-top for a moment, afterwards examining his finger-tips before speaking again.

'Jimmy Burton, the Number One, was bringing her in. She had a couple of near misses just before that and the C.O. . . . sort of . . . chucked his hand in. I've heard various stories . . . he had been kind of funny, anyway . . .'

'Mahoney says he had taken more than enough in the way of punishment. He is now in hospital, a very sick man,' Haley said and felt rather surprised at finding himself jumping to the defence of a man he knew nothing about. He watched the Sub-lieutenant's hand stray towards the bottle. 'The first sign of a crack-up is when a man starts hitting the bottle,' he went on gravely.

Booth looked up quickly and caught a faint glimmer of a

45

smile a long way back in Haley's eyes.

'I'm hitting this one back into the locker. Incidentally, it is one I brought from *Golfitt*. There is no bonded stuff on this ship. Has been none for a month. The crew are scrounging cigarettes—no duty-free—and getting by on free gift stuff.'

After the well-organised issue of duty-free tobacco and cigarettes and other commodities on a destroyer Haley was puzzled, but in a few crisp sentences Booth gave him an outline of the simple system prevailing on trawlers.

'Most of our crowd are on leave so I have been letting your lot have an odd packet each from *Golfitt*'s bond,' he finished.

After placing the gin bottle safely away in a locker, Booth turned to ship's business.

'I've got everything more or less into shape for your take-over—stores, C.B.s, and all the works. I expect Razor Blade and a paybob will be down tomorrow morning; they might even leave it until you come back. Would you like to take a quick squint through?'

Haley agreed and Booth disappeared behind a curtained doorway leading off the wardroom.

'This is Number One's berth,' his voice went on inside the room. 'I've had it cleaned up ready for the new bloke and set a couple of lads to slapping a coat of paint on it.'

'You mentioned a character called Razor Blade,' Haley said, moving towards a deep leather arm-chair and making himself comfortable. 'More details, please.'

A youthful chuckle percolated through the rep curtain.

'Lieutenant-Commander Cutter, R.N. A real old-timer. Up from the lower deck and back from retirement. He is officially Minesweeping Maintenance Officer, but is also reserve father confessor, guide, mentor and blaster-in-chief.' Booth's head appeared round the curtain. 'You see that arm-chair in . . . oh, you've found it. Remind me to tell you the story of that and Razor Blade and a very crafty, dis-

46

honest Sub-lieutenant, R.N.V.R.'

'Sounds like a bit of autobiography.'

Booth's wide grin enveloped his whole face.

'Hitting . . . salvoes,' he chuckled. 'Shan't be a tick with these books of words.' He disappeared again behind the curtain.

Haley found time to look about him, at the room which was to be part of his home for an indefinite time.

It was roughly the shape of a broad letter 'L'. The foot of the 'L' ran fore and aft, about eight feet long. There was a leather settee on three sides. The space in the opening was filled with a drop leaf table large enough to seat five or six people. The long leg of the 'L', the main part of the room, ran for two-thirds of the beam of the ship, about eighteen feet long, and the tabled section could be cut off by pulling across a blue rep curtain which hung from a brass bar.

A slow-combustion stove was placed diagonally in one corner and two large carpets, with a principal colour motif of blue, almost filled the floor. The furniture consisted of a steel tubular arm-chair, two other straight-backed armless steel chairs and the large, low club chair in which he now reclined. A small, compact sideboard, brass-railed, backed on to the bulkhead nearest the ladder leading to the hatch, and behind the ladder was a cleverly built little pantry in which gleamed crockery and glassware in racks.

'In general, a neat lay-out. Somebody used his head,' Bill decided. 'The lay-out is almost like a large yacht. Wonder what genius decided to depart from the conventional, and almost inevitable, white enamel on the bulkheads?'

They were off-white, with a definite tinge of blue; it seemed almost a reflection from the blue carpets and curtains.

Booth interrupted his reflections by coming from the room which occupied the remainder of the full beam of the ship. He had a small load of books and papers under his arm.

'Here we are, our homework for the day,' he said, deposit-

47

ing them on the table. 'But you'll find everything checked and up to date.'

Haley nodded. 'I was admiring the lay-out and colour scheme. Who dreamed it all up?'

'I did,' Booth replied. Then, realising that some amplification was necessary, he leaned against the table, started a cigarette going and embarked on an explanation.

'She has only been in commission as a minesweeper for five months. I stood by her in Aberdeen.' He paused and cocked a reflective eye at Haley. 'Ever been to the Granite City?'

Haley nodded.

'A grand place. Nothing was too much trouble for those Scots. Just ask and they'd say, "Aye, it's nae bither a' all," and it would be done. They even twisted the wardroom round a bit for me. Gave us the extra room and hid the pantry under the stairs.'

'Natty idea, too,' Haley agreed. He was puzzled again but dodged the question for a while.

'I was there for nearly four weeks,' Booth continued, a reminiscent gleam stealing into his eyes.

'What was she like?'

'Blonde, almost red, about twenty, about so high'—he indicated his shoulder—'weak, willing and enthusiastic. I had to . . .'

'The ship, you young ass,' Bill laughed. 'I'm not interested in your conquests.'

'Oh, I thought you meant the sterner facts of life. And please don't be so plural—I'm so young.'

'Young, hell! I've no doubt you got away a short head in front of a shotgun-carrying clan. What was the ship like when you took over?'

'Half-way to conversion into an Asdic trawler, then a bleat went up for more minesweepers and she was switched to join the happy throng. She had only done two fishing trips and was actually at sea, around Iceland, when the balloon went up. We were intended for the Humber, came here for Dunkirk and Mahoney pulled strings, and here we be and here we stay.'

Haley judged it an opportune moment to have one or two puzzling questions answered.

'You say "we", yet I understand you are Number One on *Golfitt*. How come?'

Booth ran his finger-nails through the ash in the ashtray for a moment or two, created an intricate pattern of curves and hills and valleys, then demolished it all with a flick of the finger.

'Lieutenant Carter was the Commanding Officer; I was Number One when she commissioned. For the first few weeks everything went fine. Then . . . after Dunkirk . . . when things got a bit tough . . . Carter got'—he paused and searched for the right word—'difficult,' he wound up. 'He would prowl about the decks in port at all hours instead of getting some sleep. Small things were magnified; we had streams of defaulters for things I would cuss 'em for and forget. He blasted me, in front of the crew, and at times became personal. In the end I asked for a change, and got it.'

He started another cigarette going and Haley made no comment. This was his chance to do what Commander Mahoney had asked. Find out some of the background, trace out some of the history of the apparent disintegration of the morale of this ship.

'I shifted to *Golfitt* two weeks ago. I was lucky, too, wasn't I?'

Haley still stayed silent and the youngster went on. 'Look, sir. You can take it from me that there is nothing wrong with this outfit. I worked 'em up. I know. I also know that Mahoney is due to have nearly three-quarters of the ship's company before him as defaulters . . . and it's all wrong . . . as wrong as hell,' he finished passionately.

'Maybe that will be levelled off,' Haley said non-committally. 'Mahoney is as puzzled as you and wants to know why and how.'

Booth brightened up. 'Do you think he will scrub the punishments?'

Haley shrugged. 'Can't say. I know he will go most thoroughly into each case. So will I before taking them before him. But that is something which will have to wait until we return. In the meantime, tell me a little of the set-up around here. What are the ships in this group, who commands them. C'mon, speak, or forever hold your peace.'

'Regan, Lieutenant, R.N.V.R., a benevolent neutral from Tralee, is Senior Officer. For God's sake don't ask me to unravel that, but he is. A character, as you will learn; and so is his ship, the *Solan*. Then comes you, then *Jacinth*, and *Pearl*. Lieutenant Anderson, R.N.V.R., is canteen boat. *Pearl* at the moment is cock ship. Two Jerry 'planes, half share in an *E*-boat, sharing most mines with *Solan*. She . . .'

'*Pearl*.' Haley almost barked the word. '*Pearl* . . .' He repeated it again.

'Sure! Do you know her, or Anderson? Before taking her he was . . .'

Haley waved his finger and the Sub-lieutenant's voice trailed away and he stared at the Commanding Officer.

'Of course, you haven't heard. *Pearl* was attacked about an hour ago, outside the harbour. I don't know all the facts, but there are some casualties.'

Both men were silent for a few moments, then Haley explained how he knew. It was Booth who pursued the theme after another short silence.

'When C.M.S.P. heard did he . . . swear . . . or did he take *Pearl*'s tally off the wall and throw it into the wire basket?'

Haley thought back for a few minutes. He recaptured the scene.

'Threw it into the basket. Why, what's the significance?'

'She's gone. So long as a ship is afloat he keeps her tally. The basket means *fini*.'

50

The youngster moved over to the small locker beneath the sideboard and brought out the bottle of gin again. Without comment he poured out two measures, looked at Haley then said softly: 'May your tally always hang on the wall.'

Haley nodded and they both drank a toast to a fervent hope.

As they replaced their glasses on the table a clatter of feet sounded overhead and was followed shortly by a pair of legs appearing in the hatch. They clambered noisily down the ladder.

'Oh, Steward, the Commanding Officer will be on board for tea; put some hot water in his room and make up his bunk.' Haley looked at the steward as Booth gave him instructions. He was an undersized, pale-faced young man about twenty-five.

'Ah've doon that. Ah can't open cases, they're locked,' the steward replied in broad Yorkshire. 'Ah'd better lay for three. Commander Razor . . . Commander Cutter is coming along the quay. He knows there's been shelling.' He stared frankly at his new Commanding Officer, then busied himself preparing the table trafficking to and fro from the small pantry.

Haley cocked an inquiring eyebrow towards Booth, who enjoyed the puzzled look for a moment, and laughed out loud. Then he embarked on an explanation.

'When the boys across the way throw large rude bricks some of them fall into the harbour. This frightens lots of nice fresh fish . . . soles . . . even lobsters . . . and the crew nip off smartly, seize them by the lower band, and we—that is, you— have the best cook in the base. His chips are yum yum and the things he can do with a sole . . . well, wait and see.'

Haley understood partly. 'But during the shelling? Don't they take cover?'

Booth chuckled. 'They have been known to wear a tin hat . . . and use it to scoop up fish.'

Haley gave a despairing shake of his head, which made

51

Booth laugh out loud again and soon Haley joined in too. The laughter was perhaps a little louder and a little longer than the humour merited; perhaps by laughter they hoped to put further back all thoughts of *Pearl*, who was gone, and of the men who had died.

'That sounds like the end of one of Booth's pothouse jokes. If so, tell it again. I want a good laugh.'

The speaker was inside the hatch and half-way down as he spoke. He paused to address somebody standing on deck. 'All right, laddie, I know my way. I didn't know you for a moment with a clean face and a cap on.'

Haley and Booth moved towards the foot of the ladder and both caught a glimpse of the young Quartermaster. He had washed his face and at a correct angle, and an inch above one eyebrow, he was wearing a seaman's cap. His turned down rubber boots were concealed under his trousers.

Haley and Booth exchanged quick glances and smiled.

'Most of his jokes smack of pothouses or worse, but being a person of coarse mental fibre I like 'em. Tell it again.'

The speaker reached the bottom of the ladder and held out his hand.

'Haley?' He gave Bill a steady, all-embracing look as he shook hands. 'I'm Cutter. Maintenance Officer. Glad to meet you. Set another place for tea, laddie.' He seemed to have an uncanny knack of separating bits of his conversation and throwing them towards different people. His last remark was to the steward dodging round the group of officers as he carried plates and silverware to the table.

'Ah have, sir. An' the Leading Hand says to say he has a lobster, sir, so tame it will eat out of your hand. But it's grilled sole and chips for tea.'

'Good! Put a lead on the lobster and I'll walk it back to the Base. How do you like your ship? Was it the story about the bishop and the chambermaid?'

The steward, Haley and Booth shared that conversational tangle almost impartially; only Haley had any difficulty in sorting out their respective sections.

'I was explaining to the C.O. the source of our fresh fish supply, sir. Somewhat unorthodox but effective.'

'Yes, I saw you off in the small boat this afternoon. You didn't wait for the "all clear", did you? I must make a note of that.'

The Lieutenant-Commander sat down in the big easy chair and accepted a cigarette from Booth.

'I have a proprietary interest in this chair, an equal right and interest in this ship, and a living, perpetual but faint hope of making a real officer of that young rascal,' Cutter continued. 'Perhaps you will succeed where I have failed. Now, to business. Everything ship-shape for your take-over? Good! I guessed it would be.'

For the next half-hour, and during the appetising meal which followed, they talked ships, ships and again ships, and quite a lot about minesweeping. Haley listened much, spoke little, and learned a lot.

Eventually Cutter rose to leave, promising to be on board after breakfast the next day to help Haley finally take over.

Bill, Booth and the Quartermaster stood in a little group on the boat deck as Cutter stepped ashore and they gave him a smart salute, Booth grinning slightly as the Quartermaster made a valiant effort to make his rubber boot-heels click.

Then Haley said he would like to go to his room to unpack. A steel door opened up from the starboard side to reveal a slightly larger door of teak, and beyond was his room.

Down the mess deck a group of seamen stood talking. They had spent the previous minute or two peeping through the hatch as Cutter left the ship.

'Gawd's truth! More bloody salutes than Whaley! We'll have pipin' and a Marines' band aboard the ship now. Bin

53

Number One of a destroyer, he has. Big-ship flannel from now on,' said one, taking a half-smoked cigarette from behind his ear.

'But Subby told him. Tich was listening at the ventilator. "This crowd's all right, sir," he says. Tich heard him. And "Commander Patrols is goin' to see it all right," he says. Didn't he, Tich?'

The Quartermaster, now off duty, nodded agreement.

'Aw, all officers is bastards. Some are big, some are little, but they are all bastards . . . all cow's sons.'

The last speaker, a thick, brawny man older than the others, was lying on a bunk reading a paper-backed novel, the cover of which showed a female with a wealth of charm and singularly little clothing. 'And shut up—the bloke's just got her into bed.' He held up his novel.

'Fat lot you'll learn from a book about that. You could nearly write one on it.'

'If he could write,' amended a thin, dark-faced man who was struggling into a jumper which had a W/T rating's badge on the arm.

The earnest seeker after sexual knowledge sat up in his bunk with a jerk but his protest was lost in a gale of laughter.

'Never mind, Jim; you can tell me about it and I'll write it for you,' Sparks chuckled. 'We'll make a fortune.'

'Saluting, piping, bloody Marines, Christ . . .' The man lay down in his bunk and resumed reading, his lips moving silently as he struggled with the words.

At the end of the stone pier Lieutenant-Commander Cutter stood in a telephone-box, speaking to the Naval Base.

'C.M.S.P.? Cutter here. I've taken a look at *Arandite*. My guess is that he'll fit in. Ambassador Booth had been performing. . . .' He listened for a while, then went on.

'I think you are right, sir. . . . I quite agree. It would be a

first-class thing. I'll do it in the morning. Meanwhile, Booth
will sail with her tomorrow.'

In his room Haley sat down to write to his wife:

It is rather an odd feeling, this being in command
[he wrote after the first affectionate preliminaries were
over]. I won't say it is confusing, but now that it is an
accomplished fact instead of something to be visualised
in the future it has had a certain effect on my ego, so
much so that I propose to use the rubber stamp I found
here, when I sign this letter. You'd better look now—
doesn't it look nice—'COMMANDING OFFICER' in
nice large type?

I can tell you little about her except that she is almost
new and I am writing at a place from which you used to
get my first post-card when I made the run down channel
before the war.

There is a bright boy on board, acting as my Number
One. He is on loan but I'm going to wangle all I know
to keep him. See? Already I am developing what *Culver's*
C.O. said was a basic accomplishment for all Commanding Officers—to be an unscrupulous wangler.

In short, I like first impressions of the ship. Of the job
she will do, and her crew . . . well, I have yet to tackle
them so I will reserve judgment.

The rest of the letter was as any letter from a husband
to a wife.

Commander Mahoney slouched resignedly over his desk
as he read the internal memorandum awaiting his signature.
It was addressed to Chief of Staff.

I propose to return Sub-lieutenant Booth to *Arandite*
as First Lieutenant in view of his previous experience on

the ship and to place Sub-lieutenant Wilton, on arrival, on *Golfitt* which will not be ready for sea for some time. It will enable him to find his feet. *Golfitt*'s Commanding Officer is a steady officer and Wilton should benefit accordingly.

'So should Haley,' he muttered as he scrawled his name across the bottom, put the memo into an envelope and tossed it into his 'Out' basket.

3

The sound of the door being unlatched and the curtain rasping back on its rings woke Haley in the morning. Vaguely he saw a figure standing near his bunk, outlined against morning sunshine outside.

'Just gone ha' past seven, sir. Breakfas' is about eight o'clock. Eggs from the N.A.A.F.I.'

Slowly Haley broke surface. It had been a long time before he got to sleep the previous night. For a couple of hours he had lain on his back, hands behind his head, reviewing the last few weeks. His departure from *Culver*, his minesweeping course, his arrival at the Base. He wondered if he was placing too grim an interpretation on events as they lined themselves up for him.

Was the ship's company so bad? How much had Carter's apparent illness contributed to it? Several times Haley had dozed off and each time some unaccustomed noise had jarred him into wakefulness again.

Once it was a stoker who clumped past his room in noisy clogs, went down the stokehold and started many bangings and clangings of steel. Later, some heavy feet thudded over his head as a quartermaster went to the wheelhouse to see the time.

Eventually Bill went off to sleep and was wrenched by a warning siren from a deep pit, swiftly through a brief nightmare in which he was trying to stop somebody screaming—and failing—to a shaking wakefulness and a thudding heart.

The siren was so close that he could hear the subdued,

mechanical whine underlying the high-pitched wavering alarm. He climbed from his bunk and wriggled into a dressing-gown. Before he had finished tying it on he could hear the drone of 'planes, followed almost instantly by the grouped barking of anti-aircraft guns. They, too, were so close that his door rattled at every shot.

Haley stepped out on deck. It was a fine, windless night and the whole harbour was wrapped in an eerie glow reflected from the searchlights. Some of them were concentrated in a cone away to the west as they pinned a 'plane flying about 15,000 feet. Others swept low, sometimes so low that they licked the top of the lighthouse at the end of the stone pier.

'That bastard up there don't mean a thing,' a deep voice said alongside him. Haley peered into the shadow cast by the bridge and saw a thick-set figure wearing a duffle wide open, a small tight-fitting woollen cap. It was the novel-reading critic of officers. 'It's the sods outside who count. That one'—he tilted his chin upwards—'makes all the fuss and the others drop the bleedin' mines.'

He lifted his cupped hands to his mouth and Haley saw the faint, concealed glow of a cigarette. It was on the tip of his tongue to bring up the question of smoking on the upper deck at night-time but he checked himself. After all, with all the illumination about from a couple of dozen searchlights the faint glow from a cigarette made little difference.

'How long does this symphony go on?' Haley asked.

'About an hour. That flamer up there flies around, creates all the fuss while the others drop the mines outside. Then he'—again there was the economical uptilt of the chin—'he drops a few bombs on the town just to show he hasn't wasted his trip, like.'

Haley noticed that although there was no familiarity in the man's tones there had not crept into his conversation one single 'sir'.

He compared this with what his actions would have been

58

on the *Culver* and had almost decided to sow a few seeds for future reaping when the sound of a diving 'plane broke up his thoughts. The rasping sound came from seawards and appeared to be under the questing searchlights. Slowly there climbed upwards thin streams of tracer, followed by a sharper, crisper bark from a gun of a different calibre to that of the shore anti-aircraft gun.

'That's the bloody order,' the Quartermaster said, flicking his cigarette over the side in a crimson arc. 'The boys have found him. Get at it! Warm his arse for him!'

Two more slowly climbing ribbons of red tracer climbed upwards and it looked like a red tripod, round the peak of which shell-fire occasionally burst.

'That's *Solan* out there,' the man went on. 'What a lad! He'd shoot at his grandmother if she flew over him in the dark.'

Halcy watched the tracer as it followed the invisible 'plane low over the sea.

'For a limited secondary armament they are putting up quite a lot of stuff,' he said.

The Quartermaster broke this down to simple words before answering. 'You mean machine-guns?' He laughed, a deep laugh which rumbled in his chest before emerging. '*Solan* is stiff with guns. He's got about six machine-guns buckshee beside his issue of a twin Lewis and a couple of Hotchkiss. We've got . . .' He broke off as they heard the hissing whistle of a bomb descending. Both stepped back to the inadequate but comforting shelter of the steel bridge as the missile whistled down. After a moment they saw a red burst somewhere in the town, saw it subside, then saw the steadier glow of the resultant fire.

'Some sort of fire bomb. Oil bomb, so they say,' the seaman said. 'Bastards.'

'You were saying that *Solan* has a number of machine-guns?'

The man chuckled again. 'Like a bloody hedgehog. Even

the C.O. has got his special job on the bridge. Cleans it himself . . . and fires it, too.'

'How come?'

'Soldiers ditched 'em when we rescued 'em at Dunkirk. All Lewises they are. Orders was that all guns rescued had to be turned in to the Base. The bloke on *Solan* said he would if he saw any guns floating about.'

Haley and the seaman shared a chuckle.

'And you were about to say that we've something or other.'

Haley saw the white flash of the man's eyes as he looked at him. It was an appreciable time before he answered.

'I was going to say we've a long way to go before we catch up with *Solan* as a shooting ship,' he said flatly.

'Liar!' Haley breathed to himself. 'You were going to say something quite different.' Then, out loud, he continued with a faint chill in his voice: 'Possibly if we put our backs into it during the course of that long way we'll catch her up.' He tried to catch the gleam from the man's eyes again and stepped out from the shadow so that the seaman could see his face in what little light there was. He could not tell whether the man was looking at him or not. Then he went on:

'Who is the gunner on this ship?' For the first time Haley put a ring of authority into his voice. It brought results.

'I am, sir.' The mark of respect came without a pause.

'Then it will be up to us—you and me—to see that we catch up with *Solan*—and pass her if necessary. Won't it?'

The 'All Clear' came as Haley waited for an answer.

'That's it,' the seaman said as he moved away from the shadow of the bridge. 'I wonder if the boys outside bumped that beauty out there.'

'You are not escaping down any by-way,' Haley thought, and returned to the main track.

'Did this ship recover any machine-guns? Were any found floating?'

The seaman waited a while before answering. After temporising by rubbing his chin with the knuckles of his right hand he admitted: 'We used to have an extra one fitted on the top bridge. Me and Mr. Booth fixed it. After he chucked . . . went to *Golfitt* . . . it wasn't wanted. The C.O. said, "Send it ashore" so I popped it into the magazine.'

'And you didn't send it ashore?'

'It sort of slipped my mind, sir. I'll do it in the morning.'

'Clever devil!' thought Haley. 'Well, here's your answer.' He turned towards his room before continuing. 'Try it over the side in the morning. If it floats, turn it into the Base. If it doesn't, recover it and'—he laid emphasis on each word— 'fit it up on the bridge.'

The Quartermaster acknowledged the little by-play with another rumbling laugh before replying, 'Aye, aye, sir.'

As Haley stepped through the door the man went on:

'I've got some coffee in the galley. I was making it when the warning went. Like a cup, sir?'

Haley agreed he would.

In a few minutes the seaman was back with a cup of coffee. It was strong, very strong, hot and sweet. After the first few sips Haley smiled at the man and said: 'From now onwards you are appointed official coffee-maker for the early hours when we are at sea.'

They exchanged smiles.

'What is your name, by the way?'

'Clay, Seaman gunner, sir. Acting Leading Hand.'

Haley nodded.

'What was your job before this business started?'

'I worked in a pub in Southwark.'

'Barman?'

'And bouncer. Tough down there on Saturday nights.' He flexed his arms. 'And when I bounced 'em, they stayed bounced.'

'Clay?' Haley let the name wander about in his mind then orientated it. It was one of the names Mahoney had

61

shown him in the formidably long list of defaulters. Well, now he had met the man; let tomorrow bring forth tomorrow's problems. He didn't look a persistent defaulter.

Haley glanced at his watch; nearly 2.0 a.m. Then he started to slip out of his dressing-gown. 'Oh, Clay'—as the man moved behind the curtain shielding the door—'do you think you could persuade the stokers, and your relief, to make a little less noise as they move about? I'm a light sleeper.'

Clay nodded. 'Aye, aye, sir. A sound from now onwards and I'll bounce 'em.'

Haley heard his deep chuckle again and he disappeared.

He rested propped up on one elbow until he finished the coffee, then lay down. Suddenly he felt extremely drowsy, stretched once . . . and the rasp of the curtain woke him.

'A . . . ha' past seven,' he heard. In the background he could hear the sounds attending the washing-down ship. The slush and swish of the hose-pipe, and clatter of hard brooms. Through it, like a stout thread, came the rumble of Clay's deep tones and a higher pitched nasal accent which eventually he pin-pointed to his Pirate of Penzance of the previous afternoon.

'After this, get that stripped Lewis up from the mag and fix it up on the bridge,' he heard Clay say. The Pirate's answer was lost in a blur of sound, a mixture of swishing water and scrubbing brooms. Then Clay's voice went on: 'We'll say nothing about Noisy's little pet. What the eye doesn't see, Tich . . . get me?'

Haley sat up in bed wondering what Noisy's pet could be, and who Noisy was. Then contemplation of the greater problems facing him pushed this one into the background.

At breakfast he found young Booth extremely cheerful and full of news.

'There was a raid last night. Usual thing—decoy and the real job dropping mines outside. News is that *Solan* and *Jacinth* beat one up and he went down half-way across the Channel. Did you hear the fuss?'

'Didn't you?'

'Unless the Hun drops one down my ventilator I hear nothing when I'm asleep. Did you hear it?'

'I was out for a bit. Couldn't sleep. Clay and I watched some shooting seawards.'

Booth stopped half-way towards his plate with a spoonful of marmalade, his questing mind racing here and there as he strove to remember any mention he had made of Clay.

'Clay? Guns? You met him?'

'We held some converse, drank some coffee, and watched the sleepless guardians of this harbour repel enemy aircraft while children slept, and no doubt snored off the result of their revelry ashore.'

It was heavy humour, but it served. Booth grinned. 'Up eight hundred, six right, you're well off target. I was stone cold sober.' He carefully spread some marmalade on his toast and equally carefully said : 'Clay is a good gunner. Given a chance, he'll make this ship sing.'

Haley held his cup out for another coffee.

'He'll have every chance,' he said. After sugaring his coffee and tasting it, he kept the cup close to his lips and with his eyes contemplatively on the bulkhead went on : 'He holds some very unorthodox but inspiring views on machine-guns and their situation on board, contagious views caught from *Solan*, I imagine.'

He glanced at Booth, and the picture was so funny that he had to put down his cup and laugh. Booth sat still with a large piece of toast held firmly between his teeth, his eyebrows curving up in surprise. Eventually he shifted the toast until it bulged one cheek, settled it firmly and licked a couple of crumbs off his lips.

'Converse, did you say? You must have wrung the man dry. Did he tell you . . .?'

Haley smiled and held up a restraining hand.

'Young boys must not ask what went on in the Commanding Officer's confessional. Top secret. I like Clay, on first impressions. Doesn't strike me as being a malcontent.'

'He isn't.'

'We'll unravel that when we get round to it. Defaulters at eleven o'clock, Number One.'

Booth nodded, his jaws working steadily at the toast.

'Er . . . how many unofficial machine-guns are on this ship, may I ask? Purely an academic question at the moment.'

'You forget, sir, that I am only a visitor, a stand-in from another ship,' Booth answered solemnly. 'I couldn't possibly know that.' A twinkle in his eyes belied the gravity of his tone.

'*Touché,*' murmured Haley.

A few minutes later, at the conclusion of Booth's racy description of some incident at the club the previous night, they were both laughing heartily when a voice came down the hatch.

'All I seem to hear on this ship recently is unseemly laughter. More of Booth's unprintable stories, I'll bet.'

Lieutenant-Commander Cutter was half-way down the ladder by the time he finished and they rose to meet him.

'Stay put, laddies, stay put. A cup of coffee, and perhaps a slice of toast'—this last to the steward who partly emerged from the pantry with the extra cup ready. 'The food we get in the Officers' Mess ashore is scandalous. Hear they had to turn out the guard last night to rescue a Wren from the clutches of a sex maniac.' His eyes were fixed on Booth. 'No scratches on your face, I see. Did you fight to the last ditch?'

Booth chuckled. 'I saw you leaving the W.R.E.N. Officers' Mess last night, sir, as I was saying good night to a friend.'

'Saying good night! Dammit, you were garrotting the girl. Still, she seemed to like it. Provided my own supper, too. Tell Clay the lobster was magnificent. Lobster and cheese. Made me dream, horribly.'

He sat in the big easy chair with the plate of toast and coffee balanced on the arm.

'*Solan, Jacinth* and the army are battling out a claim for a German 'plane shot down last night. The betting ashore is 7 to 2 on *Solan*,' he said, and for a time they discussed the raid and kindred subject of minelaying.

'Right. Let's get this take-over complete. Wilton, the new Number One for you, hasn't arrived. C.M.S.P. has inflicted this child on you for a trip or two. If you have any trouble flog him, keel-haul him, trice him up to the masthead and give him one hundred lashes.'

'Sheer plagiarism,' Booth laughed delightedly. 'You've been going on *Solan* to much, sir. It's tinged your conversation.'

Cutter chuckled, then went on: 'Right! Bring out the books, etc. The C.B. officer will be along shortly; we'll check them over, then it will be you for the high seas.'

For the next two hours they were busy, although much of the spade-work had been done by Booth in his temporary office as First Lieutenant. It was an added advantage that until recently he had been Number One of the ship and knew where to put his hands on most things.

'There, that's the lot,' Cutter growled, and looked at his watch. 'Nearly eleven. I could do the right thing by a drop of Plymouth's now.'

'We can offer you a cup of tea,' Booth said wickedly, making his way to the locker and producing the bottle.

Cutter clicked his fingers. 'That reminds me. Make out your bond demand. I'll hurry it through for you. It is demoralising for men to have to scrounge cigarettes.' He glinted his eyes towards Booth's bland face. 'And order Plymouth's gin. It's the best. I don't like the other brands,' he concluded inconsequentially.

Haley looked at Booth, who elevated his thumbs and answered: 'All made out and ready to sign.'

Bill went on.

'Defaulters and requestmen in five minutes, Number One. They need not shift from working-rig in view of sailing orders.'

'Aye, aye, sir.' Booth climbed to the deck to pass his orders to the Coxswain.

'Bright lad, acts eighteen in harbour, thirty at sea and is actually twenty-three,' Cutter said. 'D'you like him?'

'Immensely.'

'Fine! I think with a bit of persuasion Commander Mahoney would consider leaving him here as Number One,' Cutter lied cheerfully. 'He knows the ship and the crew. It would help you. We'll think it over, shall we?'

Bill felt strangely glad at the thought of Booth being his First Lieutenant. Contemplation of tackling the ship with a new First Lieutenant, a recent C.W. chrysalis, had been one of his constant and disturbing thoughts.

Booth returned with a clatter.

'Ready, sir?' he asked, and at Haley's nod called up the hatch: 'Bring 'em down, Cox'n.'

Cutter stood up. 'I'll duck out. I'll take some of these papers into Number One's room while you ladle out justice tempered with mercy.' He disappeared behind the curtain and Bill was sorry he had gone. He had a vague hope that Cutter would stay near him as an elder counsellor. It was the first defaulters' parade in which he was sitting in the seat of judgment, and not present as prosecutor or defending.

The Coxswain ushered a group of men down the ladder and marshalled them into two lines. After a brief ceremony of checking names he conferred with Booth and together they consulted the punishment book.

'Five men up for punishment, cases put back, sir. Eleven new cases to hear,' Booth said formally.

'Sixteen? Only thirteen men here,' Haley said after a brief scrutiny.

'Some are repeaters,' Booth murmured.

'Carry on, Cox'n.' The Cox'n held the book in his hand and recited the minor misdemeanours in a monotonous voice.

As he read Haley studied him. This was one of the key men on the ship. A good Cox'n could make a ship's company so far as small ships went. A bad, slack one could be worse than dry rot.

Arandite's Cox'n was slight, short, and his face had a curious pallor which threw into relief the dark line of his eyebrows and the blue-black mass of incipient beard. He kept his voice to a flat level as he recited the offences, neither condemning nor defending by a single inflection. There was a crispness about him which Bill found pleasing, and on one occasion in a brief pause, as Cox'n raised his eyes they met in a glance. It was only an infinitesimal part of a second but the two men arrived at an affinity. Their glances warmed, then the Cox'n went on again until the end.

'That the lot?'

'Yes, sir.'

All the men entered a plea of 'not guilty'. Clay, the first one, started to elaborate but Haley stopped him.

'Evidence, Number One?'

'Cox'n, sir, in each case.'

'Cox'n?'

'I only entered them, sir. I don't know any of the facts except what I was told.'

Haley began to see a little daylight ahead of him. The only disturbing thought was that behind the curtain was a regular, a man versed in the art of dealing with defaulters, both as a Petty Officer and as an officer.

'Well, sink or swim, here goes,' Bill thought.

'Hearsay is not evidence, Cox'n, and you must not tell me what you were told—that is, unless the person who told you will be giving evidence.'

Cox'n shook his head and a slight smile appeared for a moment on his face.

'No, sir. Number One—that is, the other Number One—told me to book 'em . . . he told me . . .' He eyed Haley's restraining hand for a moment then pressed on resolutely, laying emphasis on the words again as if determined to get them out despite all opposition, '. . . he told me that he knew nothing and was acting on orders from the Commanding Officer.'

The Cox'n stared straight ahead, having had his say and won his point.

'Any other evidence?' Bill felt grateful towards the Cox'n for pressing his point. It allowed a little more daylight to creep in.

'No, sir.'

Haley leaned back in his chair, rubbed his chin and finished it off with a long, slow stroke of the finger beneath his lower lip. He hoped it looked judicial as he surveyed the group of men.

'As there is no evidence I must dismiss you all,' he said eventually. Before the Cox'n could take them over Haley went on: 'Let me see that book.'

He ran his finger along the items, quickly digesting them and paying particular regard to the dates of previous offences. Then he looked up, returned the book to the Cox'n and addressed the men.

'These offences, and others against your names, seem markedly similar . . . very much alike . . . and they have all happened in the past five or six weeks. There must be a reason, but I propose to let those events lie where they are. I dismiss these offences with an easy conscience. That does not mean to say that I shall be so easy-going for any offences in the future. The three here, which should go before Commander Mahoney, I will also take no action about as there is no evidence. Carry on, Cox'n.'

Cox'n ushered the men out and Bill relaxed. After they had gone Cutter came back into the wardroom but made no mention of the somewhat unorthodox parade of defaulters and their treatment, which he must have heard. Instead, he ruffled the thick list in his hand.

'You'll want a lot of stuff. I'll have it ready for you when you come back. A bird doesn't fly on one wing,' he went on, looking at Booth. That young man reacted promptly and poured out a drink each, incidentally draining the bottle.

'That's the last,' he said. 'I'll have to borrow another bottle from *Golfitt*.'

'Then it's time I went,' Cutter said. He moved to the hatch, waited for Haley and Booth to get their caps and all three went on deck.

A neatly dressed quartermaster stood by the rail and saluted, in unison with Haley and Booth, as Cutter climbed ashore. As he reached the quay Cutter turned and looked over Bill's head.

'Ever read Shakespeare? My wife makes me read him. Says he has the answer to everything. There's a bit "the quality of mercy is not strained"!'

'Portia,' said Booth promptly.

'You probably read it on a calendar,' Cutter jeered. 'Very nicely handled, very nicely indeed, even if not according to K.R. and A.I. Good luck.' He strode off down the quay, leaving Bill glowing slightly. He felt that he had passed a test not only before a Senior Officer but insofar as the men of his crew were concerned, although he felt that basically there was nothing else he could have done. He heard Booth chuckle beside him.

'What's funny?'

'He was dead right. I did read it on a calendar, but it was many years ago.'

Bill laughed. 'All right, Methuselah. Harbour stations in fifteen minutes.'

Then he prepared for his next test—taking her to sea.

When he climbed to the top bridge a few minutes later he found that Booth had been busy. The ship was singled up to one headline and a back spring, a wire leading from the stern to a bollard on the quay nearly abeam of the bridge.

The bridge seemed higher from the water than when viewed from the deck. Bill had been up once before the previous night, just before turning in, and on that occasion he had felt just a little of the pride of command steal through the still present feeling of resentment at being moved from a destroyer to minesweeping and to trawlers.

As he reached the top bridge the feeling of pride, although it could scarcely be so clearly defined by that one word, returned to him. This was his ship, his to command, and handle. His ship, boil it down to that, he thought.

'Singled up, sir. Will you go off by the stern or by the bow?'

Haley did not answer Booth for a moment. It was a small problem, one to be settled in one all-embracing look which would take in room ahead, room astern, set of the wind off the quay, all in one or two seconds. In fact, one usually decided by the Commanding Officer before he climbed to the bridge.

But this was Haley's first attempt at taking the bridge. He had done it during his pre-war training on several occasions, but then there had been a training officer standing near to take over in the event of a crisis or a complete hash, even to offer a word or two at the right moment to turn a dismal operation into a reasonable performance.

Haley climbed to a little shelf alongside the inner side of the bridge and looked aft and forward. The seamen were lounging waiting for orders. On the quay wall stood seamen from other ships ready to let go their lines.

'I'll go off on the back spring, Mr Booth. Ring stand-by,' he said down a voice-pipe marked 'Wheelhouse'.

'Stand-by, sir,' a voice replied. A bell jangled distantly and stridenly down in the engine-room and was answered by a fainter tinkle immediately below him.

70

Haley took his station on the platform immediately behind the binnacle. The voice-pipe was a few inches from his mouth. He hesitated a few moments more while he marshalled in precise order all the things he had to do to get the ship off. Once he had her moving, rightly or wrongly, nearly five hundred tons of powerful ship would be under way and he it was who had to decide which way she moved.

He turned and saw a youngster looking at him steadily. Round his neck the lad had a pair of battered binoculars. He saw Haley looking at him and smiled.

'You are the signalman?' Haley queried.

'Yessir. Larkin's the name.'

'What is the port rule? Do we have to wait for orders to slip, or . . .'

'No, sir. Slip when ready.' The signalman looked at a watch hanging from a hook on the little chart table. 'It's a minute to twelve.'

Haley nodded. From some snatch of conversation he recalled a phrase, then a sentence. 'Mahoney means 1200 hours precisely.'

'Let go for'ard,' he called to Booth, who was hanging over the bridge side expectantly. 'Slow astern,' he said down the wheelhouse. The bells jangled and he heard the hiss of steam from the engine-room.

'Blast! I've cut it fine.' Haley thought as *Arandite* started to throb gently against the hold of the stern wire. Her bow swung off and the gap between the wall grew wider as he watched. 'Little than half a minute to be moving across the harbour.' The gap had become a wide angle and the bows well cleared the ship ahead.

'When in doubt go full ahead and hope for the best,' he remembered Payne once saying on the bridge of the *Culver*. 'At least you will have steering way on your ship.'

Without reflection, as if prompted by a hidden voice, he said sharply and loudly down the voice-pipe:

'Full ahead. Hard a starboard.'

'FULL ahead?' the voice queried below, with a world of question in the first word.

'Full ahead,' Haley repeated, accenting the 'full'.

'Full ahead, sir, hard a starboard on.'

'Let go aft.'

Booth called the order to the stern, adding: 'Take in the slack of that wire as we come up. We don't want it round the screw.'

Bill felt his heart pound slightly. 'Wire round the screw' repeated itself in his mind. Had he slipped up on some minor point?

'All clear aft,' Booth sang out. Haley glanced at him and saw him grinning widely. Beyond Booth, on the quay, were two seamen who had attended to the forward wires. Their mouths were open and their eyes were goggling. *Arandite* was already swinging past them with the forward drive of the engines and the rudder hard over.

Suddenly Haley felt cool, collected, with two or three vignetted pictures in his mind.

'Will the stern clear the wall, Mr. Booth?'

'By a mile, sir.'

'Ten feet will do,' Haley replied coldly.

Arandite raced past the ship moored ahead of her. swinging stern missing the ship's quarter by not more than a few feet. Her bow came round until it pointed almost directly towards the harbour entrance.

'Midships. . . . steady.' The bow pinned on the stumpy light-house at the end of the pier. Two black balls climbed up slowly to a yard-arm.

'We've got the gate, sir,' the signalman called.

Arandite slid smoothly across the harbour, leaving behind. her on the glassy water a knife-straight wake. From her funnel a plume of black smoke climbed out lazily and hung in the windless air; beneath it, from the exhaust pipe, a small cotton-wool wisp of steam waved bravely.

Above his head Haley saw a string of flags climb to his

yard-arm. It was their pennant numbers. He saw an opportunity to assert a little authority.

'Those pennant numbers should be up the moment we are under way, Number One. See it is so in future.'

Booth looked at him with raised eyebrows. 'In future,' he thought. 'Not this chicken. You can tell that to your new bloke.' Aloud he said to the signalman: 'Get 'em up quicker.'

The signalman looked pained and shook his head gently. 'Didn't have time, sir. One second we was alongside the wall. I takes a squint at the signal station and we're halfway across the harbour . . .'

'Don't argue, get 'em up, close up, on the jump.'

Officially *Arandite* was under way and closing the signal station rapidly.

Haley looked at the station, saw a figure come out on the verandah and peer at them through binoculars. He picked up a pair from the chart table, a powerful pair of Barr and Stroud's, and returned the scrutiny. It brought the station into startlingly close range. Bill could even see a cup or a mug balanced on the window-sill.

'Enter it in the log,' he said crisply. 'Slipped and under way 1200 hours.'

Booth leaned over the log on the chart table and Haley heard him mutter something.

'Did you speak, Number One?' Bill was still being a shade curt.

'Yes, sir. I said it is actually 1159 and 55 seconds.'

'Make it 1200. We are not timing a hundred yards sprint.'

Booth giggled slightly and opened his mouth, but seeing no glimmer of humour on Haley's face closed it and made no comment.

'Damn,' thought Bill. 'Now I'm getting to be real C.O. Why didn't I take it up and laugh about it?'

As they passed the signal station the man called through a megaphone:

'Dead on time, *Arandite*. What's the hurry?'

Bill decided that it was the moment for him to relax and become human. He glanced around the bridge and saw a battered megaphone lying beneath the chart table. He motioned with his hand and the signalman passed it to him.

'No hurry; I'm going "Dead slow" at the moment,' he called back. He lifted his binoculars again and saw the flash of the man's teeth in his sunburned face as he tilted his head to laugh. Bill went on: 'At least, my part of the ship is going slow. It's Number One's half which is in a hurry. He's on his way to a party.'

He shot a swift glance at Booth, saw he was grinning.

'Don't let your tea grow cold,' he concluded.

The man on the station reached to the window, lifted the mug then drank from it. By this time they were leaving him astern. He lifted his megaphone and faintly Bill heard 'Good luck!' He waved in reply. After a moment he turned to Booth and smiled slightly. 'That should enhance your reputation as a fast young man, Number One. What about you taking some lunch while the going is good?'

Booth nodded, thought for a moment, then said: 'We'll have it up here, if you like. It's a lovely day and we've nearly an hour before we join the throng.'

Bill concurred.

'Bunts, go and get yours and tell the steward to bring ours on the bridge.'

While waiting for the tray Bill took a quick look around his command. Now that she was away from the quay way and at sea he could gain a different perspective. From the bridge she looked much slimmer, or was it because the pencil-thin lines of the destroyer were already fading from the forefront of his mind?

His eyes swung aft and he saw the twin machine-gun move in a slight arc. Behind the shield he could see the Pirate glancing through the sights. He heard the faint series of clicks as the man brought the gun to the 'ready'. He looked immediately below him. Another young seaman was leaning negligently against the Hotchkiss mount, though there was nothing negligent about his sustained scrutiny of the sky.

Haley crossed over to the other side of the bridge. An older seaman was fiddling with the other gun, but although his hands were busy with the mechanism his eyes were on the sky. Bill stood on tip-toes and looked towards the 12-pounder gun on the bandstand mount on the foredeck. Three men stood round it. One was against the training wheel, another by the laying wheel and a third leaned against the shield looking forward. Although he could see only the back of his head Bill guessed that he, too, was missing none of the sky in the forward arc. The man's head moved in a slow turning motion as he spoke to the man at the layer wheel. Then the Layer joined him for a moment, gazed forward, slipped back to his position, calling out in a deep voice without trace of urgency or alarm:

'Aircraft bearing red two oh, low down. Couple of miles.' As he called the gun swung easily on the bearing and the third man stepped back so that he was in reaching distance of the ammunition rack.

Haley and Booth trained their glasses in the direction. It was Booth who spoke first: 'Hurricanes, two of them. Right over the stem, now, going inland.'

Haley found them after a moment, caught the glint from them as they turned in the sun.

'Famous last words—"couple of ours",' he said. Booth signalled with upraised thumbs towards the skeleton gun crew and they relaxed.

'This ship is on the top line,' he thought. 'Dammit, I should have thought of that as we left harbour.' He decided to dress the occasion slightly.

'Short burst from each machine-gun to clear guns, then keep at the "ready",' he said shortly. He heard the First Lieutenant pass the order, heard the short, ripping burst from each gun and saw the tracer climb slowly in an arc.

'Like to do a burst from Susie?' Booth asked innocently.

'Susie?' Haley turned and saw Booth fitting a stripped Lewis-gun, shorn of its air-cooling cylinder, to a mount plugged into the rail of the bridge.

'Susie?' he repeated.

'She stammers half-way through a burst, sometimes jams, so we call her "Stuttering Susie",' Booth was busy lifting a drum from a box.

Haley took it from him, fixed it on, whirled it round, cocked the gun and fired two short bursts into the air. It stammered slightly, then went on.

'Weak spring perhaps. We'll strip it down one day and have a look-see,' he said.

'Sure,' Booth replied, then he remembered the collective 'we'. 'You've got a hope, chum,' he pondered. 'Two days more and I'm off this ship.'

Haley stepped to the front of the bridge and saw Clay looking up at him. Bill took the megaphone and spoke into it.

'I see the gun didn't float, Clay. Feels quite homey on the bridge.'

He heard Clay's deep chuckle as he turned to explain the point of the joke to the men on the gun platform. Haley had not seen them before and they looked curiously at him. From where he stood they were not near enough for him to see their features but he was struck by their youthfulness. *Culver* had had a strong leavening of youth, but this ship seemed to be manned by boys and youths. The point was worth developing. He used it to establish a more easy informal atmosphere with Booth.

'This seems to be a young crew. What is the average age?'

'I worked it out once. Excluding one or two centenarians, like Clay and Noisy-the-Cook and the Cox'n, the average age is about twenty. About half a dozen of them are fishermen—R.N.R.—the rest patrol service.' Booth looked ahead for a moment. 'A good crowd, too,' he added.

'So you told me before, and so I am gathering for myself,' said Haley, with a smile. 'With luck we'll get them back into shape.'

'Again that collective 'we'. Booth nearly commented on it, but decided against. Perhaps the C.O. was using it only in a loose sense.

The steward, with a large tray covered with a serviette, broke off further discussion and between them they tackled the food.

Haley, leaning against the fore part of the bridge with a plate of prunes before him, saw through the faint heat haze the outlines of two or three trawlers.

'That must be *Solan* and company,' he said, nodding his head towards them. Booth took one quick glance, dumped his plate on the chart table and was galvanised into rapid action.

'Bunts!' he yelled, the diminutive for 'bunting tosser' or signalman ringing all over the ship. 'Bunts!' Then he grabbed a small Aldis signal lamp, sighted it on the trawlers and started flashing.

After a while one of them started blinking a reply.

'Got him! Caught him on the jump,' Booth chuckled delightedly. 'We called him first. That wipes his eye. BUNTS!' He yelled again and Haley heard the cry picked up and relayed by somebody on deck level. 'But if he starts slapping out signals I'm done. I can get by with challenges and replies and a bit of slow stuff, but *Solan*'s Bunts is hot stuff. He and our lad are great rivals. Damn!' he went on as the ship in the haze broke into a flurry of twinkling messages.

'Carry on. I can read him,' Bill said calmly. 'Just give him 't's' when I say.' He went on reading the signal.

'Right!' he replied when it ended. 'The answer will be ...' He broke off as he saw the signalman standing at the back of him and gave him the answer to pass.

'Could you read him at that speed?' Booth asked

curiously. Morse had been one of Bill's hobbies since his Boy Scout days. Friendship with a signals officer in his pre-war R.N.V.R. days had improved it and long hours with the genial Petty Officer on *Culver* had helped him to master that form of Morse shorthand used by good signallers —the abbreviations which helped speed and shortened work.

'U R' for instance would be 'you are', 'tk up stn' was 'take up station', and there were many more.

'Give me the Aldis,' Bill said. 'I'll send it. I'm a bit rusty and the practice will be useful. Is the man the other end Patrol Service or General Service?' he asked.

'P.S.,' the signalman answered, feeling slightly outraged and puzzled. 'Me and 'im passed out together. He thinks he's good,' he went on, worried at the thought of some ragged signalling passing from *Arandite* to *Solan*—of all ships.

Bill nodded and levelled the lamp. As the message went on he heard the signalman behind him chuckle two or three times. 'He's asking for repeats,' he whispered to Booth. 'The C.O.'s sending it clear enough,' he allowed grudgingly. 'Bloody liar,' he continued a little later, 'he says "Slower, please, I cannot see your light clearly." '

Haley completed his answer, handed the lamp to the signalman and said: 'He guessed at words instead of reading them. Far too many signalmen do that.' He looked severly at Bunts. 'You don't, do you?' It was a statement rather than a query.

Bunts looked shocked and virtuous at the same time.

'No, sir. Not me, sir.' He stowed his lamp away.

Haley looked solemnly at Booth. He grinned and winked. Booth answered with a grin, then they both leaned over the bridge front.

'That long signal was to the effect that our right place in the sweep formation is number two, but *Solan* asked— rather nice of him, I thought—if we would prefer to take tail-end Charlie until we get into the swing of it. It will be

78

port side sweep,' and Haley went off into technical details to which Booth listened earnestly. 'I told him I felt quite confident of assuming our right place in the fleet.' He broke off to lift his glasses towards the closing group of ships. 'Somebody is being detached,' he said.

Booth followed suit, then murmured: '*Jacinth*. She's been lame duck for a time. *Pearl* was to have sent her in yesterday.'

They were both silent for a time. 'Perhaps it was a nice clean day like this yesterday,' Haley thought, 'with *Pearl* steaming along to join the group when she was attacked.'

Instinctively he looked at the sky, half-closing his eyes, half expecting to see a diving aircraft drop out of the blue. Then he remembered the silent, watchful men at the guns and felt a supreme confidence that any aircraft would be spotted almost at once.

As he went on looking he said: 'I told him that I had Sub-lieutenant Booth as temporary First Lieutenant, local guide and mentor. It was that section her signalman stumbled over.'

He heard a commotion behind him and saw, from the corner of his eye, the signalman lift his lamp and train it on *Solan*.

As the signal developed Haley chuckled quietly but said nothing. When it was complete Bunts coughed slightly to clear his throat and intoned woodenly:

'Signal is, sir, "On your head be it. Take station astern of me. I dare not make it otherwise. Hell hath no fury like a Booth scorned." ' He coughed again, hesitated, then went on: 'There was a bit more, sir.'

'He asked you where you learned your fancy flashing and if you had heard about their 'plane,' Haley smiled. 'Tell him when you get ashore.'

He turned to Booth. 'You'd better get the sweep ready. I'd hate to make a hash of it first time.'

Booth turned to leave the bridge. 'It will be another hour

79

before we want it and I fancy it is all ready. Usually is port sweep on this beat. When we put it over I'll have Clay aft and Cox'n can take the wheel.'

Haley nodded agreement. He liked the youngster's incisive manner when a job was to be done. Perhaps it would be possible to persuade Mahoney to . . . but C.M.S.P. had too much on his plate to bother about switching junior officers to suit Commanding Officers. Still, with Cutter on his side . . . Such pleasant reveries occupied Haley until he closed the group and moved in to take his station astern of *Solan*. The other ships had not moved up when *Jacinth* had left and carefully he nudged her in until he was dead astern of the leading ship. He could see binoculars trained on him from the ship ahead and the one astern.

He rang half speed before starting to take up position, judging that to be their speed. Down in the engine-room a Petty Officer in grimy blue jean trousers and a singlet answered the telegraph muttering: 'That's the only ring since we left port. Doesn't believe in telegraph drill, this Old Man. Still, we'll see what we'll see.'

He had no time for further observations because he received several calls down the voice-pipe calling for a slight increase or decrease of revolutions, until Haley had her nicely balanced and requiring only an occasional fluctuation to keep in station.

Booth rejoined him on the bridge. 'All ready aft, sir. A nice new sweep that's only been used once. When we shoot I'll drop down and see it over.'

A hundred questions flitted through Haley's mind, questions to which he wanted answers, but he judged that this was not the time to ask any of them. He was curious to hear more details of his predecessor's last few weeks on board. Not from a morbid point of view, but the punishment book he had scrutinised early in the day pointed to an acute, sudden, irrational irritation, or something more. He wanted to hear more about Booth's desire for a shift to another ship.

But he put the questions out of his mind and turned to look round him again.

The resentment he had felt so strongly at his own transfer was still there. It still rankled, but creeping through it, softening it until it would reach final disintegration, or at least shrinkage to minute proportions, came a resurgence of the feeling of command. Maybe she was only a trawler, maybe the routine was not up to destroyer standard, maybe . . . maybe. . . . Haley found himself finding half a dozen qualifications for each limitation his rankling resentment uncovered.

He smiled slightly at the little conceit he had been guilty of in his letter to his wife when he used the 'Commanding Officer' rubber stamp. And why not? He was, when all was said and done, the Commanding Officer of H.M.S. *Arandite*, one of His Majesty's minesweepers. He ran through his mind again the little talk Mahoney had given him on the vital necessity for keeping that stretch of water open. Haley looked at it. It glistened so innocently, scarcely a swell on it, and they were little farther out than a position that would be reached by a couple of bob trip from the seaside resort he could see inshore. He had sailed down here and seen that inshore beach black with people seeking the sun and relaxation. Now the beach was bare; there was no movement on the esplanade behind it and instead of small yachts and pleasure boats dotting the water there were only four minesweeping trawlers, and astern of them a drifter lazing along like a small boy following a gang of larger lads, as if anxious to be with them but not certain of his welcome.

'That's the blood boat.' Booth followed Haley's glance towards the drifter. 'She tags along to shoot up any we cut and . . . and picks up the pieces if anybody bumps into one.' He rested his forearms on the wind-break of the bridge and looked at the drifter. 'The *Harvester* she's called, and she's had some odd harvests in the last couple of months.

81

She did good work at Dunkirk. We all had a hell of a time then. You should have seen the beaches. Millions of P.I.B.s . . . millions.'

Haley glanced at him. Although the youngster's words were mildly and humorously exaggerated there was no smile on his face.

'I see they are calling it a glorious achievement ashore. The Miracle of Dunkirk by which an army was saved. The lot I saw were disorganised rabble.' —

Haley interrupted him. 'I saw them, too; we had five days of it in *Culver*, a destroyer I was on. Disorganised? Yes. Rabble? Not on your life! Don't forget, a lot of them got back to the beaches after days and nights of footslogging or scrapping and were prepared to fight it out in the sand dunes. Given time and arms, they will still give an account of themselves.'

Booth looked at him with interest at his mention of having taken part in the Dunkirk episode but made no reply. Haley went on: 'I saw our soldiers landed in Norway, ill-armed, more than slightly bewildered, and saw them come off again. But demoralised? Never! One day—how long away, Lord knows—they'll be back with a return ticket.'

'But they were chucking their arms away wholesale,' Booth objected.

'So would you if you had to swim fifty or a hundred yards,' Haley said. 'Even at that some of them—a whole lot of them—stuck to their rifles. Those who were taken off from the piers threw no arms away. One lot we took away even wanted to go back to the outskirts of the town to collect their artillery.'

He smiled at Booth. 'I agree some of the soldiers lost items of armament'—he looked dreamily at the machine-gun mounted on the bridge—'possibly because there were some light-fingered buccaneers around . . . but not many.'

Booth threw back his head and laughed.

'All right, you win.' He suddenly became grave again

82

and Haley recalled Cutter's description of him and his quick switching from an apparent eighteen years old to a grim thirty. At the moment Booth's face was set in hard, clear lines and his eyes were looking away into space from beneath lowered lids. Quite softly he spoke:

'I want to be present when those return tickets are being used. I want to see the finish.'

Haley put his hand lightly on the youngster's shoulders.

'So do I, badly,' he said. They leaned in silence against the warm bridge, each with his own vision of the end, each realising that as yet they were only at the beginning.

'Flag-hoist on *Solan*,' barked Bunts and busied himself at his flag locker after one swift glance through his battered glasses.

'Sweeping signal,' Booth said tersely and turned to leave the bridge.

Haley heard the Cox'n take over from the man at the wheel below him and heard the seaman clatter down the steel ladder and along the deck.

'Slow ahead,' Haley ordered as one flag-hoist fluttered down. *Arandite* started to drop astern of *Solan*, Haley keeping a watch on the distance through a distance meter.

'Half speed,' he ordered when they were the correct distance apart. The little fleet spread out so that each ship was slightly on the other's port quarter.

Another flag-hoist, ordering a turn of 180 degrees, climbed to *Solan*'s yard-arm, held there until repeated down the line, then fluttered down. *Solan* swung round in a broad curve, her wake clear-cut in the water. Haley concentrated on following it, then murmured 'damn' as he saw that for some reason he was cutting down the distance apart.

A second flag-hoist slipped down from the yard-arm.

'Out sweeps.'

Haley moved to the side of the bridge to check the sweep crew aft until he could drop her astern slightly, then saw that he was no longer following *Solan*'s wake. He was going round and outside it.

Two things dawned swiftly on him. First, this course would correct his initial error and on completion would place him in the right position on *Solan*'s quarter instead of being dead astern of her, as he would have been had he followed in her wake. Second, it was the Cox'n at the wheel who was correcting the error without deviating a great deal from his last order, which was: 'Follow the ship ahead.' He gave no more helm orders until the fleet was aligned and there and then Haley decided to cut out destroyer orders in future. He leaned over the bridge rail with the megaphone and called aft: 'Let it go.' He saw the cigar-shaped Oropesa float with its short flagstaff drop over the side and draw astern. Quickly it slipped away. The crew, with a minimum of movement and noise, got the steel-shuttered kite ready and the heavy iron-shod otter-board ready hooked on, and at a signal from Booth it slid down out of sight.

A man with a sweep measure held hard against the sweep wire stood up and Booth signalled with a screwing motion of his arms to the winchman. Then he faced the bridge and held his thumbs up.

Without waiting for an order the signalman, who had been watching the group aft, hauled down one fluttering pennant from the yard-arm then looked swiftly along the fleet. 'Dead heat, us and *Solan*,' he said, his voice fat with satisfaction. 'There's the other two now.'

The ships soon settled down to a balanced speed, and Booth rejoined Haley on the bridge.

'Nice going, sir. We pipped the other two and dead-heated with *Solan*. I thought we were going to be too far inside at first.'

A faint smile took possession of Haley's face as he moved towards the voice-pipe at the wheel.

'We were . . . a lot too much inside at first. Send a man to relieve the wheel now.'

'Aye, aye, sir.' Booth leaned over the bridge to call one of the seamen.

Haley put his lips close to the voice-pipe. 'Cox'n?'

'Yessir?' The voice came back faintly.

'Thank you.'

There was a perceptible pause before the reply came back up the pipe:

'Aye, aye, sir.'

That was all. Commanding Officer and Petty Officer, both men in authority and wearing the badge of authority on their sleeves, had arrived at an understanding. Not for worlds would the Cox'n have said that it was he who corrected the error, but he knew that Haley knew and appreciated that fact.

The Cox'n smiled to himself. Haley on the top bridge also smiled. And they both shared the same sentiment: 'Things might work out yet.'

Haley had started his career as a minesweeper.

4

H.M. Minesweeper *Arandite*, ex-trawler of the same name, 400 tons net, triple expansion engines, super-heated boilers, snored along well within her full capacity, drawing after her 500 fathoms of 2½-inch sweep wire with its complicated terminus of jaw-toothed cutter, otter-board, steel kite and explosive wire cutters.

A simple task compared with the 900 fathoms of trawl wire and heavy trawl she was built to handle—and did handle—with a half-gale blowing up and Bear Island rearing its cold head not fifty miles to the north.

Many generations of wise heads had contributed their little to her all, had added something here and something there to her ultimate design, until today she steamed along at a steady five and half knots, the near perfect conception of a trawler.

Her phosphor-bronze propeller, deep down, nearly fifteen feet below, bit solidly at the green water and her cruiser stern settled a little lower. There was nearly eighteen feet of her in the water under that slim curved stern. She would hold against a gale and the rearing seas it would call to clamorous campaign against her. To aid that depth her bow cocked up haughtily with only nine feet of it in the water. Any roaring seas which climbed over it would be shaken, resolutely thrown to one side or allowed to curl over, force reduced, on her spacious fore-deck, then sent back in chastened mood to rejoin the vainly raging mass.

True, sometimes she or a sister would fall victim to an

assault and would be smothered by hammering seas which would bury her. She would find the answer. Her flared, buoyant bow would rise, tearing a gap through the smothering water, shake it, shake herself and settle down to the more orderly rhythm of breaking the force before it broke her.

True, sometimes a sister held down by seas would fail to rise clear before other ranging green mountains hurried to the kill, climbed on board, hammering, tearing and smothering, adding their weight . . . until the sister went on down . . . and down.

As often as not it was the fault of man, with his limitations which brought about the first breach in the rhythm which was her protection. Failure to give her aid with a little helm, failure to call the power of the engine, or reduce it, so that she was able to meet the forces arrayed against her with just the right amount of strength so that she could give way when necessary or use force when called for.

But that was trawling, the job for which she was built. Her destiny. Come hell, come high water, slam at full speed to the fishing-ground, fish, and, come hell, come high water, slam home again to catch the markets.

Now it was altered.

Her fish holds had been cleaned out, turned into living accommodation. Instead of the distributed weight of a load of ice or fish one solid mass had been concentrated on the foredeck and occasionally, accompanied by a shattering roar, it imposed momentarily terrific strains. Such was the effect of a gun.

She felt a little light about the bows. The thrust of the propellor was inclined to make her veer to port a little, and clumsy hands at the wheel, instead of aiding her with a small amount of rudder, would put on a lot that would start her swinging until her wake looked like a wriggling snake behind her, and turn her into a horizontal pendulum.

But the man at the wheel on this perfectly calm day had

the touch of experience. A touch—not more than two or three spokes—called on the rudder for the smallest of corrections in ample time, and *Arandite* slipped gently back on to a correct course, so gently that the change scarcely showed along her wake.

All that there was to mar such a perfect day lay in the future, either the immediate or in a long term ahead. At any moment there would come a shattering roar beneath the water which would strike her hull like a vast hammer. And that would be a mine.

Once one, round, rusted, sinister, bland, had rolled away from her stem, tossed inches clear by the plume from her bow, had slid, bobbing and frustrated, along her side, swept in threatening to touch her stern, and had rolled away to wait for another victim.

That had been in the dark of a night and the men on her, some watchful but weary-eyed on deck and others sleeping uneasily below, never knew that only a bow wave and inches were between them and a sudden, slamming crash which would have ripped and rended, sending *Arandite* reeling away to sink and for them, some of them, providing the answer to all problems.

Her designers had stolen a fraction of a knot here, another fraction there, by raking the funnel, curving the front of the bridge, reducing resistance so that the power of the triple expansion engines could concentrate on thrusting the cunningly contrived hull through the water.

The little girl, daughter of the managing director of the owning company, had clapped her hands with glee when she performed the simple ceremony of launching her at the yard on the Humber.

'Daddy, oh, Daddy, she looks like a big duck,' she cried as the still-red hull bobbed slightly against the restraining chains.

'Aye, she's like a duck, my dear,' the yard manager replied, after a thankful glance at her settling down to her designed level. 'Like a duck, and not a right angle in her.'

And now she was minesweeping, wresting a harvest of safety and salvation for other ships. Not for her the glamour of swift, pulsating action with the glory of the victory and the laurels to follow. It was hers to grope along, searching the green depths, and searching them again until she found, lurking below in them, that which carried death. And when she found it do battle with it, still in the dark green, until it was exploded, or cut free to float to the surface, a victim for destruction. Such was her allotted task so that other sisters of the sea could go on their lawful errands.

Round the coast at this moment hundreds of such trawlers were probing and searching, clearing and sweeping without thought of glory or laurels, with but one prayer:

'From things that "boomp" in the night, good Lord deliver us.'

Haley finished a cup of tea and put the empty cup on the chart table.

'Can you hold the fort up here, Number One, while I take a walk around the ship? Apart from the wardroom and the bridge, I've seen nothing of her.'

Booth grinned and settled his elbows more comfortably on the bridge rail.

'Don't get lost. If you do, ask a policeman. Our naval patrols are wonderful. Ask Clay; he's a favourite with them.'

Haley added another question to the already long list he was accumulating of queries which ultimately he proposed to lay out for examination.

On the engine-room casing, just behind the funnel, he saw three men lying in the complete relaxation of sleep. Two were stokers dressed in the inevitable faded blue dungaree trousers and grubby vest, the third was a seamen. Hanging loosely from his shoulders, so that it spread out from him, was a duffle coat stained and dirty, its original colour merged into a dingy grey-brown.

'Phew!' thought Haley. 'Here it is with a temperature at sea level around the lower eighties and they sleep on a hot engine-room casing. One wrapped as for the arctic, the others in a state of advanced undress.'

He stepped quietly over them without disturbing them, noticing that each of them had his arm through the tapes of an inflatable lifebelt. Their reason for sleeping on deck was obvious. They meant to be on the spot with a reasonable chance of going over the side if the ship struck a mine or was hit by a bomb.

His brief reflection on their place of rest and their clothing was an epitome of that mysterious, at times unfathomable, character, a naval seaman with his rigid regard for conservatism and custom.

There were a dozen cooler places on deck where they could have taken their siesta, but from the time ships had funnels it was the warm spot on deck and on that warm spot, by right of custom, they proposed to sleep, and sleep there they would.

Duffle coats, provided as loan clothing for the protection of seamen in exposed positions on the upper deck, were worn at all times on the upper deck, and unless remorselessly checked seamen would wear them over the ship's side to paint the ship, to the obvious detriment of the duffle coat.

Haley stood near the small gun platform perched on a deckhouse at the after end of the ship. He could see the lower half of a seaman's figure, but not his head and shoulders. As he stood there the man's head came round the gun-shield, a square of metal just large enough to protect the gunner's upper part. He watched him. No part of the sky was without scrutiny in sector. From almost right overhead to sea level the man's eyes swept on, slowly describing a series of perpendicular zig-zags. For just one moment he froze and his hand lifted towards the machine-gun. Haley followed his eyes and saw, clearly limned against the sky, a sea-gull planing along, wings motionless, at times just a thin outline and at others, as it banked and turned, something momentarily more sinister.

Haley turned back to the seaman who, scrutiny satisfied, was going over the rest of his sector.

'Friendly sea-gull,' Haley said quietly.

'Can be hostile when they are overhead and a bloke is dressed in his Number One's,' the man answered, briefly flicking a glance towards Haley.

Haley chuckled. 'Yes, indeed, a virulent hostility.'

His aerial survey complete, the man relaxed and turned towards Haley. He smiled, took a flat tin from his pocket and started to roll a cigarette.

'Don't mind if I smoke, do you, sir?'

'There are no Standing Orders against it, so far as I know. What is that? Ticklers?'

The man nodded, rolled a neat cigarette which he lit, inhaled the smoke and blew it out with obvious satisfaction.

'Yes, sir, we're a bit short on the others right now.' He moved a step or two to the edge of the gun platform and flicked the matchstick over the side.

'That is being attended to when we return to harbour.'

Haley spent a little time studying the man as the seaman gave another quick survey of the sky in his sector. He was about twenty-four, clean, fresh-faced, intelligent, and his well-shaped head was poised alertly on his shoulders. He had a trick of moving his eyes first then bringing his head in alignment with them as he did his zig-zag scrutiny.

Haley waited until he had completed his look-see.

'What is your name?'

'Lennox, sir.'

'I don't think I've seen you before. Have I?'

'Down the wardroom this morning, sir. Two charges. Late back from leave and neglect of duty.'

The man's face was expressionless.

Haley ran swiftly through the scene when the group of

men had appeared before him but could recall nothing except a rapid recital of names, and could think of no reason why the name should stick in his memory as soon as the man mentioned it.

He took a cigarette from his case and lit it while he searched the recesses of his mind.

'Lennox, Lennox. . . .' He allowed the name to trickle through his mind like a fistful of slowly released sand. Then it came to him. He clicked his fingers in mild triumph. It was during some of the conversation between Booth and Cutter. Cutter had asked how the C.W. candidate was progressing and after answering Booth had elaborated a little for Haley's benefit.

There was a man on board who was being observed as a potential officer for Commissions and Warrants.

'Yes, of course, you are C.W., aren't you?' Haley spoke at last. 'Nearly at the end of the three allotted months.'

'I was, and it is,' Lennox replied with a smile. 'That's answering them in that order, sir.' The smile disappeared from his face. 'I'm afraid one or two things will have blotted my copybook, sir.'

Haley declined the gambit. He was not prepared to open a discussion immediately on the merits, right or wrong, of minor crimes committed before he joined the ship, but he added to his list of things due to be discussed. He went off at a tangent, yet at the back of his mind he searched for some way of conveying to the man that events immediately prior to Haley taking command would soon be under survey and possible adjustment.

'What are you in civilian life?'

'Professional cricketer, sir. I played for a works league side in the Midlands, but I was qualifying for the county. With luck I would have had a few games this season.'

'Are you a batsman or bowler—or both?'

'Bowler primarily—spin. I go in about fifth wicket down.'

Haley saw a chance to get in a neat simile which would at once give the man an idea that his future was not being entirely clouded by recent events and yet would not be too definite.

'I think we'll have the light roller on this wicket, and that might alter the quality of the batting in the next innings. The game isn't entirely over yet, you know.'

He smiled at the man and prepared to climb down the short steel ladder from the gun platform. 'After a look at the scorebook I fancy you are down as "not out".'

They looked at each other and Haley saw a warm light steal into Lennox's eyes and they crinkled at the corners.

'That helps an average along, doesn't it, sir?'

A subdued ripple of laughter, from a small group of men sitting on a grating in the stern, greeted Haley as he walked round the deck-house. One of the men was in the middle of an anecdote and as Haley had no wish to interrupt he moved over to look at the steel sweep wire which trailed from the quarter. It was vibrating slightly as it travelled through the water and Haley allowed his thoughts to dwell on what it might be touching, or even cutting, at that second. Possibly, even as he watched it that slight vibration might be caused by the serrated cutting strand sawing through a mine mooring wire, or it might be caused by the mine wire slipping down the sweep to reach the jaws of the steel cutter, where it might go off with a roaring crash, harmless but startling.

Haley jumped as a yell of laughter burst out behind him. He turned swiftly. The story had reached its climax, and Clay, the teller of the story, was leaning back against the rail, a grin on his face as he received his due mead of laughter in reward.

'No doubt what Cutter would call a highly successful pothouse joke, judging by the applause,' Haley thought, smiling despite himself.

The laughter died as he stepped towards the group.

Clay stood up as Haley reached them.

'Quite a good angle on the sweep, sir. We beat *Solan* and the others, didn't we, sir?' he said, his eyes sweeping down the length of wire.

'We tied with *Solan,* but beat the others. But why the rivalry? Haley asked curiously.

'Us and *Solan* have always been chummy ships, sir,' another youngster explained. 'We have bets on getting the sweeps out and in. There'll be a flap when it's "in sweeps". We bet in cigarettes.' He looked at Haley rather shyly. 'At least we used to bet in cigarettes, up to a few weeks ago.'

'Here's the feeler about cigarettes again,' thought Haley. Aloud, he said: 'How long since there was an issue on board?'

Nobody answered immediately and Haley saw a swift exchange of glances between the men, then they all concentrated on Clay as if silently appointing him to take up the theme.

'Couple of weeks,' Clay said. 'The last C.O. said he wouldn't order any after . . . after something happened.'

Haley waited. 'All right, you've started the ball rolling, now carry on. Give me something to work on.' Such was the trend of his thoughts.

Clay waited to see if his opening was being accepted.

'One of the lads was caught taking a few packets ashore and Lieutenant Carter played hell and said he would order no more,' Clay went on flatly.

'Punishing the whole for a fault on the part, eh?' Haley thought. He decided not to pursue the point any further but said: 'I hope to have some bond on board when we get back. It has been ordered and Lieutenant-Commander Cutter is rushing the order through for me. In the meantime, if you are right out I have some I can let you have.'

'We're getting by on Titlers . . . and some which were got for us,' the first seaman volunteered.

Haley detected the hand of Sub-lieutenant Booth in that little act.

He returned to the rivalry.

'Why is the rivalry so keen between this ship and *Solan* particularly. Doesn't it apply to the others?'

'We can always lick them, and two of them are not in our group, anyway. Us and *Solan, Jacinth* and . . . and . . . *Pearl* made up the group at Aberdeen.' The youngster hesitated, looked at Haley from beneath lowered lids as he traced a pattern on the deck with his toecap. '*Pearl* copped out yesterday.'

'I know,' Haley replied.

It was Clay who broke the silence which followed. 'You were on destroyers, weren't you, sir? Number One?'

'I was on a destroyer,' replied Haley, stressing the article. '*Culver*. She was sunk outside Harwich a couple of weeks ago—by a mine. I was Navigating Officer, not First Lieutenant. She—'

Before he could elaborate any further there came a shattering roar from somewhere ahead and the little group jumped to their feet.

'*Solan*'s put one up!' yelled Lennox above their heads. Haley swung round to hurry towards the bridge. A further shout from Lennox halted him, then he stood poised, motionless, like a runner leaning forward slightly, waiting for the pistol.

'Floating mine to starboard.'

Haley saw it, bobbing along past the bow, coming down the starboard side not twenty feet from the ship. It looked as if it was converging on her and would hit her about the stern. Then *Arandite* swung away a little and the gap increased. Haley watched the mine breathlessly, his legs curiously weak at the back of the knees. It bobbed and swung in the slight turbulence from the ship's bow-wave and Haley could see quite clearly the horns sticking up.

It was new, shining without a sign of rust, and a newly

painted band on it stood out brightly.

As it passed the stern Haley exhaled forcibly and broke his poise. He hurried along the deck and looking upwards saw Booth's tense face over the rail of the bridge. Above him fluttered two flags from the yard-arm—'Mine to starboard'—warning the ships astern and the drifter in attendance.

As Haley reached the bridge he saw *Solan* swinging away out of formation and he had a horrible thought that she had been struck by the mine which had gone up with a roar.

'*Solan* put one up in the sweep,' Booth said tersely. 'Then that one bobbed up quarter of a cable ahead. I swung away from it. *Harvester* will get it with rifles.'

Haley found himself curiously short of breath although the distance from the stern to the bridge had not called for any undue exertion.

Booth nodded towards a beflagged dan buoy which swung and bobbed a little way ahead.

'*Solan*'s. We'll have to drop the next. I'll get it ready.' He slipped away from the bridge.

Suddenly Haley felt alone, almost afraid. He was Commanding Officer with the last word to say on board; it was up to him to make the final decisions, but with Booth gone it left a void. There was nobody to whom he could express even an opinion. Nobody to whom he could say anything even if it was merely to confirm out loud his inward decisions.

A hoist of flags travelled up to *Solan*'s yard-arm. 'My sweep is out of action'. *Arandite*'s signalman hauled up the answering pennant, then reached for his Aldis lamp as *Solan*'s bridge broke out into a furious twinkle.

Haley struggled to crystallise his ideas. Up to a minute ago he had been steaming along behind *Solan*, his ship well in hand, keeping station but he with only a vague notion of the overall picture of the operation.

How far was he to sweep? What course was he to follow?

96

What action was he to take if he, too, had his sweep disabled by a mine? Should he order the two remaining ships to carry on while he rigged another, as *Solan* was now doing?

The signal helped him out.

'*Solan* says, sir, "Continue on present course and speed for four miles, lay dans each mile, wait at the end and I will join you!" '

'Very well.' This was something concrete, a definite instruction to be followed to a logical end. But something like that should have occurred to him. *Solan*'s signal should have been a mere superfluity, just something for the log. He, as Commanding Officer of the remaining senior ship, should have taken over automatically. Such thoughts coursed through Haley's brain and he strove to think of something undone, some point to which he should give attention.

He temporised by speaking down the wheelhouse tube.

'Keep her head up; don't let her sag away to port at all.'

'Aye, aye, sir, nothing to port.'

The helmsman's answer was calm, flat, emotionless and struck an answering chord in Haley's mind. He turned to the signalman.

'Tell Mr. Booth to get three more dans ready and drop them when I say so; we won't be shortening in sweep for nearly an hour yet.'

The signalman passed the message from the after end of the bridge then jumped to cope with another flurry of twinkling light from *Solan*.

Haley lit a cigarette to help him to collect himself. Not far below the surface was a mild state of panic, a condition of indecision liable to express itself in a series of shouted, garbled orders which would achieve nothing. So he felt, and he started in to belabour himself roundly.

'Take it easy, Bill. This isn't the Commanding Officer quality Payne claimed he saw. There's nothing to be scared about. Sooner or later at this game you would have to take

97

over. It's no different to doing it on the course. Easier, in fact. Well, why panic? Have we done everything? Dans? Course? Speed? Right! Then pull yourself together. You are Commanding Officer and acting Senior Officer. Then for God's sake be one; stop assing about like an hysterical schoolgirl. There's going to be another bang soon, perhaps. Well, be ready for it. Have some orders framed, waiting. All set now? Very well, no more breathless nonsense, and stop puffing at that cigarette at twenty to the dozen.'

'*Solan* says: "Nice work. Mind the tide. It's a bit tricky, nearer three knots than two. Don't stub your toe on one. It hurts." '

The youngster stowed his lamp away on a handy shelf and snorted. 'Her Bunts is trying some of that fancy, tiddly signalling. Big ship stuff. Me and him's going to have a talk. He passed out same time as me and didn't have no more Fleet Signal procedure than I did.'

Haley chuckled. There was a youngster with sudden death at the most, severe mangling as a possibility, a long, frightening swim not too remote for consideration, waxing indignant because his friend and rival bunting tosser had started to swank about a little-known signalling procedure. Before replying he carefully, daintily traced a non-existent shred of tobacco round his lips with the tip of his tongue, and as daintily pinned it down with finger-tips before removing it. As he did it he pondered. Who is it does this with such precise daintiness? Who is it? Then he laughed. Six out of ten women smoking in a public place do it. It was a mass gesture he had recognised dimly, and was trying to identify with some individual. Of course it was a purely nervous gesture, a playing for time while one sorted out slightly confused thoughts. He laughed again.

'All right, Bunts. Between us we'll keep him on the jump. Study up all the procedure you can and we'll give him a headache.'

Bunts grinned.

'Dans all ready aft, sir.' Haley turned to see a young seaman standing at the top of the bridge ladder. 'Twenty-five fathom lines. And Mr. Booth says, sir, will you give her a bit of a kick to starboard when he let's 'em go so that they'll clear the stern?'

Haley nodded and as the seaman backed down the ladder he added: 'And ask Mr. Booth whether his grandmother sucked her eggs or blew them?'

'Aye, aye . . . sir . . . eh?' Frank astonishment swept over the man's face as he struggled with a message which had nothing to do with the errand he had just completed.

Haley repeated it to him slowly until he was certain the man had got it, but the look of wonderment on his face gave Haley another laugh.

'Nova Scotia man. Blue Nose. Dull as hell, but as good as gold.' The signalman was looking ahead as he spoke. He waited to see if his opening gambit was being swept away or accepted. Silence encouraged him. 'But a first-class sailor. We got two of 'em. Tell some good stories down the mess deck. Had to 'unt his dinner with a gun when he was a kid and got left in small boats in the Atlantic with fishing lines. Hundreds of miles out in fog he had to go, and him only twelve years old.'

He sucked his teeth in criticism of a cruel, hard world which thrust such a fate on children.

Haley pin-pointed the accent, not only of the young sea-man who had delivered the message but of the Pirate of Penzance, the Quartermaster who had greeted him on his arrival on board. Of course it was neo-Canadian, without that faint tinge of Continental accent which softened down the out-and-out northern American twang.

'Who is the other one?'

'Tich. The little fella who was Q.M. when you came aboard yesterday.'

'Good Lord, was it only yesterday?' Haley thought. 'It seems endless ages ago. Little more than twenty-four hours ago I was steaming into this place in the train and now here I am, in command at sea, sweeping mines, temporary Senior Officer of a group on the job . . . and not hating it quite so much as I thought.'

'. . . McAlister, his name is. Sounds Scotch, but he's from St. Johns. The one who showed up just now is Ross. Both nice fellas. Them and Guns—Clay—goes fishing in harbour and keeps us in fish. Fair dabs at it they are. Not so much Clay; he's learning. Says he's going to have a boat after this lot's over, fish in the winter and take people out "bob round the lightship in the *Saucy Sue*". No more pubs for him.'

'Go ahead, my son,' Haley silently encouraged him. 'You are telling me more about my crew than a dozen Mahoneys, Cutters and Booths. This is right from the fountain-head.'

'Used to get on all right with Mr. Booth, we did. The other Number One was all right, too.'

Haley concentrated on the ship, studying the course and the compass, with an occasional glance at the watch, but made no rejoinder.

Emboldened, the signalman went on. 'Some say Mr. Booth is coming back as Number One.'

Haley stayed silent, giving almost constant attention to the watch. He knew that a part of that intricate, grapevine telegraph was working. Stewards, signalmen, and W/T operators were unceasing purveyors of tit-bits of news, views and opinions which were canvassed on the mess decks, interpreted, dissected and reassembled, often bearing no relationship, in their re-erected whole, to the original matter from which their small bits had been culled.

Once he had watched Payne, in a spirit of boyish mischief, conspire with Benson, the midshipman on the *Culver*, in starting just such a 'mess deck buzz' which had *Culver*, then on a monotonous patrol from Scapa, in a mild ferment for the best part of a week.

Payne had run into a friend of pre-war days, then commanding another destroyer which stopped overnight at Scapa on passage south. Some time or other Payne had left some gear on her, including semi-tropical kit, white topee, white suits, white buckskin shoes, which he had collected from the other ship.

With the exception of the white topee the other tropical gear was stowed away in black japanned tin uniform trunks, and it was the topee which prompted Benson to say: 'They'll have the idea we are for the tropics, sir, when the crowd sees that hat.'

'And why not?' Payne had chuckled. 'It's a poor heart that does no guessing. Let's give 'em something to get their teeth into.'

The conspiracy grew.

Payne solemnly inquired from the Petty Officer steward if their was a remote chance of some emergency laundry being done for him in Scapa—'White uniforms and things like that.' He had his topee ostentatiously cleaned and dried in the drying-room. Benson left in his room a price list from Messrs. Gieves, the naval outfitters, with marks against tropical items. The engineer joined in with some jargon about expansion and contraction of oil in the tropics, the Warrant Gunner religiously checked some of his ammunition 'in case it is doubtful under heat'. And Haley helped by marking in his Admiralty list of charts such sheets as he would want for passage to the Indian Ocean, including the Persian Gulf. The wardroom conversation under they eyes of the impassive stewards, bent towards Alexandria, Tewfik, and Shepheard's at Cairo for leave.

In a few days the entire ship's company was quite convinced that within hours they would have sailing orders— for the Eastern Med in moderate opinions, India on the part of more daring spirits, and some of the reckless souls settled for a China station.

One enterprising soul tried to tell his girl friend in a letter by constant references to the Persian Market and an oblique mention that in the near future he would have to be dhobi-ing his clothes every day to keep them spotless.

'Enough!' cried Payne. 'But in the classic phrase, "it just goes for to show". I think it is time my grandmother at the Admiralty sent me a fur coat and a set of snow-shoes.'

She did the next best thing.

Culver sailed, and dreams of a hot sun, camels, sand, rickshaws and olive-coloured houris faded as her knife-like bows plunged into a half-gale flogged sea with the course inflexibly north-east.

Haley came back from his brief recollection, looked at the watch, spoke sharply down the tube to the man at the wheel, then leaned over the bridge.

'Let it go.'

The dan buoy, hanging from a slip on the stern, lurched drunkenly into the water, swayed wildly, then under the steadying pull of the weight and the tide settled down to its appointed job of marking a spot.

Immediately the dan had gone Booth and his little party set about getting another ready. Booth looked up at the bridge and saw Haley's smiling face over the edge. He stepped clear and started semaphoring. As his signal developed Haley's smile drew into a grin.

'My grandmother liked her eggs poached,' Booth sent and waited, with a faint degree of anxiety, for Haley's reaction. After all, he had known the Commanding Officer for only twenty-four hours. How far could he go with a little mild leg pulling? Would he come the heavy destroyer type and choke him off?

Master Booth had been trying all day to assess Haley, and at the same time co-ordinate sundry mixed thoughts in his mind. His first impression had been favourable, despite the fact that his introduction included a sharp criticism of the dress of the Quartermaster. Haley had not shown any marked predilection for superficial humour, but on the

102

other hand neither had he shown any anxiety to use the steel fist in the velvet glove.

Booth had a decided passion for *Arandite*. As he had commented the previous night, he had worked hard after her commissioning to make her an efficient ship, and a happy one. It was his first ship, and ships are like love affairs. A man may have a dozen, lose recollection of the sharp details of most of them, but of his first the memories stay limned, clear-cut and indelible for ever.

When Carter, the previous Commanding Officer, had become impossible to live with, irritable and irrational beyond measure both towards the crew and Booth, the youngster had spent many hours lying in his bunk before making up his mind to ask for a transfer to another ship, or to another Base.

Unlike Mahoney and Cutter, his youth had hidden from him the fact that Carter was far from fit both physically and mentally in the last few weeks of his period of command. To Booth illness consisted of an obvious acute cold, or a broken limb. The mysterious workings of the brain, its delicately poised functions and the ills to which it was heir, remained a mystery to him.

Carter had always been a quiet, reserved man, revealing little of himself or his background, but Booth had not disliked him, neither had he actively liked him, although he recognised that the man was efficient, knew his job and in the main was fair.

Well, so was the new C.O. He seemed quiet, not given to shouting and storming so far, and Booth, not knowing that they were done with Haley's heart pumping in his throat, had been impressed by the apparently clear-cut style in which the various movements of the ship had been made.

He caught a wiggle of Haley's arms from the bridge and concentrated on the reply to his signal.

'Now I know where you get the buccaneering[Booth asked

103

for two repeats of that word] spirit from. Your poaching grandmother.'

Booth chuckled and turned away to see his little crew watching the scene with interest.

Clay cleared his throat. 'We've heard that you are coming back as Number One, sir,' he opened.

'Well, you've heard all wrong,' Booth replied tersely. Damn it, he thought, everybody keeps harping on that topic. How could he tell what the new bloke would turn out like? He might be hell on wheels when he got his level. At the moment he was Number One to an officer who allowed him to run the *Golfitt*, in fact allowed him so much scope that it became perilously near slackness on the part of the Commanding Officer.

'There is a new First Lieutenant arriving today. He should have joined in time for this trip but C.M.S.P. sent me to see that you people did not get out of hand with a new C.O.,' he went on severely. 'You fellows have earned a reputation ashore which is frightening.'

Clay and the rest grinned. They were used to Mr. Booth's extravagant harangues. 'I merely came along to sort of break him in to the routine. Is that dan all ready to slip?' he went off at a tangent.

Clay caressed the slip with a small, heavy hammer until a touch would make it function.

'A touch and over it goes, sir,' Clay twisted the hammer in his hand then added with a grin: 'He doesn't want much breaking-in as regards handling a ship, does he, sir? When we came away from the wall today, I thought we were going to thump it, then hit the ship ahead.'

The little group laughed and Booth joined in. He, too, had thought while on the bridge that they would hit something at the speed they had slipped and moved away.

'You should have seen Ginger's eyes on the quay. Sticking out like doorknobs,' one of the other seamen contributed.

'All destroyer men are the same,' Clay said dogmatically. 'Two speeds destroyers got. Stop and Full Ahead.' He looked at Booth for a moment. 'The C.O. was telling me he was on a destroyer, the *Culver*, what was blown up outside Harwich a couple of weeks ago. Lost half the crew, she did.'

Booth's eyebrows went up at this tit-bit, which was news to him. Haley had told him nothing of this and he was not to know that the seaman either deliberately or by misunderstanding had created the impression that Haley had been on the ship when she was lost. But he made no mention of his lack of knowledge.

'So I understand,' Booth said. 'She did good work at Dunkirk. Was there all the time.'

And a legend was born which stayed the pace—in fact grew, gathering unto itself additional details until in the telling between seamen in the places in which they drank ashore Haley had (a) tried hard to bring a stricken ship into port, with the scuppers running with blood and all the other officers killed, or (b) had been blown over the side and had been picked up hours afterwards swimming towards Belgium.

'Drop it,' came a hail from the bridge.

Clay swung lightly with his hammer, the dan buoy dropped over, the line followed and eventually the steel weight went in with a dull klomp.

Scarcely had the buoy and its staff ceased erratically swaying when a heavy sledge-hammer clap hit the ship. There was a roar aft, and half-way down the sweep a column of water climbed skywards.

Clay, Booth and the others watched anxiously. They saw that it was well away from the sweeping gear. The wire whipped up once out of the water, then the float settled down again, plugging steadily into the disturbed water.

Booth turned towards the bridge but before he could speak there were two more shattering explosions so merged that they sounded almost like one. The tree-shaped cloud of water was twice the size of the previous one and even as they watched large splinters began dropping into the sea, pitting it all round the area of the explosion.

'Dragged two together. We've found them,' Booth said.

'Bridge calling, sir,' said the man on the machine-gun platform above them.

Booth stepped clear as he saw Haley lean over the side of the bridge with a megaphone in his hands.

'Number One.'

'Sir?'

'Could you make a little less noise when you drop the next dan buoy?'

The tones were so cold, so severe that Booth was completely deceived. He gestured vaguely towards the descending and thinning cloud of water, looked at Clay with gaping mouth, then it dawned on him that Haley was teasing. He grinned hugely and his team followed suit.

Haley went on: 'We appear to have struck the jack-pot. Sweep is not damaged, I fancy. I take it you are all rigged with a spare if we do knock it about?'

'All ready, sir,' Booth called back and Haley waved an acknowledgment.

'Make a little less noise,' Booth chuckled softly. 'Still, it wouldn't be funny if we dropped the dan weight on one right under the stern, would it?'

'It would shake the soot out of the funnel,' Clay said.

'There's no soot in my funnel,' a voice with a decided Scottish tang joined it. It was the Second Engineman. 'What's gooin' on?'

'Goin' on?' Clay asked, looking at the group with wide-eyed innocence.

'Aye, ye're bloowing up mines all aroond. Ye'll be hurrting a body before long.'

The engineman, pale-faced as with all his tribe, stood with one foot on the edge of the doorway. In the corner of

106

his mouth he had just a shred of the sweat-cloth which hung round his neck.

'Blowing up mines?' Clay continued. 'Away with yer! Have you seen any mines about here?' He appealed earnestly to his small audience. Delightedly they denied any such knowledge. This was the age-old game of engine-room *versus* the deck, as old as steamships themselves. 'It must be that l.p. big end you are always yammering about. It's knocking again.'

'Me bottom ends are all right,' the engineer said, complacently rolling a cigarette. He squinted aft over the stern. *'Harvester'*ll be picking up a load of fish after them bangs. See you get our whack from that Geordie killick on her.'

'You bet! Nice soles along here,' Clay reflected.

On the bridge Haley finished an entry in the log, took a couple of check bearings on prominent objects ashore, then blew sharply.

The triple explosion had startled him. For just a few seconds he had felt flustered, then suddenly he had found himself cool, analytical to an almost excessive extent.

After upbraiding Booth with the megaphone he took a couple of bearings, entered them in the log and checked them.

'If only my heart wouldn't thump like a damned trip hammer and my legs go rubbery at the back of the knees,' he thought. 'Still, perhaps I'll get used to it.'

'Three more for the bag,' the signalman said gleefully. 'I'll paint 'em on when we finish sweeping.' Haley looked at him inquiringly.

'We've got a row of mines on the port side of the bridge. I paint 'em,' the youngster explained. He moved to the port side of the bridge and invited Haley to see his handiwork. Haley looked. Along the outside was a short row of well painted mines the outlines of which each framed a swastika. Haley swiftly counted. Forty-eight. Forty-eight

107

ship-shattering, roaring explosions.

'This is our half-share in a Jerry 'plane.' The signalman went on to a neatly executed silhouette over which was painted '$\frac{1}{2}$'.

'Who is the artist?' Haley asked. The signalman came near to a simper. 'And did you do the crest on the front of the bridge?'

'Well, sir, Mr. Booth designed it and I painted it.'

Haley smiled and stared ahead.

Mr. Booth, half mischievous boy, half resolute man, crisp, decisive in any action, yet conceiving such a crest for a ship, a good full-blooded punch on the Hitlerian nose.

The signalman proudly creating an escutcheon, scoring the score with neatly executed pictures of mines; he himself making a jovial matter of three shattering explosions by accusing the First Lieutenant of making a noise. Haley gently shook his head. Could he have known it, the theme could be pursued through the ship. The joke about shaking the soot down from the funnel, the teasing of the engineman, the earnest desire to see that they got their share of the fish blown up by the mines.

No heroics, no striking an attitude of defiance; just sweeping up mines and making the incidentals the more important issue.

'*Solan* calling, sir.' The signalman was peering aft occasionally and answering.

'From *Solan*, sir. "Nice going. But don't be greedy. Leave some for me. I have a living to get." '

Haley went on shaking his head musingly. The signal was in keeping with his trend of thought.

Solan rejoined the group with a spare sweep rigged and once again took over the leadership. From then onwards until the blazing blue sky turned faintly pink, and the sun disappeared redly behind the dark outline of the hills, they swept methodically up and down the increasing line of dan buoys.

Five more mines surrendered their lethal potential. Two of them roared in futile fury with the accompanying flurry of water and splinters, the other three drifted harmlessly down the fairway to be destroyed by rifle fire by the drifter.

As Haley studied the area they were sweeping he began to form in his mind the picture of the operation. The mines had been laid obliquely across the channel so that they presented a long slanting threat to shipping converging on the narrow gap two or three miles ahead.

Convoys, steaming up four and six abreast, would start to thin down to a line of two, or even one, ships in line ahead. Just about where they were sweeping there would be a jostling and manœuvring among the unwieldy merchant ships. Should one hit a mine the others would scatter momentarily, like sheep shying away from a raiding dog, and in that brief moment, before the overworked escorts could marshal them into a line and resolutely push ahead at the point of that line, others would strike, shudder, and reel away stricken to add to the confusion.

Solan and her group were doing two things at one time. She was establishing the extent of the small minefield, clearing it and at the same time extending her search to cover areas at each end of the lethal box.

Haley's head had begun to ache. It had been a strain. The day had been long, full of events, some of them confusing, some frightening, all exhausting.

He felt a surge of relief ripple through him when Larkin, whose face had burned to a fiery brick-red during the afternoon, suddenly whipped his binoculars to his eyes and said crisply:

'In sweeps, sir.'

While the signalman was busy hoisting the flag-hoist to repeat it down the line Haley looked aft towards the small sweeping deck. He could not see Booth but assumed he was somewhere about. Throughout the day Booth's visits to the bridge had been few and of short duration. He seemed to be questing all over the ship, like a busy terrier in a stack-yard. Once Haley saw him, accompanied by the Cox'n and Clay, rooting under the whale-back bow. There had been a clanging of tins; roped planks and bos'ns' chairs were dragged out and untangled.

'Soon there will be much slapping on of paint,' Haley conjectured.

Later he saw his temporary First Lieutenant helping two seamen measure and cut off some lengths of canvas. In a few moments they were up on the bridge accompanied by Booth.

'Time we had a new dodger up here,' Booth offered. 'That one wouldn't stop a barmaid's whisper. Now, no homeward-bound stitches,' he went on severely. The two seamen grinned. 'We don't want it to blow away one dark night, and me up here in my best silk nightie.'

Haley contributed nothing but was highly amused at the youngster's colourful harangue and also at his possessive tone although, all things being equal, he would be leaving in a day or two to rejoin his own ship.

'A good Number One never rests.' Haley, screwing up his eyes against the sunlight, recalled one of the *Culver* captain's little lectures on the bridge. 'Put two seamen and a Number One adrift on a raft in the middle of the Atlantic and in twenty minutes he will have organised them into watches and will have them painting ship,' Payne said. 'That is, if he is up to his job.'

Haley watched the two seamen sewing for a while and saw that they were the two Nova Scotia lads. It was obvious that they were old hands with a palm and needle. Each stitch, close and tight, was sound work. As a yachtsman, knowing the value of good palm and needle work, he appreciated their craftsmanship.

When he called aft, 'Tell Mr. Booth to stand by for "in sweeps",' he was startled to hear Booth reply from almost under his feet. He looked down, then threw back his head and laughed loud and long.

Booth and a young seaman, armed with marline spikes, oil-cans and a wad of cotton waste, were working on the steering chains where they ran out from the wheelhouse, over a spindle and through sheaves down a square trough. Booth seemed to have acquired considerably more grease and dirt on his face than his young acolyte.

'Oh, if you could only see your face, Booth! A banjo and a straw hat and you could nip ashore and put on a turn on the beach.'

Booth grinned, explored his face with a grimy fist and spread oil even more impartially and generously.

'These sheaves and chains had enough coal dust and muck in them to keep us in bunkers for a week. Never saw such a mess.'

He leaned over the lower bridge where a man was warming the big winch. 'All ready, Watts?'

'All ready, sir.'

Booth nodded up at Haley, prepared to climb down to the deck. As he disappeared under the boat deck he said: 'Have you looked in a mirror recently? Sitting Bull, Mark Two. Beeg Chief Red Man. You won't half prickle tonight.'

Haley chuckled. The prickling process had already started, particularly where his hair joined his forehead, but he knew that in a few hours that would go and he would burn to a deep brown.

'Executive!' Larkin yelled, hauling down his flag-hoist.

The powerful winch clattered into life, dragging the dripping wire over its drum. Soon the sweep was on board and Larkin, watching from the edge of the bridge, with his halliards in his hand, whipped a pennant to the yard-arm as soon as Booth's hands went up.

Anxiously he looked at the other ships. On *Solan* the pennant was just climbing upwards; from the other two wisps of steam from the exhausts showed that their winches

111

were still at work pulling in the sweep.

'Us, by a few seconds, but I bet they argue. Still, they know Mr. Booth wouldn't cheat,' he muttered.

Haley found the constant rivalry, especially with *Solan*, rather stimulating and he quietly determined to underwrite any bets his men had made in cigarettes.

'Ask your opposite number if the bets are still on,' he said to Larkin.

The signalman hesitated.

'Go on, jump to it.'

'They're on, sir, but we've been playing owers, until . . . until . . .'

'Until we get into harbour, then bets, won or lost, will be settled on the nail as soon as we tie up,' Haley said. 'If the bond is not there I'll buy them ashore, but we pay or collect.'

Larkin joyously embarked on a twinkling signal which contained some private rudeness between him and his rival.

Solan moved round in a slow circle until she and *Arandite* were only fifty yards apart. Haley heard the hollow cough of the loud hailer and waited for the opening. Larkin pushed the microphone and length of flex into his hand.

'All warmed up, sir,' he said.

Haley could see that he was being scrutinised through a pair of binoculars.

'*Arandite* ahoy, Lieutenant Regan here. How d'you do?'

'Fine, thanks.'

'I take it the red face, rather like a farmer's bottom on a frosty morning, is that of Lieutenant Haley.'

'It is.' Haley sensed Booth standing near him and added, 'The dusky gentleman at my side goes by the name of Booth.' A subdued chuckle near his elbow told him that he had recorded a hit. The chuckle came back from the other ship then the voice went on, in a rich Irish brogue, pleasant, full, deep, with a delightful rising lilt in it.

' 'Tis a busy day we've been having. I didn't expect to find that stick of mines quite so soon. The Huns pulled a

112

fast one with a decoy aircraft farther up, and a couple of E-boats nipped over and laid the lot we've been dealing with.'

There was a short pause.

'Have you met the gentlemen—E-boats?'

Haley replied: 'Not socially, but . . . we have met. We had odd spots of trouble with them farther north.'

Haley could hear agitated whispering behind him and felt Booth nudge his elbow. 'Tell them they owe us a packet and a half of cigarettes each on today's showing.'

Haley passed the message and a faint howl of derision came from the group of seamen on Solan's foredeck. This was answered by some bellowed insults from Clay and Company.

The Irish voice chuckled, then went on: 'I make it a packet and a half, too, but I fear that my hired assassins think there has been some dirty work on the part of an officer I could name, but won't.'

Haley heard Booth laugh behind him. 'Insults don't matter a damn. It's the cigarettes that count.'

Haley had an idea and put it into operation immediately. 'How are you off for bond?'

There was a perciptible pause, then the answer came.

'Quite well off; ours came a few days ago. . . .' Haley anticipated an offer and determined to make the most of his idea.

'Mine is on order; should be only a few days. Could you let me have a few cartons to last out?'

'Sure! We'll drift alongside and pass them over. Better still, here's Harvester with our supper; we'll pass them to her and she can drop them aboard.'

Haley watched the drifter slip alongside Solan, pass up a bag, receive some long cartons, and back away.

He watched the drifter then turned to Booth.

'Take those cigarettes from the drifter, Mr. Booth, and issue one carton immediately.'

113

He saw a warm glow in Booth's eyes. For a second or so the youngster stood looking at him, then he nodded and said: 'Thank you, sir. That was a brainwave.'

He slipped away on his errand.

For the next few minutes *Solan*'s Commanding Officer went into the technicalities of the night's patrol. She and *Arandite* would patrol, at half speed, one section of the area leading to the gap; the other two ships, who were receiving their orders by lamp, would patrol the other. Rendezvous, ready for sweeping again, would be 0600.

'And when do we sleep?' Haley wondered. He was used to a bridge watch at night, in fact had spent long hours on the bridge of *Culver* in all sorts of weather, but there had been several others to share the long hours with the shadowy figure of Payne, hunched in his chair behind the master binnacle, always at hand to make the final decision.

'If you like, sir, I'll hold the fort from now to midnight and you can have a downer. Then you can take over for for the Indian hour.' Booth had regained the bridge and was making his offer.

Haley reflected, then amended the suggestion. 'I'll carry on for a few hours, say one o'clock, get some shut-eye until just before dawn, then we'll have everybody up and at action stations for sunrise.'

Booth looked at him fixedly.

'The men will be dozing by their guns all the time, sir. We'll work a bridge look-out rota; just before dark and the crack of dawn are the dirty bits for aircraft.'

Haley decided to submit to Booth's greater knowledge of trawler routine, but privately determined to go deeper into a watch and quarter bill as soon as possible. He nodded.

'By the way, do you go down below to your room?'

He visualised Booth having to dash up the ladder from the wardroom, two-thirds drugged with heavy sleep, and up to the bridge, or wherever his action station was.

Booth grinned and inclined his head towards the box-

114

like steel air-raid shelter at the back of the bridge.

'We have a neat little hammock rigged there. Cosy as a caravan. Hot and cold laid on, southern aspect, gravel sub-soil. All it wants to make it perfect is a blonde, about so high . . .'

'I know—weak, willing and . . .'

'. . . Enthusiastic.'

'Hard luck, laddie, but tonight it's you for a long nocturnal couch.'

'Life's hard, but I'll get by.'

Solan had moved ahead. Haley slipped *Arandite* into position astern, about two cables, four hundred yards, and the ships settled down for a night patrol which might grind on in hours of monotony or suddenly blaze into lethal activity as plumes from high-speed enemy motor-boats cut up the sea.

It was dark when Booth returned to the bridge. 'We're all nicely blacked out. I've been around with Cox'n to make certain. Guns all manned, and the hydrophone ratings on listening watch.'

'Good! Well, you get some sleep. I'll kick you at one o'clock.'

'Aye, aye, sir.'

Haley heard him settling himself in the steel box and soon a deep breathing told him that Booth was dead asleep. A seaman, duffle-clad, shadowy, stood in one wing of the bridge, rocking slightly on his feet and gently humming to himself.

'Bunts is in the wheelhouse if you want him, sir,' he said softly.

'Right!'

And *Arandite* settled down to her patrol, which brought no scares and allowed all to get a little well-earned rest.

5

For two more days and nights *Solan, Arandite* and their two
consorts swept the area during the day, and patrolled at
night in comparative peace.

Fourteen more mines were added to their bag and the
two last sweeps brought no result. Eventually Regan signalled that he was satisfied they had collected all the moored
mines in that part of the Channel and was vacating it for
the electrical sweepers.

One explosion puzzled Haley and Regan. It split the
water with tremendous, sustained shock, much deeper in
tone, and there was a measurable delay between the first
thud, which darkened the surface of the water, and the boil
and climb of the cloud of sea.

'That sounded much more like a depth-charge going off
well down, rather than a mine,' Haley said critically, and it
was obvious that Regan was puzzled. The explosion came
halfway between the two ships but well away from the
sweep.

After exchanging signals Regan decided to classify it as a
magnetic mine, but if it was so then it must have been set
extremely fine to go off at the slightest magnetic influence,
infinitely less than that found in even a small steel ship.

After some quick sights and subsequent calculations between the two ships they agreed that it was at the edge of
a circle with a two hundred yards diameter.

'They'll be going off if we plank a half-crown down for
a drink in the club,' *Solan* sent.

Booth snorted. 'If her Number One ever pays for a drink it will set all the mines off in the Channel.' He sneered openly. 'A Glasgow Scot-typical,' he added, grossly slandering the citizens of that no mean city.

But that was the only event which broke the steady monotony of sweep and patrol.

As soon as they were tied up, *Arandite* astern of *Solan*, Haley quickly made himself presentable and climbed to the quay to visit the senior ship.

'What! No frock-coat? No sword-belt with sword?' Booth's eyebrows went up in mock horror as Haley stepped on to the quay. 'What *is* the Navy coming to?'

Haley looked at him coldly. 'A wash won't hurt you, and if any soapsuds splash behind the ears or round the neck, don't be alarmed. You won't die.'

Booth grinned, quite unimpressed by the severity of Haley's tones.

'What time will you be back, sir?' he asked.

'God knows!'

'I'll see it is entered in the log. "Commanding Officer ashore with God." '

'Irreverent young devil!'

Haley then delivered his parting shot, which left Booth temporarily speechless—and that was an achievement!

'I expect a REAL First Lieutenant will arrive for the ship shortly. See that she is presentable before you hand over,' Haley said blandly. 'Perhaps you will enter that in the log also?'

Booth gaped, looked at Haley, switched his glance to Lennox, who was the Quartermaster and was thoroughly enjoying the little comedy, then went back to Haley. Before he could frame a suitable reply Haley cocked one eyebrow at him and turned away, barely concealing a grin.

'Real First Lieutenant . . . REAL . . . what the devil!' Booth bridled at Haley's disappearing back, now too far away for the retort he had framed. But Booth, always

117

against waste, decided to give it to the the the world at large.

'I hope you get a pansy-faced, mincing, comic opera sissy who faints every time a mine goes off and is sick before leaving harbour.'

Mr. Booth was eighteen years minus.

A Quartermaster and a young Sub-lieutenant were on *Solan*'s foredeck when Haley arrived. After exchanging formalities the young Sub led the way to the wardroom.

'We paid a dividend this trip all right, didn't we, sir?' he said with a pleasant Scottish accent which Haley recognised as coming from considerably farther north than Glasgow. 'How is young Booth taking to work again?'

Haley was highly amused at the 'young Booth'. If there was six months' difference between them that was all.

'I left him rather speechless, but I think he will recover,' Haley said with a smile.

'The Commanding Officer of *Arandite*, sir,' the Sub called down the hatchway, stepping over the water-board in the doorway and preparing to take the lead.

'Throw him down, neck and crop, stand not on ceremony and frisk the body for knives, pistols or other articles which may be used as missiles.'

By the time this outrageous welcome had run its course Haley and the young officer were at the bottom of the ladder and Lieutenant Regan was meeting them with outstretched hand.

'Real pleasure, old man. I must say I like the way you handle *Arandite*. Slap some alcoholic drink about, Sub.'

Haley's liking for the Irishman was spontaneous. As his drink was being poured out he studied the man who was his Senior Officer. At first he looked square and squat, but on second glance it was obvious that he was taller than he appeared. He was an inch or two short of six feet. A well-shaped head was poised arrogantly above the wide shoulders. His hair was dark, short and crisp. His eyes were blue, a dark blue, so dark that in the uncertain light of the ward-room they looked black.

'Slainthe,' Regan said when their glasses were charged. 'Don't bite it off sharply; let it roll from your tongue. Have you ever been to Ireland, Haley?'

'My father was from Bangor, and I visited there once or twice.'

'Bangor, begob, and he talks of Ireland! I mean the real Ireland, not the traitorous six counties which even now harbour and succour the enemies of freedom.'

Haley laughed. It was not the first time he had met the complete incongruity of outlook on the part of the men from the small island.

'Well, sit you down and we'll talk a piece of this and that,' Regan went on pleasantly. 'How did young Booth treat you? Not too harshly, I hope.'

Haley related in a few sentences his final small triumph over Booth and the *Solan*'s First Lieutenant roared with laughter, slapping his leg as he did so.

'Ho, ho, wait until I get him ashore! REAL First Lieutenant, eh?'

Regan looked at the youngster solemnly, then said severely: 'I'll bet a month's pay Booth knows the difference between port and starboard AT ANY TIME OF THE DAY OR NIGHT.'

The Sub-lieutenant blushed. This was something private between the Commanding Officer and First Lieutenant. 'Ask him, will you, Haley?' Regan went on.

'Surely it should be an interesting discussion between these two?'

Regan laughed, then went on in more friendly tones. 'Right, me lad! On deck and repel all boarders. Anybody with less than the rank of Captain throw down the bilges, keel haul him, trice him to the masthead and flog him. I want to talk in peace with Haley.'

Haley remembered a gibe of Booth's at Cutter, whose

conversation was sprinkled with similarly bloodthirsty threats. He wondered who was copying whom.

For the next half-hour Regan and Haley talked of ships, of *Culver*, of *Solan*, of minesweeping, and of *Arandite*.

Despite his arid comments on Northern Ireland, Regan, it appeared, was in business in Belfast, something in banking although he hailed from the extreme western toe of Ireland, from near Tralee.

He had joined the Belfast division of the R.N.V.R. and, like Haley, had dropped out, but added his name to the Supplementary Reserve shortly after Munich. Comparing notes, they found that Regan had three weeks more seniority than Haley.

It was enough. One day, or even an alphabetical placing in the C.W. list, could make one man senior to another.

Haley found Regan's musical brogue fascinating and was content to let him do most of the talking. Never at any time was laughter far below the surface and at some of Regan's sallies Haley laughed out loud.

Then Haley asked a question which wiped all the smile from Regan's lips. He stood up, crossed to the small sideboard and poured himself another drink, did the same for Haley and leaned against the table before answering.

Haley had asked: 'What sort of man was Carter? What went wrong?'

Regan took a drink and got a cigarette going before he answered.

'Two small questions yet I'd be talking for an hour before you'd understand, if then, because I don't know the answers,' he said, his voice two or three tones deeper.

'Too many bangs, perhaps?' Haley queried.

Regan shook his head and gave Haley an oblique look. 'That could upset a man with imagination. But . . . but Carter could have swept mines for ten years and laughed at the ten millionth going off between his toes.' He sat down and leaned back.

'This is only my opinion, mind, and you will hear others. But Carter killed a man, deliberately, cold-bloodedly killed a man . . . and . . .'

Haley sat up with a jerk. 'A seaman?'

'No, a German. Did young Booth tell you anything about it?'

'He did not, and while we are on that point, I found *Arandite* in a state of suppressed . . . boil; scowls, half the ship's company on Defaulters for trumpery offences, and the other half on Request men. Any connection?'

Regan looked steadily at him. 'What have you done about the defaulters? Or what do you propose to do?'

'I've done it. I've washed out the lot. I feel like throwing the punishment book over the side and starting again.'

'Good man!' Regan's tones betokened hearty approval. 'Go ahead, you'll have Mahoney's support and mine. Up to a few weeks ago that crew was one of the best in the Base, then . . .' Regan shrugged in completion.

'How did Carter kill a German? And, may I ask, what is so particularly heinous about it in view of the fact that we are mobilising a nation to do just that in as wholesale a fashion as we can arrange?' He studied Regan's face. 'And what is the connection, if any?'

Regan poured out two more drinks and resettled himself in his chair before answering.

'All the connection in the world. It seems only a few days ago—actually it was at Aberdeen, back in the winter—that Carter sat where you are now. We had just met and we were having a drink or two. Carter was a fine lad with a nice turn of humour. He seemed glad that he had been cast for minesweeping. Me? I wanted M.T.B.s, or destroyers. "One thing about this sweeping business," he says, "it's quiet, refined and we will not be called upon to shove bayonets in people's tummies." He told a funny story against himself. He once was asked to do away with a pet rabbit, botched the job, was ill for a couple of days and bribed the baker's boy to finish the thing. Yet that same Carter did this.'

Regan's mind was a long way from the wardroom as he went on talking. For the next few minutes he gave Haley the details. *Arandite* and two other ships were sweeping along a channel leading to the French coast a week or so before the Dunkirk evacuation. They had with them a drifter to shoot up any mines. One of the trawlers hit a mine and her fore part opened like an over-bloomed flower. In a matter of seconds the water was covered with wreckage and injured men. The drifter moved in and was picking up the men when a German 'plane swept down and machine-gunned drifter and swimmers. It circled, swept back and machine-gunned again. On its third run it dropped a bomb right alongside the drifter, which had doggedly stuck to its task.

Arandite, racing in to help, got a full burst from her machine-gun into the 'plane, which rocked, rolled over and dropped into the sea.

'The drifter, barely afloat, was on fire in two places, her deck full of dying and dead men, her own and the trawler's. *Arandite* closed her, took off the men, dead and alive, and put a couple aboard to help cope with the fires. Then she went searching for the pilot of the machine.'

Regan sat forward, his hands clasped as he went on with his story.

'They saw him, still alive and waving, about fifty yards fine on the bow. Carter went straight for him, missed him first time, then . . . went full astern, full ahead, full astern half a dozen times with Booth yelling aft and half the crew draped over the side with heaving lines.' He paused, finished his drink and started a cigarette.

'The pilot never came out of that boiling water. Booth says he showed up two or three times, and they heard him yell as the screw pulled him down the first time. Then Carter made for harbour, cold, hard, and he stayed that way until . . . until they took him ashore last week.'

Haley made no answer for a while, then said, 'But I still don't get the connection.'

'I doubt if Carter had a decent sleep from that day on. During Dunkirk he drove himself like mad, did twice as much as any of us, four times as much as they asked of us ashore. He went off balance completely, snapped and snarled at small things, and the hardness became brittle.'

Regan leaned back and looked at the bulkhead above him.

'We were clearing up a very naughty little field near the Gap and the Hun was being quite offensive while we were doing it. Half a dozen times in a day he would slip over and machine-gun. Nothing serious, but annoying. *Arandite* put up three mines in nearly as many seconds. One went off abeam, away from any sweep, like that joker we had yesterday. Carter broke away from formation. I signalled him, lamp and radio, but he was high-tailing for home when the Hun 'planes, two of them, swept in low over the sea.'

Haley's mind flashed back to the patched-up holes in the bridge and he visualised the two-'plane attack. With only her limited armament *Arandite* could not meet the double threat on her own, no matter how steady and resolute her shooting.

'After breaking away Carter went to bits. It seems he ran round the bridge like a demented woman, then collapsed. Number One took over and was turning her to rejoin when the last attack came. He and some others were killed.'

Regan's last sentence came harshly, suddenly, and brought the story to a jarring finish.

It was Haley who broke the silence. 'I know everyone was being overworked, but did nobody notice that he was ... that he had gone ... was ... ?'

Regan shook his head. 'Much of what we know now we didn't know then. From being a cheery cove he changed to a silent, cold man. But he was efficient. Bits of the story came from Booth, but only afterwards. He asked for a

123

change and got it on grounds of incompatability.' Regan grinned momentarily. 'Sounds like a divorce, doesn't it?'

'And where is Carter now?'

'Hospital.'

'And condemned as a coward, among other things, without having had a hearing.' Haley's tones were cold.

Regan's eyes blazed and Haley felt them boring into his.

'Condemned is a hard word, my bhoy.' His tones developed a real Irish brogue. 'But I am concerned only with effects, not causes. He was a weak link. A ship lost its efficiency, an officer and men were killed—unnecessarily—and a weak link is a weak chain.'

Haley thought: 'You go to hell with your generalisations.' Aloud, he went on in tones still cold: 'You will have little cause to complain about *Arandite*, on the ground of inefficiency, or of her strength as a link in your chain.'

Regan's blazing eyes suddenly dissolved in a warm smile. He put his hand on Haley's shoulder.

' 'Tis a wild Irish fighting man yer are, and me a man of peace with the dove itself on me shoulders,' he laughed.

Haley found the mood infectious and joined in, feeling rather ashamed of himself for his slight flare-up. 'At least, when I've broken myself and my new Number One in, I hope you find us on the top line. There is . . .'

'Holy Pete, I'd forgotten that! You have a new lad coming and he a greenhorn, I've no doubt. What a pity you can't hang on to Booth. He's a great man. He and my dogsbody bicker happily for hours when they are together.'

He related in high humour some anecdotes of the two when their ships were commissioning together at Aberdeen. If all Regan told was true they should have been arraigned half a dozen times for barefaced theft and fraud in obtaining extras for their respective ships.

'It was Booth and my lad gave me those,' Regan said, pointing to some attractive hunting prints on the wardroom bulkhead. They were some excellent Lionel Edwards prints which captured all the fascinating chilly November countryside.

'You hunt?' Haley asked.

'I do, but don't run away with a picture of me in a top hat on a three-hundred-guinea hunter,' Regan laughed. 'We have six couple of hounds of indistinct parentage—I wouldn't be denying a trace of harrier in two or three of them—and as like as not the horse I would be riding would have the mark of the plough trace along its flank.' He looked solemnly at Haley. 'We fit climbing irons to our horses. Man, when one puts its head at a bank, cat-leaps to the top, changes feet, and covers the next ten feet like a cat —that's a thrill.'

Regan was away off on his hobbyhorse and Haley was content to let him talk, fascinatingly, with a wealth of rich exaggeration wherein lay most of the humour of his stories.

He had just completed an almost fantastic anecdote of a baby-eyed Irish horse dealer and an incredible deal he had carried out, and they were both laughing when *Solan*'s First Lieutenant came to the top of the hatch and called down in a loud voice:

'There is a . . . a . . . person here to see the Commanding Officer of *Arandite*. Shall I bring the person down, sir?'

Haley and Regan looked at one another questioningly as the sounds of a scuffle came from the top of the hatch. Then the Number One came down, grinning all over his face, followed by Booth with a sheet of signal pad in his hand.

'This came a little while ago, and the van is waiting on the quay. I . . . what shall I do, sir? It seems . . .'

Haley checked him as he read the signal. It was addressed:

'Chief of Staff, Commanding Officers *Golfitt*, *Arandite* (repeat) Group Officer, *Solan*, Paymaster Commander Sub-lieutenant Booth, RNVR, will transfer from *Golfitt* to *Arandite* on appointment as First Lieutenant from

125

p.m. today. Transport will be available as required.'

It was from Commander Minesweepers and Patrols. Haley passed the signal to Regan without comment.

'We've got one, too, sir,' *Solan's* First Lieutenant said with a grin. 'I was bringing it down when this person dashed on board.' He held out a similar sheet. He turned his grin over to Booth, who was standing at the foot of the ladder leaning slightly forward. His chin was thrust out pugnaciously and his elbows were held out slightly from his side. He caught the grin and snorted.

Haley slightly tilted his head as he glanced towards Booth. Obviously this youngster was put out and equally obviously did not want this transfer. Well, he himself did not want to inherit anything or anybody who had grievances. That atmosphere was but barely beneath the surface in the ship at the moment. With a completely new First Lieutenant he could tackle the problem from the letter A.

'I'll see Mahoney about this as soon as I can. Has the new Sub-lieutenant arrived?' he asked.

'He has and is moving in on *Golfitt*,' Booth said. 'He's got some nice silver-mounted suitcases.' He sneered.

'We do pick up bits of gossip from Transport Wrens,' *Solan's* Number One said dreamily to the ceiling. Regan silenced him with a glance, handed the sheet of signal pad back to Haley. When he spoke his words had all the smooth diplomacy of the Irishman.

'And you telling me not half an hour ago that you were hoping to have a REAL Number One after today. Well, you've got your wish, Haley. You've got one that can tell the difference between port and starboard in daytime or in the dark of the night.' He glanced blandly at his junior who blushed furiously then fell head over heels into the trap.

'It was a momentary error, sir. I was looking aft and for just a second . . .'

'Tell me more, sir, please,' Booth asked winningly. 'I am

126

a PERSON'—he heavily accented the 'PERSON' and embraced *Solan*'s Sub in his earnest search for knowledge—'always willing to learn. I accept it that port is left and starboard right, but perhaps another opinion . . . ?' He trailed off on a rising note.

Regan judged the moment ripe. 'By-and-by, but . . . this transfer . . . there is justice in the world. How did you wangle it, Haley? *Golfitt*'s going to be good and mad.'

Haley continued the diplomatic juggling for a while, finally deciding to put all his cards on the table.

'I think I detect the hand of the fair Cutter in this. He hinted that Mahoney thought that as Booth knew the ropes on *Arandite* it would be a sound move to transfer him back to help me get her into shape again. But,' he went on cunningly, 'if Booth thinks the job is too difficult . . .'

'Too difficult me foot!' Booth snorted. 'It's this chopping and changing me about without asking me that gets under my skin. Still, if it's done it's done and I can't argue.' He relaxed his somewhat pugnacious attitude and leaned against the ladder. 'Every darn' seaman on the ship seemed to know it was coming off. All yesterday they were hinting at it. Bunts, Clay, Cox'n, Lennox—they all had a go.' He imitated the accents of the seamen, carrying his mimicry to excess. ' "I heard tell as how you was coming back to us, Mr. Booth." "They do say you are coming back to us, Mr. Booth." '

It was *Solan*'s Number One who added the note which completely demolished Booth's already dying resentment. Booth, in fact, in the few minutes following the reading of the signal found himself forming a hazy liking for the idea. It was not without its attractions. Returning to his first love, his first ship, and picking up threads he had helped to weave into her original pattern.

'From odd bits I've heard, if you read "hoping" for "heard" and "they say" you'll be near the mark. But why

127

any crew in its right senses should want you around . . . well, I'll give it up.'

The stage was set for a youthful wrangle between the two. Regan and Haley exchanged smiles and Haley thrust out his hand towards Booth.

'I'll be frank, Number One. I was one of the hopeful ones. It will be a tremendous help.'

Booth surrendered completely. He took Haley's hand firmly and grinned. 'I think you will find I have anticipated things slightly in the log, sir,' he said.

'How so?'

Booth giggled. 'I've entered in the log: "Commanding Officer ashore with God, hoping to find a REAL Number One on board on his return." '

'Holy Pete!' said *Solan*'s youth, in awe. 'What's going to happen when C.M.S.P. inspects ship and reads that lot?'

'Nothing to what will happen when Group Officer inspects her,' said Regan sternly. He switched quickly. 'This calls for a drink. It's on you, Number One. Pour 'em out.'

'Another overdraft in Glasgow,' jeered Booth. They all raised their glasses. 'To *Arandite*'s Number One.'

'To *Arandite*,' Booth echoed softly. 'And her Number One who knows port from starboard, day or night.'

Solan's Sub looked piteously at his Commanding Officer. 'I demand the truth, sir. This story will be repeated ashore with embellishments far removed from the truth.'

'So be it,' Regan said calmly. ' 'Twas in the dark of the night, on the bridge, and he in command. I was dozing . . .'

'Snoring,' the youngster murmured.

'Dozing,' Regan went on firmly. 'Sort of cat-napping. One eye open, so to speak . . .'

'And your mouth—wide,' the Sub-lieutenant inserted.

' "Port two turns," says the brave officer of the watch. "Port two turns," says the hero on the wheel. "What in hell are you doing?" yells me brave officer and me awake like

128

a flash. "Port two turns you said, sir," argues the lad on the wheel. "The damned ship's swinging to port as fast as she can go," shouts the officer, him being addicted to bad language. "Yes, sir," says the bhoy on the wheel. "She should do, sir, and her being half hard over." '

Haley, Booth and the young Sub-lieutenant were hanging on Regan's lips at his racy story.

'There was silence for a while,' Regan went on, 'then the brave officer of the watch, him that defies death every night, says softly: "So she should. Sorry. I meant two turns to starboard." And us missing Number Ten buoy by a coat of paint,' Regan concluded.

'We hit it and it was that which woke you up,' the youngster said calmly. 'You were dreaming, sir.'

'You lie in your throat,' Regan said fiercely.

'I didn't allow enough for tide,' the youngster added, 'and made a slight mistake. I was over-tired, having too much responsibility thrust on me, what with the Commanding Officer being dead asleep most of the night . . .'

'B'God, it's the masthead for you! Trice him up, keel haul him, flog him through the fleet, a hundred lashes for each ship.'

'Two hundred alongside us, please,' Booth asked urgently. 'We like our little pleasures wholesale.' *Solan*'s Sub closed on him with clenched fists and a determined look in his eyes.

'Begob, they'll wreck the ship,' Regan said placidly as as the two wrestled fiercely on the settee. 'It was grand meeting you. Are you for the beach tonight? There's a film on, a Western. I love sheriff's posses and "stick 'em ups".'

'Sure, and I think I'll take my family away while your ship is still whole.'

'Don't give it a care. They can have the return match in your wardroom another day.' He looked benevolently at the two dishevelled youngsters who were now lying breathless alongside each other on the settee, grinning amiably.

Standing near *Arandite,* on the quay, was a light motor van, grey painted with the Admiralty insignia of the anchor in red on its wings.

'The chariot, waiting for me and my one clean shirt,' Booth said. 'I like the line in drivers; just what the doctor ordered for a tired naval officer.'

Haley looked at the girl behind the wheel. It was the girl who had picked him up at the station a few days before, the girl who had lightly teased him about *Arandite* catching up with *Pearl.*

As Booth leaned his elbows on the door and prepared to embark on his favourite sport of impressing young ladies as a preliminary to ultimate mild conquest, Haley studied her face.

It was immobile, almost frozen. Apart from an occasional movement of the eyes she made no response to Booth's overtures. There were dark shadows beneath her eyes, blue shadows as if she were tired, lacked sleep. Her mouth was pursed up in a pathetic attempt at bravery.

Booth retreated slightly and turned to his Commanding Officer. Jabbing a finger towards the girl he said, in a high-pitched, fair facsimile of a film tough guy, the tones flat and coming from the corner of his mouth: 'De dame's dumb, Boss. Maybe I'll loirn her to speak. Wassay I give her the once-over lightly?'

A faint smile crept over the girl's face, played for a moment round her lips as she looked at Haley then disappeared, and she resumed the blank expression. It came and went so quickly that only Haley saw it.

Booth turned inwards towards the driving seat once more. 'Maybe I ought to do sumpin' about yer, babe. Get tough or sumpin'.'

'Maybe you ought to do something about getting your luggage from *Golfitt,*' Haley said coldly. 'But I suggest you clean up a little before you start wandering off the pier. You seem to have brought quite a lot of the dust from *Solan*'s settee ashore on your face. Filthy, isn't he?' Haley turned to the girl for confirmation.

'Revolting,' she replied, and the smile struggled for air again but gave up the ghost after one attempt. 'Like all small boys. They can't keep clean.'

'Small boys, huh?' Booth snorted. He divided a pugnacious look between Haley and the girl and climbed up on that doubtful starter, Injured Dignity. 'If you don't mind waiting a moment I will be with you,' he said and moved towards the ship.

Haley watched him smilingly, then called softly: 'Don't forget, behind the ears as well.'

Injured Dignity failed to come under starter's orders. Booth's back registered extreme outrage, then he made a flying leap for a funnel stay, grabbed it, swung like an agile monkey, with only touch of his foot, down to the deck and stalked towards the hatchway with long hurried strides. As he disappeared Haley turned back to the girl. He caught her looking at him gravely from big grey eyes. For a moment he was at a loss for a conversational opening. For a second or two he even contemplated following Booth on the ship. After all, he had no common ground for conversation with the girl. Or had he? And did he want to mention *Pearl* or did he want her to bring it up? He used an old subterfuge to break the ice.

'Cigarette?'

'No thanks. I haven't time.'

'You have time; it will take him quite a while to prepare himself in all his glory.'

The girl accepted a cigarette from his case and the lighting of the two smokes bridged a few more seconds.

'Bright boy, isn't he?' Haley continued.

The girl nodded. 'Quite harmless. I know his type.'

'And quite amusing, too.'

'This is sheer fencing,' Haley thought. 'Either I go on board or say something about . . .'

131

It was the girl who wrenched the conversation away from the almost banal.

'Did you know that *Pearl* had gone when I drove you down to the ship?' she asked flatly.

'I knew she had been hit, but not to what extent.'

'Could you not have given me a hint?'

'Not so easily as that. I hadn't spoken half a dozen words to you ...'

'But you knew I was very interested in *Pearl* ... you knew I was friendly with Andy ... her Commanding Officer, Lieutenant Anderson.' The girl's mouth twisted bitterly and she turned away to stare through the windscreen. Her lower lip quivered slightly, then she bit it so that all the blood drained away.

It was on the tip of Haley's tongue to snap back a rejoinder that at that time he had other important things on his mind, but the bitten, quivering lip stopped him. The girl was obviously suffering deeply. He put out a hand and let it rest gently on her arm. She made no motion to shake it away.

'All the way down to the ship I wondered if I should tell you or not,' he said softly. 'If you remember, you were teasing me about the standard of this ship and her crew. I just could not ... somehow. When did you learn?'

'Shortly after I left you. We received a call in Transport for a van for the ... some were dead when they were picked up.' The lip started quivering again.

'Couldn't you go on leave for a while until ... ?'

A pathetic little smile crept over her face. 'A Transport Wren ask for leave because a ship has been sunk?'

'But ...'

'We were friends ... no more.' She locked looks with Haley. 'He was engaged to be married to a girl in his home town. We were friends ... no more.' The emphasis was harsh, flat, as if she wanted the point driven well home without any further doubt. Haley did not pursue it. He went off

132

at a tangent into safer territory.

'Have you taken a Sub-lieutenant to *Golfitt*?'

'Yes, and came on here to pick up your young officer, Sub-lieutenant Booth. Is he coming back to you as Number One?'

'Everybody has their problems. He is going to be mine.'

'He's no problem. Just jump on him, good and hard. I've been doing it successfully for weeks.'

'Oh, you've met before?'

' "Met" is scarcely the word. We have exchanged fragments of conversation,' she said with a suggestion of chill in her voice. 'Mine were little fragments, widely spaced.'

Haley chuckled. This was better. Away from the danger point, the recollections which brought bitten, quivering lips.

'I'll make it a priority job to see that he does not pester you,' he said solemnly. Then he jumped in to the defence of Booth. 'Actually, he is quite a nice lad, a bit inclined to think . . .'

'Inclined to think that all girls will fall at his feet in the first ten seconds of a meeting,' she broke in. She looked at Haley rather shyly for a moment and went on : 'He is rather nice, isn't he? Don't for goodness' sake tell him but some of the girls call him the officer with the bedroom eyes.'

Haley contributed another laugh.

'I must file that away for future reference. Don't worry, I won't let him know my source of information. But I'm glad you don't really dislike him.'

A soft smile came to her mouth. 'He keeps his hands to himself, doesn't paw people,' the girl said. Haley suddenly conscious of his hand still resting on her arm, pulled it away almost violently. 'I don't mean that,' she went on. 'But some of the officers think they have a right to . . .'

'Don't tell me. I think I know.'

On an impulse Haley said : 'Please come on board to tea tomorrow.' A second afterwards he regretted it. It was leaving himself wide open for a crushing retort.

It was the sort of offer she had undoubtedly had dozens of times. He waited for the slam. She bit lightly at her lip, looked up steadily at Haley, then smiled.

'Thank you. I would like to. You have to ask permission from King's Harbour Master, but it is a formality.'

'Good! I'll get rid of Booth.' He saw her eyes widen. 'Alternatively, could you bring another girl?'

'I could, but I would prefer not to. Let him stay; he will make an excellent . . .' She paused.

' "Chaperon" are you striving for?'

'Something akin to sparring partner would be a better description.'

'Good! And I will be referee. Where can I meet you?'

'At the gate to the pier.'

The clatter of feet from the deck of *Arandite* claimed their attention. Booth had slipped into his second best uniform and a clean collar, and as he adjusted his hat they could see that his unruly hair was plastered well down. He climbed sedately to the quay, his face solemn.

'I'm ready,' he said shortly.

'This looks like a scene from the French Revolution,' Haley said lightly. 'Into the tumbril, aristo!' He stepped to one side for Booth to climb in beside the girl. 'To the guillotine. Let there be berlood, gallons of it.'

The girl laughed lightly as she trod on the starter and neatly engaged a gear. Haley put his head inside the little cab and said, 'Until tomorrow, then.' He caught Booth's puzzled look and went on: 'I have a job for you tomorrow afternoon, Sub. This young lady is honouring us for tea. I want you to meet her at the gate.'

He stepped back, the girl let her clutch in and the van started to move away. Booth's expression, a mixture of violent curiosity, frank outrage and bewilderment, was wonderful to behold. They reached the gate before he decided that he could sacrifice dignity on the altar of curiosity. Looking straight ahead of him, he said in even

134

tones: 'What has he got that I haven't got?' It was leading with his chin with a vengeance and the girl was too much woman to let such an opportunity pass.

'He's grown up,' she replied tartly. 'And he has eyes.'

Young Mr. Booth was much too inexperienced to know that he was beaten before he started at this form of oblique dialogue, the unquestioned territory of woman from the time she learns to walk and talk.

'Eyes?' he queried, turning the full blast of his long-lashed weapons on the girl, something for which she was waiting. 'How do I get about? With a white stick and a seeing-eye dog?'

'I wouldn't know.' This was said coldly. 'But he doesn't flutter his at everybody.'

Booth curled. He was caught in the act of doing just that. It was scarcely a flutter, but he was guilty of lowering his eyelids in pronounced film-star fashion.

The girl whipped the little van expertly alongside *Golfitt*, and Booth climbed out.

'Will you wait a few minutes? I shan't be long.'

'Yes, sir,' she said primly, with a significant glance at the one gold ring on his sleeve. There and then Booth decided that come the morrow he would meet her at the gate, conduct her on board with cold dignity, then leave her and Haley alone in their glory while he went ashore.

But that was not to be.

Half an hour before the girl was due on board Haley was called on board *Solan*, where he found Regan studying a chart and a sweeping graph spread over the wardroom table.

'I wanted to compare a few notes with you,' Regan said. 'We have to go to the Base for a conference with C.M.S.P. and some heavy brass at three o'clock. Something about those mysterious bangs away on our beam. Now, I worked it out that . . .' And to Haley's credit let it be said that the girl and his social engagement disappeared in a moment as

135

he became engrossed in the details of the last sweeps.

Booth struggled with mixed feelings when Haley told him a little later that he would have to entertain the Wren by himself.

'I don't know how long I will be; it may be a hour . . .'

'It may be for years, and it may be for ever. . . . Don't hurry back; I'll manage,' Booth said.

Haley looked at him coldly. 'If you can't, I'll ask *Solan*'s Number One to come over and help you.'

'If he shows a nose on this ship this afternoon,' bridled Booth, 'I'll clap him in irons. I'll . . . I'll . . .'

Haley broke in on the threats. 'Save it!' he said tersely. 'Get me that spare chart on which we kept the sweeping tracks, and the log.' He hurried away to root out a clean collar. Booth was similarly employed when Haley returned to the wardroom and saw the log and rolled-up chart on the table waiting. He grabbed them, called out to his First Lieutenant and shot up on deck. From the depths of Booth's room came shouted advice about 'using *Solan*'s chart' and a half-heard comment about 'the picture'.

Regan and Haley were ushered into Commander Mahoney's office and were introduced to three other officers sitting there.

They were a Commander, R.N., a Lieutenant-Commander, R.N., and a Lieutenant, R.N.V.R., the latter with green piping between his gold rings showing that he was Special Branch. Immediately the introductions were over Mahoney took charge.

'These officers are down from Director of Minesweeping's office. D.M.S. is very anxious to hear more about those mines which pooped off on your beam. Those cross-bearings you gave me may provide us with a vital clue. You first, Regan.'

Regan explained succinctly where, when and how, to the best of his knowledge, the explosions took place. He amplified by referring to his chart. He also recalled the mine which went off well away from any sweep, and also well outside any magnetic influence exerted by trawlers, when Carter decided to bring *Arandite* in.

'There's a point there,' the Commander broke in. 'This sweeper . . . *Arandite,* or whatever her name is, swung away from formation. She jumped into full speed at that point?'

Regan thought for a moment. 'Yes.'

'How far from her was the mine, and was it on her beam, abaft or forrard of it?'

Regan closed one eye, contemplated the ceiling, then gave his opinion. 'Roughly abeam, starboard side.'

'I think I can help a little, sir,' Haley broke in. 'My Cox'n says there were definitely two. One on the starboard quarter, the other abeam. The first might have been mistaken for one going off in the sweep as they were getting it in. But he is definite that it was at least half a cable away from the sweep. He showed me roughly the angle and it was broad on the quarter. He is so certain because he was watching the sweep, which was vibrating badly having been damaged.' He stopped, and the green striper, looking at him keenly, said : 'Go on, leave nothing out. This *is* interesting.'

He and the Commander exchanged looks.

'I don't know if this point is of any value, but Clay, my leading seaman, described the damaged sweep as rattling like an old Ford as it came in.'

The visiting Commander leaned back and sighed with a measure of contentment.

'Better and better. Where was this? Anywhere near the others which have gone off similarly?'

Haley unrolled his sweeping-chart on which Booth had marked off their sweeps, courses, mines exploded, and kindred detail extracted from a rough graph kept on the bridge. They gathered round the chart and Haley felt his back hair tingle and knew a flush was creeping over his face.

There was a wealth of neatly, even cleverly, executed drawings, all relative to sweeping but outrageous in the extreme.

137

There was nothing he could do. They were grouped round the chart.

The areas marked off as British protective minefields stood out like sore thumbs at a bridge party. A few mines were drawn in and in the circle of each there was a face of a beaming Winston Churchill, complete with cigar. Across the areas was written 'Friendly mines, I've no doubt.'

Areas of suspected enemy mines had an equal number of faces of Hitler drawn on the mines, and bore the legend: '*Achtung!* Addled Adolf's export brand.' But the most outrageous drawings were where the explosions had taken place. They were correctly marked in, timed and bearings given, but Booth had very cleverly embodied in the lines of an explosion female figures in a state of advanced undress, captioned with such phrases as: 'Priscilla the Pip', 'Lulu', and where the double explosion had startled them he had converted a small oblong into a house, with two seductive faces peering from the windows and a notice inviting one to 'Knock twice. Ask for Nellie.'

Haley wanted a large hole to open up in the floor. He gaped at Regan, who had a wide grin threatening to split his face in two. There was no help there. He found Mahoney's face equally devoid of comfort. The Commander Minesweeping was wearing his best poker countenance.

'I'm sorry, sir. I . . . I was in such a hurry . . . I . . .'

The visiting Commander sat back in his chair with the chart held before him. At last he started to shake with silent laughter. This gathered force until he threw back his head and roared.

'Lovely, simply luvverly grub! I must have this, Pat,' he said to Mahoney. 'D.M.S. will howl.' He turned to Haley. 'Are you the artist?'

Haley dumbly shook his head. Slowly it was dawning on him that they found the exquisite drawings extremely amusing, and were far from being incensed.

'Brother Booth, unless I miss my bet,' Mahoney said.

'Let me have another peep.' He leaned over to look at the chart, muttered out loud 'Knock twice. Ask for Nellie,' and broke into a chuckle. 'The beauty of it is that every position is accurately marked. I like the pin-point on Lulu's what d'you call it.'

Despite the incongruity of the illustrations they found the information valuable as Booth had embodied details taken from Carter's log and sweeping-graph. But Haley was extremely glad when the Commander rolled it up and put it behind him.

'I will have a . . . a . . . more orthodox chart copied for you, rely on me, but this I must keep. Damn it, I can dine out on this alone inside the Department for a month. Your Number One is a genius.'

'That scarcely describes what I shall call him,' Haley said grimly.

For a little while longer Haley and Regan answered questions and elaborated points, and the more the talk went on the more Haley realised that minelaying and minesweeping were major forms of offensive and defensive warfare.

It was the Lieutenant, R.N.V.R., who finally provided the break. He had been taking notes copiously throughout the cross-examination and after a glance at the Commander and Mahoney he said:

'Much of what you have told us this afternoon confirms what we suspect. This is very top secret at the moment—that right, sir?' He appealed to the Commander for confirmation and received a nod. 'We have, from Intelligence and sweeping reports, built up a picture which points to the Hun now having a mine exploded by sound.' He leaned back and consulted his notes, and Regan broke in.

'Glory be! Do you mean if I sing in me bath I will set off a mine?'

'I haven't heard you sing, so that may be a possibility. We'll arrange a trial. If it works you can swim around rendering arias from opera,' the Lieutenant replied gravely.

'With illustrations by his Number One,' the Commander interjected, chuckling.

The Lieutenant continued with a disarming smile. 'It's not quite that. It seems that the beat of a propeller sets them off. We've arrived at that, with almost complete confirmation today. We have been puzzled why trawlers seem to set them off, even at half speed, and destroyers and larger ships are occasionally immune, but sometimes get blown up.'

Regan answered that one.

'Even when a trawler is sweeping her engines are going full bat, and there is little slip with their prop. They are built to tow, don't forget, like a tug. My propeller sounds like the *Queen Mary*'s when I'm giving it the full wick up.'

'And a destroyer's screws kick up a useful shindy when she increases speed suddenly,' Haley added. 'On *Culver* there was 30,000 horse power turned on the two props. For a minute or so it was like the anvil chorus if one was down below.'

The Lieutenant, R.N.V.R., clicked his fingers in triumph.

'Everything fits, sir,' he said, 'fits to a "T". You see? The trawler towing and the destroyer suddenly increasing speed give off roughly the acoustic value of a steadily plugging merchant ship . . . and up one goes.' He turned curiously to Haley. 'Did you say your ship was *Culver*?'

Haley nodded. 'She was, until a few weeks ago. I left her to come here, just before she . . .'

'I know. She was one of the first, if not the first, H.M. ship to go up from one of this type of mine.'

Haley suddenly felt that minesweeping was no longer a secondary, poor relation sort of service to be admitted apologetically. He felt as if it was a personal mission. One mine discovered, swept, blown up or destroyed by rifle fire would be a personal triumph. One less *Culver* lost, more lives saved.

'Can I offer you two laddies some tea?' Mahoney said, standing up. 'I'm going to give these folk a mild treat. I'm taking them home. Some kind friend gave my wife some . . . er . . . essentials, and the poor dear has been extending herself making some cakes today.' He looked blandly at Regan, whose return stare was equally bland.

Haley remembered his guest on board. He glanced at his watch and was appalled. She had been there an hour at the mercy of the outraged Booth.

He hurriedly apologised, explaining that he had a guest on board, and the understanding C.M.S.P. ordered a car to hurry them back to their ships. As they left he put an arm over each of their shoulders.

'I can't say a lot now,' he said, 'but the balloon is going up at any moment. The boyos the other side are all set, so I understand, to hit us with everything including the kitchen stove. You go to sea tomorrow morning. I've regrouped you; *Jacinth* joins you, Regan, instead of *Pearl*—I've made the signals. I can promise you nothing but hard work, and a lot of heartbreak in the near future.'

And that was akin to another speech made by a fighting leader who promised nothing but blood and tears, with victory at the end no matter what the price.

Haley was silent until the car nearly reached the ship, and after a brief attempt at conversation Regan made no more excursions into Haley's introspective mood. As they climbed from the car alongside *Solan* Regan said: 'The group will now be us, you, *Jacinth* and *Sheila* in that order. *Sheila*'s C.O. is a chief skipper, a Fleetwood lad, very keen, very good type. Are you for the beach tonight?'

Haley shook his head.

'Good! Come on board and I'll ask the others to join us.'

'Better still, you and the rest come to me. My duty-free and bonded stuff has arrived. We'll christen it.'

'Right ho! You make the signals, I'll round 'em up.'

Haley accepted a smart salute from his quartermaster and dived down into the wardroom. Booth and the girl were

141

leaning over the table examining an album of snapshots. There was no sign of enmity between them. The girl was laughing, with a trill in her voice.

Booth stood up. 'I was showing some snapshots of . . .'

'Of Priscilla, or Lulu or Nellie, or some of your other girl friends,' Haley broke in grimly. Before Booth could collect himself to reply, although it was obvious that the shafts had gone winging home, Haley made his apologies and for the short remainder of the afternoon set himself out to entertain his guest. Booth joined in manfully and earned his fair share of smiles and laughs, but Haley, not without humour, detected an occasional abstracted silence on the Sub's part.

'Good! Let him stew for a while,' he thought, although as the memory of his complete and utter embarrassment faded slightly the humour of the situation—and of the chart —appealed to him.

Eventually the girl, after a quick look at her watch, rose to go. Booth quickly offered her the hospitality of his room to powder her nose and Haley leaned back on the settee with a cigarette going. Before Booth emerged from behind the curtained door, leaving the girl to her intimate rites, he heard a whispered conclave and Booth came out with a grin on his face like that of the proverbial cat and cream. It disappeared like the gleam on the sea being wiped away as the sun disappears behind a cloud.

'About the chart,' he whispered. 'I shouted after you not to use it, to rely on *Solan*'s . . . I . . .'

'You'll be delighted to know that it is now on its way to Director of Minesweeping, Admiralty, W.C.1,' said Haley truthfully. 'Conveyed by the hand of a Staff Commander.'

Booth's mouth dropped open. He sank down on the settee facing Haley.

'No,' he said in a shocked tone.

'Yes,' Haley retorted remorselessly. 'It was the subject of much discussion at a sweeping conference full of brass hats, and I've no doubt it will be further discussed in London.'

'Did Commander Mahoney see it?' asked the unhappy Booth.

Haley nodded, striving to keep his face completely straight. 'He did, and he expressed an opinion which was on all fours with that of the other officers.'

Mr. Booth looked a distinctly unhappy young man. Any further talk on the chart was brought to an abrupt close when the girl came out. A shaft of sunlight coming down the hatch lit up her face and again Haley was struck by the shadows beneath her eyes, but the grim little tightening of the lips had softened. 'So be it,' Haley thought as he watched her frank look answer the somewhat bemused one Booth was bestowing upon her. 'A few more fencing matches with Master Booth, and your wounds will heal. You are in the war like the rest of us. You'll get over it again and again.' Aloud, he said: 'Can I trust you with my Number One? I shall want him tomorrow morning. We sail.'

'What, again?' asked Booth, startled.

Haley nodded. 'Again. And I should make the most of tonight. We're going to be busy,' he went on, pushing along his little conspiracy.

Booth jumped in like an eager swimmer. 'I won't come back, sir, after escorting Heather to the gate,' he said airily. Haley noted the ready use of the girl's name and tabulated it under the heading of progress. He nodded and led the way on deck.

'We sail at midday pre-cise-lee. Tomorrow is Sunday, so a nice clean collar for Divisions. Have a good time.'

He watched them walk along the quay wall, two clean young people both barely out of their teens, both deeply embroiled in a war not of their seeking, both at the moment as near to the enemy as anybody in the country with the exception of the R.A.F. aircrews.

143

6

A summer sun gilded the sea as the little fleet steamed out in line ahead. It was a brave little fleet, four trawlers and a drifter, each with pendant numbers flying and an occasional hoist of signals adding an extra splash of colour.

Commander Mahoney, standing on the balcony of the hotel, watching them steam across the harbour, kept his face impassive but deep in his heart he longed to be on the bridge of the senior ship. He had mooted that point the previous night to Chief of Staff but the refusal had been sharp almost to the point of brusqueness.

'Can you trust the Senior Officer to do the job properly?' C. of S. asked. 'You can? Then there is no point in you sailing with them.' He had looked off into space before adding any further comment. 'I'd like to be going out, but *anno Domini,* the merciless bitch, has caught up with us.' He glanced at Mahoney's lined, tanned face. They were old friends, had served on half a dozen foreign commissions together before Mahoney had decided to retire with the rank of Commander, away from the frustration and intrigue of pre-war naval service. 'If things go the way some people fancy we'll get all the excitement and scrapping we want.' The two old sailors were standing shoulder to shoulder now. 'You know what it will mean, of course?'

'I've a vague idea.'

'It will mean that anything that will float and carry a gun will go out, do its damnedest to sink or damage enemy troop-carrying craft until . . .'

'Until . . . sunk,' Mahoney finished softly. 'And then we won't stop them.' In his mind's eye he could see *Solan*, *Almarina*, *Morning Glory* and all the other little craft, built for peace, closing in towards a solid phalanx of enemy craft, escorted by *E*-boats, destroyers, aircraft. Outnumbered, outgunned, out-speeded, overwhelmed, but with depthless courage they would go in until only the merciful sea, leaving the bits of wreckage, would witness their end.

'I used to wonder, when I was a kid, what the men of those days thought when they knew the Spanish Armada was coming up the Channel. It must have seemed a pretty hopeless sort of job for them to face,' Mahoney mused.

'Something the same as we think now, I imagine,' Chief of Staff said. 'With a predominating bitterness against the damned politicians who saw to it that there was a shortage of ships and men and ammunition.'

'And one day—maybe this is it—their change of mind will be too late, and the contribution too little.'

Chief of Staff nodded slowly.

The confab the night before had turned into quite a stag party. The Commanding Officers of *Sheila* and *Jacinth* had come on board, curious to meet *Arandite*'s new C.O., and had been joined by *Harvester*'s skipper.

Sheila's captain was, as Regan had described, a young fishing skipper from Fleetwood, a man with a wealth of good Lancashire humour and not a trace of the inherent inferiority complex so often to be found in those professional men when they were in contact with R.N.V.R. officers.

Haley had not met a lot of it; there were no fishing skippers within the destroyer orbit but he had heard other R.N.V.R. officers talk about it, and Regan had waxed eloquent on the topic.

Their attitude was a curious mixture of resentment born of two grievances, neither of which held much water. In pre-war days they had joined the R.N.R. with rank of skipper, a warrant rank, had done minesweeping courses, and when war broke out were given command. Then a lot of them found that men who had not joined were making small fortunes fishing for a ravenous market while they were on a glorified Petty Officer's pay.

Their other grievance was that they had to work in close intimacy with R.N.V.R. officers who, they felt, were far beneath them in experience as seamen and handlers of ships.

Haley gathered that Regan had stood for no nonsense when he was a unit officer in charge of two trawlers.

'Lots of them are merely sea-going fish gutters—ditch crawlers—with the vocabulary of an oversexed but backward baboon,' was one of his savage summings-up. 'When a skipper is good he *is* good, but when he possesses the inferiority devil he *is* bad.' Haley remembered Mahoney's somewhat similar judgment.

But Flood, the captain of *Sheila*, was a quite well-educated young man who had brought his intelligence to bear on his pre-war fishing trips, with the result that he was probably one of the highest paid fishing skippers out of his port.

'My father wanted me to take a collar and tie job ashore,' he chuckled, telling the story during the evening, 'and had the shock of his life when he found that I had shipped away on one of his own trawlers as a deck learner. But I think he was secretly pleased. With luck, I'll be a director when the war is over.'

Some of his anecdotes of fishing life were fascinating and Haley found him a good talker. It was well on into the evening that it dawned on Haley that Regan was doing but little talking, rather leaving Haley to push ahead and get acquainted with his two colleagues who would command ships in the reconstructed group.

Jacinth's captain was the exact opposite of *Sheila*'s Commanding Officer. He was a R.N.V.R. Lieutenant who had

146

Merchant Service Second Mate's and Mate's tickets and had actually been a midshipman, R.N.R., in his career. He had swallowed the anchor between the late '20's and early '30's and had crashed into the Admiralty at the outbreak of war, until at last, in desperation, they gave him a commission.

His pet possession, which he kept framed in his room, was an initial reply from somebody in the Admiralty to the effect that they regretted that he was too old (at thirty-five) and advised him to apply for an A.R.P. job.

As the entertaining evening progressed Haley had ample opportunity to study the two men. Flood, the skipper, was a calm, impassive man who seemed to sum up each word and sentence before speaking but, once committed, spoke without hesitation. He had blue eyes which looked out from beneath fair, rather bushy, eyebrows surmounted by a crop of crisp, fair hair.

Meredith, *Jacinth*'s captain, was a short, dark volatile Welshman. He declared vehemently that he was a man of peace with a dove nestling on each shoulder yet in the same breath displayed an inherent pugnacity by utterances indicating that anything to be done against him would be completed only over his dead body.

Both, in their own way, were martinets on their ships, Flood by an impassive method of stating flatly the way he wanted something done—and getting it done that way. Meredith, on the other hand, owned a flaying, volatile tongue which could produce an almost grotesque form of exaggeration. At first this had inflamed his crew almost to a point of mutiny until they realised that there was not an atom of venom in the man and that, given his choice, he preferred fighting senior officers on their behalf rather than combating their little peccadilloes.

Haley was both highly amused and interested at one part of the evening when Meredith described how he took the ship over from a Sub-lieutenant-skipper combination.

147

The combination, in a pathetic attempt to maintain some sort of discipline, had made an unfortunate mess of things. Added to which there was a smooth, slick young bully on the ship who got the youthful mess deck complement completely under his thumb, albeit he was in reality a coward, as are all bullies.

Meredith's slightly sing-song Welsh voice was full of laughter as he described how he took over. He joined the ship after one of Mahoney's pep talks, accepted the Sub-lieutenant as his Number One, mustered the crew on the foredeck and read them what he called the Riot Act by Articles of War out of Meredith. Haley could imagine him doing it, teetering slightly forward on his toes, his hat tilted well on one side, his pugnacious chin jutting out.

'I told 'em,' he related, with a wealth of gesture, 'that all the smart tricks they had been pulling were raw amateur stuff. I'd done it all myself twenty-five years before, with a bloody sight more finesse. I didn't mind them trying to pull fast ones, but I would be insulted if anyone tried pulling a crude one. There was going to be one boss on the ship and that was me.'

The Welshman chuckled and earned a roar of laughter at his story of how he dealt with an erring quartermaster whom he caught dozing on deck late one night when he returned on board.

He crept round the wardroom, giving a graphic illustration of what had happened.

'He should have been put on a charge and all that tripe. Not me! "Sleep on, beloved," I thought. I found a big empty ash-bucket on the deck. Up on to the boat deck I climbed, and I dropped the bucket with a hell of a bang a few inches from his head. Before that I had quietly pinched his revolver. He jumped'—Meredith illustrated with a cat-like leap—'fifty feet into the air, and as he came down I spluttered something like German into his ears and shoved the revolver against his ribs.'

148

When the laughter had died down Meredith went on: 'Every time that seaman sees an ash-bucket now he breaks out into a cold sweat and trembles.'

It was Regan who urged the Welshman to tell two or three stories, which gave Haley a greater insight into the volatile little man's character than anything else he heard or saw.

'Tell Haley about your ladder,' Regan urged, sitting back to listen.

Apparently during the Dunkirk operation a paddle steamer minesweeper had been hit with a bomb and badly damaged. She was put alongside the wall in the inner basin and left there during the turmoil. She was so badly knocked about that she was destined for scrapping and was bought by a syndicate of local business men with an eye to profit.

Meredith's men had gone raiding in daylight with a small boat and had stripped various refinements from the paddler, including some chests of drawers, wardrobes, and a magnificent ladder, complete with rail, which they had taken back to their ship. Unfortunately for them, the taking of the ladder was observed by one of the business men, who stalked the crew and reported the matter to the Base.

Meredith was sent for, was given a dressing-down by Mahoney and was ordered to return the steel ladder to the paddler. He returned on board and after a few investigations he was last seen tearing back towards the Base with his hat tilted well over one ear, a sure sign that a squall was blowing. The business man was invited to the Base again and was asked to repeat his accusations, which he did vehemently. He had seen, with his own eyes, he said venomously, the seamen taking the wide steel ladder away towards Meredith's ship. Meredith then swore that he had searched the ship from stem to stern and there was no steel ladder on board. He had questioned his crew thoroughly and they were equally adamant that they had not removed a steel ladder from the wreck.

'I got into a flaming rage with him,' Meredith related

complacently. 'Mahoney had to cool me down but I got in some tidy shots about seamen fighting for a bob a day and other people grieving about their dividends.'

He leaned back and finished his drink. 'And it was quite true, too. They had not taken any steel ladder. Mahoney was like ice and got an apology of sorts from the fellow.'

'Go on, finish it,' Regan prompted.

'When I got back on board Number One and a couple of the lads were fitting a beautiful ladder to the bridge, doing away with the old wooden thing we had. It was a peach, like a liner's.'

Haley looked slightly puzzled and wondered what was the point.

'You see, it wasn't a steel ladder at all. It was a brass ladder, covered with oil and grease, but when we cleaned it up we found it was brass.'

When the laughter had died down Meredith said: 'One day I'm going to tell C.M.S.P. the whole story.'

The other anecdote was about his way of disposing of the bully. After watching the man with growing exasperation for some time he called him to his room, told him to take an afternoon's leave and to be waiting at three o'clock outside a pub known to all seamen in the Base.

'We'll go for a little walk from there to a place where it is quiet, and you and I will settle it man to man. If you win, all well and good, but if you lose—and I'm going to knock your block off—you'll put in a request for a shift and I'll o.k. it.'

The man never turned up, but his transfer went through.

Haley, perhaps somewhat fancifully, identified each ship with the personality of her Commanding Officer. *Solan*, flying two or three strings of signals, was first away from the quay wall, followed by *Arandite*. Haley dropped her in behind *Solan* and watched the other two.

Sheila came away from the wall with little fuss, and

steamed in a slow half-circle in readiness to take up station. *Jacinth* looked as if she was going to be late, but suddenly there was a burst of activity on the bridge and almost in the twinkling of an eye she swung away from her berth, turned sharply and raced into position with a white bone in her teeth.

Characteristic of each captain, Haley decided, and remembered something that Meredith had said the previous night.

'I hate this minesweeping business. I would like something about thirty knots, with a lot of guns, an all-Welsh crew so that we could quarrel happily then go out and take it out of the Huns' hides. For minesweeping you want the mentality of a ploughman—an intelligent ploughman, maybe—that placid outlook—fix a mark and plod up to it, fix another and go on plodding.'

Haley decided that there was something of the pirate-buccaneer in Meredith, and Regan agreed.

'He wastes—no, that's not the word—he uses up more ammunition than any three ships in the Base. He'll shoot at anything that moves in the night or flies close to him in the day, and questions afterwards. Mahoney swears that he yells "Enemy in sight!" every time the French coast becomes visible.' He ran his hands through his hair and went on. 'What a gunboat officer he would make—but he would die within a month, chasing something right into Boulogne or Calais.'

As Regan's group went out of harbour in neat line ahead at eight knots another group followed shortly. Behind them came two groups of electric sweepers, smaller trawlers adapted with anti-magnetic sweeps.

'Something big on?' Booth asked from the wing of the bridge.

'Minesweeping,' replied Haley shortly. His head ached slightly from the amount of drink he had shifted the previous night and he felt short-tempered with his First

151

Lieutenant. As it was Sunday morning he had ordered Sunday Divisions, crew in Number Ones on the foredeck. Master Booth, arrayed in a very Number Ten seagoing outfit, had looked a little shocked when Haley had told him what he wanted.

'We're going to sea this morning,' he objected.

'And we're having Divisions an hour before,' Haley replied tersely. 'Lets get this straight, Number One. It is what I want which goes on this ship from now. I am not concerned with what went on before.'

'Aye, aye, sir,' Booth replied. And Divisions were held. It was the first time Haley had seen the entire crew mustered before him. He looked them over, walked down the ranks with Booth a formal pace behind him.

Almost at the end of the rear rank, standing next to Clay, was a wizened man dressed in a deplorable uniform, grubby in the extreme. He had a nut-cracker face. It was obvious that there were few teeth in his head, and his features were creased in a multitude of heavy lines. Only the eyes were bright as they returned Haley's scrutiny. They were a cold grey, a grey usually found only in newly broken steel.

'Your name?' Haley asked stopping by him.

The man muttered something in a husky whisper.

'Speak up! What is your name and what are you on the ship?'

Before Booth could offer any enlightenment Lennox, next in line, said, looking straight to his front: 'Butler, sir. He is seaman cook.'

So this was the producer of exquisite fish dishes and golden brown chips.

Haley turned coldly to Lennox. 'I spoke to this man,' he said.

It was Clay who took up the battle.

'He can't talk much, sir. We call him Noisy for that.'

Haley accepted the new speaker without comment and

152

Clay went on, emboldened: 'Best cook in the Base, sir. Never gives any trouble.'

A slight frown creased Haley's forehead. He could think of no reason for Clay's defence of the man. He felt he had arrived at an impasse. Now he decided that if he passed on without pursuing the point he would lose, yet he did not want to delve any deeper. The Admiralty had accepted the man, drafted him to the ship as a cook, and that was that. Haley strove to find a question which would give him what stage people call a good exit line.

'How old are you?'

The ancient whispered something in a husky wheeze. Lennox leaned forward until his ear was not far from the old man's lips.

'He says "just over forty", sir.' Lennox's face was impassive but he failed to subdue a twinkle.

Haley met his eyes, looked at the old man for a moment, then made his exit line.

'You wear very well,' he said. 'Perhaps it's your own cooking.'

Poor stuff, but it served and a subdued chuckle rippled along the ranks. As Haley turned away he saw a grin slip from Booth's face.

After his inspection Haley spoke briefly to the men, trying to explain to them that he had some idea of the difficulties of the immediate past and assuring them that they would get a fair crack of the whip from now onwards, provided they, too, pulled their weight.

He felt it was not a very inspiring speech. He had heard Payne give much better talks with less to go on, but he felt the better for having made it.

Booth had been singularly quiet and subdued all through preparations for sea and Haley thought he still felt slightly resentful over their friction about Divisions. But it was a different matter that was worrying the young First Lieutenant. After his opening gambit about the fleet sailing he maintained silence for a little longer, then burst out: 'I'm sorry about that chart, sir. I never dreamed that anybody would be seeing it except you and me. Lieutenant Carter used to find them rather . . .'

Haley meant to say: 'Damn Lieutenant Carter! What he liked and what I like are presumably two different things.' Instead, he turned swiftly and encountered Booth's troubled blue eyes, limpid, almost swimming.

'All right, bedroom eyes,' he laughed. 'Forget it. The Brass Hats—and Mahoney—thought it was one hell of a joke. The Commander from D.M.S. roared with laughter and pinched the chart. It's gone to London and your name will become famous.'

Booth smiled rather undecidedly. 'Really?'

'I assure you they were delighted at Lulu and Priscilla. Now watch for a practice shell from *Solan*. When it goes, get a short burst in from each machine-gun which will bear.'

Here was something for Booth to get his teeth into and he bustled about contacting the men on the guns.

Suddenly there was a bang and a flash from *Solan* and shortly afterwards a smoke shell burst off on the starboard side about forty-five degrees high. Almost as soon as the dull 'plop' had sounded thin red lines of tracer threaded the little knot of smoke as *Jacinth*'s gunners opened up. *Arandite* and *Sheila* followed suit seconds afterwards.

'Strike a light! That *Jacinth* is mustard. We and *Solan* will have to watch our step. And where did he get all the guns? He must bristle with 'em,' Booth said, impressed.

Haley looked bland. 'Acquired them, I suppose, like certain other ships.' He remembered in a flash something he had overheard Clay mention outside his room on the first morning on board. 'What was wrong with . . . er . . . Noisy's pet today? Doesn't he play except on special occasions?'

Booth stood clean bowled. 'Noisy's pet? His pet? I didn't know . . .'

Haley smiled knowingly. 'I know a lot more than people

154

give me credit for, Number One,' he said mysteriously.

The signalman made it sound much more impressive and pontifical when he repeated it later to Clay.

' "I knows everything that goes on on this ship, Number One," he says, a bit fierce-like. "Everything, including Noisy's pet." '

Bunts looked a little bit troubled for a moment.

'Do you think he knows about our "sippers" in the Daddy's sauce bottle?' ['Sippers' is a small contribution from each man's tot of rum, either to a mess-deck chum or to be used to settle a debt or bet. Occasionally, on small ships where supervision is not so rigid, 'sippers' are saved in a bottle for a special occasion. It is wrong, and both men knew it was wrong.]

'Leave it to me; he won't find it,' replied Clay confidentially, then went on with slightly less confidence: 'I wonder how he found out about Noisy's pet? You haven't been opening your big mouth, have you?'

Larkin indignantly denied any such delinquency.

It soon became obvious what the overall picture of the operation was. Regan's group began sweeping immediately to the west of the entrance to the Gap, another group swept up to their area, and two units of two ships each of the electrical sweepers plodded down the whole length.

Within an hour *Almarina*'s group got among some mines, and heavy thuds shook the still air. Ater the first two or three sweeps Haley found himself getting edgy, impatient, waiting for the first roar which would show that they, too, had found mines.

The afternoon wore on monotonously without any result, and once Regan signalled 'Coy, are they not?' But the meticulous regard for accurate sweeping was not relaxed for a moment. Haley found that once they were in sweeping formation he could keep *Arandite* in station with an alteration of five revolutions up or down every few minutes, and he watched *Jacinth* and *Sheila* astern of him doing the same. Time and again he checked them with a Stewart distance meter and found that they were never more than a few yards out of station.

'Good God! Look at that lot!' The impious and startled exclamation came from Booth as he pointed ahead towards the east. Through the haze there loomed up the van of a convoy. Haley had seen any number of convoys in the North Sea and they were no novelty to him, but to the extremely narrow channel this one was bunched so closely together that it seemed, from their foreshortened viewpoint, that some of the ships were almost touching.

'We'll have to get cracking to get out of their way,' Booth went on. 'They'll be on us before we can finish the lap.'

Solan obviously had similar views. A flag-hoist fluttered to her yard-arm. Larkin glanced at it and repeated the hoist down the line.

'In sweeps.'

By the time the sweeps were on board and stowed the destroyer leading the convoy was almost abeam of them with its double-lined flock close astern. A rough count showed about forty ships, with possibly more to come from the haze.

As they left the narrow channel girded on each side by treacherous sand-banks they started to move up from a formation of two abreast to four abreast, and the destroyer fussed about at the focal point of the change. Half-way down the line, between it and the French coast, another destroyer was dashing to and fro with a large white bow wave showing that whatever she was doing she was doing it quickly.

Solan and her group moved out to seaward of the convoy and lay stopped, rolling ever so slightly on the glassy sea.

Haley watched the merchant ships juggle for position and marvelled slightly at the comparative ease with which they dropped into position even though there was an infinite variety of ships.

156

He saw Larkin suddenly duck down to the radio office voice-pipe and after listening repeat tersely: 'Air-Raid warning—Blue Gate area.' He sucked his teeth momentarily then added, 'That's us, sir.'

Haley felt his heart suddenly pound. He looked at Booth who, after one glance, moved swiftly round the bridge, viewing each gun position. Two quick orders sent the full gun's crew tumbling up on to the 12-pounder. Scarcely had they taken up their positions when the air started pulsating to the uneven throb of aircraft.

A smothered ejaculation escaped Larkin's lips as he peered through his battered binoculars.

'Look, sir, there's hundreds of the bastards . . . hundreds of 'em.'

Booth and Haley trained their glasses in the same direction. For a moment Haley could see nothing except a smother of tiny bits of grit, or flies, on the lens.

Then one of the bits of grit flashed. They were 'planes; orderly formations of them, flying at about 12,000 to 15,000 feet. The glasses began to tremble and Haley locked his fingers in a tight clutch on them in an attempt to keep them steady. As he watched a group wheeled away from the formation at a broad angle. He followed it for a while, then an obstruction got in his way. He dropped his binoculars and saw that a stanchion was in line with the 'planes. They were lower, still dropping, and were bent on attacking the convoy still shuffling into formation.

Bang! A few seconds pause then bang! again. Haley jumped and looked round. Two dun-coloured clouds were rolling away from *Jacinth*'s bow and as he watched there was another flash and a bang.

The destroyer on the beam of the convoy opened up, the leader following suit.

Haley, watching through his glasses, saw three puffs suddenly appear in the sky below and ahead of the dropping formation. They would be *Jacinth*'s.

'Open fire!' he rasped at Booth. Booth yelled an order and in almost the same second *Arandite*'s gun barked viciously and Haley felt the hot back-flash and smelt the cordite.

All the ships and opened up by now and the approaching enemy 'planes seemed to be running into a sky full of little clusters of cotton wool.

' "G10" from *Solan*, "to be obeyed as soon as read," ' came from Larkin.

'Full ahead!' Haley ordered, and telegraph bells clanged. *Arandite* started to throb as a sound of steam hissing into the cylinders came from her open engine-room skylights. From the corner of his eye Haley saw Larkin using his Aldis lamp.

' "Position to best advantage on beam of convoy. Let them have it." From *Solan*, sir. Christ, they've got one!' The signalman's flat intonation suddenly soared up as one of the 'planes, now quite distinct and not more than a mile away, lurched, tilted over on to one wing, righted itself, then dropped steeply seawards with an ominous red glow and a streamer of smoke coming from its front.

The roar from the 'planes was almost deafening and was punctuated by the frequent but irregular crash of gunfire.

Haley suddenly found himself icy calm, giving each phase of the attack a rapid appraisal and thinking ahead like a flash to meet it. Booth was doing admirably with the gun control, primitive as it was. Now to handle the ship to best advantage. *Solan*, he could see, was closing the destroyer on the beam of the convoy. *Arandite*'s best place was in the gap between the two destroyers, and Haley gave an order which took her into an irregular, weaving half-circle. On one of his turns he saw *Jacinth* steaming full tilt straight towards the 'planes. In addition to her 12-pounder she seemed to be throwing fiery tracer from at least half a dozen points on the ship.

The 'planes split up, wheeled right and left, one part rolling over to run along the length of the convoy, the other aiming to cover the top of the van.

A nerve-shattering clatter came from immediately beneath Haley. Port side machine-gun had opened up. He saw a stream of tracer come from the guns aft, both lines converging on a 'plane whose course would take her ahead of *Arandite*. It must have been hit, but it raced on, engines rising in a roar, and swept over the milling ships.

There was a dull thump and Haley felt *Arandite* jar slightly. He looked quickly and between the destroyer and the leading merchant ship a plume of water rose.

'Near miss,' Booth yelled. 'Leave it. There's one coming up the side.'

The youngster dashed madly across the bridge as *Arandite* altered course again. The starboard machine-gun opened up, followed a second later by the guns aft. Then Haley felt a series of rapid little blows in the small of his back as a ripping clatter slightly deafened him. Booth had joined in with Susie. She coughed once in the middle of the burst, then went on heroically shedding her empty cartridge cases over Haley.

As *Arandite* turned they heard a heavy metallic crash. One of the merchant ships reeled away, rolling almost to its beam ends. The smoke and shower of debris had scarcely reached its peak height when it was followed by a huge rose of flame which savagely reared up once, died down momentarily, then came up again, this time in a steadily increasing, sullen, billowing sheet of dark red flame topped by a cloud of thick black smoke.

'They've hit a ship—they've hit a ship!' Larkin was repeating in a blurred, excited, almost hysterical voice as he crouched down behind the canvas bridge front, only his eyes above the rail.

'Shut up! Keep your eyes open for signals,' Haley snapped. Along the line several more bombs fell, sending spouts of dark water upwards. The opening attack wavered away as the 'planes roared off to reform, and only an

159

occasional bark of a gun came as somebody tried a long-range shot.

Haley heard a clatter on the foredeck and looked over. The steward, sweating profusely, was heaving away at a hoist getting up more ammunition. The 12-pounder crew were heaving shells and projectiles up on to the platform while Clay was vigorously kicking out of his way a clutter of stained brass shell-cases.

A stoker seized some boxes of .303 cartridges and started dragging them along the deck.

Then Haley realised that all at once it was quiet, a soft, early summer evening, with a faint flecking of cloud in the sky and only the distant roar of 'planes, so distant that he had to seize and hold it to identify it.

The first wave of the attack was over. When was the next to come? He felt his knees go slightly shaky at the back. He found himself breathing sharply, in little jerks, as if he had been running and was short of breath. His lips were dry and he found he was unable to moisten them.

'Two ships hit, so far as I can see. One on fire, the other moving inshore,' Booth reported. Haley looked at him. His face was streaked with grease and sweat. His tin hat was tilted well back and his blue eyes were flashing with excitement.

'Damn him, I believe he enjoyed it all,' Haley thought irritably.

'They're coming again.' Larkin's voice was cracked. Then he remembered something of the drill he had been taught.

'Aircraft bearing red eighty, angle of sight . . . and *Jacinth*'s stuck into 'em again. There's three of 'em at her.'

The roar of planes was distinct once more. Away out, well to seaward of the convoy, *Jacinth* was spitting fire and 12-pounder short range H.E. at three 'planes which were obviously concentrating on this lone ship well away from the protective barrage of other ships.

160

Then Clay opened up once more as the 'planes came within a thousand yards. In seconds the machine-guns from bridge and aft were sending up their deadly strings of tracer. Haley, glancing aft, saw one line starting from a point well down, much lower than the gun-mounting aft. He moved slightly and saw that it was coming from a single gun barrel resting on the steel half-door of the galley.

Noisy was in action with his pet.

By one of those tricks that sometimes happen in action one 'plane came on without anybody firing directly at it, just as a leader of a charge will get through while men behind him are killed because each of the defenders assumes that somebody else will drop him. Haley felt, as much as heard, the thud of its engines and looked up swiftly. He could see only the sharp edge of the two wings and the thicker parts which were the engines. As he watched he saw something fall away.

'He's hit,' he thought. Then he realised that it was not part of the 'plane. It was a bomb. *And this 'plane was coming directly at Arandite.*

'It will hit the bridge. It's bound to get us amidships.' The thought raced through his mind.

'Starboard! Hard over!'

'Hard to starboard on, sir . . . hard over.' The Cox'n's voice came back, calm, comforting like a cool draught on a hot day. Haley suddenly realised that down below, shut in that little box, with only a few small windows to allow him to see what was going on, was the Cox'n.

'You all right, Cox?'

'Everything's all right, sir.'

Haley watched the bomb coming straight towards him. There was a sudden vicious rattle as if a boy had thrown a handful of heavy gravel at a window. The 'plane was now right ahead, the bomb travelling with it and dropping all the time. A heavy twang came from near Haley's head. The roar of the 'plane, only a few feet above the bridge, was

161

almost unbearable and Haley found himself crouching and cringing like a child sheltering from a heavy hailstorm. Something swished over the bridge, charts and signal pads whirled up in a mad flutter, and *Arandite* reeled away, her bow surged upwards. She righted herself as the bomb went off below the water less than the beam away. Water cascaded down over the forepart and the bridge, and Haley came up from his crouch to find his head singing and a drumming noise in his ears.

Half a dozen quick vignettes flashed through his mind. He saw Booth reeling about the back of the bridge with his hands to his face. The signalman was down on his hands and knees like a praying Mussulman. Water sloshed about the bridge and dripped from everything. A loose stay whipped and cracked in the air.

Up the voice-pipe from the wheel came a calm voice.

'A near one that, sir.' Cox'n was reporting in his own way that he was still all right. 'I think somebody's been hit for'rard.'

Haley staggered to the front of the bridge. Clay and another man were trying to get the head of one of the seamen up from between his knees and from between his hands. Haley saw blood coming from the man's fingers.

He shouted something unintelligible to the gun platform and Clay, wrestling with the man, stopped in response. He put his cupped hand to his ear, then his deep voice rolled back.

'He's bitten his bloody tongue, sir.'

Haley laughed slightly hysterically. He reeled away and looked towards Booth.

'I got half the damned Channel smacked into my face,' Booth said, wiping his face with a sleeve. 'That one was near enough. I smelt it as it went past.'

The signalman climbed slowly to his feet and exhaled noisily like a small boy who has been holding his breath under water for a long time.

He looked apologetically at Haley.

'I forgot to breathe,' he said in self-reproach, and straightened himself, painfully rubbing his stomach.

Booth quickly looked at the bridge. 'He sprayed us well and truly as he came in. The funnel got most of it. It's like a watering-can.'

Haley's eyes were on the chart table. Two ragged holes about a foot apart let daylight in. The bullets had travelled on, slashed through the log, splintered long furrows on the flat table and buried themselves in the canvas-covered splinter mats round the bridge. Silently he followed the line of their travel. When the harsh rattle, like thrown gravel, had sounded he was standing near the chart table almost in line with the ragged furrow. The bullets must have passed within inches of his chest.

He shook himself and fought off the faint tingle which stole over him. They missed him and that was that. Trying to assess by how much was just taxing imagination.

'See what other damage there is, quickly—they'll be back to find out what casualties there are. I know one'—the giggle came out despite his attempt to smother it—'one of the 12-pounder men has bitten his tongue.'

Booth's eyebrows arched then he, too, giggled.

Haley used his binoculars to sweep swiftly along the convoy.

Nearly two miles away, indistinct in the haze, the tail of the long line of ships was still engaged in fighting off aircraft he could not see and could only faintly hear.

Occasionally an orange flash ripped through the haze as a destroyer or other escort fired, and no doubt the sky was full of tracer.

Solan seemed to be stopped, or moving only dead slow, and was letting the convoy pass her while she swung slowly in the tide. Distantly he heard the dull bomp of a gun, the short ripping bursts of machine-gun fire, and heard the snarling roar of an aircraft diving in to attack. Although it was some way off, and obviously not directed at *Arandite,* Haley's thigh and stomach muscles contracted protectively. He followed the direction of the sound. Well to seaward of the convoy, framed in the climbing water plumes from two near misses, was a ship, indistinct in the scattering spray. A lurid flash from her gun was followed by another dull bomp and lazily curving tracer climbed from various parts of the ship to come to a cone point in and around an aircraft wheeling away in a climb. From a small black spot a little distance from her a plume of black smoke edged away, increasing in size as it went, looking like a large dark feather carelessly thrown on to a sheet of glass.

'That's *Jacinth.* She's got one . . . there's a sod in the drink.' Larkin's voice broke like a schoolboy's. '*Jacinth*'s got one!' he yelled again, hanging over the front of the bridge and gesticulating for the benefit of the 12-pounder crew. Booth was on the platform examining the now inarticulate tongue-biter. He saw Haley appear at the front of the bridge and cupped his hands round his mouth.

'Not serious; a deep bite and bleeding freely. I can't stop it yet,' he called.

'Stop screaming,' Haley rasped at the signalman. 'And I'm damned if I know how to stop it, either,' he pondered. 'Tie it up, I suppose.' The picture of the seaman with a large bandage on the end of his tongue flickered through his mind and he laughed sharply.

There came another sullen roar as a 'plane swooped in on *Jacinth.* The 12-pounder went bomp . . . pause . . . bomp, and her machine-guns clattered again. She disappeared as the harsher, deeper thump of an exploding bomb came over the water. The dark, ominous plume climbed upwards and Haley felt his heart jump and start thumping. Then *Jacinth*'s jaunty bow came through the column of smoke and spray. Once again her gun barked and she threaded the aircraft, which was turning away in a flat half-circle, at the end of the deadly fiery necklace.

'Hard to port,' down the wheelhouse pipe. 'Emergency full ahead.' Haley raised his head. 'I'm going over to *Jacinth*. Short range H.E.,' he called. Clay and his crew jerked into activity, Booth slid down the steel ladder and scuttered along the deck.

Jacinth was steaming in wide circles round the remnants of the wrecked 'plane still smoking in the water. The attack by the two remaining 'planes was keeping her too busy to allow any attempt to pick up the bomber's crew, if they still lived.

The method of attack was obvious. One was diving in from ahead, crossing the bow at a wide angle, and immediately afterwards the other came screaming in from the quarter. No trawler had sufficient armament to beat off attacks of that sort resolutely pushed home. It was purely a question of poor bomb-aiming which was saving her. How much damage they had done by gunfire it was hard to say.

As *Arandite* throbbed over Halcy closely watched the two aircraft wheeling away fairly low down about a mile away. They straightened up, climbed slightly, then the one attacked from the bow came tearing down in a shallow dive. *Jacinth*'s bow was pointing that way. The other delayed its turn, swept wide out, then started its roaring dive. The two aircraft and *Arandite* were describing the outline of a broad arrow, with *Arandite* as the centre stalk.

Haley swung his ship slightly and steadied her. 'Open fire,' he rapped to Booth. 'That one, fine on the bow.'

Booth yelled and *Arandite*'s 12-pounder crashed. There was the smell of cordite and the hot flash. The gun barked again and Haley saw the two burst slightly ahead of the 'plane. From beneath him and from aft lines of lazy tracer curved towards it. The range was extreme but the tracer was reaching well ahead and must have been zipping at right angles across the nose of the 'plane. From *Jacinth*'s stern came two more streams of tracer and Haley saw some of it hit and kick away at an angle.

The cross-fire upset the pilot. He swung—it looked almost like a jerk—and the silhouette altered, first to a full view of the machine as it banked acutely, then to the razor edge.

'It's coming for me,' Haley felt himself gulp.

'Turning away—doesn't like it,' Booth yelped and jumped towards Susie. She fired one short burst and jammed. Haley saw the small line of tracer, like a little stream of angry wasps, following the line of the 'plane dropping in a curve long before they reached her. Clay got in two more shots under her tail, one bursting close enough to make the 'plane rock and swerve violently.

The solitary machine attacking *Jacinth* apparently had no more bombs, and after a sustained, ripping burst wheeled upwards and away.

Haley watched them through his binoculars until they were but minute outlines. He dropped his viewpoint to include *Jacinth*, now only a few hundred yards away. Small figures were scurrying about the gun platform and Haley saw the flash from empty shell-cases as they threw them down on to the deck.

A light twinkled agitatedly from her bridge and Larkin scurried to cope with the signal.

'Cover me while I pick up a Jerry swimming for home,' *Jacinth* sent. There was a pause, then: 'Thanks, chum, they were getting fussy.'

Jacinth moved in a half-circle towards the now barely discernible wreck of the bomber, stopped, and Haley saw some activity among a small group on the foredeck. Then she moved on, blotting out the wreckage on the water, and stopped again. The same little group converged on one spot. Haley saw part of the tail assembly, twisted and torn, rise above *Jacinth*'s rail. There was the flash of an axe two or three times, then *Jacinth* signalled 'O.K.'

As the two ships turned back towards the convoy Haley used his binoculars again. The first merchant ship hit, now burning furiously, was drifting inshore. From a huge, vicious

166

rose-coloured base which billowed and rolled a thick, black cloud of smoke stretched greasily, keeping low on the water until it joined the haze.

Further inshore, and more easterly, another ship was moving painfully and slowly, her stern well down and her deck showing in a list. Even as he watched her she gave a lurch and her stern settled deeper.

'She's going to sink in the Swept Channel unless they hurry her along.' Booth was using his glasses too.

One of the escorting destroyers had similar views. She tore through the slowly moving lines of ships, dodging across the bows of one, swerving under the stern of another, until she closed on the crippled ship.

A gentle smile played on Haley's lips as he mentally went through the orders which were being given on the destroyer's bridge. It might look alarming from the bridge of a trawler or a merchant ship but he knew that the destroyer captain had assessed his gaps, judged the speed of the ships in a couple of seconds and could, in fact, have cut it considerably finer yet done no harm.

But whatever its intentions the destroyer was too late. The merchant ship's bows rose slowly and the angle of the deck became even more acute.

'There she goes!' It came involuntarily from Haley. He saw men scramble across her decks, jump into the water. The water boiled under the destroyer's stern as she backed away. A small group tried to get a lifeboat into the water. One end of it dropped; it hung perpendicular, then the men also jumped. Slowly, almost imperceptibly, the ship slid backwards into the water. There was a dull rumble; a cloud of steam and smoke came from her engine-room skylights, was quenched, came up from the the funnel in one large gout, and she settled with scarcely any fuss at all.

When only the top of the bridge and the masts were visible the ship remained on an even keel.

'She's on the bottom.' Haley almost whispered it.

'And in the fairway, smack in the middle.' Booth was almost as quiet.

The destroyer moved in swiftly. Sleek, soaking figures were helped over her side and in a few minutes a furiously boiling froth appeared under the destroyer's stern as she turned away.

Suddenly there was a sharp clank. The water darkened around *Arandite*'s stern about a hundred feet away from her, then the darkened patch climbed upwards and there was a terrific roar. *Arandite* shuddered slightly.

'A bloody mine!' Booth's voice cracked in excitement. The destroyer reeled but tore on shaken but safe apart from a few electric globes. Her course took her close to *Arandite* and Haley could see the little group on the bridge. A light twinkled. Larkin jumped to answer.

'From the destroyer, sir. "Who threw that brick?" '

Haley chuckled and pondered. '*Vindex*, old V. and W., nearly a pensioner back for her second war. Um, Lieutenant-Commander . . . er . . . er . . . damn it, I forget, but a lad noted for his cheery ways.'

'Make the answer: "Same chap. A man named Hitler," ' he said and listened to Larkin's clatter with the lamp. The destroyer was some distance away when her light flashed again and Haley read the signal over Larkin's shoulder.

'Rude, isn't he?' it said.

Only a few stragglers were left, now hurrying to join the main convoy four or five miles ahead. They were being ruthlessly shepherded along by an escort trawler, the smoke billowing from their funnels showing that they were putting their last ounce into the task.

'Always some stragglers.' Haley watched them through his glasses. 'I suppose this is an eight-knot convoy and it left the Thames about midday. By three o'clock this little bunch were lagging along behind, giving tail-end Charlie no end of work.' He spoke with feeling. 'All the afternoon he's been chivvying them along, asking them to close up, but

168

would they? Would they hell! Now there's a few bombs hanging about they scuttle like frightened sheep and produce a couple of extra knots.'

'And produce some extra smoke, too,' Booth said crisply. 'That might start the Big Boys the other side chucking over some of their heavy stuff.'

'Is that what they do?'

'They haven't done yet, but we were warned a couple of weeks ago that any smoke might draw shell-fire.'

Solan emerged from the haze created by the burning ship and started calling her flock together. Soon, from her yard-arm, hoists of signals were fluttering.

' "Out sweeps",' Larkin intoned.

'So be it, but if we finish a lap that's all we'll do to-night,' Booth said, leaving the bridge.

Solan set a course to carry the group close past the new hazard in the channel, the newly sunk ship whose masts and bridge stood up forlornly above the smooth water. Almost at once a mine blew up in her sweep. She cut another which bobbed menacingly down *Arandite*'s starboard side. *Solan* swung out to replace her damaged sweep and *Arandite* took over the lead.

The sunken ship was almost abeam when there were three crashing explosions almost merging into one another. They were in a line diagonally across the course the minesweepers were steering but were nowhere near *Arandite*'s or *Jacinth*'s sweeps.

'I knew it . . . I knew it!' Booth shinned up the ladder to the bridge excitedly. 'That damned smoke and the burning ship has started them off. They're shelling us.'

Haley stood against the front of the bridge, his chest pressed firmly against the woodwork. Bombing, gunfire, mines and now shells. And his head ached atrociously from the clatter of his guns and the near-miss earlier in the afternoon. He kept his eyes on a transit bearing ashore, murmured an alteration of course down the voice-pipe, then

169

closed his eyes momentarily. Should he order 'In sweeps' and move out of the target area? But what was the target area? Was it the burning ship, or the tail-end of the convoy, now still smoking furiously but a couple of miles away? Or were they, four puny trawlers and a drifter, the target?

Flatly, distantly, he heard the sound of gunfire and the thin, reedy noise of diving aircraft.

'The Hun's having another go at the convoy,' Booth said, peering through his glasses. A deeper, duller explosion reached them. Haley looked round, caught Booth's eyes on him and shrugged. A bomb? Another ship? They could not see through the evening haze.

Then came gunfire, closer, sharper, and the gravel rattle of machine-guns.

'Stragglers.' Booth sounded like a BBC commentator. The comparison stirred a little wave of humour in Haley. In almost the same informative tones he continued the technique: 'Aircraft now in square four . . . the ball has gone out to the wing . . . a half-back tackles . . .'

Three thudding explosions jarred *Arandite* and three separate plumes of water climbed upwards, but this time between *Jacinth* and *Sheila*. The second of the three momentarily hid *Sheila* and Haley caught his breath. Then he exhaled forcibly as he saw her jaunty bow come through the dropping, thinning water.

He saw the barrel of the 12-pounder swing upwards and outwards uncertainly as Clay and his trainer searched for a target.

Haley felt rather than saw Larkin and Booth watching him. At the same time he visualised what was happening the other side.

A strutting major or colonel would put down his telephone. 'The stupid Britisher would take through a convoy. Our glorious Luftwaffe sank some, our wonderful mines will sink others, but the impertinent Britisher sends insulting little ships to clear them up. Those I will shell and sink.

Heil Hitler. Open fire.'

'It's us,' Booth said with just a suspicion of a tremble in his voice. 'And if one lands on us . . .'

'The general effect will be the same as a hit from a bomb.' Haley kept his voice well to the back of his throat. It sounded harsh, brittle. For God's sake shut up! Leave the bridge, or something. Stop making me brave, stop making me think of things to say to show that I am not going to be deterred by bombing, shelling, or anything. I'm going on with the sweep until we complete the lap. Where in hell is *Solan*? Why doesn't he signal? He is Senior Officer. A damaged sweep doesn't put him out of court.

The gunfire and duller thomps were renewed. Aircraft. That was something tangible, something to shoot at. In the 'plane was a man who could be scared, made to waver. These damned shells dropped without warning, and dropped close. Another fifty yards and that last salvo would have got either *Jacinth* or *Sheila*.

'Flagstaff and blockhouse in transit, sir.' Booth had regained control of his voice. 'That's the end of the lap,' he added with a shade of reluctance.

Haley made no reply for a while. Then he turned to Larkin. 'Make to *Sheila*: "Signal me when blockhouse and Flagstaff are in transit." Then call *Solan* and ask him if he wants me to do another lap. No! Say: "I intend to start another lap."' He pondered. 'Shall I add "if you approve"?' but changed his mind. 'Get them away and never mind the tiddley procedure stuff.'

Larkin shook his head in silent indignation.

'Stand by to shorten in, Mr. Booth.'

'Aye, aye, sir. Stand by!' Booth climbed down the ladder. As he reached the deck there were three more heavy, sullen explosions. Haley could not at once locate the inevitable towering plumes; then he saw them. They were well inshore, in line with them but at least half a mile over.

If the gunner dropped his sights slightly next salvo . . .

'From *Sheila*, sir. "Bearings abeam now." *Solan*'s calling, sir.'

Click-clack went Larkin's lamp trigger.

'From *Solan*, sir. "Call it a day. No overtime pay on this job!"' Larkin sounded almost cheerful.

Haley felt a surge of thankfulness. He leaned over the after end of the bridge with the megaphone in his hand. Booth, with an attentuated sweeping crew, was watching him.

'Stand by. In sweeps.' Booth waved his hand in acknowledgment.

The signal fluttered to *Arandite*'s yard-arm, was repeated down the line, and soon the big winches were heaving in the dripping sweeps.

Haley saw a motor-launch closing *Solan* and lie-to a few yards from the trawler. *Solan* signalled asking if there were any casualties; if any they were to be transferred to the M.L.

'Is a bitten tongue a casualty?' Haley asked the world out loud. 'Could be! Tell Cox'n to stand by to ship that man with the cut tongue to the M.L.,' he told Larkin.

The M.L. went first to *Jacinth* then sheered away and came to *Arandite*. The injured man stepped aboard with a little parcel under his arm.

A young Lieutenant was on the bridge of the M.L. and Haley spoke to him as they dropped alongside each other.

'Did *Solan* and *Jacinth* have any . . . any casualties?'

The youngster nodded.

'Three wounded on *Solan* . . . two wounded and'—he jerked his head at a blanket-covered figure lying on the M.L.'s foredeck—'from *Jacinth*. She's got a couple more, but they are only scratches and they want to stay.'

He looked critically along *Arandite*'s length, up at Haley and smiled. 'You've been in quite a battle, haven't you?' Haley wondered how much the remark was related to the glance along the ship's length.

'For a time. Why, does it show?'

'You look a bit pepper-pottish about the bridge and the

funnel, and your port side boat deck—and boat—will want darning before you can do much with them.'

Haley gave the boat deck and boat a quick scrutiny. From where he stood the damage was not obvious although he could see some fresh white splinters.

'That one must have given you a shave and a haircut,' the M.L.'s captain went on pleasantly, pointing a finger to the bridge rail over which Haley was leaning. From the splinter mat a large jagged piece of metal protruded near the top. Inches more and it would have gone scything across the bridge. Haley touched it. The edge was like a razor. He shivered slightly.

The M.L. moved away with its cargo of wounded.

'See you in the morning. I expect I'll be out with a few replacements.' He waved, then as she gathered speed he called through a megaphone: 'C.M.S.P. was watching the battle from his balcony. I gather he was rather pleased.'

'What had he to be pleased about?' Haley thought irritably. 'It might have looked ...'

'Aircraft ... high up ... hundreds of 'em!'

Larkin pointed with a shaking finger and Haley screwed up his aching eyes. The aircraft were miles away, flying in ragged formation back towards France. Above them weaved tiny little gnats—gnats with a vicious sting. R.A.F. fighters taking their toll from enemy bombers which had been ... been where? Doing what? What was their target? London, Chatham, London's docks?

While the convoy had been fighting its way resolutely through the narrow gap the big attack, the heavy air-raids which everybody knew would come, had started. But where? London ... and London meant Madge. Haley clenched his fists.

'*Solan* calling,' port side gunner shouted.

'*Solan* and *Arandite* take M patrol, *Jacinth* and *Sheila* take S beat.'

'And the Lord have mercy on any *E*-boats which come

173

rambling along S patrol,' Booth murmured, 'and some of that mercy for *Sheila*, because that fighting Celt must be at boiling point now and would tackle the *Von Hipper* by boarding party.'

Haley turned on Booth irritably.

'The captain of *Jacinth* is a very fine officer,' he said coldly. Damn! Why am I snapping at that kid all the time? He's probably feeling as jittery as I am. Here goes—I'll make some amends. 'But I'll settle for a quiet patrol tonight.'

Fates were kind. *Solan* and *Arandite* patrolled the dark oily waters without incident, but away in the distance they saw star shells soaring upwards from about S patrol and heard two or three distant thuds of gunfire.

'Probably somebody opened a door in Calais, so *Jacinth* accepts it as a hostile gesture.' Booth sounded rather weary. He stood upright, bent and flexed his arms. 'He had a hell of a nerve careering off today, and starting a war on his own.'

Haley smiled in the darkness.

'You career off to your little cubby-hole for a couple of hours, and don't snore or I'll cut your throat.'

'Me snore? ME?'

'All right, get to sleep.'

And soon, despite his protestation, Booth was softly snoring in the little air-raid shelter. The humour of the situation made Haley chuckle. Throughout a number of air attacks everybody had forgotten the shelter; nobody had ducked into it. Now a youngster was sleeping the sleep of the justly tired in it.

Arandite throbbed ahead, slowly running down the glowing wake of *Solan*.

7

The war tempo increased. The sky seldom seemed empty of high-flying aircraft leaving behind them a delicate tracery of filmy white trails, some cutting a straight line across the sky, others weaving as the fighters strove for an opening. Frequently a darker trail broke from the more-or-less orderly pattern, went downwards, the smoke thinning and widening into indeterminate proportions with always the pin-point black and red at the beginning of it until it disappeared ashore, or came to an abrupt termination in a small white splash.

It was difficult to believe that war was being fought out in the heights at nearly three hundred miles an hour while below a plodding convoy, moving at less than ten miles an hour, or a group of ships sweeping at half that speed, carried on their warfare at the same tactical speed as that used by Sir Francis Drake.

Frequent air-raid warnings brought little or no reaction. From the shore there came the thin heart-startling banshee wail. Anti-aircraft guns opened up, puffs of smoke punctuated the progress of the raiding 'planes, and sometimes a duller crump and a shower of smoke and debris climbed, framed against the background of dwellings.

It became a matter of expert assessment. 'Planes flying at 12,000 feet or higher were out for some other target. Some town full of non-belligerents, of little men and women who had no means of hitting back.

Portsmouth, Plymouth, London—all were being repeatedly raided and toll was being taken from the raiding 'planes. Watching a fight moving across the sky, Haley remembered one day the words of Lieutenant-Commander Payne. With French airfields in the hands of the enemy, only a few minutes away from the British coast, raids would be frequent and heavy. The R.A.F., sadly maligned for its apparent non-appearance at the Dunkirk evacuation, would want every machine.

And so it was. The German machines above them, black silhouetted against the cloud-flecked sky, seemed to be flying in tight formation in complete peace. Then, from the direction of the westerly sun, a stream of angry hornets swept down on them. From the heights came the clock-clock of short bursts of gunfire. Bombers dropped out of the formation, some wheeling away and retracing their direction. Others came down in an ever-steepening dive.

As Haley and Booth watched they both saw a tiny white speck below the fight, a speck which seemed scarcely to move. Then gradually it took shape. It was a pilot dropping by parachute. Haley saw Clay swing his 12-pounder round until he got the dropping man in his sights. There was an eager invitation in the glance he threw up to the bridge.

'Train that gun fore and aft. He may be one of ours.' Haley rapped it out.

Clay trained the gun with obvious reluctance. It had not occurred to him that British pilots could be at the losing end of an aerial fight, and might have to drop through the air with only a thin, strumming bag of silk between them and a shapeless death.

In the succeeding weeks they swept the same area time and time again during the day, and patrolled it at night. And went on cutting mines and blowing them up. A mine drifting close by brought no reaction other than a hoist of flags to warn the ships astern and to inform the patient plodding *Harvester* that there was work for her.

176

Three times they had to break off sweeping, drop out to seawards to let convoys go past, and each time the convoys were attacked by air and by shelling.

The ominous line of wrecks, twisted masts, shattered bridges, grew larger each side of the channel and bombed or mined ships were thrust, sinking and useless, out of the fairway.

Clay summed it up one afternoon to Booth when he said, not without humour: 'I think, when I get my boat after the war, I'll start a 'opping farm out here. There's nearly enough poles up.'

It complicated sweeping, involved devious twists and sharp turns which in the swift tide caused inevitable gaps in the swept area.

It was this which led to a tumultuous row between Meredith and Regan. Twice they had swept an area defined by a series of broad 'S's' caused by newly sunk ships and twice they failed to search the area completely.

Regan altered formation from four ships almost in line to two pairs sweeping abreast. *Solan* took *Sheila* and *Arandite* worked with *Jacinth*.

A scorching signal came down from *Solan*, directed mainly towards *Jacinth* although it was Haley's fault, if fault there was. He allowed a little too much for tide and squeezed *Jacinth* in until it looked as if he was bound to wrap his sweep wire round the masts and bridge of a wreck.

On a previous run they had set up two mines and it was obvious that in and around the area between two wrecks either an *E-*boat or aircraft, or both, had laid a new field. It was just the place where a ship would try to slip through in an effort to avoid the congestion caused by the now almost inevitable bombing and shelling which came with the re-formation of the convoys after they had come through the gap in single line. So Regan was determined to search it thoroughly for moored mines before turning it over to a pair of electric sweepers.

To give *Jacinth* a little more room Haley swung away. It was touch and go and only Meredith could assess from his bridge whether he would clear the wreck or not. He decided not and wheeled away.

As *Arandite* turned round ready to join up with *Jacinth* for another sweep he was surprised to see *Solan* and *Sheila* moving in to cover the area. *Jacinth* lay stopped, her sweep shortened in to the rail and a wisp of steam coming from her exhaust.

Haley watched through his glasses and saw with a considerable admiration the *Solan* swept down without a deviation and *Sheila*, keeping close station, cut the wreck so finely that the slight wash from her Oropesa float lapped the shattered bridge of the wreck.

'Ten feet more and he would have been well and truly hung up.' Booth had been an interested spectator. Before Haley could make any reply there was a shattering explosion and *Sheila*'s otter-board, kite and sweep wire went careering skywards. A mine had been laid not a hundred feet from the wreck. *Sheila* dropped away to recover the remains of her sweep and *Solan* signalled *Arandite* to take over, and in almost the same spot *Solan* put up two close together.

Haley was surprised to receive a signal:

Wait for *Sheila* who will join you when she has rigged another sweep.

Why not *Jacinth*, lying stopped and rolling, with her sweep intact? He signalled to *Solan* and suggested it. The reply was terse:

'Take *Sheila*.'

Two days later they slipped into harbour for a few hours for stores, ammunition, bunkers and new sweeping gear. Haley felt tired, not with the tiredness that can be refreshed by a night's sleep but with the weariness which comes with staleness and with the taxing of physical and mental strength beyond normal.

As Booth hurried about seeing that all was fast Haley gave the shore view a tired scrutiny. There were harsh gaps in the row of houses along the sea front. Masonry tumbled in untidy heaps where once there had been houses. He slowly shook his head and wrenched his mind away from the reflection that perhaps it was the same in London, in North London where Madge . . . If anything happened he would be told. Until then . . . sweep on and dodge the things that go bomp in the night.

He turned and saw Cutter coming along the quay with a working-party from the Base camp. Cutter had laid it down that as soon as a ship came in the crew were to get as much rest as possible. To ensure this he had organised working-parties to meet each sweeper. They put stores aboard, bunkered, replaced broken sweep gear, leaving the crew only the job of eating and sleeping—which they did admirably.

A Petty Officer chivvied the working-party on board and Cutter spoke to Haley.

'You've got two days—nearly. Out tomorrow afternoon to sweep before a convoy comes through. Pleasant dreams.'

Haley sank down on his settee. He ought to take a bath, a nice, warm, comforting bath. Lie in it until the water cooled off, then turn on more hot and let the water work its will. He ought to write letters. He should write to Madge. What was there to write about? 'Dearest, I am quite well and fit.' And beyond that, what? There was something to be said for a stereotyped kind of letter already printed so that all one had to do was cross out the unwanted sentences. 'I am well.' 'I am not well.' 'I am short of money.' It took an effort to stand up and pull over his head the sweater he was wearing. Once the initial inertia was overcome he concentrated on the thought of a bath.

There was a knock at his door. In response to his invitation it opened and Meredith stepped in. He was dressed for the shore; clean white collar and presentable uniform.

'You going to a wedding? Or a funeral?' Haley asked. Then he saw Meredith's face. It was set in tight lines; his mouth was like a slit, the lips bloodless, and in his eyes burned a fiery light.

'*Solan*. And you are coming with me.'

'Not on your life! No social visit for me. I'm going to have a bath and turn . . .'

Meredith threw a small file of papers on to the table.

'Read those,' he snapped. Haley looked at him wonderingly, picked up the papers and read.

On the top was a signal.

S.O. *Solan* to *Jacinth*. As you seem scared to tackle it close to the wreck keep clear. I will do it.

Haley was still puzzled but Meredith recalled for him the incident when they were sweeping round the wrecks.

'I may be the world's worst sweeping officer,' Meredith said, passionately thumping the table, 'but no jumped-up Irish swill eater is going to call me a coward in front of my crew.'

Haley tried, futilely, to minimise the trouble.

'I don't think Regan meant . . .'

'To Hell with what Regan meant! You can read, can't you? I was too close to the wreck. If I had wrapped my sweep round the wreck you would have heard him yell a mile away.'

'It was my fault. I ran you too close.'

'It was nobody's fault. It happens every day; misjudge a tide, or some other factor, and you have to go back again to do the job, as we would have. We're going on board *Solan*,' he wound up flatly.

Haley wearily slipped his coat on and they went to *Solan*.

Regan's greeting was outrageously Reganish.

'Boarding party, eh? Out pikes! Get the plank ready.

180

You do look beautiful!'—this last to Meredith.

Meredith looked at *Solan*'s grinning Number One.

'Lieutenant Regan, I want to talk to you.' He trailed off. Regan jerked his head and the young Sub-lieutenant disappeared.

'What's on your mind, Taff?'

Meredith's reply was to toss on to the table his signal pad and a sheet of paper clipped to it. After a quick glance at Haley and the Welshman Regan read it. As he went on he started to bite his bottom lip. He flicked over the signal pad and read on down the foolscap sheet. When he had finished he rubbed his forehead with his fingers.

'Actually, it was my fault,' Haley started. 'I cut in too close and squeezed *Jacinth* on to the wreck. We would have cleaned it up next time.'

'Sit down.' Regan jerked his head towards the settee. Haley sat but Meredith remained standing. 'SIT DOWN!' Regan rapped it out. Meredith stuck his chin out. He stood formally, with his cap tucked under his arm, staring straight into Regan's eyes.

'Oh, God, they're going to quarrel. They're going to make it an issue,' thought Haley miserably. 'Two fiery types, each highly inflammable and at explosion point.'

Regan's voice was flat and harsh. 'Very well, stand up. Had you come to me in a different way I would have said outright that I was in the wrong. When I sent that signal I was tired and'—he strove for a word—'exasperated. For some reason, I can't explain it now, I wanted to get under your skin. Presumably I did.'

'Go on.' Meredith was equally unyielding.

'You want to make an issue of it? Let's get it clear. A Senior Officer has called another officer a coward.' Regan began itemising the points on his finger-tips. 'Called him a coward in front of his crew. That officer has redress—you want redress. You shall have it.'

'Look, you two. You're both making a mountain out of

181

a molehill. It was my fault, completely my fault. I didn't give *Jacinth* enough room. Meredith was quite in order in swinging away.'

Regan looked coldly at Haley.

'Undoubtedly it was your fault. But that is not the point at issue. It is my signal.' He waved a hand vaguely in the air. 'It wasn't even logged as a signal, was not even sent by the signalman. It was Number One who had the lamp. However, give me a few minutes to dress and we'll take the matter to Mahoney.'

Haley tried once more to take on the mantle of peacemaker.

'Surely we can argue it out . . .'

'There will no be argument. I'll dress and we'll take the matter up properly.' Regan reached the bottom of the companion. 'Help yourself to a drink if you want one. I'll be as quick as I can.'

When they were alone neither of them spoke. Haley thoughtfully twisted a broken matchstick in an ashtray and Meredith stood, feet wide apart, staring at the bulkhead. Haley felt too tired to line up the points. Somewhere, he felt, there was a more simple solution than taking it to C.M.S.P. What view he would take was difficult to determine. He might decide to take an official standpoint; an accusation of cowardice against an officer was a serious matter. Or he might give them both a severe dressing-down. In either case it would leave a nasty taste.

Haley rested his elbows on the table and cupped his head in his hands.

'You think I should have taken it and said nothing.' Meredith sounded pugnacious. Haley lifted up his head and saw a troubled light in the Welshman's eyes.

Haley shook his head. 'I think a flaming row would have settled it without making it an official matter. I do not for one moment think that Regan meant to question your courage, or your ability. As he said, he was tired, irritable.

182

Aren't we all? And he just sent one . . . well, just one of those signals.'

'A flaming row? What do you think I came here for?'

'In Number One's, with gloves and clean collar?' Haley said wearily. 'And when did you start logging all Regan's signals? Good God, we'd want a dozen signal logs to put them all down.'

'I logged that one.'

'Because it annoyed you and you wanted a row.'

'I logged it because it cast a reflection on me in front of my crew. Do you think it lost anything in the telling down the mess deck, and will lose anything as it is repeated among the other ships?'

'Oh, this can go on forever,' Haley thought wearily. 'It can be endless and however it ends officially the aftermath will stay with us.'

And it lasted just a few minutes.

Solan's Number One came tumbling down the companion. 'Commander Mahoney's coming aboard, sir. Where's the C.O.? There's a ton of brass on the quay.'

He shot up the ladder again to warn Regan.

Haley looked at Meredith.

'Tailor made, isn't it?'

Regan clattered into view, followed by Lieutenant-Commander Cutter, Commander Mahoney and another Commander. *Solan*'s Number One came last.

After greetings had been exchanged Mahoney sat in the one arm-chair. Haley felt acutely conscious of his stubbly chin and his sea-going uniform, and a similar uneasiness must have come to Regan because he rubbed his hand across his chin and apologised for his appearance.

Cutter looked at Regan and ran his tongue over his lips. Regan took up the cue. Soon there were glasses nicely filled in front of each man.

'Now, this is the sort of job I like,' Mahoney said. 'By the way, this is Commander Luke, Flag Officer's staff, and believe it or not, he was once my Number One—and the biggest thief in the Navy.'

Commander Luke accepted the compliment with a wide grin. 'You chaps have been having quite a picnic, I gather. We've heard . . .'

'This is my story,' Mahoney cut in, 'and I'm going to have the pleasure. Fill his glass again to stop him stealing my thunder.'

He idly picked up Meredith's signal sheet, glanced quickly at it, gave the attached sheet of paper an equally quick glance and tossed it back on the table.

Haley gulped and looked swiftly at Regan and Meredith who, by a curious quirk, were sitting side by side on the settee.

'Do you listen-in at all, you fellows? Y'know, to the BBC?' He eyed the bulkhead in a detached manner.

Haley, Regan and the others exchanged quick looks.

'Sometimes, sir, when we get a chance, which is not very often.' Regan was the spokesman.

'Pity!' Mahoney settled himself comfortably in his chair, watched his glass being topped up, then went on : 'Remember that convoy which came through and was heavily attacked from the air?'

'Which one, sir?' Meredith allowed a smile to play about his lips as he asked the question.

'The first or second big air attack.'

Haley remembered, so did the other, but made no reply as Mahoney went on : 'On board the senior escorting destroyer was a quite famous broadcaster. When he got back to London he did a description of the passage and much of it was his story of the attack.'

Mahoney stopped and looked at the little group.

'Which of you went careering over to France, fighting a private war with a few German aircraft—and shot one down?'

'*Jacinth.*'

184

It was a simultaneous explosive ejaculation from Regan and Haley. Regan amplified it: 'Private war was right, sir. He was damned nearly in Boulogne.'

'They were there to be shot at,' said Meredith aggressively.

Mahoney and Luke chuckled in unison.

'And shot at they were, I gather. You have been credited with two-and-a-half 'planes shot down. I don't know how you will work it out. But this is the point: the broadcasting laddie dwelt for some time in his talk on the trawlers which put themselves between the diving aircraft and the convoy. . . .'

'We were there already, sir; we had just finished a sweep,' Regan said.

'Don't spoil the story for a h'porth of fact. His version was that you inserted yourself between aircraft and convoy, and that the first shots came from you. That caused the aircraft to split and made it easier to drive off the attack. That's his story.'

'Trigger-finger Taff!' laughed Regan. 'You did pop a few off at around fifty thousand yards' range,' he added, looking at Meredith.

'It was three thousand, and they were damned close at that.'

'At any rate, Flag Officer listened in and was quite impressed.'

' "Thrilled" is the word,' Luke murmured.

'Added to which he has seen the news-films taken from the cliffs and you show up well in them, too.'

'Where is all this leading?' Haley thought. 'It's all fine and dandy, but that doesn't bring a ton of brass down to a few minesweepers. And wait until Regan and Meredith present their little time bomb.' Momentarily he allowed his mind to wander, then came back to hear Mahoney saying:

'It has suddenly made the BBC minesweeper-conscious. They want to send a man out with some sweepers to do a chin-wag on it. The news-reels want similar facilities, so as one of you seems to have a clean collar'—he looked pointedly at Meredith—'and that bespeaks a degree of respectability, I've agreed that the little outfit will sail with you tomorrow.'

He looked at Regan. 'Can you guarantee to set off a few mines for them?' he asked with a mischievous glint in his eyes.

'I think so, sir; we've some left in the Gap round the wrecks.'

'Won't make you nervous, will it?'

'Scared stiff, sir. I'll have to borrow a clean table-cloth.'

'Meredith's laundry seems to have come back; try borrowing from him.'

His shrewd eyes went quizzing from one to another, then he waved a hand towards Luke.

'I felt I wanted some fresh air, and to see what a ship looked like at close quarters, so I brought him with me. He wants two things. More details of that scrap, and to discuss ways and means.'

For a while the Commander took notes, then he and Mahoney stood up.

'I've some work to do,' Mahoney said. 'By the way, Mrs. Mahoney was saying last night that she would like you to come to tea sometime. We'll have to fix a day.'

'Why not tonight?' Haley suddenly blurted it out.

Mahoney looked startled. 'Tonight? I'm . . .'

'I mean, you and Mrs. Mahoney come on board my ship to dinner.' He was committed so he dashed on. His glance included Regan and Meredith. 'I'm sure I can put you all in my ward-room.'

'If I was invited I could put my hand on a leading seaman who would find a couple of lobsters and a sole or two.' Cutter spoke shamelessly to the ceiling.'

'You're in, *ex officio*.' Haley laughed.

'Mrs. Mahoney will be delighted. Have *Jacinth* keep a

186

gun or two loaded in case there is a raid.'

Meredith looked fierce. 'If an R.A.F. Air Marshal shows up tonight he'll be shot at.'

Mahoney reached the bottom of the ladder. He stood with one foot on the lowest step.

'Nothing else, is there? Nothing you wanted to see me about?'

'Yessir.'

Haley felt himself go cold as Meredith spoke up. The fool! Was he bound to start things now, when everything looked so rosy?

Mahoney stood, impassive, waiting.

'A complaint, sir.'

Regan's jaw was square and all the colour had drained from his face as Meredith rapped out the words.

'A complaint?' Mahoney's eyebrows were arched.

'Yessir, Lieutenant Regan seems to think'—he paused, then went on—'he wants to hog all the mines, sir. As Number Three in the line, I don't get any. I haven't had a decent mine for a week.'

Mahoney's face dissolved into a multi-creased grin.

'Simple,' he said, turning to Regan. 'Bung him in the lead for a few trips.' He turned back to Meredith. 'Is that all? Was the clean shirt for that?'

Meredith laughed. 'It's the only one on board, sir. And it belongs to my Number One.'

'It's Number One's prerogative to have a supply of clean shirts. See that he gets a cut at the decorations for providing the shirt.'

'A D.S.O., nothing less, sir.'

Meredith stepped back as Regan went on to lead the way on deck. As he passed Meredith the Welshman clapped an arm round Regan's shoulder and shook him slightly. Regan paused, a smile lit his face, warmed his blue eyes, and he gently prodded Meredith on the upper part of his arm with his clenched fist.

187

When Regan returned to the wardroom Haley expected him to make some comment to Meredith but all the Irishman did was to slip a hand under Meredith's elbow and pilot him to a seat. For a few seconds they gazed at each other, Meredith's eyes crinkled at the corners, Regan's widened in a broad smile. Peace was declared.

'One for the road,' Regan said. 'Do you think we ought to have a whip round the ships for the odd knife, fork, spoon and trimmings for Haley?'

'I've a silverish tray you can borrow, beautifully engraved. . . .' Meredith chuckled.

'Engraved "Euston Hotel"; I've seen it,' Regan countered.

They sat nursing their drinks for a minute or two, lifted them, drained them, and Meredith stood up.

Then he let out an anguished howl.

'Hell's bells! Where's my papers?'

A feverish search failed to unearth them.

'Could the Staff Commander have picked them up with his notes?'

'No.' Regan was firm about it. 'He used a notebook all the time.'

'Perhaps Cutter swept them up with his stores list?' Haley volunteered.

'Let's hope so. If he finds them perhaps he'll have enough savvy to bring 'em back.'

Meredith looked miserable. 'I hope so, indeed. I was a damned fool to have written it.' His mercurial Celtic temperament had him plunging down into the deeps.

'Forget it,' Regan said at last. 'We all write—and say— things we shouldn't.'

Mahoney leaned back in the car and carefully tore into strips a sheet of signal pad and a memorandum.

Detecting Luke's eyes on him he smiled as he put the shreds into his pocket.

'Something which might have been discussed on *Solan*. It's not important now.'

The party was a conspicuous success. When Booth heard it was in the offing he went into mysterious conferences with Clay and an engineman. Time pressed and Haley had no opportunity to go down the wardroom until just before his guests arrived. When he did his eyebrows shot up.

Booth and the engineman had rigged concealed lighting in one corner of the wardroom and it was partly concealed behind a large bunch of mixed Michaelmas daisies and copper-coloured leaves. Another large bunch stood in the centre of the table in what looked suspiciously like a cut down 12-pounder shell-case. It was obvious that *Jacinth* and *Solan*'s wardroom had been raided for the best of their glass and silverware. A final touch was a sheet of buff correspondence paper across the bottom of the electric light shade, which softened the lighting to a warm, golden glow. The general effect was extremely pleasing.

'Bless the lad,' Haley thought. 'He certainly has an eye for effect. It must be the artist in him.'

Another surprise awaited Haley when he went on deck. Lennox, the Quartermaster, was on duty in what Haley suspected was his Number One uniform. His canvas belt and gaiters had been scrubbed hard. Near him stood Clay, leaning against the rail with studied nonchalance.

'Like the flowers, sir?'

Haley smiled and said, with emphasis, that he did.

Clay anticipated the inevitable query. 'Came from a garden ashore. Empty house. People ducked from the raids. Me and Tich nipped smartly ashore and seized 'em by the lower band.' A reflective look stole over his face. 'There's something I want to say to one of the coppers on the gate when I meet him . . . off duty,' he wound up, significantly.

Clay moved away. Lennox looked at Haley, one eyebrow cocked quizzically. 'The policeman asked which was the bride.' He clicked his tongue. 'Suicide, practically.'

As the picture of Clay and the hard-bitten Nova Scotia seaman returning on board with huge bunches of flowers and leaves in their arms conjured itself into Haley's mind he had great difficulty in preventing himself from laughing. The next thought saved him. It came to him that Booth must have tremendously good will-power over such tough men to influence them into doing something completely beyond any call of naval duty. His reflections were broken by a sudden movement by Lennox and a shout from the other side of the ship. Haley hurried round, and the next effect of Booth's conspiracy showed itself.

Regan and Meredith stood at the shore end of the gangway. And what a gangway! In short notice a ladder along which had been nailed two broad planks was flanked by stanchions from the boat deck and through them were rove lengths of brand new manilla rope. A far cry from the usually shaky ladder which served minesweeping trawlers.

'Big ship stuff,' said Meredith, eyeing the luxury. 'But no Marines? No band? Who rigged this little lot?'

Haley looked to Lennox for enlightenment.

'A couple of us rigged it this afternoon, sir. Mr. Booth suggested it as ladies were coming on board.'

And for this a couple of seamen had given up their afternoon 'Stand Easy', had sacrificed an afternoon of sleep so that their effort could bring a little credit to their ship— his ship. Or was it to please Booth? Haley had no time to reflect. A car pulled up on the quay and from it climbed Mahoney and his wife.

Although the party was ill-balanced Mrs. Mahoney helped to make it a complete success by combining the age-old wisdom of woman in letting the men talk, together with her wide experience of naval officers. She fitted like a glove.

Later in the evening she and Haley sat alone while the

190

others battled out some complicated manœuvre which involved the use of most of the ashtrays, two match-boxes and the entire top of the table.

Mrs. Mahoney accepted a light for her cigarette, leaned back and said: 'I must compliment you on your lighting. Wardrooms are usually hard on women.'

Haley placed the credit where it was due.

'Oh, yes! That is the artistic young man; draws pictures on charts, I believe.'

She looked up mischievously. 'I would like to meet him. Is he on board?'

Haley chuckled. 'Ashore, I'm afraid. On an affair of the heart.' He leaned back, too. 'Those watercolours in the room you used—they also are his.'

Mrs. Mahoney turned her head sideways to look at Haley. 'Pat'—she flicked a glance towards her husband—'says he varies from fifteen years old to thirty, according to the mood and the job.'

Haley nodded. 'And tonight he's about twenty, roughly his correct age. And meeting fierce opposition.'

'I would like to meet him. I paint, happily rather than expertly.'

The battle on the table ended and shortly afterwards the party broke up.

Next morning at breakfast Haley passed his thanks to Booth.

Booth nodded, then grinned expansively. 'I nearly brought my girl friend down last night to see the illuminations.'

'Which girl friend?'

'There is only one,' Booth said firmly. 'THE girl friend, Heather. You know, the Wren driver.'

'Take your pleasures sadly, don't you? I thought you chewed lumps out of each other every time you met.' He looked shrewdly at Booth. 'She is beginning to forget . . . *Pearl*?'

191

Booth made intricate little patterns in the ashtray before replying. 'Sometimes I wonder. I can get her laughing when she spars with me. Then for no reason she'll start to cry, silently.' He wiped out the pattern. 'I don't get it.'

'Women are difficult to understand,' Haley said sententiously. 'Perhaps in that lies their charm.'

Booth shrugged. 'I've been working on a pastel drawing of her. Like to see it?'

He brought it from his room and Haley was struck by its brilliant execution. Booth had caught the deep, pensive, almost tragic look in the girl's eyes. Yet on the lips was a faint smile, provocative, challenging, as if to say: 'Draw ME, not merely the outer mask. Draw me as I feel . . . if you can.'

'Where did you learn to draw?'

'Mother taught me. She's really good. I've had no other lessons.'

Later in the day Haley went on board *Solan*. As he went down the wardroom he heard Regan explaining to the BBC man and the cameraman: 'We'll sweep across the Gap'—running his hand across the chart—'a couple of laps round the wrecks and be through by the time a convoy is due through tomorrow afternoon. Hullo, Haley! Meet the cameraman and the radio man. BBC is going with you. And who is to lead this fleet? None other than the Channel Scourge, Sir Francis Meredith, in person.'

Meredith looked up quickly.

'Oh, yes you are, chum,' Regan went on. 'You'll be in the lead, *Sheila* next, then me and Haley will be tail-end Charlie. You see,' he went on quickly, 'if we pop up a few it will give the cameraman something to shoot at, and you'—he looked towards the young broadcaster—'you will have a seat in the third row of the grandstand.'

The extremely *blasé* cameraman, who had been sitting on the settee nursing a large-sized drink, stirred slightly. 'What are we likely to get?' he asked in a bored voice.

192

'Some mines going up, with luck. Possibly, although I hope not, an air attack.'

'Is that all?'

What the hell DO you want?' Meredith broke in passionately. 'Chorus girls with nothing on except saucepan lids on their tits? We're minesweepers, not the front line at the Windmill Theatre. If one or two go up under your stern you'll think of something else besides pretty pictures.'

Embarrassment struggled with indignation on the cameraman's face, and indignation won by a short head.

'Keep your shirt on,' he answered shortly. 'You may want to sweep mines, but I'm thinking in terms of pictures.'

'We don't WANT to sweep mines; we hope we don't get any.' Regan's tones were dangerously mild although a suspicion of mimicry had crept into his voice.

It was the BBC man who brought peace to the room. 'I saw you the last time I went through this bit of water and'—he glanced obliquely at the cameraman—'it was quite exciting enough for me.'

'All right, I'll settle for a few pictures of mines blowing up,' the cameraman replied, his voice just a shade short of direct surliness. 'I'll get on board the ship I'm to sail in.'

Regan sent him off in charge of his Number One to board *Arandite*.

'Just as well he isn't sailing with me,' Meredith growled, watching the two disappear up the companion.

'He'd be liable to get a close-up of Calais harbour with trimmings,' Haley answered wickedly. 'Meredith firmly believes that if there is no war in his vicinity it is his bounden duty to go somewhere and provoke one,' he explained to the broadcaster.

'Liar! I'm a man of peace,' Meredith retorted.

'I loved the line about the saucepan lids. Do you think we could arrange something like that? Y'know, a few Wrens pirouetting on a mine with the old do-das on the whatsits.' The broadcaster was deliciously bland. 'I'd chance it. It would simply make the talk.' He accepted a drink and a cigarette from Regan. 'That laddie told me some hair-raising stories, coming down in the train, about his shots at Dunkirk.'

'We all had some hair-raising shots at Dunkirk,' Regan said.

'All of you?'

'The entire troupe. Haley was on a destroyer. I had this ship and Meredith tried hard to land his and turn it into a tank.'

'I touched ground for a few minutes and that has been turned into a long story,' Meredith chipped in. 'I was watching . . .'

'You were chasing a Stuka at the time,' Regan said flatly. 'Taking a trawler with a draught of eighteen feet into sixteen feet of water.'

Meredith smiled sweetly with a reflective look in his eyes. 'I got him, too—right in the pantry. He dissolved in mid-air'—he gestured with his hands and Haley was struck by the grace of his moving fingers—'like a dandelion being blown by a child . . . puff . . . finish. Just the dead stalk left.'

'Almost poetry,' the broadcaster murmured. 'I feel I am going on the wrong ship for material.'

Meredith squinted at him shrewdly, ever alert for a jibe, but accepted the remark without comment. He reached for his cap. 'Sail in half an hour, Regan?'

'Half an hour to the dot.'

After his footsteps had died away on deck the broadcaster said: 'A fighting man from the hills, I think. One of the small dark people, by his accent.'

Regan nodded and poured himself a drink.

'Now he's gone I'll tell you about his Stuka at Dunkirk. For days some troops had been building a sort of pier of barges each night and shipping wounded troops from it. Every morning the Hun came over and blew it up again. We heard they were Welsh troops, Welsh engineers and odds

194

and sods. It looked as if they might be written off as the Germans closed in.' Regan paused. 'A shallow draught paddler tried, got in close and was hit, troops and all.'

The broadcaster leaned forward, listening intently.

'Up comes Meredith, pushing half the Channel in front of him for a bow wave and towing half a dozen lifeboats. He smacked those boats down close to the remains of the pier with inches to spare. The troops piled in and a Stuka came over for a last crack, saw the empty pier and decided *Jacinth* was his meat. It was the last decision he ever made. He was crippled with the first barrage from her, and as he limped away towards the French coast Meredith went chasing after him. You heard him. He got it with almost the last shot.'

Regan stood up. 'The cheek of it! Ten knots chasing a hundred and fifty!'

'All singled up, sir,' *Solan*'s Number One called down the companion.

'All right.' Regan held his glass up to his eyes, judged the last drop and tipped it back. 'The Wrens ashore here tell a wonderful story of *Jacinth* coming alongside that night with troops on board singing in Welsh.'

'I've heard Welshmen sing, fifty thousand of them at a football match,' the broadcaster said. 'As you say, wonderful stuff, no single harmony but full four-part choral singing. It must have been really stirring.' He tilted his head to one side and looked ingenuously at Regan. 'What is his full name, did you say?'

'I didn't, but it's Lieutenant Owen Meredith.'

Jacinth led the group out through the harbour gate and swung away for the Gap to try, fruitlessly, one lap before autumn darkness set in. Then they split for patrols for the night.

Haley had little to say to the cameraman but Booth chattered away quite cheerily to him until the man decided to turn in on the wardroom settee.

'He's going to take a couple of shots of the crew getting the sweep out in the morning,' Booth informed Haley. 'Six to four they all shave and part their hair.'

Haley snorted. 'Get some beauty sleep; we can't have you looking wan and haggard in front of the camera tomorrow.'

' "Pale and interesting" is the phrase you are struggling to say,' Booth retorted with dignity.

' "Fat and artful" is nearer the mark. Go, get some sleep, film star.'

Booth ignored the insult and settled down for a couple of hours' snooze.

By a strange twist lap after lap was completely blank although Regan, who was still Senior Officer, switched from four ships formation to two pairs. Haley expected to find the cameraman disgruntled and bad-tempered, but he was quite philosophic. He and Booth got along like a house on fire and Haley smiled when he saw the cameraman carrying out his promise and taking pictures of Clay and his merry men handling the half-ton or so of ironmongery at the stern. A little later Booth was the central figure in a dramatically staged group round a machine-gun while the camerman shot it from an almost prone position.

Haley sent a rude note aft:

From C.O. to God's Gift to the Ninepennies. I think you are wonderful. Better than Garbo. Can I have (1) your autograph (2) your fair body on the bridge for a while?

Booth arrived looking very dignified and up-stage.

'The camerman said he wanted to get in a bit of background stuff so I was assisting him,' he said stiffly.

'All right, Garbo, you can vaunt to be alone up here for a while. I'm going to have my morning look-see.' Haley was dangerously meek and conciliatory. 'This is a voice-pipe.

It leads to the man at the wheel. You know—he guides the ship.' Booth's eyebrows were arched high. 'You are now on the bridge alone, in command, the centre of the hub of this little universe. The fate of the nation depends on you. Lights... action... roll 'em!'

Haley slid down the bridge ladder, leaving an extremely indignant Booth seething in solitude.

But the cameraman got his little epic after all; not a world-shaking one, not even one which merited more than five lines tucked away at the bottom of a column in the inside pages of the newspapers:

> The Admiralty regrefs to announce the loss of H.M. trawler *Sheila*, Chief Skipper Robert Flood, R.N.R. There were some casualties. The next of kin have been advised.

The destroyer and leading ships of the convoy were nosing down to the Gap when *Jacinth* and *Sheila*, sweeping in pairs across their track, put up three mines in rapid succession. *Solan* followed with another. The explosions were so close that Haley thought it was the now familiar salvo of shell-fire.

'Any more there?' called the destroyer.

Regan answered: 'Maybe. We will sweep in front of you until the last minute. Hope for the best.'

It slowed the convoy down so that it became an impacted mass of shipping, a mushroom of vessels as the head of it spread out, slowly growing larger as the long stem of ships in single line added its quota.

Large-scale day raids had proved too costly for the enemy and the sporadic daylight hit-and-run visits had come to have little more than a nuisance value. The German air fleet, its wounds gaping and open, had changed to night raids, but a convoy was a different target.

'Hell, how those ships bunch!' Haley said. 'A bomb on

that lot couldn't fail but get one of them. We'll be lucky if we get away without an attack.'

Meredith had simply hurled *Jacinth* and *Sheila* about and was belting away as hard as he could go in a long, slanting line across the track of the convoy, aiming to cover as much of the course as he could yet cutting delay to a minimum. Regan and Haley were astern but to one side on a similar course.

The destroyer correctly assessed the manœuvre and started the convoy moving at half speed.

'Floaters astern of *Sheila*, sir.' Booth had his glasses pinned to his eyes as 'Mine to port' climbed up to *Sheila*'s yardarm.

'*Solan*'s got a hoist up too, sir,' Larkin called from the wing of the bridge. Soon there were at least half a dozen floating mines, sinister little specks right in the path of the convoy.

Regan, on *Solan*, flashed a message to the destroyer advising avoiding action for the convoy, suggesting a slight alteration of course which would take the ships partly down the area they had swept during the day.

'The Hun has probably put a mixed bag here,' he explained to the broadcasting man. 'We have swept this area for magnetics. Now we cut into this little lot of moored mines, put here to complicate matters, and I hope not, but I'm afraid there will be some other types which . . . er . . .' He stopped and looked keenly at the man. 'I don't know how much of this you will be allowed to say.'

'It will be censored.'

'Well, we are meeting a new type about which we know little. It just goes off bang. We don't know why.'

All four sweepers were driving as hard as they could to minimise delay to the convoy and had practically reached the end of the run when the first shattering roar came. *Sheila* lurched. Her bow climbed laboriously up a steepling mushroom of water. A cloud of smoke belched from her funnel.

198

She settled back, wallowing heavily.

'*Sheila*'s bought it!' *Solan*'s Number One yelled. Regan studied her through his glasses, saw the flash of an axe as somebody cut the sweep adrift. She was still rolling slowly and heavily but on a fairly even keel, and the bow wave died away to mix with the debris and specked water from the explosion. A light twinkled from her bridge.

'Mine. Under the engine-room. Will report damage later.'

Regan rapped out : 'In sweeps all ships.' He turned to the broadcasting man, who was standing discreetly at the back of the bridge but missing nothing. 'You can stay up here but keep well out of the way, please.'

Jacinth swung off the track and her sweep was racing in. Regan and Haley were whipping theirs in. The convoy plodded on, bearing as far away to one side of the channel as they could from the little group of bobbing mines and minesweepers. *Harvester*, the drifter, was well astern on the wrong side of the convoy to be of any help.

'We'll sink 'em by rifle fire,' Regan rapped. 'Make it.' The signalman clattered away with his light. 'Now ask *Sheila* how long she will last.'

Staccato rifle-fire came from *Jacinth* as she attacked two of the mines. *Arandite* disposed of another which went down tamely, riddled with bullets, and she was turning to tackle another when *Solan* signalled 'Leave it.' Haley saw why. The tide was taking them clear away from the channel.

'First things first,' Haley said quietly. 'Leaving them to the drifter.' He watched the cameraman perched up on the little searchlight platform. The man's eyes were bright and his head was darting about like an excited sparrow's. In his hand he held a camera which he was winding. He craned round to look at *Sheila*, then looked down and saw Haley watching him.

'I think I got some of it. The smoke and water was just coming down when I got my camera up.'

'Warning . . . Gate Area,' Larkin intoned. 'That will be us,' he informed the cameraman. 'They come over in hundreds. Want a tin hat? You'll want it up there.'

Soon Haley picked up the uneven drone of aircraft. This was a target the Hun could not afford to let go by.

'About a dozen,' Booth called, after peering through his glasses. 'Low down, on the beam.'

The crack of gunfire came sharply over the water, followed by the lighter thump of another gun.

'Destroyer beat *Jacinth* by a second. He'll be mad,' Booth grinned. 'Open up, sir?'

'Open up.'

Clay was waiting, tense, eye to eyepiece which framed a dozen dancing gnats.

Crack! There was an exclamation from the cameraman. The flash and explosion had taken him by surprise.

'Jesus! I thought we'd got one,' he said, scrambling for a foothold again.

The gunfire intensified as the merchant ships joined in, and the rippling fire from machine-guns became almost unbroken. Curving lines of tracer reached out to the aircraft. *Arandite* shuddered to the crack of her 12-pounder.

As Haley, crouched in one wing with only his head above the rail, watched the attacking aircraft, *Sheila* came into his view. He saw a flash from her 12-pounder and a line of tracer climb slowly from her stern. He heard a faint whirring above his head and saw the cameraman with his camera trained on her. Then the man swung it to follow the now wheeling aircraft. A plume of dark water climbed up between them and *Sheila*, and back the camera swung.

Slowly and ponderously the convoy rolled past, ship after ship, each one contributing its quota of noise and missiles at the snarling, diving aircraft. A tiny M.L., almost out of sight behind its own bow wave and back-wash, tore along the line of ships, its guns spitting as it raced. The leading destroyer was flat out, tearing along between the front of the ships and a point half-way along. From its multiple pom-pom came an almost incessant fringe of flame and tracer. An escort trawler tried, more or less effectively, to guard the centre section and it was towards this part that Haley took *Arandite* to increase the protection over the long line.

A group of three 'planes, flying in tight formation in a shallow dive, defied the storm of tracer and flashed in at the broad head of the convoy. There was a dull clang. A shower of rust and sparks showed momentarily just behind the bridge of one, momentarily because it was lost in a second by a greater upheaval which split the midships apart. The bridge lurched and jerked forward. Behind it a shower of debris, splintered woodwork and steel shot up in an inverted climbing cone, followed by a billowing column of smoke and steam. For just a fraction of a second the whole hung poised, motionless in the air, as gravity fought and won against the force of the explosion. It was as if the bomb had called: 'Look! See what I've done in one-tenth of a second!' then let everything drop back in crumpled ruins.

The ships astern swung right and left from the wallowing ship. From her riven, canting decks men slid in ungainly haste into the water and to them raced the little M.L. Two men slithered slowly, without movement on their part, to the torn gap in the lower bridge, hung together as if they were jointly summoning up enough courage to jump, then like part of a slow-motion film, they tilted as the deck raised and fell into the water in a limp, effortless half-curve.

The nearest 'plane was half a mile away, wheeling off to re-form with the others for another attack, when a man climbed slowly to his feet on a small machine-gun platform behind the funnel.

The gun wavered uncertainly, then from it came a short burst of tracer. It wandered off, aimed at nowhere in particular, until the light died from it like tired fireflies. The man sank to his knees, stayed there for a moment, scrabbled to his feet, and half stumbling, half running, made a flat dive which carried him into the water well away from the ship's side.

A last defiant gesture, or a stunned brain, fumbling in bomb-fuddled mists vaguely remembering? Did it matter?

Half-way down the line a ship slowly wheeled away from the convoy, losing speed all the time. There was no apparent damage as she slipped away in a long curve towards the shore, towards the serried rows of masts and bridges of other ships which had dropped out, dropped clear to sink.

Arandite ceased firing as the 'planes drew out of range, and Haley searched for *Sheila*. He saw her drifting in the tide, clear of the convoy, her stern almost awash, her bow cocked well up looking like a picture drawn by an unskilled artist. As he watched he saw figures move on her deck, saw somebody lean over the bridge and gesticulate.

The air attack switched to the back portion of the convoy and Haley marvelled as he saw the 'planes, four of them, race in through the tracery of fiery bullets and puffs of high explosive shell. One reared up, like a horse violently reined in, fluttered for a few seconds, then swung away in a long arc downwards.

The others pressed home their attack, and plumes of water climbed upwards harmlessly from misses. Then came the dull, metallic clang of a hit. Over the top of the plumes of water, flying barely above mast height, a 'plane weaved along the length of the convoy, more or less safe from a concentration of gunfire by its proximity to the ships it was attacking.

Two flashes of gunfire came from *Jacinth,* and lines of tracer whipped over ships' bridges as she followed the 'plane.

'The merchant blokes will be pleased! Scare 'em more than the bombs,' Booth said.

Haley, watching the approaching 'plane through his binoculars, suddenly called: 'Watch him! He'll swing out before he reaches the destroyer. Let him have it then.'

The 'plane did swing out, climbed slightly before it reached *Arandite*, swung its nose right and left as if searching for a fresh victim, then dropped it and dived for *Sheila*.

Clay's 12-pounder barked viciously . . . and again. The machine-guns pinned the 'plane in a centre of lethal fire but still it went on towards *Sheila*, who was beam on, stopped, and very low in the water.

Haley saw the bomb leave, travel in a flat trajectory towards her bow. He saw the splash as it landed almost alongside. He saw also the tracer hitting, smashing its way inside the 'plane.

The 12-pounder flashed once and with the 'plane only yards away. 'Plane and ship disappeared in one crescendo roar as *Sheila*'s magazine exploded. From the thinning fan of smoke and water *Sheila* rolled clear, her keel showing. She lurched slowly back in a ponderous arc. Her bow was gone completely. The tottering mast broke off and fell across the bridge. The shattered, twisted plates framing a gaping, smoking hole reached heavenwards for a few seconds, then the remains of the little ship slipped backwards with so little fuss that it was difficult to believe that she had gone, that she would not rise and steam onwards, leaving behind the heaving, frothing water.

'Full ahead.' Haley's voice was cracked and strangled. 'Hard a'port.' 'Steady.' He looked quickly at Booth. The youngster's face was frozen; his eyes stared at the wreck-cluttered spot only a few hundred yards away.

'Keep your guns going. A couple of hands stand by with lines,' Haley rapped. He missed something, some intangible fragment which had made up the recent whole and searched in his mind. Then he heard it again. It was the almost incessant bumble-bee whirring of the camera. He looked up. The cameraman was slowly swinging his camera from the bridge to take in the wreckage-flecked water.

'Damn you—DAMN YOU! You've got your pretty pictures. No chorus girls. Just men dying. Room in the two-and-threes . . . come and see the brave sailors . . . chocolates . . . cigarettes . . . matches. . . .'

The cameraman saw Haley's eyes fixed on him in a stare.

'Jesus,' he said softly, winding his camera spring by sheer reflex action. 'Jesus!'

'Can't you say anything else besides "Jesus"?' Haley's voice rasped and snarled.

'She went like that,' the cameraman said softly, gesturing vaguely in the air with one hand. 'Jesus!'

'*Solan* calling.' Larkin's voice sounded thick, as if he were speaking with his mouth full. ' "Pick up survivors then resume position on convoy beam," sir.'

Jacinth tore through the edge of the wrack and twisted woodwork, Meredith's eyes on a shimmering, silvered, slim object a couple of hundred yards away. As he watched he saw a figure climb painfully and lie half in, half out, of the shattered aircraft.

'Who's on the wheel?' He almost snarled it.

'Cox'n, sir.'

'Keep her straight, dead straight.'

'Aye, aye, sir.'

He glanced down on to the foredeck and saw his First Lieutenant and two seamen coiling a heaving line with a grapple hook at the end of it.

A quick glance aft showed *Arandite* circling slowly through the wreckage of what had been *Sheila*. He stepped to the bridge side, squinted through his glasses at the half-submerged 'plane, although it was so close that the indentations of the rivets and the splintered perspex of the cockpit could be seen. He saw the figure move, slowly, painfully, sit upright and half raise one arm.

'Not a hairsbreadth out, Cox'n. Keep her straight.'

'Aye, aye, sir.' After a moment the Cox'n added, diffi-

204

dently: 'Still got full ahead on, sir.'

'Keep it on.'

Meredith leaned over the bridge front. His Number One looked up.

'You won't want that. Drop it.'

'I'll try to hook it . . .'

'Drop it!' Meredith barked it and the seaman allowed the line to slither slowly from his hands to the deck. He looked questioningly from the First Lieutenant to the bridge.

The 'plane, a bare fifty yards ahead, slowly disappeared from view as the bow hid it. Suddenly Meredith smashed his hands violently on the bridge rail. He jumped to the voice-pipe.

'Hard to starboard.'

'Hard over, sir.'

'Full astern.'

The ship began to shudder as the astern drive fought against the forward motion. Her bow swung away to starboard in a quick half-circle aided by the pull of the propeller. There was still forward weigh on the ship.

'Hard a port.'

'Hard a port on, sir.'

Back swung her bow. She stopped almost in her tracks, rolling slightly from the violence of change of motion. The wreck of the 'plane was right alongside the foredeck. The two upraised arms of the German airman were almost touching the rails. After one quick glance towards the bridge the First Lieutenant and the two seamen jumped to the rail. One cocked a leg over, grasped the man, and between them they heaved him, sobbing and collapsing, on to the deck.

Meredith dropped his head downwards on his chest, and shook it quickly, blew forcibly.

'Cox'n.'

'Sir?'

'Very good. Full ahead, two turns to port.'

'Two turns to port, sir. Thank you, sir.' After a pause: 'I thought for a minute . . .'

'Blast what you thought. Two turns to port.'

'Aye, aye, sir.'

Number One clambered back to the bridge. 'He's all in, sir. He's only a kid.' The First Lieutenant, speaking with the worldly wisdom of the advanced age of twenty-four, talked as he would of a schoolboy caught smashing a greenhouse. 'I'll bet he isn't twenty.'

'What did you expect? A hairy Tarzan? Keep him below.'

'Yes, sir.' Number One turned back at the top of the bridge. 'Scared the bags off me for a moment. I thought you were going to . . .'

'To hell with what you thought! It's what I did that counts.' Meredith wheeled swiftly. His voice was high-pitched, sharp with a jagged edge. Number One flushed and dropped his eyes. He climbed backwards down the ladder. As he reached the bottom and turned along the deck he heard Meredith say softly above him:

'Number One, I did mean to.' Meredith faced forward again.

The First Lieutenant shrugged his shoulders. 'I thought so, the mad devil. But what's he crying for now?'

The broadcasting man on *Solan* moved away from the corner of the after part of the bridge and stood beside Regan. He said nothing but watched the Irishman's face intently. It was frozen into hard, unyielding lines as Regan watched *Arandite* steam in slow circles, then leave the wreckage-cluttered spot without stopping.

Arandite's light flickered.

'From *Arandite*, sir. "No survivors." ' The signalman placed his light back in its box softly as though afraid he would make a jarring, disturbing noise.

Regan turned away. The tail-end of the convoy was passing with its attendant escort of two Asdic trawlers. Astern of them, motionless, three ships lay in grotesque, almost obscene angles, barely clear of the fairway. Not far from one a destroyer moved slowly. Suddenly her forward guns barked and Regan saw the flashes of explosions on one of the ships, close to the water-line. The guns barked again and water bubbled and frothed; a dark, sullen gout of smoke and steam came from the ship's funnel; a last defiant gesture and she lurched, settling lower in the water with a slight list.

The destroyer crept in closer. Once again the guns barked. A few moments later the destroyer turned away and leapt into high speed, the bow wave climbing and creaming nearly to her rail.

' "V.M.T. for your help. She'll go down now." From the destroyer, sir.'

Regan nodded, caught the questioning look from the BBC man. 'Very many thanks for your help,' he interpreted. He looked over towards the barely discernible discolouration of the water which had shortly before been *Sheila*.

In the distance there was the sound of gunfire. The air attack was being resumed; more ships would be sunk, more men would see an orange flash, feel the hammer thud about them, and the water would boil and froth and for them all questions would cease to be questions.

'Hoist "G formation, port sweep," ' Regan said shortly. The flag-hoist climbed fluttering to the yard-arm. '*Jacinth* take the lead.'

'Are you going in now?' the BBC man asked diffidently.

Regan shook his head. 'We're out here to sweep mines. Everything else is incidental.' He gestured with his arm towards the line of wrecks. 'See that stretch of water? That is what we call the Gap. You saw the convoy come through. Well, stop that gap with mines and what happens?'

The man nodded slowly.

'So we keep it open. Find them, cut them, sink them. Not very glamorous, is it?'

The man was looking out over the water and did not

reply immediately. He gently chewed his top lip. 'Now I know what dying like a very gallant gentleman means,' he said softly. 'He fought to the last, didn't he. His gun and the bomb went off together.'

Jacinth swept past, her sweep close hauled. *Solan* swung in behind her and *Arandite* completed the group. Soon they were plodding along at five knots, sweep floats creaming into little wakes on each ship's quarter.

Until darkness came they heard, sullenly, from a great distance, the faint boom of gunfire away to the west, where the convoy fought doggedly on. With them was *Almarina* and her group.

Occasionally plumes of water shot skywards in salvoes of three as the German long-range gunners groped for the sweepers, trying to keep the Channel clear.

'Is there anything they don't try?' the BBC man asked.

Regan laughed. 'When it gets dark they'll try to sow a few more mines with *E*-boats and aircraft, but otherwise we've had the entire works today. We don't get much money but we do see life.'

'. . . and death,' concluded the broadcaster softly.

8

Haley hoisted his suit-case to the rack and sat down in a corner seat. A week's leave finished and behind him, gone like a flash. He glanced through an evening paper, learned that Mr. Molotov and von Ribbentrop had become blood-brothers, that a Senior Officer had suggested arming air-field guards with pikes to slay German parachutists—Haley grinned and thought of the hot-eyed, efficient, grim party of German prisoners they had brought back on *Culver* and imagined what would happen if a bunch of past middle-age volunteers met a group of those resolute young men.

Another item met his eyes. Some genius from Hampstead, N.W., submitted a scheme for fitting close-mesh steel nets over buildings to catch bombs. A steel mesh would have been useful on *Sheila*, wouldn't it? Or on one of the merchant ships. A bright idea! The bomb would go bouncing up and down harmlessly, like a clown on one of those spring things they used. Why not develop the idea a spot further —increase the tension of the spring and toss the bomb back?

He learned that football crowds for the forthcoming season would have to be restricted in size. Hell, that's bringing the war home to the workers!

Haley tossed the paper impatiently away and lit a cigarette. The workers were a sore point with him. He had taken *Arandite* into dock, leaking from a dozen seams, rattling like a handful of peas in a tin.

Arandite will enter dock and blow down for boiler

clean [Cutter's signal had read]. Defect lists, kept to essential minimum, to be in my office for approval and consultation with Admy Overseer by 10.00 hrs Wednesday 28.8.40.

Booth had had the right idea. In the column for defects he had inserted briefly '*Arandite*'.

'Sound idea, Number One, but I'm afraid we'll have to settle for the obvious and vital defects.'

'Still stands,' Booth answered, chewing his pen. 'She's all defects.'

'Nevertheless, pick out your favourites and write them down. That's no proof positive that we will get them done.'

After Booth's ambitious list had been ruthlessly pruned by Cutter and a *blasé* Overseer a group of workmen had descended on the ship. It was Saturday morning and Haley had expected them to blaze into a scurry of activity; to start right in to put back that which was broken or bent or would not function.

The first thing they had done was to cluster round the galley door pestering Noisy for boiling water for tea. Haley found, not without amusement, that Noisy could repel hard bitten seamen with a series of sibilants seldom above a whisper.

The morning had progressed without sounds of activity and it was midday when Booth stormed into Haley's room, bearing a tangle of fishing lines and followed by an indignant workman.

' "Cut your defect list to the bones," Cutter said. "We haven't the men to do them." Five days they allow us and I found two workmen sleeping on the engine-room casing and another fishing for eels over the stern. They'll start work after lunch at overtime rates.' Booth choked and spluttered. 'I asked this . . . this . . .'—he enveloped the workman in a withering glance—'if he thought it was helping to get the ship out by catching eels and . . .'

210

'Them lines is mine,' the man said doggedly. 'Nobody's got a right to pull 'em in.'

'Pull them in? I'll chuck them down the stokehold,' Booth seethed.

But the workman won. A vehement man who introduced himself as a shop steward had produced the Overseer, and a chastened Booth had had to return the fishing lines—and apologise to the workman.

He had spent the remainder of the afternoon in sporadic wordy warfare with the workmen.

'If I was on your ship I'd do six months for you,' one man glowered, but kept a weather eye on Clay, who was standing nearby expertly flexing his muscles and with a yearning look in his eyes.

'If you were on this ship you'd sweat blood and cry yourself to sleep, collaborator,' Booth had snarled. It was the latest and most fashionable form of insult.

'Collaborator! That's good,' Clay chuckled to Ross. 'I think it's something lousy from France,' he elaborated. He watched the workmen from the corner of his eyes. 'Couple of quid those bastards get for this afternoon. Much as you and I get for a week. And what do they do? Sit on their fannys all day.' He got his reactions. A workman glared vaguely in his direction. 'Yes, you I'm talking about, wage-slave.'

To Sub-lieutenant Booth Clay had contributed what he considered the ingredients for a delectable afternoon. 'I'll make a pot of tea and get a couple of 'em down the mess deck.' He eyed Booth expectantly. 'I can always pick an argument with 'em over the Arsenal—or the Spurs.'

The elemental solution appealed to Booth but with reluctance he vetoed it.

'We'd have the shop steward stopping the war. Sorry, but it's a good idea.'

Haley had to take a firm hand as the afternoon wore on. He sent for Booth and told him that the sporadic sniping would have to stop and that he would be held responsible for seeing that it did stop.

It was Ross, the slow-moving, quick-thinking Nova Scotia seaman, who got in the last and devastating broadside as the liberty party were leaving the ship.

He was remaining behind as one of the small Care and Maintenance party, and with two or three others he leaned over the rail uttering mild jibes.

'Mind you have her nice and ready for us to take out for two quid a week, and no overtime,' Clay called out, determined to have a parting shot.

'All fixed,' Ross drawled loudly, turning his head so that the workmen could clearly hear all he had to say. 'I heard the Old Man say we were having the guns taken off. We're being fitted with better armament. A secret weapon.'

Clay showed a violent interest and Haley, in his room, had found himself listening despite himself.

'It's a fact. When the German 'planes dive on us we're going to stop 'em in their tracks with the new thing.' Ross's drawl was even more drawn out. 'Yessir, stop 'em dead to rights.'

Clay and the party listened and even the workmen were all ears.

'We're going to mount a shop steward on the fo'c'sle. That'll stop 'em.'

It was crude, almost brutal, and the workmen writhed impotently, but the liberty party laughed loud and long, making the squawking sea-gulls rise from the quay in fluttering protest.

Haley smiled to himself in his corner seat at these recollections.

He tried for a few minutes to become interested in a copy of *Men Only*, recognised some hackneyed pictures of nudes in the middle pages, remembered Benson and his collection of art studies now at the bottom of the North Sea. He tossed the magazine to join the discarded evening paper and sat back as a whistle shrilled. The train jerked and slowly gathered speed.

Leave had been a complicated affair of ravelled emotions. He was tired, far more tired than he realised, when he left the ship and journeyed homewards. His brief telegram, 'Charing Cross, 8.15', had told his wife enough.

She was there, waiting at the barrier, and unaccountably he had felt shy and restrained as he greeted her. They just looked at one another for a moment; all he saw was a pair of grey eyes searching his face, questing behind the outward appearance, then they held each other tightly, motionless, with no obvious demonstration of emotion.

As they won a taxi and it climbed towards North London a warning wail shredded through the drone of the motor engine.

'Not now, not tonight,' Haley protested.

'Nearly every night now, dear. We never get them in the daytime.' She snuggled up closer to him. 'We haven't had anything close to us up to now. The docks seem to be their target.'

Through the night they had heard the drone of enemy 'planes and the sound of inadequate anti-aircraft gunfire.

'We can put up a better barrage than this ourselves,' he complained. 'Why, when all ships open up with the shore guns . . .'

'Yes, dear, I've seen something of what happens.'

Haley looked questioningly at her. Suddenly she sat down on the settee by him and held one of his arms in both her hands.

'I was frightened. I realised that you were in all that. When I saw your face it looked so drawn and tired . . . I didn't sleep that night.'

'What ARE you talking about?'

'You haven't had my last letter? About the picture?'

Haley shook his head.

'Nor about the broadcast?'

213

'Yes, I heard that. Rather good, I thought.'

He and Regan had listened to the broadcast a week or two after *Sheila* had been lost. The man's voice had sounded deeper, richer, not so cold and detached as when he had been on the ship. He made the most of his subject and Haley had found himself feeling tight about the eyes and the throat as the man talked.

Almost confidentially, as if talking across a dinner table, the man had gone on:

'Do you remember the last time I talked to you I told you of a convoy and its passage down Channel? I told you of some little ships which threw themselves between the attacking aircraft and the convoy. Since then I have been to sea in one of those little ships during just such another attack. I was with them when they deliberately put themselves as living buffers against the attack. Yet that isn't their job at all. It was, as one Commanding Officer said, "an incidental". Their job is to sweep mines.'

Although Haley had lived through it he found himself gripped by the narrative as the man talked on. He kept his voice at a calm level as he described *Jacinth*'s headlong dash towards the aircraft. He gave an impeccable thumbnail description of Meredith, 'a short, dark man of the small dark people, a fiery, fighting Celt', and when he came to describe *Sheila*'s end Haley felt the man was living it again.

'. . . and THAT convoy went through, as had the others, not because that wild man of the Welsh hills blazed away, not because another man and his crew died like gallant gentlemen, dying without counting the cost, but'—he paused—'but because those little ships had done, and are doing today, their humble little job of clearing mines, sweeping the Channel clear, and will go on doing it as it is being done all round the coast. Good night.'

Haley put his arm round his wife. 'I heard him. Rather good, I thought, but . . .'

She lit two cigarettes and gave him one.

'I'd better tell you what was in my letter. I had a 'phone call a week ago. It was from the man who broadcast. He told me he had been to sea with you and asked if I would like to go out to dinner with him.'

She watched Haley's face for reactions, saw none, and went on : 'He took me to dinner and asked me to the studios to hear his broadcast. Then he rang somebody and we went to a little place in Wardour Street, a very small cinema, a trade place I think they called it. There was a man there who had been on your ship. They showed us the whole film . . . not the bits that went out to the cinemas, but everything. I thought . . . I thought for a dreadful moment it was your ship that was blown up. Then I saw you looking right out of the screen . . . it was dreadful . . . not you, but the ships. Just that smoke and she was gone. But you looked so tired, so drawn . . .' She stopped and drew on her cigarette. 'I came home and cried all night.'

'Because I looked dreadful?'

She refused to be drawn.

'It was probably shadows. I hadn't shaved, anyway. You should see young Booth when he has been at sea a day or so. . . .'

She shook her head, went questing into the future.

'How long will it last, dear?'

'How long is a piece of string?'

By this time she was holding him tightly as she whispered : 'Take great care of yourself, won't you? I'm so frightened.'

Despite the mild crudities of pre-leave jokes, the night had not been one of unending passion. In the darkness they were content to lie close to each other, content to draw comfort from close proximity. Haley had found it difficult to get to sleep. For a long time he lay still until her measured breathing indicated that she was asleep. Carefully he climbed out of bed, lit a cigarette, pulled aside the blackout curtain and looked out at the night sky. Away to

215

the east searchlights were questing in a wavering cone. Occasional thuds of gunfire came faintly, and nearer he heard the uneven, unsynchronised drone of aircraft.

A gentle hand placed on his shoulder made him jump.

'Startle you, dear? I didn't mean to, but I knew you were not asleep.'

So they sat and talked, and in the darkness he lost the feeling of shyness, of diffidence, which had been with him from the time he met her at the station.

But in the daytime it would come back. He found himself in abstract moods thinking of the ship, or of *Sheila*, or Regan, and when his wife broke into his thoughts, through the barrier he had unconsciously erected against present events, he felt a mild irritation. He even showed it at times, then was furiously angry with himself because he saw she was mildly hurt.

Once they had quarrelled. Not a satisfying quarrel of flaming outrageous give-and-take ripping phrases, with an equally satisfying make-up of kisses, but a cold, subdued quarrel which manifested itself in short, clipped sentences of bare essentials. It last a day and part of a night. He was adamant, she was hurt and bewildered, and neither would or could make a move to establish peace until in the dark of the night he felt her shake quietly as she dissolved in tears.

The train rattled through the darkened countryside as Haley sat back in his corner, indulging in mental accountancy. He must have dozed because when he sat up with a jerk he was only one station away from the Base.

During the remainder of the journey he stood in the corridor looking out over the sea. There was no moon but by the faint starlight he could see the white tops of the waves whipped up by the brisk breeze. Was it barely two months since he stood in a train looking out over that same stretch of sea? Two months in which such a lot had happened?

216

When he arrived in the wardroom he was pleasantly surprised to see the stove glowing faintly to offset the chill of the early autumn night, and some sandwiches were on a plate. As he descended the companion Booth came from his room.

'Welcome home,' he said rather sourly. 'Good leave?'

'Splendid, such as it was. And you?'

'Not bad. I came back yesterday.'

Haley looked at him in surprise and Booth grinned. 'It was a double-barrelled reason. I wanted to see if the defects were done and . . . and . . . well'—he hurried it out—'I wanted to see Heather. We don't get much time ashore nowadays'—shifting the responsibility elsewhere.

'And, in that order, how are things?'

'Defects? Like the poor, still with us. Heather? I'm worried.' He leaned back in his chair and stared into the open stove for a few moments. 'I can't get the idea that she has . . . sort of . . . well, put Anderson's death more or less behind her. Did you know that they had one hell of a row the day before he sailed?'

'No, but I never met him, and she has barely mentioned him to me since. After all, that phase was before I came here.'

'Well, they did. They had been friendly for months. She was crackers about him, and he was completely gone on her. Or, at least, she thought so until—until the day he went up.'

Haley made no reply but studied the youngster closely. It was obvious that something had provoked this confidential mood in Booth. Right! Let him get it off his chest. Time to tackle it was when it was all in the open.

'They had a row. He sailed and she expected it would be the usual make-it-up-and-be-friends when he came back.' For a moment Booth looked up. 'As you know, he didn't.'

Haley began to see daylight. 'Pretty damnable for her, I agree, but she can't—in fact, she won't—grieve about it all her life. It will fade.'

'Oh, no! The point is that she received a letter from him in which he told her that they could not go on. He was engaged to a girl in his home town and the banns were being put up shortly. He was sorry, and all that muck, hoped it wouldn't hurt her too much, and that was that.'

Haley visualised the problem as a common one. An officer had become friendly with a girl while he had another at home, by no means a unique situation, and things reached a point where the officer felt he had to break things off. He tried staging a row and followed it up with a letter while the iron was hot. A bit cowardly, but there it was.

'Bit of a dirty trick, but it would have been a dirtier one to go on sort of kidding her along. Don't you agree? I've no doubt that a short course of your bulldozing methods will effect a cure in time.' He looked straight at Booth. 'Would it be impolite for me to ask the extent of your feelings?'

Booth looked at him. 'This is the real thing for me.'

Haley threw back his head and laughed. 'Aberdeen—two, if my information is correct. Harwich, again two. But you were there only ten days, so that handicapped you. And, let me see, from snatches I've heard from that ardent historian, *Solan*'s Number One, you have not been the complete embryo celibate here.'

Booth bridled. 'I'll knock his block off when I meet him. When it comes to raking up the past I've got a good two handed rake. We'll have a go one night and you can be judge.'

'Entertaining, if not edifying,' Haley said, drily.

Booth stood up, leaned his elbow on the small shelf above the stove and stared down into the fire. Then he turned round. Haley saw him struggling against an inherent shyness, a reluctance to lay bare the depth of his feelings or the details of his friendship with the girl.

'Look, sir, this is real; it's different, somehow. I can't explain how, but it is.'

218

'They all are until the next, or until one cleverer than the other hooks you securely,' thought Haley with a flash of cynicism.

'And not only on my part,' Booth went on. 'When I went on leave I . . . I nearly didn't go. The night before she had a long fit of weeps; then she said that so long as I was around she felt she could cope, but without me . . . I couldn't get her to explain, either then or yesterday. She didn't know I was back until I went to the Wrennery for her, and she had another go of crying. It beats me.'

Haley offered him a few hackneyed words of comfort and gradually the conversation turned to ships, and the clock hands crept to the early hours of the morning before they turned in.

Booth's gloomy estimate of the number of defects rectified was partly justified. In the morning Haley found that the ship was still in the hands of the workmen, who were busy on a job in the engine-room. An estimate from the foreman said two more days, possibly three.

'Bribery, corruption and alarming inroads into your cigarettes and liquor,' Regan claimed when Haley went on board to explain. 'Probably some cash included. Here you are, alongside the quay like a gilded hell-ship while we brave the terrors of the deep. But I've been saving up an odd defect or two and we are having two days in as well, Honest days off,' he said soberly. 'I've heard the story of the fishing lines. Wish I had been there.'

Haley laughed. 'Meredith would have been the lad for that situation. The workmen would have gone dashing up the quay with Meredith and party close behind with cutlasses. Nearly came to that with my crowd.'

'Me bhoy, we must handle the workers with silken gloves, otherwise they'll declare a separate peace and where will we be then?'

Later in the day Regan called for Haley and they went for

219

that rare treat for naval men in wartime, a walk into the country without a chance of a hurried recall. They walked for several miles over the rolling hills of Kent, which were just beginning to surrender their luscious green for the more varied autumn hues, from rich yellow to golden brown and an occasional dash of deeper red. The faint breeze rippled shadows softly across fields of still uncut corn and in the distance, like a single thread melody, they could hear the drone of a tractor.

By tacit consent ships, and all that goes with them, were not mentioned. Instead, Regan talked entertainingly about his native Ireland—'Not the traitor city where I earn me honest crust,' but the true, tragic island itself, of the strong winds of the Atlantic which whipped Tralee, of the people with their strangely contradictory outlook, of hunting. 'There's nothing to beat it, Haley, my bhoy. A day with the hounds and you soaking wet nine miles from home. Then a hot bran mash for your horse, a hot bath with a generous handful of mustard in it, and a glass of the cratur itself before a fire taking the best part of a hundred-weight of peat and some salt-soaked wreck wood to give it the bit of flame.'

Haley found it was almost like listening to music to hear the Irishman and his nostalgic thoughts. The miles rolled away although they intentionally walked in a wide half-circle so that the Base would not be far away when they were tired.

They came to the top of a rise overlooking a heavily wooded valley. On the opposite side of the vale a small village clustered round its square-towered church, and slightly beyond the group of cottages was a large house, partly ivy-covered.

For a few minutes they leaned on a gate looking out over the view, and neither spoke. It was Regan who broke the silence.

'That is England,' he said softly, nodding his head towards the village. 'Unchanging, unruffled. Wars, pestilence, even death—it takes them all in its stride, covers the wounds with a decent clothing of greenery, and goes on.

'It's all a monument to a sublime conviction that ultimately everything will come right. So long as England has faith—that's the BIG thing, Haley, FAITH—nobody in the world can lick us.'

Regan's voice was deep in his chest and he spoke with such sincerity that Haley bit back a jibe he was going to make about the hateful oppressors grinding the faces of the poor Irish.

'Nobody, least of all a half-doped, propaganda-whipped nation of semi-automatons. They just haven't got it. See that house?' He pointed with his stick to the large manor on the opposite hillside. 'See that winding avenue of trees? All oak trees, and the babies of them are a couple of hundred years old. That's faith for you. The faith to plant an acorn in the ground'—he pushed a hole in the soft earth with the point of his stick—'and knowing that it will grow into a vast oak.'

He gestured expansively, and Haley felt a slight thrill go through him at the magnetism of the Irishman's eloquence.

'Englishmen learned to do that when ships were wood, good oak. They knew that oak would be wanted and planted acorns. They also knew that they would never live to see them grow to that size, but their sons' sons would, and THEIR sons would want them.'

He stepped away from the gate and widely extended his arms.

'That's the unbeatable quality the English have. The faith to plant acorns. You may die, I may die, and a lot more of us besides, but that ingrained faith will live with those that remain . . . and nothing will lick it.'

He stood silent, then shrugged his shoulders. 'Begob, they'd burn my effigy and cut off me head from the knees up if they heard me talk like this at home,' he said, but

221

Haley saw that he was merely trying to come up from the depth of his emotional mood by a purely shallow gesture towards the traditional Irish vehement spleen against the English, something to be expressed in noisy, wordy condemnation only.

They started walking along the ridge and Regan told Haley about the village and the manor house.

'It stood out against Cromwell, which endears it to me, in any event; there are cannon-balls from his guns still embedded in the walls. The lady of the house defended it while her husband was away with Prince Rupert—and him needing a haircut, no doubt.'

He laughed out loud. 'Make no mistake, if the square-headed, ambitious lads across the way DO land here the lady of today will slam the door in their faces and set the pots a-boiling with lead in the kitchen.' He shook his head gently. 'She's a fiery lady and no mistake. She held a twelve-bore against my midriff while her pint-sized army hedged me in with pitchforks, and them contemplating the best way in under a man's breastbone.'

Haley detected another story and strode along in silence.

'It was shortly after Dunkirk, and me off for a walk with an ache in me heart for something green without a ship in it,' Regan went on. 'I was walking along that lane you see running behind the house when out pops a lad with a double-barrelled gun. "Oy!" says he, and me squinting down the barrels. "Ye're far from home," he says. "I am," says I, "and a stretch of water and the whole damn' British Navy between me and it."

' "What d'ye make of it, Harry?" he says, speaking to the hedge, and a bush stands up, it being helped by a man who was holding it. "Bloody Jerry, without a doubt. Let's take him in," says the bush.'

Haley stopped and raised his eyebrows. 'Were you in uniform?'

'I was, and I tried to explain I was a naval officer.'

222

' "Not in them wriggly stripes, you ain't," says the bush. "Our'n are straight, and you ain't got no English accent, anyway. We'd best let Missus see you. Move." '

Regan grinned widely. 'I moved, and them with a couple of rusty twelve-bores with a trigger-full of an uncertain two pounds. Into the big house we go. "Tell the Missus we got another one," says the bush to a neat little maid who answered the door. "Wait," says she, with regard for the niceties, "and don't clump around the hall in your hobnail boots." And there we waits, me trying to squint down two guns at the same time, and it can't be done,' Regan said categorically.

' "Bring him in. M'lady will see him in the dining-room with the other one." And they marches me across the hall and into the dining-room. There, sitting all regal in a chair, with another twelve-bore across her lap, was a white-haired lady, not all that old, and in front of her a German pilot.

' "Do you speak English, too?" says she, coolly giving me a look down her barrels.

' "I do, madam, of the purest," says I.

' "Join your friend," she says, waving a generous chunk of air away with the gun from under me chin. I joined him although he was no friend of mine.

' "Are you a parachutist, too?" she asks.

' "God forbid!" says I. "Ten feet off the ground and I've me heart in me mouth and a prayer to St. Bridget herself on me lips." '

Haley visualised the scene and chuckled quietly to himself. He strongly suspected that Regan, from sheer devilry and curiosity, had deliberately allowed the situation to develop to the point it had reached.

'At that she laughs,' Regan went on, 'and explanations followed. The police had telephoned round that a German pilot, having a morning look-see, had lost an argument with a Spitfire but his final crash had been lost in the morning mist. Her bright boys had found him and brought him in.

223

That gave them a surging ambition, so they roped me in also.

'I stayed to lunch and I've been back several times. I've an open invitation, and she with a charming daughter and a daughter-in-law. There's an American pilot comes down sometimes—he's in the Eagle squadron—all Yanks—and we have great arguments deciding what part Ireland has played in the history of the land of the Almighty Dollar.'

Regan looked at Haley. 'You being a married man, I'll take you along one day. She's a great hater of war.' He shook his head softly. 'Lost her husband in the other one and it's odds-on she's lost a son in this.'

'Who doesn't hate war except a few pugnacious Irishmen who poke their noses into a fight which has nothing to do with them,' said Haley, flatly.

'It's public; you can't afford to be selfish about it,' Regan grinned. 'About liking wars. I sometimes think Meredith is rather fond of it. He certainly helps himself to as much as he can.'

Haley shook his head. 'I doubt it. Did he tell you about the pilot he picked up?'

Regan nodded. 'He did. It was almost like confessional. He said he meant to chop him up with the screw right to the last second, and nearly tore the guts out of *Jacinth* in stopping her. Only Meredith could have stopped her like that. I wonder if . . .'

He stopped and rubbed his hand across his chin.

'Go on.'

'I wonder if Carter changed his mind the last second but failed to stop her in time. I've thought a lot about it since Meredith told me about himself. He said he woke up at nights sweating; the ship wasn't stopping and the German was disappearing under the stern.'

'Celtic imagination working on his subconscious.'

Regan shrugged. 'It's started me thinking a lot. Wonder what we would do? Who can tell?'

They walked on in silence, two men with a problem on

224

their minds. When does war end and murder begin?

Haley found Booth on the quay the following morning brooding over a long 'T' girder and something which looked like a steel megaphone closed in at each end.

'They say they are going to fix this to the bow,' Booth submitted, nodding to some workmen who were rigging a staging round the stem. 'It's fifteen feet long. With that stuck out we'll look like a blasted swordfish. It will be fun for you coming alongside, won't it? You'll be able to wipe people off the quay.'

The workmen could offer no explanation except that they were to fit the contraption to *Arandite* and had a similar one for *Solan.*

'All the ships are going to have it,' the foreman volunteered.

Mahoney cleared up the mystery when Regan and Haley called on him later in the morning.

'Good! Glad you've dropped in,' he said. 'Had a good leave, Haley? We've managed to find Regan a little work here and there while you've been away. Who has all the cigarettes?' He accepted one. 'Seen Cutter this morning? Oh, well, he's near your ships somewhere. I've news for you children. No more sweeping in daylight. The last convoy has gone through here. In daylight hours, I mean,' he hastened to add. 'Some routing genius has at last discovered that it is asking for trouble to send them through under the German guns in daytime.'

'That should have occurred to them after the first convoy was shelled weeks ago,' Regan growled. 'But they didn't have to sail on them, sir.'

'True, and by the same token those guns can hit my ships also.' Mahoney stood up and moved to his large wall chart. 'So I'm amending the drill.' He covered an area with his hand. 'Here we'll sweep once a week and put a nightly anti-minesweeping one-ship patrol.' He touched the Gap

225

with his fingers. 'Here we'll sweep and patrol by night, and the ships can move in under the cliffs during the day, reducing movement—and smoke—to a minimum. By that arrangement you will have some protection from the anti-aircraft guns ashore.'

Regan chuckled. 'Wait until Meredith hears about this! He got into an argument the other night with some army officers and ended up by offering to send his gunner ashore to teach 'em how to shoot.'

Haley was only half listening. He was visualising the intricacies of sweeping in and around that narrow Gap, narrower than when he had first done it because of the new wrecks on its flanks.

'It's going to be a bit tricky sweeping it at night-time, sir,' he said, studying the chart.

'Hm hm, but it's going to be done,' Mahoney said flatly. 'It's night sweeping or lose more ships by day. We can't afford to lose the ships—or the men.'

'What is that new toasting fork business they are sticking on the ships, sir?' Regan asked. 'With that poking out from the bows . . .'

Mahoney laughed. 'It won't poke out from the bows. It will be hinged and will be stowed inboard when not in use and will be straight up and down the stem when you are sweeping. It's a hammer or knocker sweep. In brief, it is an ordinary pneumatic drill hitting on a diaphragm inside that cone, and that will—or is supposed to—set off those new mines the Hun has. They are definitely acoustic mines.'

'And will they go off under the stem?' Regan's face was bland.

'The hope is that they will not. If they do, then you must come back and complain to Cutter, who will issue a new hammer.' Mahoney was likewise bland. 'Seriously, for a moment. I'm told that they will give you rather more than a hundred yards immunity from either beam. In effect, you will be travelling in a circle of safety roughly two hundred

226

yards in diameter so long as you have your hammer down and buzzing away.'

For the next half-hour or so they went into the technicalities of sweeping and the problems involved in doing so by night.

'And now shall we have a cup of tea?' Mahoney asked, ringing his desk bell.

'That's nice,' he said a little later, putting his cup back on the saucer. 'I must pray tonight that some kind fairy will put some sugar in my Wren's stocking. We're getting low.' Mahoney looked at Regan with complete detachment. 'There are fairies about, you know.'

Regan grinned.

'Oh, yes! This is one of the little moments I like,' Mahoney went on. 'It's all strictly under the bonnet at the moment and it's very wrong of me to tell, but I can't resist. It will be out tomorrow, anyway, in the *Gazette*. You have got a Distinguished Service Cross, Regan, and you, Haley, have got a Mention in Despatches. Congratulations to both of you. They are honours well earned.'

Regan and Haley exchanged glances. Regan's face had coloured up at the totally unexpected news.

'What for, sir?'

It came from both of them simultaneously. They both stopped and looked at each other again.

'Tck, tck,' Mahoney clicked. 'Such modesty does you credit. But, seriously, you've both earned it over and over again.'

It was Regan who spoke up, voicing the thought that was in both their minds.

'Meredith, sir. He's done . . . he's been . . .'

Mahoney smiled and held up his hand. 'Meredith's name was put forward with another recommendation. I'll be seeing him so that I can explain. He has been recommended for accelerated promotion to Lieutenant-Commander for command of a larger ship. That will be almost a certainty

227

in a month or so. I will be sorry to lose him, but I feel that those flaring qualities of his can be better employed. He is Asdic trained. Did you know?'

'Yes, sir. He was standing by *Jacinth* in Aberdeen to take her over as an Asdic trawler when she switched. He'll find the extra money useful. He has a family as long as his arm,' Regan concluded with a chuckle.

'Well, not quite. He has four boys and a girl. One for each year of his married life.'

'Energetic lad,' Regan murmured.

'Did you say something? No? I believe he has been heard to threaten his crew that if they didn't buck up their ideas he would ship his family in their stead. He'll find all the work he wants on escort duty. Do you realise what it means? The Germans have all the French coast ports. They have the Atlantic on the doorstep a few steaming hours away from our convoy routes. And we'—Mahoney looked at Regan—'all southern Irishmen don't think the same as you and I, Regan. We have no Queenstown now, so protection for those same convoys will have to be a long haul.'

Haley diverted the conversation away from the ticklish point.

'How long before Meredith will go, sir?'

'Couple of months, so my informant at the Admiralty tells me.'

'She doesn't wash the doorstep of the Big Front Door, does she, sir?'

Mahoney looked astonished until Haley explained the *Culver* captain's mythical grandmother at the Admiralty. Then he laughed. 'No, no! Mine merely empties the waste-paper baskets. Much more profitable, I assure you.'

Outside Base Haley saw Heather sitting in a car reading a novel. He crossed to talk to her. She greeted him with a soft smile.

228

'I seem to detect some improvement in my Number One recently. Can I attribute it to you?' he asked lightly.

She picked up the mood. 'Purely an illusion.'

'Do you mean there is no hope for improvement, or no scope?'

'Not a shred of hope.' She closed the book and slipped it into the pigeon-hole in the dashboard. Her fingers stayed with it; without lifting her head her eyes rose to Haley's.

'He thinks rather a lot of you.' Her fingers came up to stop any comment. 'I think he would listen to any advice you gave him.'

The statement was tinged slightly with a query. 'Where is this hare leading us?' Haley thought. 'We'll give it a run to see its line of country.'

'Please!' There was an undercurrent of urgency about her. 'Please give him good advice. He does so want it. He so badly wants things putting in perspective.'

'Anything in particular?'

'Anything he tries to discuss with you.'

'He is more likely to give me advice. I've never met a more informative young man. But give me a lead. What am I to say? Marry the girl and make an honest woman of her?'

The girl sat still. Only her eyelids moved. Her head was poised, chin tilted, features frozen, but her eyelids dropped slowly, remained down for a second or two like a child submitting to the first wooing of sleep. Haley scarcely heard her next sentence.

'Marrying him would be so simple, wouldn't it?'

Haley felt he was floundering out of his depth but he blundered on. 'Easy as falling off a log. But don't you believe the legend of simplicity. Getting married is a most complicated business.'

She nodded and echoed quietly, 'Most complicated.'

'Anyway, I'll try to do what you ask.'

He could see Regan waiting some way ahead and was thankful when a Staff Officer came out to enter the car.

As Haley had expected, sweeping in the twisted, narrow Gap in darkness was far from being a picnic. To him fell the dubious honour of being the first to entangle his sweeping gear round a wreck. There was some excuse for it because the wreck on which he was caught up was not visible above water.

After considerable difficulty the gear was freed and he steamed on to join the vague bulk of *Solan*, who seemed to be waiting for him at the end of the lap. Haley was vaguely surprised that he had not had at least one pungent signal from Regan.

'Maybe he is towing a ten-thousand-ton wreck and doesn't know it,' Booth said, almost prophetically, as he watched the dim green light bobbing and nodding on the sweep astern.

And so it was. As *Arandite* closed *Solan* a blue light twinkled from her bridge.

'I have established close relation with an underwater obstruction,' Regan sent.

' 'Strewth!' Larkin muttered when he had stumbled over the delivery of the signal. 'Can't we think up a few long words for him, sir? I'd like to make her Bunts sweat.'

'Could we try: "It is the inevitable sequel to the presence of an inefficient subordinate." ' Haley chuckled at Booth's suggestion. 'There are enough "i's" and "e's" in it. Yes, make it from Number One to Number One.'

Larkin embarked joyously on a high-speed signal, using as low a blue light as he could manage, and for once did not snarl when he several times received 'IMI', which means repeat. Finally he put his lamp down.

'That's larned 'im,' he said with deep satisfaction. 'Bet

he could beat his eyes with a spoon, they're sticking out so much.'

By trial and error they learned to judge distances in the darkness and soon it became a point of honour to clip a wreck as closely in the night as they had done in the daylight.

It was Booth who advanced a novel suggestion, but could have bitten off his tongue a second afterwards. By the dim light on the chart table, he had been browsing through the complicated directions for use with the new hammer sweep. He came out from behind the canvas cover and queried: 'The book of words says we should carry a large red flag when using the knocker. How-come night-time? What do we hoist? A large red light? It would be an idea. The Huns would think it was a new address for the *bon femme* and come dashing off in hundreds.'

'No doubt knocking twice and asking for Nellie,' Haley said drily, and Booth retired to one corner of the bridge muttering criticisms of people who hit below the belt.

As each ship was fitted with the new sweeping device so the destruction of mines increased. Their explosion in darkness was a far more impressive, awe-inspiring moment than in the daytime. One went off quite close to *Solan* and Regan and his Number One quite distinctly saw the underwater flash from the explosion a split second before the sea climbed up in a tall column of lighter shadow.

Meredith came into his own as *E*-boats made sporadic attempts to lay new fields and repair the holes made in the existing ones by the sweepers. The fights were short in duration, if fights they could be called. Two or four *E*-boats would come stealing over in the darkest hour, make a swift run, lay their mines and tear away in a flurry of foam and noise.

Seldom, if ever, did thay stay and fight, much to the disgust of Meredith and his bloody-minded gunners.

'Can't say that I blame them much,' Regan said to his

Number One. 'I don't think I would want to linger about with a load of mines liable to go off if some interfering trawler squirted a stream of tracer aboard.'

So what they saw mainly in the dark was a sudden spurt of water splitting into a twin plume of bow wave, a short, sharp ripping burst of tracer, and then it was the usual drill: shooting at a small and disappearing target usually going away behind a thin smoke-screen.

Mahoney worked them hard. Out four days, in a day, store up and out again. Possibly the worst part was hearing the enemy aircraft droning over each night for some inland target. Occasionally one would go back overhead, limping, its engines labouring heavily as it struggled to gain height. One machine struggled out from the English coast with fire pouring from an engine, losing height as it crossed. Its flight took it over *Jacinth* and *Arandite*.

An orange flash lit up *Jacinth*'s forepart as she opened up with her 12-pounder and Haley, hearing Booth whinnying beside him, and guessing that Clay was on the gun with his eyes to the sight and a longing in his heart, rapped out: 'Open up. Range is about 1,000 yards.'

The shell in *Arandite*'s gun was a star-shell, fused for 2,000 yards in readiness for *E*-boats. Clay let it fly well ahead and followed it with two or three rapid rounds of H.E. The star shell burst above and in front of the aircraft and showed it struggling along with one wing well down. It was going along with a peculiar jerking motion, nose-down, jerk-up, nose-down, jerk-up, as the pilot fought to keep it on a level course.

Little bursts of orange broke round it as *Jacinth*'s and *Arandite*'s shells reached it. It is doubtful if either of them really hit it, but the barrage bursting round his nose and under his tail must have upset the pilot.

He pulled the machine round in a slow half-circle which developed into a descending spiral. It increased and tightened until, as the star-shell burned itself out ahead of it,

232

the 'plane went into a steep, spinning dive and crashed into the water about three or four miles away. The distinct sound of the smack as it hit the water came to the ships. Then they saw a faint flicker of flame rise again, subside for a moment, then burst into one great, ruddy rose opening from a bud to overblooming blossom in a few seconds.

'Across two minefields. One of ours and one of theirs, on the slender chance of there being a survivor? No.' Haley made up his mind and signalled *Jacinth* to resume station on his beam.

In the early hours of the morning German aircraft began hitting the Base. They heard the thin, wailing cry of the warning and in a matter of minutes the sudden lurid stabs of flame came from anti-aircraft guns. The 'planes raiding the Base were flying much lower than those bound farther inland. They dropped their bombs in a dive and swept back towards the French coast quite low over the water.

At first Haley thought it was a diversion raid while other aircraft laid mines but as it developed in intensity he realised that it was a real one bent on doing damage.

Slowly they plodded on up and down their laps while a few miles away they could hear the dull crump of bombs and see the angry, flickering flames from half a dozen fires.

Daylight seemed never to come but at last a faint tinge of colour lightened the darkness in the east, disappeared and came back with renewed confidence to start another day of light, another day in which one could see the damage, assess the heartbreaks and the gaps and reduce fears from the looming gigantic proportions to something more manageable.

As they closed up to return to harbour they could see a dingy, dun-coloured pall of smoke hanging over the Base. The wind was trying its best to disperse it but from the ground fresh reinforcements rolled up to add to the murk.

Nobody spoke as they slid alongside the quay. Haley used his binoculars as soon as the drifting clouds of acrid smoke allowed him to make out any details. *Solan,* in her berth, seemed all right. Figures moved about her deck. Two other ships astern of her also seemed to have escaped damage. One or two buildings on the short pier had been hit and their jagged scars stood out starkly.

He swept the shore line. Some buildings were roofless; their windows gaped like open eyes, and from them slowly climbed tenuous threads of smoke. Where others had been were merely heaps of rubble. Back in the centre of the town the smoke column seemed to be at its thickest.

'It sure has copped it,' Ross said softly to Clay on the fo'c'sle head. 'I wonder if that bastard we got done some of it?'

A grey-faced, tired, unshaven Cutter met them on the pier. 'Detail a party to go ashore to help in rescue work,' he said shortly. 'The naval barracks had two hits, the Base had a near miss and is partly wrecked, and up in the town it is hell.'

Booth rapidly picked out eight men and it was then that the full scale of his worth came to Haley. Although he was a youngster he seemed to have at his finger-tips a complete assessment of each man and his value for a job.

'Clay, Lennox, Ross . . .' He rapped out names and Haley saw that each one was a man who had shown some form of personal initiative. He realised that in a quiet way Booth had organised the ship so that at sea or in harbour the crew was departmentalised; whatever the captain wanted Booth had ready in his mind the group of men for the job. In addition to fundamentals, like handling the sweep or the guns, there were the right men to use for stores, painting, or the dozens of jobs to be done. Momentarily he allowed his increasing affection for Booth to show.

'Go with them. I'll organise things here. And don't run into trouble,' he said, and slipped his arm round Booth's shoulders.

It was at the end of a long, heartbreaking day that Booth led back on board his dirty, dishevelled working-party. They were dead-weary, smelled of fire and smoke, and they had seen things which had turned their faces into frozen masks.

All of them had seen ships blow up, had fought and indirectly killed in the heat of a fight, but the tasks they had performed in the brief twelve hours had searched out and outraged time and again all their emotions.

'Tot each all round,' Haley said crisply as they clambered over the rail. Booth said nothing. He watched his weary party disappear down to the mess deck. He looked once at Haley then slowly he, too, disappeared below.

Haley shook his head and followed him. Booth had gone to his room and Haley poured out a stiff drink and waited for him to emerge from behind the curtain. Time passed and Booth did not appear, so Haley went to the doorway, tapped softly, heard a smothered exclamation inside, and pulled over the curtain.

Filthy; water and debris-stained as he was, Booth lay face down on his settee, his head hidden in his arms. Haley collected the stiff drink and went into the room.

'Drink this, laddie, you need it,' he said, putting his hand on Booth's shoulder. Booth shrugged it off.

'Had anything to eat?' Haley persisted. 'That means you've been nearly twenty-four hours with only one meal.' He decided to take a strong line. 'We'll get a hell of a lot of this before this war is over. Now, come on, knock this back, have a bath and get some sleep. God knows we all need it.'

Booth suddenly swung his legs to the floor. He sat up without looking at Haley. His face was streaked white where tears had furrowed through the grime.

'Heather's dead,' he said dully. 'Bomb hit her car last night. She was on the quay . . .' He trailed off and gulped.

Haley made no reply. For a moment or two he could formulate no collected thoughts in his mind, although a hazy

235

thread ran through it: 'Can't be! Only a few days ago she was here, on board, titivating her hair against that very mirror. She can't be dead.'

Instinctively he again slipped his hand over Booth's shoulders and pushed the drink on to him. Booth looked at it hesitantly, then drank it back in one straight gulp. Suddenly he swung back to the settee, buried his face in his arms, and his shoulders started to heave.

Quietly Haley stepped from the room, drew the curtain and left the man to his grief . . . and Booth was all man.

From Regan and from Cutter Haley heard the details of the night attack. At first it was thought that it was merely a diversion while other 'planes laid mines at sea. But it increased in intensity. The Germans mixed in two or three land mines, showered the town with incendiaries and dropped a number of oil bombs which started large fires. By a touch of irony the bomb which hit the naval camp dropped just as the ratings had been brought from their comparatively safe shelters to form working-parties to help fight fires. The death roll was high and many of those who escaped being killed were wounded and suffered from shock.

It was there that the ships' working-parties had to clear up wreckage, put out the innumerable little fires which started as air was allowed to get in to smouldering debris, and it was there that they had to delve to recover the bodies of men they knew, men against whom they had played football, men who had worked with them in storing ships, with whom they had drank and played darts.

'She must have been blown off the wall by blast some time during the night,' Cutter theorised to Haley when he asked him about Heather.

'We found the car end-up in the water. A couple of men broke open the roof and she was still at the wheel. There was no sign of damage so it doesn't look as if she was actually hit by anything.'

Meredith dropped on board for a few minutes. He had been up to the Base. 'It was in a bad shape, mainly blast, and fortunately nobody was there at the time. I left Mahoney cussing blue lights because his favourite teapot and crockery was smashed.' Meredith grinned and went on: 'He'd found another lot because he had some tea on the way as I left.'

Meredith reached the quay wall and was walking away when he remembered what it was he had come to *Arandite* about.

'The damned Pongos are going to claim that 'plane we bumped off.' He worked himself up into a state of indignation. 'It would have got home if we hadn't slapped a few into him. I'm going to argue it out, anyway.'

Does it matter who shot it down? Haley thought wearily. Does it matter who paints a swastika on a gun, or a 'plane silhouette on a bridge, or on a Mess wall? Did the Germans on return paint a baby's pram on their 'planes, or a church, or a school, as signs of their triumphs? Did some pilot make a mark on his fuselage to show that he had wiped out a young Wren? Gradually the day adjusted itself. Shore-officers and ratings told their stories, talked of the bigger and brighter bombs which fell nearer to them than to any-body else. As night-time came the bombs which had fallen twenty hours before ceased to be the topic. Although nobody put it into words, it was the hours to come which filled their minds. Would there be another raid? Would there be more shattered buildings? More roaring fires? More twisted, sil-ent bodies under debris? Would it be, this time, one with one's own name on it?

Haley turned in early in the evening and woke, savagely, every nerve tingling and his heart pounding, to the sound of the wailing warning. He got out on deck to find there was gusty wind blowing with occasional showers of rain whipping the ship.

Usually the German 'planes arrived almost with the last

237

warble of the warning. He crouched behind the deck-house and listened but could hear no sound of droning engines. Two or three times his keyed-up ears picked up a faint moan but he soon identified it as the wind twanging a stay.

Suddenly a group of searchlights switched on. The light reflected from the low clouds filled the Base with an eerie green-white reflection. They groped through the cloud, swung out seawards, concentrated on one point and crept slowly from west to east. Then Haley heard the intermittent throb of 'planes. It grew louder. Guns on the cliffs and on the fringe of the town suddenly opened up but their bursts were well above the clouds. He heard the whistle of bombs through the air, crouched lower and waited as the whistling stopped.

The bomb burst in a quick flash somewhere in the town. It was followed by several more thudding explosions. Then came an uncanny silence as the guns stopped and the drone of the 'plane died away.

Haley decided it was a diversion raid and shrugged himself inside his duffle. He might as well sit this one out in the warm wardroom. He pulled aside the blackout curtain over the companionway and was surprised to see the light on below.

Sitting in the arm-chair was Booth, slumped back, head on his chest and an empty glass in the hand which hung limply over the arm of the chair. It was the first time Haley had seen him since he softly pulled the curtain over the First Lieutenant's doorway some hours before.

'It's a good way as any to sit out a raid,' Haley said quietly, and he moved towards the sideboard and poured himself a drink. Booth made no answer and Haley thought he had dropped off to sleep until he saw a glint from beneath his lowered eyelids. 'Can I pour you one, Number One?'

Booth raised his arm, surrendered the glass without moving any other part of his body. Haley poured a drink and gave it to him.

238

'Warning wake you up? For me, it's nearly as bad as the bombs.'

Booth raised his glass and tossed the drink back in one quick motion, and his hand slipped down to the side of the chair again.

'You got some sleep in, I hope.' Haley made himself comfortable on the settee with his knees tucked up under his chin. 'I told the steward not to disturb you.'

'Kind of you.' Booth's voice was hard, flat, and he spoke with scarcely a movement of the lips. Haley looked more closely at him, then turned his gaze towards the bottle on the sideboard. It was more than half full and he had opened it that midday for Cutter. He studied Booth but gained no definite impression.

It was Booth who spoke next, and the thing he said was more startling than if a bomb had gone off alongside the ships.

'She was going to have a child.' The flat, emotionless level of the sentence made it a delay-shock for Haley. It was some while before the import of the sentence made its full impact. It took him a little time to absorb it and connect it with anything else in his mind. When it did shape in his brain, and he got the whole force of it, he sat up with a jerk. There was no need for him to temporise.

'Good God! When did . . . how do you know?'

Booth slowly lifted his other hand. In it he had a letter which he handed to Haley.

The other took it slowly, glanced at the first page and turned it over to see the signature.

'Do you want me to read it . . . all?'

Booth shrugged. 'Why not?'

Haley read on.

Dear Man,

When I sat down to write this letter I had made up my mind. You were my one hope of saving myself, not for myself but for Mummy and Daddy, for the others who love me and whom I love. I had planned it out to the last detail. A quick surrender to you, then we would get married and I could go away, home or somewhere else. Please try to understand, my dear. In the past few weeks you have come to mean such a lot to me. Why didn't we meet a few months ago? Why didn't Fate arrange it so that it was you I fell in love with months ago, instead of somebody else? And now my resolutions have gone. I can't do it. Because you would know, and knowing would hurt you.

You see, I am going to have a baby. Do you need to ask who is the father?

So I am writing this letter to you in order that you will understand why I have been so beastly towards you in the past few weeks, yet all I really wanted was to slip into your arms. . . .

Haley looked up and found Booth's eyes on him. They were burning with a hot glow from right down inside them. Booth said, almost harshly, 'Read on.'

I am going away from here. I don't know where. I dare not go home. But I'll go somewhere. Please, please do understand that I am telling you all this because I became fond of you, and it was too late. . . .

Haley put the letter on the table. He looked at Booth. Somewhere in the recesses of his mind something flickered. 'Please give him good advice.' Was it this the girl had hinted at?

'Had you asked her to marry you?'

Booth shook his head like a young bull worried by flies. 'N-n-no, not exactly. I had mentioned it. I wanted . . . I meant to have a talk with you about it. I . . . I . . . thought perhaps you would give me some advice on how to go about

240

it . . . what to say . . . the right thing to say.'

Haley picked up the letter and looked at it again. There was only one question he could ask and it provided the answer.

'Anderson?'

'Who else? For God's sake, she didn't go whoring all over the Base.' Booth was slipping from the frozen grip he had on himself. 'Do you think she would have to look at her diary to find out who would be the father? Damn it all . . .' Booth beat his thigh with a clenched fist. 'It did not matter . . . I would have married her . . .'

Booth's voice trailed into a strangled sob.

Haley rested his arms on the table and let his head drop into his cupped hands.

Two kids, just two young kids, getting their lives so tangled up. He thought of the girl sitting in her quarters alone, writing of the secret that she had kept for two or three months. Two or three months? He did some quick mental arithmetic. *Pearl* had been sunk . . . three months . . . a bit over.

He looked up. 'Booth, look at me.' The flat, hard tone, the surname, not 'Number One', jarred Booth's head upwards. 'I want a straight answer. It was Anderson? It could not possibly have been you?' His eyes bored into the youngster's.

The answer came equally flat and hard.

'No. You'll have to take my word for it.'

'I will.'

Haley's eyes dropped once more to the letter. Certain phrases developed an extra emphasis. 'A quick surrender to you . . .', '. . . I can't do it . . .', 'I am going away from here . . .' I'M GOING AWAY FROM HERE! Had she? Was it a bomb which sent her toppling over into the dark waters? Or had she in the tortured recesses of her mind seen a way out, a solution to all the problems which had kept her awake, twisting and turning in her bed?

241

He heard Booth ask a question.

'Do you think she drove over the wall deliberately?'

Haley made no answer, and after an interval Booth repeated it with greater emphasis.

'From what Cutter told me she was caught in a stick of bombs which hit across the pier, and it is highly probable that the blast blew her over.'

'Nobody saw it happen.'

'But a lot of people knew she was there. She had just finished a job.'

'Nobody saw it happen.' It was a dull repetition, as if Booth wanted to get the thought out loud, brought into the open so that something or somebody could demolish the nagging idea in his head.

'A number of people died last night. Nobody SAW them die, but they are dead, as you know.'

Booth stood up. For a few seconds he kept his hands clenched and straight down by his sides. He moved towards the sideboard, poured himself another drink, looked at Haley, who shook his head, and tossed the drink back in one quick move.

'How many is that?' Haley kept his voice level.

Booth shrugged.

'It's not going to do any good getting mildly blotto. Look, sit down and we'll thrash it out from the beginning.' Wearily Booth moved back to his chair and slumped down.

It was such a simple story when broken down to its elements as Booth by degrees told it, and of his part in the later stages.

She was the only daughter of a country doctor. At first they were adamant, frowned heavily and fearfully at her suggestions that she should join any of the women's forces. Surely there was plenty of work to be done at home? Bandages to be rolled, flag days, no doubt, and first-aid classes. By sheer persistence she had broken them down and gone off

242

triumphantly to join the W.R.E.N.S., at just over twenty years old.

She met Anderson and he overcame her shyness, persuaded her to go on board for tea one day and she found him amusing, very correct, and later very attractive. It came as something of a shock to her when he told her that he was engaged to be married to another girl and was in fact preparing to put the banns up.

But the bigger shock was more deliberate in building up; a frightening suspicion became terrifying certainty, with nobody to turn to.

'It explains the fits of crying she had in the past couple of weeks,' Booth said at the end of his long, halting narrative. 'Oh, God, why didn't she tell me? I could have done something.'

And what could you have done? Haley thought. Just what would your reactions have been if she had come to you and announced, 'Oh, by the way, I am going to have a child.' He had been close enough to Booth to know that all his talk of weak, willing, enthusiastic victims in the feminine world was just so much talk and no more. He doubted whether in any of his affairs he had done anything but indulge in a little cuddling and kissing in the dark. His thoughts slipped along until he visualised the mental torture chamber in which the girl had lived alone, day after day trying to do her job normally and to appear just normal. Instinctively he knew that her self-confessed scheme to catch Booth had been little more than a passing idea. Somehow he could not see her going through with it, thinking out all the implications and all the subtle lying it would involve.

And now there was no need. She was dead and young Booth was carrying his tragic load.

'I don't quite see what you could have done,' Haley said.

'I would have married her just as quickly as possible.'

Haley shook his head. That would not have been the

end. It would have been just the beginning, the start of end-less doubts, deception bringing in its train an ever-increasing weave of unhappiness, and ultimate disaster.

And now she was dead. Did she find the answer herself? Did some ironic quirk of fate find it for her?

The thin, steady wail of the 'all clear' came from above and Haley realised that he was tired; his eyes were heavy and his head ached. He stood up and Booth followed suit. Suddenly Haley took the letter in his hand.

'I imagine that only you and I know this. She will be buried with the other casualties. Shall I . . . ?' He nodded towards the faintly glowing stove.

Booth looked at him from beneath lowered lids. Gently he gave assent with one faint gesture. Haley thrust the letter into the dying embers, watched it char and turn brown. There was not enough heat in the fire to start it burning so he touched it with a match. It flared, and died down until only a twisted, blackened shape remained with oc-casional twisting red-gold threads showing. Soon they faded.

'Now, get turned in. We'll be off again in the morning.' Booth made no movement, so Haley stepped up to him. 'There is nothing you can do now, or ever; you'll just have to let time take charge. Take my advice, get some sleep and . . . no more . . .'—he nodded towards the bottle on the locker. Shall I put it away, or leave it out and trust him? Leave it out. He will have to battle this thing out on his own, as thousands of others will have to do in this damned war.

'All right. See you in the morning.' Booth moved towards his room. As he pulled aside the curtain he looked at Haley, now at the bottom of the companionway. 'You do think that only we knew? She would scarcely have told . . .?'

'Not for one moment. That letter'—he jerked his head towards the stove—'was the first time she had unburdened her mind. She was going to run away . . . or something . . . but I'm certain that she told only you.'

244

'And you,' Booth whispered.

'All right. And me, and . . . we don't talk.' He adopted a brisk tone. 'Now get some sleep.'

A secret it remained. It was the first casualty among the Wrens, and the girl was buried with the other ratings killed in the raid. The Wrens made the most of the emotional moment. Her coffin was covered with flowers from Wren friends, Wren officers and Base staff. Booth and Haley were at sea when the mass funeral took place and it was not for a few days that they were able to go to the little churchyard in which one corner will be forever naval, the corner where the naval casualties of two wars slept the sleep of eternal peace.

Haley stooped and read the inscriptions on some of the wreaths. 'From Commander and Mrs. Mahoney'. 'W.R.E.N. Officers' Mess'. One bunch of white lilac, now fading and turning a dingy brown, had a label tied to it: 'Billy Boy'. That was all. Haley looked up at the sky in a vague attempt to concentrate sufficiently to identify anybody he knew by that name.

'She used to sing "Where have you been all the day, Billy Boy?" when I met her and—well, it became her name for me.'

Booth stood with his hat tucked under his arm, looking down at the newly turfed grave.

'If there's any knowing she'll know who sent it. Nobody else will, and she'll know I understood.'

Haley felt his throat grow tight and a tingling came to the back of his eyes. Silently they left the churchyard and walked back to the ship.

9

Autumn slipped into winter, a bitterly cold winter with a long series of savage gales followed by a succession of snow-storms which left the countryside gripped in a thick layer of frozen snow.

Sweeping became what Meredith had once described as soul-destroying ploughing. It became a slugging battle against an enemy never seen, except for an occasional glimpse of an *E*-boat or the faint shape of an aeroplane picked out in a searchlight.

The one highlight was Meredith's departure. Because *Solan* and *Arandite* were both in for temporary repairs *Jacinth* had to take out a scratch team to search through the Gap and its approaches before a convoy slipped through in the darkest hour. *Jacinth* did the job with complete thoroughness but instead of dropping out to seawards and waiting for the convoy to pass before starting a slow patrol *Jacinth* went cruising. At least, that was Meredith's description. In actual fact he took his ship through a narrow slit between two rapacious sand-banks, neither of which was buoyed, and surprised two *E*-boats lying nice and snug in the lee of one of the banks.

Meredith had long held the theory that they used to sit peacefully there waiting until the patrol had passed, then slip in and lay their mines. Once or twice he had supported his theory by loosing off star-shells over that area without conspicuous luck. There was a lot to be said for his view, because a number of wrecks in the vicinity gave the *E*-boats a nice screen behind which to hide so that the shore detectors could not pick them up.

'It was a lovely scrap,' Meredith related to Regan and Haley when he got into harbour. 'Pity I was on my own. With you two with me we would have cleaned 'em up. You see, they had to cross my bow to get to open water, or chance going over the banks. One tried a dash, the other tried the banks. I caught the second one as he bumped and slid over.'

Regan and Haley exchanged amused glances. Had either of them been out with *Jacinth* there would have been no journey through the narrow slit, to begin with, but they said nothing.

Fascinated watchers from the shore, on the signal station, and the army guns, saw a naval fight in miniature clearly illuminated by *Jacinth*'s star-shell, and confirmed that Meredith had hit one *E*-boat severely enough to create a doubt about its safe arrival back in its base. The other had been well riddled with machine-gun fire. It was all over in a few minutes and the only damage Meredith sustained was a series of small holes about the superstructure.

When he said farewell to Regan and Haley the night before he left he suddenly became unaccountably shy.

'I'm really sorry to leave you chaps. Can't you persuade Mahoney to let us do the patrolling around and about, and stick the L.L. ships on sweeping? After all, they had to have destroyers around here for that work. There is enough to keep us busy. Why, we could have a fight a night, enough for everybody.'

Regan looked at Meredith's brand new two and half rings on his sleeve, newly shipped that day, and laughed.

'With you as Senior Officer. Why, we'd be raiding Calais in a week, and be prisoners or *non est* in ten days.'

Meredith grinned and looked at his sleeve. 'You can still be boss. I'd arrange a patrol of my own.'

'Not more than half a mile from Boulogne harbour. Go away! Get your big ship and start winning the war.'

Meredith became serious. 'Somebody'll have to start winning it; it's pretty grim at the moment.' He looked at Regan and Haley. 'You fellows have laughed at me and my theory about where the *E*-boats side out. Well, I've shown you. What they've done before they'll do again. Remember that.'

They missed his pugnacious outlook after his departure, but a few weeks afterwards received a letter from him, written to Regan but for joint perusal, which gave them one of their few laughs.

The long succession of bitterly cold snow-laden winds made going ashore a tribulation and Regan and Haley developed the habit of visiting each other and just sitting in idle comfort.

Sometimes Regan would talk amusingly of life in his Irish backwater, and Haley would describe some of his long cruises in his yacht. But often they would just sit in comfort before each other's wardroom stove, Haley reading and Regan tying innumerable fishing flies.

One evening Regan tossed over Meredith's letter.

'Read that,' he said, 'and pray for the Clyde.'

Meredith, after a long leave, was standing by a new corvette, one of the 1,000-ton maid-of-all-work escort ships being built in a Clyde shipyard. From his letter he seemed to have started a prolonged guerilla warfare with eyerybody, from managing director of the yard downwards, and was holding his own.

After all [Meredith wrote], I've got to take her to sea and fight her, so I want things my way. I've got a good Number One, at least, he feels good. He's a Scot; this is his home town. He stands six feet and a half, is as fat as a boat-hook, and half the time I can't understand him. He has to spit it on the bulkhead and I wait till it dries, then I read it. But he speaks the lingo here, so we get along and get things done.

Haley chuckled. He pictured Meredith, a bare five feet five, storming about the dockyard with his tall First Lieutenant in tow.

'In a couple of weeks he will commission her. Let's send him a telegram: "Adolf. Let battle commence." Did you ever meet such a pugnacious man? If there are two ways of doing a job, and one involves a scrap, he'll pick the fight from choice.'

Regan did the honours with the drinks and shook his head. 'How wrong you are! Meredith was dead accurate when he called himself a man of peace. He IS a man of peace.'

Haley's face registered frank disbelief.

Regan settled himself in his chair. 'Did he ever tell you he was afraid of the dark? Well, he was. Terrified of it. Now, you figure out what he must have gone through on those night patrols and it as dark as Reilly's pigsty, that being a hundred feet deep in a hillside. Something to do with his childhood, some lasting fright he had.'

Regan tested his drink and looked at Haley from under his eyelids.

'He once told me of his early days at sea. He was on a small windjammer aloft and in the dark. Alone, just him up top and the whole world gone from him. He fought it through panic, clung on with his legs and deliberately let go with his hands, defying that something to come out of the dark and do its damndest, got back on deck, and fainted flat out.'

'What happened then?'

'I gather he had his backside kicked for sleeping on watch. He is a typical Celt, with a streak of the mystic and a free-riding imagination, which can be a curse. Of course he doesn't get panicky now in the dark—you can laugh but I'm convinced that the reason for his constant scrapping and searching for fights at night-time is all part of whistling in the dark.'

'You mean . . .'

'Just this: the steady grind of a patrol or a sweep was torture to him. The darkness held too many things for him which were there only in his imagination, terrifying things he couldn't describe or explain. Flush an *E*-boat and that was something tangible, something to shoot at. Difficult to explain, but that is my opinion.'

'I can realise that to anybody afraid of the dark it can be terrifying.' Haley stopped, then went on quietly: ' "From things that go bump in the night, good Lord deliver us." '

'That sort of thing didn't worry him a lot. He classed them with *E*-boats. Do you know, I feel that he will do one of two things—burn himself out chasing the tangible to fight it, or go out in a blaze of glory in some impossible scrap.'

'From your story I think there must be a tremendous hidden source of self-discipline. He'll possibly tone down and end up with half a sleeve of gold and a chest full of decorations.'

'Possibly.' Regan went off at a tangent. 'How's your Number One? We don't see much of him these days. He and my Jimmy used to scrap all over the ship.'

Haley pursed his lips and whistled softly. 'Quiet, far too quiet. He took the death of that young Wren more deeply than I thought.'

'Ara, he'll snap out of it. In a couple of months he'll be eyeing some girl's torso with a wicked gleam in his eye and a notion in his head, and her knowing what's going on behind his eyes.'

'I don't know—he's got me worried.'

'Work him, laddie, work him to death. Don't give him time to brood.'

'He's doing that himself without any help from me. He hasn't been ashore for a month. He's shut away in his room now, slaving away at some painting. I don't know what it is. He caught the steward peeping at it a couple of weeks ago and slanged him like a bargee. Indirectly, I heard

250

it's something red and black.' Haley shrugged. 'I can think of nothing . . . nothing to help him.'

'He's young and youth works out its own cures.'

The broader picture of the war became something vague and indistinct to Haley. With the feel of the grasp of the hand of friendship still fresh in his fingers Hitler leapt on Russia like a mad dog. The tempo of the air-raids increased. Other towns shared with London the horror of being selected for repeated raids, were hit on succeeding nights, but while the structural heart of the towns were plucked out the spiritual heart remained.

For one brief flash Haley saw a moment or two of the former high-spirited Booth. He called everybody Comrade, but it was only a flash.

It was a week's leave, a week of unrelenting rain and gusty wind, which drove it home to Haley how tired he was and how taut were his nerves. When he reflected he counted up that he was averaging about four hours sleep a day, and that was not in regular doses, small as they were.

Although they did little wire sweeping, confining themselves to searching for acoustic mines, it was a considerable strain manœuvring in and round the wrecks, now marked by low-lighted green-flashing buoys, and patrolling the channels leading to the Gap. The monotony was exhausting. After what seemed an age of slowly patrolling along a channel the inexorable clock would show that only an hour had passed.

At times Haley would rest his aching head on his arms, but he found that this practice had dangers. He would have to wrench himself back brutally from sleep, a wrench which was almost physical.

The little minesweeping force lost two ships that winter, both to mines, but each one went down so slowly that the loss of life was small.

For weeks the electric sweepers had combed a stretch,

followed by the larger trawlers, and only the occasional mine showed a small profit for the almost endless hours of monotony.

'And if we relax just once,' Mahoney said grimly when they were discussing things in his office, 'they would build up a field which would take us nearly a month to clear.'

His words were strangely prophetic. Damage, defects and other causes reduced Mahoney's little force to a bare half-dozen. The succession of gales suddenly stopped, giving way to bitterly cold weather with snow which froze as it fell and stayed frozen.

In two nights E-boats and aircraft laid a formidable field of mines which narrowed the Gap to a couple of hundred yards.

'And possibly less,' C.M.S.P. said tautly. 'They may have filled that little hole with delayed action or tickers, and you know what that will mean if they start going off in the middle of a convoy. So—into battle!'

First they thoroughly swept the centre of the Gap. Mahoney was right. It took three long nights of frustrating, temper-fraying sweeping to clear it almost a yard at a time.

Moored mines were mixed with devilish cunning right in the path of any electric sweepers attempting to clear the magnetic and acoustic mines.

Sweeps were blown out of the water with exasperating frequency and poor *Harvester*, the drifter, had a harassing time beyond description, either exploding mines by rifle-fire in the first pale light of dawn, or ranging alongside heaving trawlers to ship new gear over.

Almarina limped back to Base leaking like a basket, with steam gushing from a dozen seams in her boilers after two mines had gone up close to her stern. She was getting her sweep in preparatory to making a turn and must have dragged two together. They went off with a colossal roar, deluging her with solid water. Haley, looking astern, saw her disappear and it seemed a lifetime before he discerned her bow

252

coming through the flurry of water and debris.

A fault in her electric sweep spelled the doom of *Penguin*. Her mine went off under her stern also. She lifted up slowly, settled down and went on settling down with a grim persistence until only her bow and bridge remained. The men had plenty of time to get away and were on their way to a drifter when she gave her final farewell curtsy and slid under, so gently that she scarcely disturbed the water.

Another L.L. trawler, an old Aberdeen ship which had defied the North Sea for nearly thirty years, met a more violent end. An overlooked floater, possibly one which had broken away from its mooring in the gales, blew her bow off in one flat, shattering blow. She went in less than a minute with another shriller blast as the cold water met her boilers. By a miracle the loss of life was small—only two men—because like all mine-sweepers, they were either on watch or, if catching a cat-nap, were on the engine-room casing.

Four days saw the back of the field broken. Four days of uneasy steaming close to the cliffs, watching every aircraft during the few hours of grey day and four nights of steady soul-destroying sweeping.

'And that makes it worth while, I suppose,' Booth said huskily as he leaned over the bridge, peering into the black night through his binoculars.

Haley forced his weary eyelids apart and followed suit.

Creeping past them, without a glimmer of light to show they were there, went dark bulk after bulk as a convoy steamed along the route.

'If they had tried it last night a couple of them would have stumbled over the doorstep,' Booth went on.

'They wouldn't have come through last night. They would have been turned back. They came on because Base signalled "Channel swept",' Haley countered wearily.

'Four nights of sheer, bloody torture, two ships gone and another damaged so that somebody could say, "Channel

253

swept," somebody sitting on his backside in an office ashore. . . .'

'You're talking nonsense, Number One. It had to be swept; somebody had to do it. That somebody was us. Who passes the signal that it was done is quite immaterial. We did it . . . and that'—he gestured unseen in the darkness towards the line of ships sliding silently by—'that makes it worth it.'

It took a couple of weeks to clear completely the field and although the hills ashore were still covered with a thick, frozen mantle of snow and the wind, light but steady, was bitterly cold a pale sun shone nearly all the time, and they had the whole phase of a moon.

Twice at night-time they were shelled by the big guns from the opposite side as they groped after the extreme fringe of the minefield, and once a raiding E-boat came close enough to be shot at.

'If I had Meredith here now I'd give him a free hand to wander about out there,' Regan said thoughtfully in one of their few short stays alongside the quay. 'The Hun is not going to like us clearing up all his naughty mines. He'll be over as soon as this moon has gone.'

Mahoney held the same opinion and reduced night sweeping to a minimum, concentrating his small force into a series of screening patrols.

'Heaven help you if E-boats come over bent on real mischief,' he told his little group of Commanding Officers. 'They'll blow you out of the water. We should have at least four destroyers here for the outer patrols, but the Big House says "no", so we must make do with trawlers.'

'Somewhat cheaper, speaking in terms of losses,' Regan offered drily.

'What economists would call "sparsely populated",' Haley said.

'Under-populated,' *Golfitt*'s C.O. amended.

'We'll concentrate on patrols and try to cut the mine-

254

laying down to a minimum. In this weather they don't like relying on aircraft; their accuracy is open to doubt. So long as the E-boats you meet are minelaying you won't have much of a fight, but if they bolster them with gunboats you'll have a bellyful.' Mahoney looked at the group. 'Did you say something, Regan?'

'Yes, sir. I was toying with the idea of inviting Meredith down here with his new battleship. It strikes me it is just his meat.'

'Meredith will get all the meat he wants in the Atlantic. The sinkings are appalling. It's the same story. Not enough ships—not enough. Talking won't help. Good luck.'

Outside the Base Regan shrugged into the collar of his thick bridge coat. 'Cold, but brisk. Feel like a walk?'

The iron-hard roads rang under their feet until they reached a stile at the entrance to a valley. Regan and Haley paused and looked back at the deep V of steel-grey water visible between two cliffs.

'That's it. There's the arena. Looks peaceful enough, doesn't it? Peaceful until the gladiators start scuffling about.'

'*Morituri te salutamus,*' Haley murmured.

'Bit morbid, but it fits. "We who are about to die, salute thee." Will that do, my erudite captain?'

'It will pass, fellow gladiator.'

Gradually Haley saw which way they were heading and confirmed this when they rounded a bend. He saw in front of him the little church with the village clustered round it and beyond, through the leafless trees, the grey manor house.

'Are we going visiting?'

Regan nodded. 'That I have in mind. We've just drifted this way. I promised to bring you along one day. This is it.'

Progress was slow. It seemed as every body in the village knew Regan. He stopped to tickle a well-wrapped-up child shyly peeping over a gate, exchanged a few words with its mother, got as far as the local shop, brazenly accused the apple-faced woman, to her huge delight, of mixing sand with her sugar and paused outside a wheelwright-cum-joiner's place from behind the doors of which came sounds of feverish activity.

The old man who opened the half-door cackled in a high-pitched laugh when he saw Regan. 'It's me prisoner again. Half a jiffy while I load me gun.'

' "The bush",' Regan introduced briefly. 'Stalked me like a Red Indian, had me dying of fright for an hour, and him with blackberry trees wrapped round him.'

'Blackberry trees!' the old man squeaked scornfully. 'It was a bit of blackthorn, and blackberries don't grow on trees. And how is life?'

But eventually, travelling hopefully like Stevenson's tramp, they arrived at the gates leading to the big house.

Great Oaks. Haley read the modest little square stone set in the solid gateway. A snug, compact creeper-covered lodge guarded the entrance to the long oak-bounded drive and Regan, after a reasonable pause waiting for an answer to his ring, opened the heavy iron gate and they walked up the drive.

Mrs. Lambert's heart-warming welcome affected Haley more than he cared to admit; more than he could analyse accurately. He found Regan's description of her fitted like a glove. Although her hair, piled on the top of her head in a curiously attractive way, was white, her figure and movements were youthfully lithe.

Soon there were tea-things laid before them as they sat in front of a large, arched fireplace, and Haley had the odd feeling that, despite the fire, and the hard-packed snow outside, spring was not far away. Possibly it was the glint from the pale winter sun creeping through the flowered curtains, or the warm tints of the furnishings.

Once again he laughed at the story of the arrest of Regan by the villagers.

'I am still not certain in my mind whether he was scared, or merely teasing us,' Mrs. Lambert said.

'I was scared, all right. Who wouldn't be?' Regan said, stretching himself luxuriously. 'There she was with a fierce glint in her eyes, a longing for blood in her soul, and a double-barrelled gun sticking in me throat.'

'It was empty and you knew it, and I was trembling like a leaf. We thought you were all parachutists come to wipe us out.'

After tea Mrs. Lambert showed Haley round the house, in which modern amenities had been skilfully embodied in order not to spoil its more ancient and more dignified features.

'It goes back nearly five hundred years, always in the Lambert family. Originally they had an estate in Scotland also, which might explain why most of the Lambert wives have been Scots.'

'And you have kept up the sequence?'

'Yes. I'm from Aberdeen, although I thought that long residence south had taken away my accent.'

'It's an intonation rather than an accent.' Halcy chuckled. 'You should meet my First Lieutenant. He has a soft spot for Aberdeen—and memories of some quite modest conquests there.'

Mrs. Lambert was thoughtful. 'I've heard a little about him. Lieutenant Regan has mentioned him. Is he getting over the loss of his friend?'

Haley shrugged. 'He is quieter, keeps more to himself, but . . . Well, he's young and . . .'

'And we imagine that you young people never permit your wounds to go deeply, or to hurt mortally, and we are so wrong. Youth doesn't go under quite so quickly but it can feel just as deeply, and just as long.'

Haley felt that she was musing out loud, was finding a reason, even an excuse, for something other than Booth's problem. Confirmation came in the next few seconds.

257

She accepted a cigarette from him and after he had lit it she said evenly: 'I tried to place a young one's problem on a plane of my devising, and I was wrong. Oh, so wrong!' She walked a little way along the corridor before speaking again. 'I was selfish, too, and that is even worse.'

'And now you have discovered that, you have put it right?'

She tilted her head and a bleak look came over her face. 'Only partly, I'm afraid, but I hope to . . .' Suddenly she shrugged her shoulders. 'Unpardonable of me. I'm trying to unload my problems on you, and you have enough, surely. Come, I'll show you some of the history of Great Oaks. It stood out against Cromwell, you know. The lady of the house then was quite a character. She refused to surrender it to the Roundheads, armed her few servants and withstood a siege. I've no doubt she used a gun herself. What are you chuckling at?'

'You seem to think she was no end of lass because she took a gun to a Roundhead, and you were prepared to do just that yourself, except that you took one to a squarehead and a crazy Irishman.'

Mrs. Lambert laughed. 'But I was petrified with fear, especially when the men said they had caught another.'

'Probably she was, too.'

'Possibly. Well, this is the lady.'

They stopped before a dark painting, a portrait of an aquiline-nosed, haughty woman who seemed to stare out from the frame with a question hovering on her lips.

'I can imagine her doing it,' Haley said, after a long scrutiny. 'She is what Booth would call a "ten-minute egg".' He intercepted Mrs. Lambert's querying glance and interpreted the Americanism. She gave a little trilling laugh.

'I must try that one on Hank. He is a pilot in the All-American Eagle Squadron of the R.A.F. and visits us in between turns of duty. Yet, from all we know of her, she was a gentle creature given to doing much good. Possibly she kept that face for appearance sake, just to create an atmosphere, an illusion of being—what did you call her?— a ten-minute egg.'

After showing Haley some Cromwellian relics and other pictures of the Lamberts through the ages she showed him into the oak room.

'Everything in here, panelling included, has been made from oak cut on the estate,' she said. 'That is not all. When a Lambert is born an acorn is pushed into the ground. When one is married, oak, cut when he is born, is made into something for him. There are Lambert oak tables all over the world. Some of them sailed in the old wooden warships. The avenue of oaks was planted when Great Oaks was built—one hundred and fifty of them. Many have been cut, but if you care to count them you will find that there are still one hundred and fifty trees there.'

As they walked out of the room she turned to Haley and said, with a bright smile, 'It is what Hank calls "traadition".' She gave the first syllable a long-drawn value with a slightly nasal twang.

'A growing monument to faith, too, surely.'

Mrs. Lambert stopped. One finger poised over her bottom lip, then a gentle smile crept across her face. 'Do you know, I've never heard it called that but I suppose it is.'

Haley told her of Regan's conception of it and as he talked she kept her grey eyes on him in an unblinking stare. When he finished she breathed: 'Wonderful . . . wonderful! It helps me enormously.'

Regan had only a hazy idea of what she was talking about but realised that somehow the picture of Great Oaks standing for an undying faith in something had shaken, if not cleared away, some doubts in her mind.

'It certainly is a wonderful thought in these days of shifting, unstable values,' he said steadily.

She put a hand on his arm. 'If ever you feel your faith

259

being shaken, come here, walk among the trees and have it restored. Promise?'

Back on board *Solan*, as they were having a final drink, Regan said: 'That's a great little family, the Lamberts. There's a daughter—she's a Wren—and a daughter-in-law for you to meet. Sometimes I get a hint of a family tragedy behind it all.'

That night Haley spent some time lying in his bunk, his mind idling from one event of the day to another, before he dropped off to sleep. Patrols . . . nights of weary-eyed vigilance . . . great oak trees crashing down . . . being made into tables . . . the young have their problems . . . was he young? Or did he come into the aged class? 'We who are about to die, salute thee.'

10

The late winter gales brought lashing storms which washed away the packed snow in dirty yellow streams. They also complicated the night patrols, which became hours of weary tossing and rolling, with the ships groaning every second as they painfully pitched and tossed.

Booth voiced an intricate complaint.

'If we got somewhere it would mean something, but as soon as we get there we have to turn round and start back. And so it goes on. Nobody but a fool, or a ship on patrol, would be out in this stuff.'

It certainly seemed that nobody the other side was stupid enough to attempt precise navigation between minefields, known and guessed at, to arrive at a point at which to start laying more mines. Nevertheless the British kept on patrolling, climbing the short, steep punishing seas, thrusting a dripping bow into a creaming sea, shipping it on board in a rolling crash, listening to it rushing madly along the deck, listening to the clatter of the flood doors monotonously clanking as they swung open to release the water from the decks. For days on end everything was wet. Mess decks were swimming with a foot of scummy water which sloshed to and fro searching nooks and crannies for hitherto ignored cigarette-ends, bits of paper, grease, until the whole was a slimy flood.

Haley's room fared a little better than the wardroom, which was dripping wet and had all movable furniture lashed into one corner. Haley watched a seaman stagger forrard with a large tin of something which steamed, and again he marvelled at the grim persistence of the silent cook who never seemed to fail to produce something hot, something unidentifiable, but something comforting from the small steel box which was his domain.

Once, as Clay arrived on the bridge, just after the dawn of a wild spindrift-lashed day, with some hot coffee, Haley asked him how it was done. Clay shook his head. 'I don't know, sir. I just don't know. The little bastard just shuts himself away in the galley. His stove roars away red-hot, and he opens up the lee door for a while, dishes out what he's made, and shuts himself away again until the next grub time comes round.'

It was *Jacinth*, the fighting ship with the pugnacious aura of Meredith still vaguely surrounding it, which ran into trouble, yet lived up in part to her reputation. After a wild day of lashing wind, a sudden calm came with a fiery red sunset lighting an angry sky. The sea dropped from its foam-crested, racing violence to an uneasy oil swell in a few hours, a promise of more turbulence to come.

And the enemy seized the opportunity to slip three or four *E*-boats over under cover of first darkness.

Jacinth, rolling heavily with *Golfitt* not far astern, surprised the first pair, illuminated them with star-shell and went into action. The captain who succeeded Meredith was an experienced minesweeping officer but lacked the Welshman's instinct for detecting a trap or a feint. Taking *Golfitt* with him, he wallowed and rolled along the length of his patrol after firing some short, futile bursts at the *E*-boats, completed the beat, and returned blissfully unaware that other *E*-boats had slipped in behind him and had laid the foundation of another minefield across the Gap with several short sticks of mines.

It was *Golfitt*, using her hammer purely as a precaution in the morning as she moved away from the patrol area towards the protection of the cliffs, who set up two mines in an oblique line across the Gap.

Mahoney's bitter snarl was something to hear as he whipped the other ships out to sweep. He boarded *Solan* in sheltered waters for a quick conference of C.O.s.

'I'm not blaming anybody. A man is just as good as his best and *Jacinth* and *Golfitt* did their best. They beat off some *E*-boats and finished their patrol. But Meredith would have fired off every star-shell he had and would have been darting all over the show. Still, there it is; a field God knows how big and a convoy comes through tomorrow night.' He looked at the little group of Commanding Officers. 'You'll have to use every moment you can. If visibility is down, use your own judgment and sweep by day.' He smacked his hand down hard on the desk. 'But Sweep Those Mines. I want no excuses.'

'Just like that, like sweeping crumbs off a table,' Regan said. 'We'll split it. You take *Jacinth* and I'll take *Golfitt*. When they go in we'll take *Almarina* and *Morning Glory*, if they'll float, and we stay out until the job is done.'

Two hours before the convoy was due through the Gap the four ships swept down in line abreast for a quick last search, a manœuvre of no mean performance in view of the twisting, unlit channel along which they had to go while each ship was little more than a vague dark bulk on the beam of the other.

They swung away to the south of the convoy route and lay, engines stopped, rolling in the swell. To the north of them crept a long line of shapes, unseen, proceeding along at a steady seven knots—the convoy passing through.

Completely clearing the field took longer. To begin with, the weather broke, short, furious secondary gales which blew for twenty-four hours, paused, filled their lungs and blew again, lashing the ships, aided by their consort, blinding rain.

Regan sent *Golfitt* and *Jacinth* in for stores, bunkers and a needed rest, and *Solan* and *Arandite* started off on their patrols, each confident of meeting a relief ship when the first leg had been completed.

Arandite reached the end of her patrol length and was swinging round to return along the beat when tracer bullets cut a fiery trail well ahead of her bows. There were sudden flashes, another line of tracer cut in from a wide angle and Haley heard the deeper note of a quick-firing gun of some description.

There was no need for him to sound Action Stations. As he swung *Arandite* towards the focal point of the firing he heard the quick rattle of machine-guns being cocked, and saw shadowy figures moving near the 12-pounder platform. Soon he was in closer range. He saw the flash from guns and heard the whine of shells and the higher pitched sobbing wheeew of lighter missiles.

'*Solan!* She's run into a real ambush. They're putting up a show this time,' he said to Booth. 'Open up as soon as you see target.'

Haley strained his eyes through the binoculars, trying to determine a darker, more solid, portion of the darkness which might be a ship.

'What the devil is he doing out here?' he queried to the bridge at large. 'He should have been at least five miles away now, and well to the south-east.'

'Picked 'em up on the hydrophone and jumped them,' Booth offered. 'There's one! Fine on the starboard bow.' His voice soared up to a cracking yell as he continued: 'Green 25, shoot!'

The 12-pounder barked, the star-shell fused for two thousand yards, burst and shed a brilliant pink-white light over a large area. Streaking across it they saw the low, lean hull of an *E*-boat. Clay got in two quick shots, cursing his gun crew meantime, and vaguely Haley wondered how he found it possible to concentrate on his sights and curse. The machine-guns, loaded almost entirely with tracer, sent their parabolic

264

lines screaming towards the racing boat, each line converging to a point near the enemy craft. Suddenly it swung stern on to them and disappeared as quickly as if somebody had wiped it out, like rubbing a chalk drawing off a blackboard.

'Ducked behind a smoke-screen. Keep shooting—increase your range four hundred yards each shot,' Haley snapped. Astern and to port of him now he could still hear the crackle of machine-guns, the occasional bark of a 12-pounder, and a fresh radiance lit up the sea as a new star-shell soared and burst.

'They're belting away at *Solan*.' Booth said, peering over the after-end of the bridge. 'I can't see her, but—There she is! THERE SHE IS—THEY'VE GOT HER—SHE'S ON FIRE!'

Haley leapt to his side, followed the vague outline of Booth's arm and saw a sudden tongue of flame come from the trawler's bridge a mile or two away from him.

'Hard a port . . . midships . . . steady.' The Cox'n's emotionless voice repeated the orders and *Arandite*'s lifting bow pointed towards the other ship. Haley saw a flash from her 12-pounder and tried to pick up her fall of shot as a clue to the whereabouts of the attacking *E*-boats, but failed.

All at once the burning trawler, so clearly lit up by the flash of her gun and the glare from the burning bridge, suddenly faded away. Shreds of mist streaked across their own bow and they smelled a peculiar, acrid smell. Almost before they could identify it they were out of the enshrouding mist.

'*E*-boats' smoke-screen. But where the hell are they?' Haley swung his glasses in a quick arc.

A high-pitched yell came from the port machine-gunner: 'On the beam, sir.' In the same instant he opened fire, hosing a shadowy, low shape which came out of the smoke-screen at almost the same time as *Arandite*, and not more than two or three hundreds away. It was travelling full out doing three of four miles to *Arandite*'s one. Quick orders followed and the 12-pounder snapped in two shots close enough to

265

spray the *E*-boat's bridge. It swung round in a quick circle and dodged behind the smoke-screen once more but got in a long, and accurate, burst from a gun on its bow a second before it disappeared. They heard the shots hit somewhere after and saw the faint flashes from the bursting projectiles.

'Watch him! He'll be through that screen again anywhere,' Haley rapped. 'They mean business tonight.'

He raised his glasses to scrutinise the burning trawler and saw that three jets of water were arcing up from the deck over the burning bridge.

'Switch the minesweeping lights on for five seconds . . . off . . . then on again. We don't want her shooting at us,' Haley ordered Larkin. 'Any sign of them?'

'No, sir, but I can hear one drumming away behind the screen.'

'Put a star-shell over it, short range.'

The shell whined away into the dark and burst behind the screen, showing that it was a long, curving, low-lying, tenuous shroud encircling the two trawlers in a wide half-circle.

It was the stern machine-guns which gave tongue first, firing straight back along their wake.

'Two of them,' Booth shouted. The perfect *E*-boat ambush. They would split as they raced in, and with her limited armament training aft the trawler was easy meat. If she turned she was beam-on for a raking fire from both and stood a chance of being torpedoed. This was it.

'Can't train the gun,' Clay boomed appealingly. Both beam machine-guns tried short bursts but the tail of tracer slipped harmlessly well to each side of the *E*-boats, now racing in with twin plumes of water climbing high from their knife-edged stems.

Haley strove to evolve a manœuvre which would give him a fighting chance. He would wait until they split, swing with them and give of his best at one of them. He watched them through his binoculars closely as they were outlined in sharp relief against the dying star-shell, decided that the one edging to port would be his best bet. The order to swing to port was hovering on his lips when he heard a 12-pounder crack and in a second or two saw a column of water climb steeply up in front of the *E*-boats. Crack! Another column climbed; tracer ripped across the dark water at right angles to their course, started hitting the *E*-boat on his starboard quarter. His own stern machine-gun spoke again, firing at the craft on his port quarter.

Haley saw a lot of fireflies dancing in his glasses. Almost immediately they became elongated, and he heard the bullets scream over the bridge, and hollow thumps came from the funnel. He ducked behind the futile cover of the painted canvas surround as some bullets ripped through it with faint thuds. As he stood up again he saw both *E*-boats swing away, their stern wash, nearly as high and as long as the boats themselves, disappearing in a trailing, lengthening tail of smoke-screen. In seconds they were gone.

He looked off towards his beam to see if he could sight the ship which had joined in at right angles, but darkness defeated him.

As he swung his glasses to the burning trawler Larkin said: 'That ain't *Solan*, it's *Almarina*.' He turned to Haley. 'It's *Almarina* what's on fire, sir.'

Arandite steamed a tight circle round the other ship; there came a twinkle of blue light from a spot well away from the bridge. Larkin answered:

'Fire under control. *Morning Glory* is out there somewhere looking for *Solan*.'

At the end of an hour, after a widening search, which identified *Morning Glory* as the rescuer, *Arandite* considered the *E*-boats had gone and Haley closed in for more details from *Almarina*.

Almarina had left *Morning Glory*; each was to search for its Senior Officers to join them in patrol. They came on the three *E*-boats which had apparently waited until *Solan* and

Arandite had completed their first leg, then moved in to lay their mines. *Morning Glory* hit one hard with her second shot, saw it limp away and went after it. 'That was the first one we shot at dodging away in a smoke-screen,' Booth volunteered. The two others jumped *Almarina* and set her bridge on fire. They were working the Indian trick—a smoke-screen in a circle—and dashing through it at intervals when Haley showed up.

While they were clearing up the loose ends over their loud-hailers one of *Arandite*'s look-outs sighted something in the dark. There came a flashing challenge and *Solan* joined the throng.

Daylight showed *Almarina* with a badly burned bridge and a lot of holes above water, but her steering gear was intact. *Arandite* was similarly well punctured, but not seriously.

'And a nice way to have a fight,' Booth said rather pleasantly. 'Nobody hurt. We'll leave a message on a buoy inviting them over again some dark night.'

Solan had been singularly quiet after a few inquiring signals but when the ships were steaming slowly close under the cliffs *Arandite* received a signal which startled Haley.

'Explain why you were two miles off patrol last night at 2300 hrs. I estimate your position was . . .'

'He's right, too; we were about there,' Haley said with a puzzled frown. 'But he knows what we were doing. Damn it, we were scrapping with *E*-boats.'

He embodied those facts in a reply, but the first signal puzzled him. Was this to be another instance of Regan being tired, sending a scorching signal and forgetting it after some sleep. He remembered the message which had sent Meredith flaring over the top in a temper.

His answer came when he entered harbour a few days later. It came from Mahoney. After greeting Haley he said: 'Sit down. Now, this kind of war, minesweeping and anti-mining patrols, has one object in view—to sweep up mines and if possible prevent them from being laid. Judging from this'—he touched a wide open chart—'three of you enjoyed a damned good scrap and left the Gap and twelve miles of fairway unwatched.'

'But, sir, I saw a ship on fire and thought . . .'

'That was the problem of *Almarina* and *Morning Glory*; they were in company on their way to patrol—a patrol you left unguarded—and in doing so nearly ran into an ambush.'

'I thought *Solan* . . .'

'*Solan* remained on patrol and did not find any of you for more than a hour. Time enough for *E*-boats to lay a formidable array of mines.'

'Very well, sir.' Haley considered it impolitic to argue although he was seething with temper at what he felt was an injustice.

Regan had reported the details of the fight as gathered from the other ships, and had reported that they were well away from the patrol area. In any event the movements of the ships would be detected on the screen at Operations ashore, but Haley doubted if the fact that the fight took place off the patrol area would have been stressed unless Regan had done so.

He passed *Solan* when returning on board and sat in his room for more than an hour considering his approach to Regan, something he was determined to do although he recognised that as Senior Officer *Solan*'s captain was quite in order.

Booth broke in on his unpleasant reverie, knocking at his door to report that the ship was all stored and ammunition-stocked again. After making his report Booth lingered.

'*Solan* bumped into a couple of *E*-boats last night,' he said. 'Her Number One says they were all shaped up for a minelaying run at the far end of the beat . . .' He paused, fiddled with his cap, and added: 'Our beat.'

Haley made no answer, but he flicked a quick glance at

Booth, standing by the door quite expressionless. Go on, young man, add your petty criticisms. Say you think it was wrong of me to leave the beat to help a ship being attacked and on fire. Go on, say it! Speak up! It was as if he had willed Booth to speak.

Booth sat down on the breakwater in the doorway, twisting his cap in his hands. After fiddling with the badge for a moment he looked up. '*Solan* saw the *E*-boats at the same time as he saw *Almarina* on fire. He went after the *E*-boats, but they ducked away behind smoke. *Solan* chased 'em for a while, then came back at a rate of knots.' He leaned back against the open door. 'They thought it was we who had caught a packet.' Booth suddenly slapped a streak of dust off his cap. 'They thought we were on fire . . . and they went beetling off after *E*-boats. To hell with you, Jack, I'm after glory and my feet are dry!'

'*Solan* was quite right.' Haley jerked it out. The jagged fragments had dropped into place. 'I would have done the same.'

'We didn't. We thought it was *Solan* on fire and we went in.'

'And left the beat open for a minelaying raid—minelaying which *Solan* prevented. Furthermore, we had our supply of *E*-boats laid on, right on the spot.'

Booth grinned. 'They were there, all right. It was what the steward calls a "reet good do". If they come any closer Clay is going to fix a bayonet to the 12-pounder.'

Haley was only half listening. He was trying to formulate in his mind an approach to Regan. He could see that had he gone on board *Solan* when he passed her when returning to his own ship there might have been recriminations, possibly a row, and he felt glad that he had decided to think things over.

'That's an idea,' he said vaguely. 'You might indent for some cutlasses. You can lead the boarding party.' Haley got up decisively. 'I'm going on board *Solan*.'

Regan was ashore but his First Lieutenant did the honours.

'Captain won't be long, sir. He said if you came on board I was to clap you in irons, fill you with gin and throw you down the bilges. Bear witness I'm trying to follow out orders. Say when, sir.'

When they were settled the Number One said: 'Quite a battle you had, wasn't it. I've had a look at *Almarina*. Burned a bit about the bridge and a couple of men nicked, but all things considered she got off lightly. You breezed up just in time, they tell me.'

'Breezed up comes near to being the operative phrase. At one time a couple of them had got me just where they wanted. *Morning Glory* showed up just in time.' Haley looked at the smiling youngster sitting opposite him. 'How far did you chase your little party?'

'Not so far. We buzzed a few long-range shots at them.' He looked at the remains of his drink. 'The Old Man got into quite a flap. We heard the shindig, cut corners and saw what we thought was you on fire. Then we spotted the *E*-boats starting their sneak run. He wanted to . . . to sort of come over to you . . . and chase the Hun. . . . We belted back once we'd chased them off.'

Haley detected the slight note of defence. Behind the almost off-hand phrases he imagined the struggle Regan had had within himself. Go to *Arandite*'s assistance, or leave her to fight it out and chase the *E*-boats off what was Haley's patrol? He had it on the tip of his tongue to uphold Regan's decision when he heard *Solan*'s Commanding Officer speaking on deck, and heard him start to descend the companionway.

'Ha, ha! I spy strangers. I said "irons and down the bilges", Number One.'

'He fought desperately and overpowered me, sir,' the First Lieutenant grinned. 'So I settled for a gin. One for you, sir?'

Regan gave Haley a quick, penetrating look before accepting his drink.

'Been cohabiting with the intelligentsia?' Regan queried.

Haley nodded and smiled. 'I've been to the mat for the best of three falls with C.M.S.P. this morning.' Regan's eyebrows climbed slightly. 'And he won on a technical knockout,' Haley finished drily.

'Try to find some work to do, Number One; your conscience should be worrying you at the ease with which you get your money.' Regan wrinkled his nose up at his First Lieutenant. 'This ship looks like a perishing Jiddah pilgrim ship.'

Number One looked mildly indignant but took the hint.

Regan cut corners and went right to the root of the matter which was in both their minds. 'Mahoney doesn't miss a lot. After ten seconds of reading my report he wanted to know this and that about that and this. You were more than two miles off patrol, you know.' Regan's eyes were cold and staring.

Haley nodded. 'I know.' He settled down deeper in his chair. 'It was rather stupid. I realise that, but . . . well, I thought you had run into a spot of trouble, so . . .' He completed the sentence with a shrug.

Regan grinned and his eyes softened. Haley found the grin infectious and followed suit. 'By the same token, Lieutenant Regan, what in hell were you doing in MY patrol area?'

'Who's been sleeping in my bed?' Regan chuckled. ' "I thought you had run into a spot of trouble, so . . ." ' The mimicry ended with a shrug.

They sat looking at one another without speaking and from them both emanated a growing warmth which fused them together into a common bond, a bond of deeper friendship which needed no words to explain it.

It was Regan who broke the silence. 'I've been finding out why *Almarina* and *Morning Glory* ran into that lot. It

272

seems they cut corners to meet us and ran into three *E*-boats waiting until we had met and gone on our patrols again. At the other end of the beat were three more. You would have met them about half-way along your beat—on your own.' He pursed out his bottom lip. 'That would have been fun, wouldn't it?'

Silence reigned again for a short while as they visualised what might have happened.

'They certainly mean business,' Haley said at last. 'Two stabs in three nights.'

Regan nodded. 'C.M.S.P. has worked out a variation. It's to be one-ship patrols with irregular timing, never fewer than three in or around the Gap so that they won't be able to work out a time-table. Search behind buoys, alter speeds, turn back on your course—anything except the regular half speed up and down the beat.'

He poured out two more drinks and handed Haley one. 'Anybody who runs into trouble from now on will have to sweat it out until the other ships are certain that it is not a feint to draw them off. Did C.M.S.P. mention this to you?'

Haley grinned. 'No. We discussed other things and I left rather hurriedly.'

Regan searched in his pockets and tossed over a sheet of paper to Haley. 'Have you seen that?'

Haley read it. It ran :

In view of the recurring attacks by *E*-boats on minesweeping trawlers while doing patrols [to blazes with that; it is we who do the attacking, Haley thought] Flag Officer has impressed on the Admiralty the necessity for additional armament. The Admiralty agrees that the standard armament of one 12-pounder and three .303 machine-guns is scarcely adequate to provide protection against aircraft and *E*-boats and trawlers will enter dock as duties permit for fitting of twin .5 machine-guns or .8 Oerlikon guns. Ratings from each ship are to be detailed to attend short course under direction of Auxiliary Vessels Gunnery Officer.

Haley read it through twice. 'Such a nice lot of words, eh? I like the modest bit about three .303 machine-guns. How many have you got actually?'

'Three,' Regan replied flatly. 'Three officially—nine actually. And you?'

'Seven. Twin point fives? Isn't that a two-man gun, something like a miniature pom-pom?'

'I believe so, but I fancy the point eight Oerlikon. It's like the cannon job the Hun 'planes have.'

And they fell to a technical discussion about ways and means of wangling the guns of their choice. And ultimately got them so sited that there was no arc of the circle round the ship on which two twin guns could not bear. For a small ship, plus the unofficial machine-guns, it was a formidable armament.

Booth, in a rare moment of mathematical enthusiasm, worked out that (including Noisy's pet, which Haley had never seen, diplomatically closing his eyes to its existence, but which he knew was an ex-army Bren) the ship could in a moment of anger put nearly four thousand shots into the air in one minute.

'With most of that tracer we can compete with Blackpool for illuminations,' he added complacently.

11

'A little accountancy over the past few months shows that the Hun has had a dead loss in this section of his business if we weigh ships mined against an estimate of mines laid.'

It was Mahoney speaking. He had circling him in his room in Base most of his Commanding Officers. They were a fair cross-section of the Wavy Navy, expanding every day and with startling clarity showing that scratch any Englishman and just below skin deep you will find a sailor.

Included in the little group of officers were men who in peace-time were in banking, law, journalism, motor sales, teaching and insurance. But the dark blue brass-bound uniform with its traditions, the Service for which it stood, had fused them into as compact a single-minded group of officers as one could find anywhere in the Navy.

'There has been nothing spectacular, but the steady grind shows a splendid profit. Let's hope it keeps that way. It hasn't been easy for you fellows. We are still grossly undermanned, but other ships are coming—sometime. In the meantime, keep ploughing.'

Haley murmured something to Regan.

'Did you say something, Haley?'

'Yes, sir. I remembered something Meredith once said about minesweeping being closely akin to ploughing and I thought of the bit, "the weary ploughman homeward plods his way".'

'You might try "the ploughman homeward plods his weary way",' Bolter, the schoolmaster, the new Commanding Officer of *Almarina*, showed a twinkle far back in his eyes and he stroked his chin as he cast his doubt upon the waters.

'Which is correct?' Lister, *Jacinth*'s barrister-cum-yachtsman-cum-captain, asked earnestly. He had a deep, suave voice and Haley had frequently thought he would like to hear him working on the flexible minds of a jury.

'Haven't the foggiest,' Bolter said. 'I believe it can be twisted round a few dozen ways.'

'What DO you teach your small boys?' Lister asked severely. He and Bolter, the two academics of the mine-sweeping force, were great friends and were always flaying one another in public debate.

'A few things which they write on walls—a little lower down than when you did it, possibly—and a little dog-Latin with which they ultimately bamboozle bemused clients for large fees.' Bolter was deadly sweet.

'We will discuss the point some other time.' Lister refused to be drawn. 'I think we will find that the accent should be on "dog".'

Mahoney joined in the general chuckle. He liked to hear his captains enjoying a mild slanging match, even at his bi-monthly conferences. He felt that they were at ease, and from such mental relaxation would frequently come a sound suggestion, or a constructive criticism, which would be still-born, stifled in a more formal talk.

'Whichever way you like it, it's ploughing away wearily, and that will be your lot for the coming winter. In the past summer we've worked very well with the shore screen. We know now the moment a group of *E*-boats leave the other side, and with the self-evident code the time-lag in informing you is down to seconds. You won't have to grope in the dark for them. . . .'

'No chance to ram then, sir?' Regan was deliciously bland and Lister coloured up profusely at the laughter the apparently innocent remark had provoked.

One dark morning a month or two back his young and rather inexperienced First Lieutenant had roused him from a cat-nap on the bridge with the news that an *E*-boat was crawling towards them. Still half asleep and fiercely gouging open his eyes, Lister peered through his glasses, saw an *E*-boat's bow wave only a few hundred yards ahead.

Two star-shells went winging on their way. The enemy was savagely sprayed with gunfire and Lister swung in to ram as the star-shells lit up the water. With only feet to spare he swung away from the battered bridge of a wreck, which at low tide was above the water and, in fairness, in the darkness did look like a motor craft as the seas broke over it in creaming whiteness. It was a heart-jarring moment; travelling at full speed *Jacinth* would have ripped the bottom off herself and would have gone down like a stone.

It was Haley who offered the blushing Lister some comfort.

'You are not alone in that, Lister,' he smiled. 'An escorting destroyer challenged your wreck the other morning, got no reply, and tore in with everything blazing. We were lying half a mile away and my Number One, who had the bridge, asked them if they had permission to knock our wrecks about. The destroyer was very terse.'

Lister gratefully retreated behind the laughter.

'Now, gentlemen, to arms. We've had an easy time through the summer and in the early autumn. We have, you know,' he reiterated against the murmur of disagreement. 'In fact it is two weeks since we exploded a mine in this sector and the Gap is the widest it has been since Dunkirk. That doesn't mean the Hun is going to leave it like that. So . . .'

And for the next hour the talk was of minesweeping and patrols, with everybody contributing something to be acclaimed or rejected in the light of experience.

Finally Mahoney stood up. 'There's too many of you for me to offer tea, but I think we'll adjourn to the Officers' Mess, where I've no doubt they have the wherewithal.'

277

Probably a similar conference was being held about the same time a bare twenty miles away across the water with a Korvette Kapitan, stiff and dignified, presiding and a Luftwaffe representative present, because that night the Base was heavily raided with fire bombs and land mines, while at sea a group of *E*-boats crept over under cover of an air-raid smoke-screen and amplified by their contribution the deadly sticks of mines put down by aircraft.

It was a grim-faced Mahoney who called a conference on *Solan,* and this time there was no joking.

'The Gap is closed, closed tight,' he said shortly. 'Nobody is to blame; it's just that they've won the last move. Glory, you were going on boiler-clean leave. It's postponed. I'll want every ship. You'll have to take a chance, if visibility is low, and sweep by day.' He allowed his eyes to run over the little group. 'The Hun isn't going to like this, so he'll make it as difficult as he can.

'Keep Maintenance posted on your requirements, enter harbour for bunkers at first daylight, those below two-thirds top up today, and you'll sail at 2200.'

A thin smile stole across his face. 'There was another item I was hoping to tell you—one of my little pre-*Gazette* and C.W. list secrets—which should have provoked a party. Still, here it is.' He stopped and lit a cigarette. 'Lieutenant Regan will be Lieutenant-Commander Regan, Temporary, R.N.V.R., as from a.m. tomorrow. Congratulations, Regan.' He thrust out his hand and Regan took it.

Regan survived the slaps on the back and the spate of 'yes-sirs' which they all tagged on to the shortest of sentences and soon the conference broke up. Haley and Regan went ashore for a couple of hours. There was not time for a walk out to Great Oaks but they cut inland, and neither of them broke the silence, each communing with his own thoughts.

'I hope this extra half-ring doesn't mean a move,' Regan said at last. 'At least, not immediately. I'm just beginning to like this place and to get used to it.'

Haley smiled wryly. 'I suppose the war is the same in any other place. We just think that our bit is tougher than any other. Remember Meredith's last letter?'

Regan nodded. Between the lines in the Welshman's last missive they had read that convoys in the Atlantic were undergoing a grim time.

'I doubt if any of us will go the whole war staying in one place. Promotions will follow—you'll probably get a half-ring soon—and kids who are now Subs will get command of our little ships.' Regan was staring out over the country as he mused. 'When this war started, the hidebound brass-sleeves would have been shocked at the thought of an R.N.V.R. officer being Senior Officer of an outfit.'

'The "volunteer" element is rapidly disappearing, judging by some of the youngsters coming along now. Lister's Number One is a typical specimen. He is a conscript, has had a fair education, was picked out for C.W., is commissioned, and I've never met a more indolent, insolent youngster in my born days. Lister should jump on him, good and hard.'

'*Golfitt*'s new lad is not so hot either—not a patch on the kid you should have had instead of Booth. Speaking of Booth, he seems to have brightened up slightly. I think you and I have the pick of the bunch so far as Number Ones go.'

Haley nodded. 'They're vintage, *circa* 1939–40. Booth is toying with a new love affair, I believe. He says little, but I fancy there is a Wren in the offing. . . .'

Regan chuckled. 'These youngsters take their beatings happily, don't they?'

'Yes, Grandpa.'

From then until the early winter it was a steady grind of patrolling and sweeping. Sometimes the enemy filled a hole in the field as soon as it had been swept, but grimly the little force stuck to the task.

By degrees the Gap was cleared and the edges of several permanent fields were trimmed down. Single-ship, irregularly-timed patrols brought occasional encounters with E-boats but these minor clashes became little more than coldly checking their run as they left their French bases according to wireless reports from the plot, timing their arrival and greeting them with a flurry of star-shell and tracer.

The E-boats, fitted with acutely sensitive hydrophones, picked up every move of the trawlers at several thousand yards range, so close combat was very rare.

It was Bolter who hit upon an effective form of counter-attack. After studying a number of W.T. reports he arrived at a formula based on what he called the hidebound Hun's meticulous regard for regularity. It certainly seemed that various Senior Officers in charge of E-boat groups did conform to a set pattern in their approach and put a virtual signature on their preliminary manœuvres before running in.

Bolter approached it as he would a mathematical problem, which in fact it was. On his first W.T. report that E-boats were leaving harbour he steamed full speed to a point well up-tide of where he estimated they would strike. He followed their progress from successive W.T. signals and by judicious touches of slow ahead allowed the tide to take him down so that he arrived silently at the Gap just as the first of the unsuspecting E-boats turned at right angles for a minelaying run.

Jacinth hit the first one with a frenzied burst of gunfire which took it completely by surprise, and followed this up with 12-pounder pursuing fire as it limped away behind a protective smoke-screen. There was no doubt that the E-boat was badly damaged; subsequent W.T. reports of its progress back to harbour showed that it was being carefully shepherded by the remaining boats and was travelling slowly.

And *Jacinth* resumed its patrol complacently.

It was a trick the other ships adopted frequently but without the conspicuous success achieved by *Jacinth*.

'If Meredith had been on it he would have had it in tow in ten minutes,' Regan said with bitterness. 'Lister looked on it as a problem, for which he found a solution, and he called it a day.'

'If Meredith—or you—had been there the other E-boats would have turned in protection and sunk you in less than ten minutes,' Haley argued. 'Lister did his job. How was he to know it wasn't a feint? Live up to your half ring, man!'

Regan grinned. 'It's difficult. The weight makes me feel humpbacked down to my calves. But I wish we could get one right in our sights like that, at less than a hundred yards, and him not knowing we were there.'

'You can have it all! I'm pleased if they push off home and write it off for the night.'

Nevertheless Haley and Regan tried the trick several times, Haley with Booth whinnying tensely from the chart table as he worked out the converging angles. Possibly it was tried too often and the Germans guessed the truth, wholly or partially.

They did manage to sow some mines, either from the air or from E-boats, or both, throughout the winter, their best night being that before Christmas Eve, a dirty, squally night with driving flurries of rain and sleet.

Arandite found the mines in the grey dawn and as visibility was low, both straight up and across the water, Haley signalled *Almarina*, his consort, and they swept through the day, rolling heavily but managing a dividend of nine mines, which went up with sullen roars and plumes of grey water.

'Just like the bloody Germans to put this lot in my stocking,' Clay boomed as they launched dan buoys from the reeling deck. 'I hope some sod puts a few outside their harbour for them to mix in with their puddings.'

'They're getting them, all right,' Booth said confidently. He was wet, cold, and in a bad temper. All being well, this morning should have ended their patrol and they would have been back in time to retrieve something from the wreck of Christmas. He had a party laid on ashore and was feeling anything but full of goodwill towards all men. 'Get the next one over without the wire being wrapped round it like . . . like . . .'

'Like a Christmas tree,' one of the seamen offered brightly.

'Like a bird-cage,' Booth snarled.

The short afternoon wore away and each time they approached the signal tower booth watched it for a twinkle of light which could mean that they were being called in and relieved. But just as darkness came he saw two or three plumes of smoke rising raggedly above the breakwater, and other sweepers came out to join them in a multiple-ships search sweep.

Booth kicked the signalman's lamp-box under the chart table and glowered at Larkin. 'Keep that damned box out of the way. You'll have somebody breaking his legs over it in the dark.'

'I 'ad it 'andy if me lamp was wanted,' Larkin explained in injured tones.

'Don't argue with me. Keep it under there where it belongs.'

Haley, crouching in the weather corner of the draughty bridge, smiled commiseratingly at the youngster's outbreak. He was wet, cold, had been on the bridge for most of the day and most of the previous night. And now it looked as if he was doomed to spend another night of slashing rain and sleet on the heaving, creaking bridge, trying to pierce the darkness with eyes which seemed to be ringed with red-hot wire.

Booth took a stand near a copper voice-pipe but after a

moment he shut the cover with a slam.

' "Holy night, peaceful night, calm and still," ' he raged. 'Some fool has got that going on the mess-deck radio. I'll bet it's the love-sick stoker with the red hair. "Calm and still." I ask you!' he demanded of the world at large. And there was nothing calm and still about the scene before them. A short, steep sea kept *Arandite* pitching like a see-saw. At the same time she gave a wicked little rolling wriggle which turned her progress into a series of corkscrew motions. As far as they could see, there was only a succession of froth-topped steep waves, each a dingy grey, now turning almost black as the last shred of daylight slipped out of the sky.

'Carry on, Number One, you haven't missed a thing yet.' Haley wedged himself in his corner and peered at Booth. 'You are expressing my feelings quite adequately.'

Booth grinned in the darkness. 'It is a bit bloody, though, isn't it, sir? Couldn't the Hun have given it a rest for just one day?'

'Expecting too much of him, aren't you? Where's *Almarina*, Bunts? Tell her to take R patrol; we'll take M. Rendezvous 0700 for sweeping orders.'

Larkin made the getting out of his lamp-box a terrific job, involving much grunting and stooping, but eventually he got the signal away. Another signal passed to *Solan* and *Arandite* settled down to her job.

'Wind's going to drop, I fancy. It will be flat calm by midnight.' Haley looked at the cloud-laden sky. 'Some more rain coming, and that will beat the sea down.'

'And blow up a real stinker by morning,' Booth growled.

' "God rest ye merry gentlemen, let nothing you dismay," ' Haley hummed softly, and grinned at Booth's snort.

The wind did drop to a gentle sigh with only occasional flurries of cold rain and sleet, and the hours dragged on the bridge. Neither Haley nor Booth attempted to get any sleep until midnight. After they had turned twice on their tracks,

283

and the W.T. was silent on *E*-boat reports. Haley felt he could no longer keep his eyes open. His head was nodding forward with a violent jerk and to get it upwards again required an effort which was almost painful.

'I'm going to get my head down for an hour, Number One. Call me when we are abeam of Number 12 buoy. I'll decide what to do then.'

'Aye, aye, sir.' Booth peered at the luminous face of his watch. 'Merry Christmas, sir. It's Christmas Day.'

'Same to you, with brass finishings. Don't forget, Number One, 12 buoy.'

For a short while after lying down in the small air-raid shelter on the bridge he felt curiously wide awake. Christmas Day . . . wonder what Madge . . . she'll have finished the little tree . . . always had a tree . . . she'd open his present . . . perhaps even now she was thinking. . . .

'Four *E*-boats 185 degrees Donset point, 12 miles, sir'— Larkin's hoarse whisper crashed through Haley's deep sleep —'and Number 12 buoy just coming abeam.'

Haley sat up stiffly. 'Have I been to sleep?'

'Yes, sir. Number One said to call you.'

Haley dragged himself up from the deep slumber, clambered to the front of the bridge and allowed the cold wind to play on his face. Booth's muffled voice came from the screen over the small chart table.

'Looks as if they are aiming for Starfish Bay. That's against tide, so we can't drift down on them.'

They listened to the flat, emotionless voice of the Wren ashore calling the movements over the W.T.

'. . . 185 degrees . . . six miles . . .'

'Steady course; they're about four miles off. We'll meet 'em in twenty minutes,' Booth said, emerging from behind the curtain. He grabbed the megaphone. 'Clay,' he called out to the bow, 'what have you got up the spout?'

It was a superfluous question. It was always star-shell ready at night, but Booth was too experienced an officer to take things for granted. He checked all guns which were manned and ready and reported to Haley, who was standing silent at the front of the bridge.

Suddenly the course of the *E*-boats altered. Booth ducked under the curtain again and in a moment called out: 'Looks as if they are going to sit behind those wrecks just east of Starfish Bay. Two miles off now, sir. Think they've picked us up?'

'Probably. We'll open up at 2,000 yards.'

Any hope of surprise was gone.

Arandite rocked on leaving behind her a wake over the heavy but unbroken swell. It was pitch dark and somewhere ahead of them were four or more enemy boats feeling their way through the same darkness. Their engines had no doubt been picked up by the *E*-boat hydrophones, but *Arandite*'s indifferent apparatus would get no burning noise from the *E*-boats until they were under 2,000 yards away.

'. . . 190 degrees . . . three miles . . .' The girl's voice came over the repeater on the bridge without a single alteration in the inflection, and Haley wondered if she knew that little over a mile separated the craft she was reporting from another ship racing to intercept.

'Hydrophones got 'em now, sir. Green 40.' Larkin accepted a message from another voice-pipe.

'Engage.'

Booth rapped out an order. They heard the star-shell whine away after the rap of the gun; another followed as they peered into the darkness. A sudden pin-point of light increased to a spreading white radiance as the star-shell burst. Higher and to the right of it another grew into a descending canopy.

'There they go!' Booth, eyes pinned to his binoculars, snapped an order down the voice-pipes to the machine-guns.

Allowing for the slight time-lag in the W.T. signals, Haley had estimated that when the star-shells burst he would see the *E*-boats at less than 1,000 yards away. As they were aware of his presence he could hope for nothing closer. And it was at about 800 yards that *Arandite*'s guns opened up. It was extreme range for the .303 weapons but their flow of tracer looked impressive and the heavier Oerlikon cannon shells were capable of doing serious damage to the thin hulls of the *E*-boats at that range.

'Damned smoke-screen again,' Haley growled as they saw in the bright light of the star-shells a wisp of misty refuge spread quickly across the water as the *E*-boats swung behind the screen.

'I saw some Oerlikon hitting the second one and I think we sprayed his bridge with .303,' Booth claimed.

'Watch the plot; tell me which way they go,' Haley ordered. He raised his voice. 'Clay, keep pumping star-shell over. Start at Green 45, increase to 65 and finish at Green 90. Mix them 2,000 to 4,000.'

'Aye, aye, sir.'

'. . . 185 degrees . . . three miles. . . .' The girl's voice threaded through the darkness.

'Going away from us, sir. About Green 50, more than a mile away.' Booth's muffled voice came from the chart table.

They were into the first fringe of the smoke-screen. Although they could barely see its twisting, tenuous shapes in the faint light from the distant star-shell they could smell it —acrid, throat-biting.

'Last shell off at 4,000, sir,' Clay hailed from the 12-pounder.

'Check, load and wait, 2,000 yards.'

'Going away fast now, sir; two miles. . . .'

'. . . . 185 degrees . . . four miles.'

Haley made a quick calculation. Booth, who could see the *E*-boats, and the girl working from a plot ashore, were differing by only half a mile—little more. It's going to be hard for you to get through now without being shot up.

We've got you taped, mister, taped from the time you cast off in Calais. . . .

Crash! The bridge was momentarily lit up as if for a flash-light photograph. Haley heard Booth give a smothered exclamation and the canvas screen over the chart table billowed violently. Larkin cannoned heavily into Haley, mumbling and spluttering something unintelligible. In a split second Haley realised what had happened. One of the E-boats, probably temporarily stopped after being hit, had stayed sheltering behind the smoke-screen and hidden from the shore plot by her closeness to the wrecks in Starfish Bay.

As he staggered round the bridge he saw her tearing to-wards him but on a course which would carry her clear of him by a hundred yards. Haley swung *Arandite*.

'Starboard three turns.'

Arandite's bow followed the arc being described by the E-boat to keep only her bow in line as target if the enemy sent off a torpedo.

'Why the hell aren't we shooting? Booth! BOOTH! Number One! Engage! Open fire!' Although he received no answer from the First Lieutenant the guns aft and on the starboard beam opened up, and the tracer from both craft made a fantastic criss-cross pattern over the dark water. From somewhere aft he could hear—and feel—cannon shell thudding into the ship. The 12-pounder barked sharply and a column of white water climbed suddenly up in front of the E-boat, then burst into white radiancy. Clay had let fly with star-shell, aiming it at the enemy craft.

Again the 12-pounder barked and a second later the high explosive shell burst above the racing motor-boat. Some-where beneath him he could hear subdued thuds merging with the harder crackling noise from the Oerlikon. The E-boat twisted round hard and went racing back over its course, and Haley swung *Arandite* to keep her bow pointing approximately towards it. As it altered course the E-boat

287

stopped firing, but resumed once its turn was complete. The tracer was short and hit the water. Then Haley heard it go overhead in a slobbering whine, which dropped to a harder clatter as the gunner altered his sights and started hitting again.

From somewhere aft he heard a deafening, crashing whistle of escaping steam and saw over the after-end of the bridge a white cloud climb from somewhere behind the funnel. He scrambled towards this, stumbling over Larkin who appeared to be reaching under the chart table for his signal lamp.

'Get out of the damned way,' Haley snarled. 'Number One! NUMBER ONE!' Where the hell has Booth got to? Why has he left the bridge? 'Larkin, find Number One for me at once.' Haley heard somebody struggle noisily across the steel casing below him, heard a steely clatter of a spanner, and the roaring, ear-shattering sound of steam died down. In comparison, the silence was almost cathedral-like.

'Hit main steam-pipe, sir,' a hoarse voice called up. 'Engine-room side of main valve.' Vaguely Haley recognised the voice of an engineman and at the same time he realised that *Arandite* was slowing down. There was no longer the slight tremble beneath his feet as the bridge vibrated from the drive of the engines.

'Let me know all the damage as soon as you can,' he called.

Wisps of acrid smoke-screen drifted past the bridge like a shredded veil. The guns were silent. Haley cupped his hands: 'Keep your eyes skinned, aft. Open up if you see anything.' He waited for the thin hail of acknowledgment and added, 'Is Number One aft with you?'

'No, sir.'

Haley moved towards the front of the bridge and stumbled over a figure crouched against the chart table. 'Bunts! Larkin, where are you?' He broke off as he caught a faint reflection of light from buttons coming from under the half-

288

open duffle coat. 'Number One! Booth, what's up?' He bent down and found Booth lying crouched on his side with part of the wrecked chart table across his chest. 'Christ, he's been hit!' he jerked out. 'Bunts! BUNTS!' There was no answer. He stooped, got his arms under Booth and partly lifted him from the wreckage. Booth moaned slightly. 'Got half the Channel . . . in . . . my face,' and he moaned again and went limp.

Haley let him go back slowly. He jumped to the front of the bridge. 'Clay, send one man to the bridge. One of your supply party. Number One has been hit.' He thought swiftly, reviewed his small force in his mind and quickly moved to the back end of the bridge: 'Aft! Send one man to the wheel. Keep two to your gun. Jump to it!' Then to the wheel voice-pipe: 'Cox'n, I'm having you relieved. Come up as quickly as you can.'

In turning away from the back end of the bridge he found another figure half in, half out, of the little steel air-raid shelter. It was Larkin, lying on his back breathing jerkily and stertorously. He did not respond when Haley spoke to him. A clatter of feet climbing the ladder behind him made Haley turn. It was a seaman.

'Find the torch—in a box on the front of the bridge; keep it shaded but see how badly Mr. Booth and Larkin have been hit. Oh, Cox'n'—to the shadowy figure which joined them—'you see how they are.' Haley staggered to the front of the bridge, every nerve in his body jangling and jumping as if galvanised by small electric shocks. Every little wave that overtoppled itself in a short line of white suddenly became the bow waves of an *E*-boat. He found that his fists were tightly clenched, that his hands were trembling, and that the backs of his legs felt curiously weak as if he were about to go down on his knees.

'Donset Point 185 degrees eight miles.' The girl's voice came monotonously from the repeater. 'One E B Donset point 185 degrees five miles,' she went on, her flat, emotionless voice seeping through the turmoil in his brain like the sound of a dripping tap. Subconsciously he analysed her information. If the first lot were three strong then they must all be on their way home, or going farther out for another attempt elsewhere. How many did she say at first? He searched his memory without success.

The girl provided the answer. 'Three E B 185 degrees Donset point eight-and-half miles.'

Behind him he heard the subdued murmur of voices as the Cox'n and his helper worked at Booth and Larkin. He turned and saw the faint glow of the hand-shaded torch reflect back from a dark, shining, red smudge on the bridge deck.

'How badly, Cox'n?' Haley snapped it out.

'Can't really see, sir. Mr. Booth is able to answer us. Larkin is unconscious and is bleeding badly from a hole in his chest.'

Haley quickly decided. For the time being the enemy had dodged back to try elsewhere, farther west. *Arandite* was rolling steadily, beam on to the sea, creaking loudly with a faint rising and falling musical note from the eyelet holes in the canvas, and from the rigging as the wind stole through.

'Get them down to the wheel-house. I'll have a look there. Keep the light as low as possible.'

He saw the figures of the Cox'n and the seaman bunch into one dark mass as they bent over Booth. He heard a moan and a stifled exclamation.

'Mr. Booth says leave him here, sir. Shall I get Bunts down?'

'Yes.'

As they struggled towards the ladder an engineman reached the top of it.

'Chief says, sir, he can't do anything. Main steam-pipe is cut engine-room side of the valve. Proper mess, it is. Can he knock the steam back to 150 pounds?'

'Will we be able to use the main engines at all?'

'No, sir. Shell blew a piece of main steam-pipe clean away. Lucky it wasn't the valve.'

Haley shook his head irritably. The niceties of the problem could wait. Either he could move or he could not.

'Tell the Chief I want to see him.'

'Aye, aye, sir.'

He bent over the dark figure which was Booth lying close to the canvas screen of the bridge.

'How do you feel, Booth?' Haley bent down to catch the reply. The first part was mumbled and he bent closer.

'. . . something hit me in the face . . . thought it was water . . . I can move everything without pain . . . face feels numb . . . and my hands are cold . . . can't feel my fingers . . .' Haley whipped his duffle off and started to wrap it round Booth. Groping in the dark he felt for the man's arms and started to put them under the duffle. His fingers traced down the arms to the wrists, then he felt a bundle of wet rags— rough bandages. Something hard was sticking from them— splinters of wood. Booth moaned as Haley's exploring fingers felt their way about. He found two short lengths of line tied round a wrist as a rough tourniquet; they were wet and sticky. Beyond them the warm, shapeless mess of . . . Haley stood up with a jerk as his outraged nerves jumped in frenzied tingles. It was the bleeding, shattered stumps of Booth's hands he could feel. He staggered back two steps as the full force of the tragedy struck him.

Both Booth's hands were gone.

A dark figure climbed up the ladder.

'Cox'n here, sir. Larkin's got a big lump on the side of his head and a slice of wood sticking in his chest. It doesn't seem to have gone in deeply, but I haven't attempted to move it.'

Haley wiped his forehead with the back of his hand. It felt cold. Unconsciously he explored his forehead again and found his hand warm and sticky. With a forceful shrug of the shoulders he pulled himself together.

291

'Torch.' It was a rasping whisper as he reached for the faint silvery glint of the light in the Cox'n's hand. 'Take the front of the bridge.' It came from far back in Haley's throat. As the Cox'n moved to obey Haley went down on his knees, shading the torch with his hands until only a faint glow escaped over the deck. This he directed on to the bloodstrained, torn sleeves on Booth's duffle, let it travel on past the twisted, knotted piece of signal halliard and . . . Although he had steeled himself to look a shudder shook him again.

It was as if Booth had dipped his clenched fists into a pot of rich red paint and kept them clenched. From them hung shapeless shreds of bloodstained flesh.

'Fingers are . . . cold. . . .' Booth's murmur was so quiet he scarcely heard it. 'Perhaps I'd be better down below.'

'In a moment, laddie.'

'Thought half the Channel . . . smack in the face . . . like when . . . the bomb . . .'

Haley allowed the thin glimmer of light to travel upwards to Booth's face and again a shudder ripped through his frame. Booth appeared to be wearing a red mask over one side, a mask in which the eye was only a dark hole. The other side was ripped and bleeding from a number of oozing cuts.

'Get . . . torch . . let's have a good look. . . .' Booth moved slightly as he tried to sit up, and a moan escaped from between his twisted, broken lips.

'Get the torch! God! I'm shining it right in his eyes. Can't he see it? Open them! Open them wide! I've got it inches from your face. Open them. . . . Open your eyes!'

Haley heard someone screaming it, steadied his shaking hand, and realised that the screaming was inside him, was not escaping, was still going on inside him although he had his lips tightly clipped, the bottom one jammed between his teeth.

He slid a hand beneath Booth's head and lifted him

slightly, just enough to bunch his duffle into a sort of pillow.

'Just lie quiet for a moment. I'll have you moved down below. You'll be warmer down there.'

Booth squirmed slightly, like a tired child preparing to drop off to sleep A sigh escaped him. 'Quiet . . . it's quiet up here . . . like a church . . . can hear music . . . Holy night . . . calm . . . damned stoker, love-sick. . . .' His voice trailed off to nothing.

Haley stood up, unaware that he still had the torch on and that it was shining down on the youngster.

'Is it bad, sir?' The whisper came from the Cox'n.

Haley came to with a jerk, switched the light off. 'I can't tell . . . can't tell.'

'He was bleeding badly from the hands. Said they were cold so I whipped a couple of tack lines round his wrists. It stopped the bleeding. Nasty mess, his fingers.'

'Nasty mess? There aren't any fingers . . . there aren't any eyes . . . there isn't any face . . .' The voice began rising hysterically inside him again. Resolutely Haley silenced it.

'We'll have to get him down to my room. Get a couple of men. Try not to jolt him too much. Give him one tablet of morphia under the tongue, wrap as much bandage as you can round each hand, and a put a piece of gauze over the face. Is that clear?'

'Can I take the man from the wheel, sir? We've no steerage way.'

Haley remembered. 'Yes, and afterwards go round the ship, find out all the damage, report to me on the bridge.'

12

The wind was rising a little, just enough to whip an occasional sea into a tumbling, frothing line of gleaming whiteness, but for a long time such things had lost their power to make Haley's heart jump.

Crouched in one corner of the bridge, with his shoulder jammed against a support, Haley allowed his head to drop wearily to meet his slowly rising arm. He wanted to see the time and it required a big physical effort. First he had to catch and hold the idea. See the time. Slowly the mental process took charge of his arm, a laborious effort starting with a heave of the shoulder to overcome inertia. Once the movement was started his arm came up painfully and wearily. Then his head went down gathering pace, like a lift dropping into space, to finish up with a jerk on his chest. In that fraction of a second interval his eyes seized the opportunity to close. It required another effort to open them, concentrating everything on that one small task. They opened with a jerk, wide and staring, and brought the luminous face of his watch into focus.

Nearly five o'clock.

For more than three hours—nearly four—they had been drifting along silently, rolling heavily but steadily in the uneasy swell. Haley had exhausted himself mentally in working out the innumerable problems involved. He had to carry in his head a clear-cut picture of the chart of the area. After one look at the tattered remnants on the broken chart table he realised that it was almost useless, anyway. And the welter of blood and broken flesh spattered over it made it too revolting for him to consider.

So he drifted, each problem being brought out, assessed, then placed back among the hundred other things to be remembered.

The tide would take them one mile roughly south-west, keep them hovering for a short while, then change, and the drift would be reciprocal—north-east. Tide was . . . ? Call it two-and-a-half miles an hour, but the wind was north-east and about fifteen miles an hour, which would slow down the drift. So the drift would be . . . His tired brain lost the trend of his calculations and in retracing them another problem, urgent and frightening, battled its way to the forefront.

They had no lights; the dynamo was out of action. No steam; therefore there was no degaussing, no protection against magnetic mines. The ship was just a mass of magnetic influence drifting over what . . . Even now, at this second, they might be creeping into the orbit of a rusted cylinder of flashing death.

Small noises about the ship, the clang of a steel door, started his jangling nerves off again. Vaguely he centralised the beginning of the nerve-storm. Something would clang, or thud, and a lightning-like stab would pierce him between his shoulders, rip through his body, and end in jerking, convulsive movements of his toes and fingers.

'Cox'n, pass the word to those stokers to stop slamming things about. I want no noise.'

'Aye, aye, sir.' And the vague figure of the Cox'n, keeping company as much as watch on the bridge, faded away.

He pinned in front of his eyes a memory-picture of the chart, wearily raised his arms until they were before him in the darkness as if they held something about two feet square.

Now! Hold these facts! He swayed slightly. Number 12 buoy . . . drift was . . . mile-and-a-half; give it a maximum of two miles with bit of wind behind it . . . now back . . . on this reciprocal they would miss that long, narrow box of suspected enemy mines . . . always suspected, although it was swept four times a week . . . always suspected . . . Suppose some aircraft had bossed his run, dropped wide, dropped a stick away from the sweep, away off the swept and buoyed Channel . . . then that would be in their path . . . right now they might be nearly over one . . . even now the complicated mechanism of a mine might be beginning to tremble. . . . Somebody touched him and he jerked violently.

'Coffee, sir?' It was Clay, self-appointed whacker-out of hot drinks, pridefully conscious that nobody could make better coffee in the still watches than he.

'Thanks, Clay.'

'There's a drop of you-know-what in it, sir.'

Another generous sip of the scalding fluid identified the rich taste of rum. Haley felt it start something stirring and comforting as it went down.

'Just the stuff!' Clay melted away from his side and Haley turned to speak to the top of the ladder. 'Clay.'

'Sir?'

'Don't raid the sauce bottle too much. See that you have some left to celebrate.'

Dead silence from the top of the bridge ladder; Haley thought the man had gone. Then he heard a soft but deep-toned 'Aye, aye, sir. I'll watch it.' And shortly afterwards: 'I've taken a look at Mr. Booth. He's sleeping, I think, because he's breathing steadily.' The voice came from the level of Haley's feet. 'Hit pretty badly, isn't he, sir?'

Drift? She can drift back on this course for four hours in safety . . . nothing until the Carlisle banks, stretching out like an open hand . . . five hours if the wind holds her up . . . but if it changes? . . . ten minutes and they'll be ashore on the lower jaw of the Gap . . . but it won't change . . . they'll drift . . . and drift . . . unless some aircraft or *E*-boat has been wide with a stick of mines and they run over them. . . .

Always that thought . . . whatever the problem he had in his mind, that thought worked its way into the weave . . . like . . . what was it that ran through something? He remembered. Madge doing some fine stitching, and a long, silvery hair from their Persian cat, Binks, somehow got caught up in the work and remained, like a streak of silver. Madge. She would be sleeping now . . . perhaps dreaming. Downstairs the small Christmas tree she had decorated was . . . Or would she be asleep? Would she be lying awake, knowing somehow that something was wrong? Nearly five o'clock. His sister-ship would not worry if they did not meet at the junction of patrols. Not until 0700 at rendezvous would they wonder, and start to search. On the shore plot he was still visible as a green dot slowly moving south-west and north-east. That green dot was *Arandite*. Reliable ship, *Arandite*; nothing spectacular, bit off patrol tonight but he knows the job. Seems to have chased those *E*-boats away. So the Wrens on the plot would chatter. Occasionally the Staff Officer in Charge would peer at the plot. Fine! fine! *E*-boats have beetled back home. Looks as if they got in a run farther west; might be a minelaying run. Ships left a hell of a gap there. What about some coffee, my dear? Let C.M.S.P. know about that suspect run. That's *Arandite*, mooching about Number 12 buoy. *Arandite*; that's the young officer with the marvellous eyes. He looks at you and you go all ga-ga.

Bedroom eyes . . . But now his eyes are . . . Haley felt a surge of near-panic and choked it back. Perhaps it wasn't too bad. Perhaps Booth had his fists tightly clenched—yes, that was it! That was why he couldn't feel the fingers. Pain made one clench the fists. Perhaps the cuts and the blood made his face look worse than it was. By the time a doctor had cleaned it up it would be just deep scratches. But the dark red hole . . . no glisten of white from the eye. . . .

'Sparks, get this signal coded up; keep it as short as you

297

can. Tell me when it's ready. Right?

'To FOIC (Repeat CMSP). Engine disabled . . . approximate position 0530 five miles 60 degrees 12 buoy, drift approx 75 degrees one mile an hour.'

A thought struck him. 'Are your batteries all right?'

'Yes, sir.' Sparks sounded aggrieved. 'I always keep them topped up.' After a pause he added : 'Main set is useless, sir.'

There was a long wait during which Haley rocked slightly to the roll of the ship; he did not sleep because he was vaguely conscious of subdued activity in the ship. Once he heard a quick rattle as somebody cocked a machine-gun. From the 12-pounder platform he heard quiet voices, and through them the deep booming tones of Clay. It was the Indian Hour, the hour when anything might happen. A clear hour at dawn, and a look-see aircraft might be ambitiously prowling anxious to strike a blow for Adolf Hitler.

Meredith had once been jumped by an *E*-boat which had been hiding close in under the cliffs, repairing a defect, perhaps. . . . Meredith, the fighting Celt who was afraid of the dark . . . or was it of something in the darkness? What could be in the darkness? The thought grew, expanded. He shrugged it away. It came back probing, finding a crack. . . . Meredith, who called minesweeping ploughing . . . the weary ploughman homeward plods . . . leaving the world to darkness and to me . . . leaving the world to darkness, the darkness which seemed to gather shape, seemed to swoop down in tangible form, writhing and twisting, hiding something behind it . . . something which shouldn't be there . . . something which crept closer . . . closer . . . malignant. Haley crouched in a corner, his eyes probing the dark bridge and beyond. The solid bridge support at his back gave him comfort. Funny how he always ducked behind the bridge support and its canvas cover when an aircraft raided them. It didn't stop the cannon shell which shattered the chart table and smashed Booth's face. . . . Steady! Steady! There's nothing more you can do until you get him to a doctor.

'Sparks, add to that signal: "Two casualties, stretcher cases." ' Should he mention Booth's hands and eyes? Was it important to the ambulance men and doctor who would meet them?

'Flashing light fine on the bow, sir.'

Haley jerked painfully. There was the lightning stab across his shoulders, from the spot between his shoulder-blades, like a stone starring a glass window.

'How long have you been there, Cox'n?'

'Little while, sir. I didn't want to disturb . . . I thought . . . perhaps . . .'

'I wasn't asleep, if that's what you mean.' Haley rasped it out.

'No, sir.' Cox'n sounded non-committal. 'Main steam-pipe broken. Large piece blown away. A number of can-non-shell holes in stokehold and engine-room casing, some in the funnel, three below deck-line but above water-line. Several holes in the wheel-house, low down, and one in your berth, sir.' Cox'n finished his recital of damage. Super-fluously he added, 'The ones below deck-line I've plugged.'

'That the lot?' Haley asked, after he had identified the flashing light as a buoy.

'Not quite, sir.' Cox'n paused. Should he try a little humour?

'Well? Go on.'

'One made a mess in the galley. Smashed up a few pots, and upset the cook's tin of dripping over the stove. The fire was put out with an extinguisher. That helped the mess.' Haley heard a soft chuckle. 'Real proper mess it was.'

'Message gone, sir.' Sparks's voice came faintly up the tube.

Haley and Cox'n stood or crouched in silence, and gradually Haley co-ordinated the small chorus of noises, identifying each one before allowing it to slip back into the comparative anonymity of being part of the whole. The gentle clat-clat he identified at signal halliards hitting against the canvas side of the bridge. It was regular, like the tick of a grandfather clock. A deeper, more subdued thud; he knew that one—it had puzzled him for weeks when he first took over the ship. At sea and in harbour it had sounded . . . faintly thub-thub . . . a deeper-toned clock. It was a steel weight at the bottom of the black-out canvas at the stokehold door. Thub-thub . . . thub . . . A more irregular noise defied him. It was a swishing slap, irritating, puzzling. He tried to concentrate on the mass of problems. Drift? Roughly a mile . . . nothing in the way for a few miles . . . nothing but . . . swish-slap . . . swish-slap . . . let's hope that there are no magnetics laying waste . . . swish-slap. Painfully he heaved himself from the corner and lurched round the bridge . . . and it stopped. Haley stood in the middle of the small area . . . swish . . . slap. . . . Got it! He caught a glimpse of white sea through the wreck of the chart table; a strip of canvas hung loose, curled in the wind, wiped across a stanchion.

'Got you!' Haley reached up and tore it away with a loud ripping noise.

'I wondered where that was coming from, sir.' Cox'n sounded faintly congratulatory. 'I was thinking to have a look myself.'

'So the noises were worrying you too, were they?' Haley lurched back to his corner. 'Are you hearing things? Thinking things, feeling things, but saying nothing, keeping it all to yourself behind that dark, sallow face of yours? Are you wondering about magnetic mines? Are you wondering. . . .'

'It was annoying me.'

'I know, sir; like a tap dripping in the night.'

Like a tap dripping. A small thing, a tapping window-blind cord, a rattling window, can become such a big thing. A strip of canvas flapping became bigger, more threatening than .

'Solan calling us on R.T., sir. Shall I switch it over?'

Sparks's voice chattered up the voice-pipe. Haley picked up the hand microphone set from its little box. Crackling, metallic, distant, he heard the voice. It was Regan's; no mechanical device could hide the rich intonation.

'Fulcrum calling Snowflake, Fulcrum calling . . .' He slid the switch over. 'Go ahead, Fulcrum.' Switched back again. Faintly but clearly the voice came. 'Hold on, Bill. I'm practically there.' There was a pause and Haley was on the point of switching over to answer when the voice went on: 'Are you O.K., Bill?'

Bill? In all the time of their friendship Regan had never called him that. Always 'Haley, me boy,' or '*Arandite.*' He slipped the switch over. 'Yes, I'm all right. Switching off now.'

Slowly thoughts began forming in his mind. What was *Solan* doing away up here? He should have been eight to ten miles away. Had Regan intercepted their signal? Left patrol? He looked at the time—nearly six o'clock. Patrol was nearly over. But what of his sweep? Mahoney would play the devil.

'Bridge? Sparks here, sir. They're sending a tug out for us. E.T.A. 0730. *Almarina* is being told to cover us in.'

'Very well.'

'Sir, there's nothing about *Solan* coming. . . .'

A quick surge of exultation swept through Haley. 'There doesn't have to be, Sparks. But he's coming just the same. Cox'n, get a tow up ready.'

Suddenly Haley felt curiously wide-awake and no longer felt alone. The feeling reached a point of near-exhilaration. A little longer now and they would be under tow.

He felt a thud throb through the hull although its origin was a long way away.

'That's a mine, sir. Somebody's put one up.'

For some time Haley stood as if frozen, staring into the darkness.

It must be an acoustic; Regan would be using his knocker. Or a contact; one they had overlooked—they seldom swept as far off the Swept Channel as this. Regan, hurrying through the night, through the darkness, might have . . .

'Ship bearing Green 150, sir.' Haley recognised the yell as coming from Ross, the Nova Scotia man with the cat's eyes.

'Can you see it, Cox'n?'

'No, sir.'

'Bunts . . .' Haley remembered that Larkin was lying below with a piece of jagged wood in his chest. He scrabbled for the light from the box, leaned it on the rail, flashed a challenge, waited, and as he waited he heard the quick rattle of the gun being cocked aft. A faint flash of light came from a spot a little off the line on which he was flashing. He flashed again; the code reply came back. Then: '*Solan* to *Arandite*. Stand by to tow.'

Solan's Number One sipped at his scalding hot coffee and did a simple sum in hours and minutes as he stared out into the darkness. Soon he would be giving the Old Man a call. Then it would be sweeping at six knots all day, but knocking only. Thank God for that! He could get a long nap in. So no cold sweeps to get out, with the wind whistling *Annie Laurie* round your what's-its-name. Half an hour more on the bridge, three or four hours sleep, finish sweeping around 1500, enter harbour 1640, bath, dash ashore, tea in the Officers' Club and there would be that nice little Wren officer number for the Officers' Christmas dance. Luv-verly! Nicely rounded in her uniform, round where the Lord meant her to be round—or was it curved? Who cares? There may be gold in them thar hills . . . perhaps a bit of Christmas prospecting. . . .

302

'Yes, Sparks?'

'*Arandite*'s in trouble, sir. She's signalled Base. She's . . .'

'Send it up the pipe. Hey, Sleeping Beauty'—he nudged a hunched-up figure in one corner of the bridge—'call the captain.' He hauled away on the string down the voice-pipe, took the signal from the brass cylinder, and went under the canvas cover of the chart table. In a short time he had plotted where *Arandite* was lying helpless. He made a large cross on the chart, then whistled incredulously.

The canvas cover billowed as Regan moved inside it.

'Here, sir,' the First Lieutenant said tersely, putting a pencil point on the spot. 'And look at this lot.' He ran his finger along the oblong shapes of two minefields in the centre, on which were large '?'s'.

Regan worked for a moment with his dividers, talking quietly to himself. 'Seven miles . . . three across the minefields, and us stubbing our toes . . . course across the fields . . . N. 70 E. . . .' He tossed the dividers down and wriggled from under the curtain.

'Wheel? Steer North 70 E. Full ahead.'

'North 70 East. Full ahead, sir.'

Solan throbbed and rolled over the uneasy sea, cutting through a darkness nearly as solid as the water.

'How far now, sir?'

'Mile and a half. Keep your eyes skinned for Number 12 buoy. We'll work from that.'

The throbbing roar close in on the beam shook the ship and a swift, pattering hail of water fell over the bridge.

'One.' The young First Lieutenant counted softly.

'Sparks, switch over R.T. I want to talk to *Arandite*. 'Over, sir.'

Regan picked up the hand microphone. 'Fulcrum calling Snowflake.' He paused. 'Fulcrum calling Snowflake.' A faint voice came back to him as he slipped the switch over. 'Hold on, Bill, I'm practically there.' Was that Haley's voice, faint, metallic, and shrouded in a blanket of crackling

303

noises? 'Are you O.K., Bill?' He listened, smiled and switched off.

'Get your playmates ready to tow, Number One.'

'Aye, aye, sir.'

A sullen, ship-shaking roar came from the darkness ahead and a grey column climbed solidly towards the sky.

'Two.' The First Lieutenant grinned in the darkness. 'How many for the full set, sir?'

'You never get the last one.'

Regan concentrated on staring into the darkness. There was a possibility that Haley, or he, would either over- or under-estimate the drift and he would pass her in the dark.

'Ship right ahead, sir.' The look-out allowed a spark of triumph to illuminate his voice. 'She's flashing, sir.' The signalman grunted to himself as he lifted his Aldis lamp. Clever bastard, eh? Always trying to get in the first call.

'Challenge, sir,' he said. 'Lamp isn't trained properly.'

'Stop being pernickity. Make the reply,' Regan snarled.

'Reply made, sir.'

'Now send : "Stand by to tow."'

Manœuvring to make fast the tow was a small epic on its own. The problems were manifold. Regan had to take care that his knocker sweeper did not put up a mine on the outside of his circle of immunity but under *Arandite*. Both ships were wallowing heavily and twice the light grass rope fastened to buoyant pellets drifted past out of reach of the seamen on *Arandite*. Eventually they got it, made fast their tow to it, and *Solan*'s big winch made short work of heaving it across. During the operation they drifted slowly but inexorably north-east.

'All fast, sir.' Number One's faint hail came to Regan on the bridge.

'Slow ahead.' The long, painful half-circle tow to get back to the Swept Channel and comparative safety started at crawling speed. Regan raised his revolutions a few at a time until both ships began a steady movement.

'Now where in hell are we?' Regan mused out loud.

'English Channel, eastern end,' Number One offered brightly. He was still glowing from the 'Very well done, Number One', which had come down from the bridge when they made fast the two at the second attempt.

Regan snorted. Drift? Maybe half a mile . . . too far south and it will be across the tips of two minefields, and her as helpless as Shamus O'Connor on a Saturday night. Too far north and it will be all along the skirt of a field. And the damned darkness like a black blanket.

'Turn that genius of yours to picking up a buoy.'

Again it was the look-out, anxious to add to his little triumph, who first saw the pin-point flash.

'Fine on the port bow, sir. Flashing light.' Regan tried with his binoculars, wiped the mist from them, picked up the light and grunted. He ducked under the canvas cover of the chart table and communed with his parallel rule and dividers.

'Two miles and us as safe as the Bank of Eire,' he muttered. 'But two miles . . . hm. . . .' He came out from the cover.

He checked the course, altered five degress, and for some time studied the effect on the two ships of tide, wind and drift.

The darkness became tinged with a faint pearly grey. First the sea boasted outlines which half an hour before would have merged into the jet blanket. Above it, the sky competed with a uniform grey-black but the line between the two became definite; an horizon. Daylight was stirring ready to do another few short hours of duty.

'Ship right ahead, sir.' Number One was using his glasses from his corner of the bridge. 'Two ships. One looks like the tug.'

Regan kept his signalman busy. First he warned the tug to remain where she was. To attempt to take the tow over

305

now would mean hazarding another ship over the mine-fields. Then to *Almarina* a slightly more complicated signal. She was to drop in close astern of *Arandite* so that her knocker's circle of immunity would overlap with *Solan*'s —a cradle of safety for the stricken sister.

Almarina wallowed past, dipping her rails under, and in the increasing daylight they saw her crew sheltering in the lee of deck-houses but on deck, curious . . . and ready.

'Tow's parted, sir.' The thin, high-pitched wailing cry from aft brought a curse from Regan and sent his First Lieutenant scrambling down from the bridge and hurrying aft in a limb-hazarding dash.

Haley thrust against the front of the bridge with his chest. 'I'm going below for a moment to look at Booth and the signalman.'

'Aye, aye, sir.' Cox'n moved from his corner to the centre of the bridge, an unconscious assumption of authority.

The main light was off but his emergency battery lamp was on with a towel thrown over it to subdue the light to little more than a glow. Haley moved the towel and looked at Larkin. He was lying on the settee, flat on his back. His mouth was half open and he was breathing jerkily, his lips moving in time with the breathing. Haley lifted the blanket. The clothes had been cut away; a substantial pad and band-age covered the wound. On the man's face, extending up to his hair and probably into it, was a large purple bruise. The swelling had pulled his face slightly out of shape, as if it had been pressed in a mould and cooled before resuming normal.

Haley allowed the blanket to drop back gently. He pulled down one eyelid; no blood. Vaguely he remembered that it was a possible sign of skull fracture if an eye was badly bloodshot.

He turned to Booth. The pink-tinged square of gauze over his face looked like a hideous mask. Haley stood swaying. Would another look help him? Would it tell him anything? Very gently he lifted the gauze, found it was sticking to the more substantial pad of bandage and lint beneath. He lowered it. By lifting one side of the blanket he could look at one arm. That, too, was covered, tinged red, showing nothing but a round shape of bandage and gauze. He replaced the blanket, stepped back quietly. A long-drawn-out sigh escaped from Booth.

'All . . . nicely wrapped . . . up . . .' he said. Haley felt a tingle start down his back, reach to his arms and legs.

'Like a dog's dinner. Lie quiet, sonny.' 'Oh, Christ, why did I have to disturb him? He was sleeping peacefully and I . . .'

'Dark in here, isn't it?' Booth squeezed the words out with an effort.

'Not so dark, laddie. I've got your face covered; you've got a lot of splinters in it. Guarding against infection. Look, go back to sleep. We'll be in soon. *Solan*'s . . .' He stopped, remembering that Booth knew nothing of events. It would mean explanations; others would follow. '*Solan*'s going to take over our sweep while we pop you into sick bay for a few days.' He picked up the white box of little squares of morphia, rather like small tablets of chocolate. He peered at the directions. 'One every four hours . . . or if pain is acute give half a tablet more.'

'I'm going to pop a pill into your mouth; don't bother about swallowing it. Just let it melt.' He slid a generous half-tablet under the boy's tongue.

Booth moved it about for a moment, sighed deeply. 'It's a bit cold in here; can't feel my hands.'

'I'll put an extra blanket over you and switch on the steam heater. Now get some sleep. . . .'

'Can you . . . hear . . . music . . . like an organ?' Haley bit his bottom lip. Then through the stifling heat of the cabin he heard, subdued, so quiet that he had to strain his ears, the deep moan of the wind through a ventilator, a higher

307

whine through some small hole somewhere, a metallic chunk as something rolled to the movement of the ship; it was the weight on the black-out curtain alternating with the metallic chunk. And the whole did sound like distant, rolling music from a church organ.

'Yes, I can hear it. Somebody in the mess deck using the gramophone . . .' Oh, God, please make him go to sleep.

'Stoker . . . love-sick . . . silent night . . . calm . . . still . . .' Booth's voice slipped away on the last word into a sigh; his breathing became deeper.

'Sir! Sir, below.' The whisper was harsh, strident down the voice-pipe near Booth's head. Haley whipped his hand over it. He breathed rather than spoke up the pipe, his eyes resting fearfully on the boy's face. 'Yes?'

'Tow's parted, sir.'

'Coming up.'

At the door he found he had the other half of the tablet in his hand. Swiftly he slipped it into Larkin's mouth.

Solan came round in a wallowing, rolling circle which carried her to within thirty yards of *Arandite*. Once again the grass rope floated by, was grappled, the tow passed. Haley saw a figure, head and shoulders above the rail of *Solan*'s bridge. That would be Regan, watching, making the most of every chance, but not shouting a string of confusing orders.

When the tow was fast the figure moved. One arm was raised in brief salute to Haley and the two ships gradually gained speed once more.

Clear of the minefields, *Solan* moved over towards the squat, powerful tug. The tow was transferred and the tug, made confident by the wealth of experience behind it, surged forward. Haley found it curiously comforting to watch the tug's broad, low stern rise to a sea and slip along over it like a peacock dragging its broad tail over a lawn. It seemed as if the tug were saying: 'Look, I'll smooth them down and take you in just like that. Easy!'

The little procession steamed steadily on in the grey morning. A vague outline became a signal tower which broke into a flurry of winking signals. Haley picked up his lamp, but somebody ashore with forethought had decided that signalling was to be confined to tug and to *Solan*. Then the piers, with foaming water breaking over their feet; and soon the shapes of houses ashore.

Solan and *Almarina*, keeping close station to provide an immune circle for tug and ship, dropped astern when the harbour mouth gaped widely. The tug shortened its tow.

'They're leaving us now, sir.' The seaman on the bridge, who had relieved Cox'n, nodded his head towards the trawlers. *Solan* was swinging away; *Almarina* was stopped.

Haley picked up his Aldis lamp. His eyes were red, dry, burning as if they were set in white-hot sockets. Every move required a tremendous effort. He rested the lamp on the rail, peered over it until he dimly focused *Solan*. His finger pressed the trigger; he saw an answering flicker. 'Regan, you wild Irish loon . . . "don't leave station" . . . you said, always keep on patrol, says you. From Haley— you called me Bill, remember? From Bill to Regan. I was nine miles from home in the dark of the night and me horse foundering under me, Regan. I was afraid because things were going bomp in the dark, afraid and alone. And then you came out of the darkness.' Haley clicked the trigger. '*Arandite* to *Solan*. V M T.'

His throat was tight, and something was there choking it. Two wet spots fell on the back of his hand, although the sky above was dry.

13

'He's a hard-hearted bastard.' Wilcox, 'Hostilities Only'
Patrol Service A.B., rolled himself a cigarette reflectively.
' "Get them off the bridge," he says, just like that. "They're
bleedin' all over the bleedin' ship." ' Wilcox cast a quick
eye round the mess deck in a rapid assessment of his audience. Interest secured, he lit his cigarette and continued.
'Not a bleedin' squeak from him and us likely to go up
any time. *Solan* takin' all the risks to pass us a tow. Did he
sing out "Thanks, chum"? Did he hell! Did he come down
off the bridge when they took Number One and Bunts
ashore? Did he bleedin' hell! Just stands there looking like
a—a —bleedin' statue. Then him and that doctor goes
down the wardroom knockin' 'em back at a rate of knots.'

Wilcox, a comparative newcomer to *Arandite*'s crew,
detected a flaw somewhere. His monologue was going on
uninterrupted. By mess deck custom he should have been
fighting to get a complete sentence in, struggling to overcome the inserted contributions of half a dozen others. He
looked round. The half-dozen or so men were standing
still just looking at him. From one to another his eyes
travelled, meeting bleak, unsympathetic looks. He reached
Clay, who was resting his elbows on his bunk, an upper one
of two. Vaguely Wilcox remembered something which he
felt might create some support for himself.

'All officers are bastards, anyway.' He appealed mutely
to Clay. He found the deadly silence oppressive. 'They don't
care a goddam cuss about us.'

Clay spoke slowly but clearly. 'Who said so?'

'You did.'

'When?'

'A lot of times.'

'I did not.'

All the ingredients for a mess debate were laid out ready for the mixing.

'God blimey, I've heard you say it a dozen times or more. "All officers are bastards," you said. "Some big, some little, but all are bastards" and . . .'

'When did I say the bit about them not caring a goddam cuss about us?'

'Well . . . you said . . .'

Clay felt the ground was secure enough beneath his feet. 'You calling me a liar?' He stood up slowly and flexed his muscles.

The formula followed its mathematical shape. Wilcox floundered desperately until Clay trapped him. 'That's the second time you've called me a liar.' The original issue was lost.

'So you are if . . .'

Smack! And Wilcox sprawled awkwardly on the floor, a thin trickle of blood flowing from a cut over his eye.

'What's going on?' Cox'n, copper rum jug in hand, turned at the foot of the ladder.

'Wilcox fell over himself.' The reply was flat, requiring no further confirmation, but Cox'n sought for one. He looked quickly round the mess deck and from each man got a nod. Wilcox clambered slowly to his feet, testing his eyebrow with the back of his hand. Cox'n caught and held his eyes.

'I tripped.' The admission was surly. A quick examination showed that it was not a bad cut.

'Get it cleaned up; there's been enough blood about today. C'mon, line up. Up spirits, my lucky lads. This is the stuff to warm your toe ends.'

Clay smiled gently as he reached into his locker for his enamel mug. He lifted the sauce bottle and glinted at it. The contents were low, nearly at the bottom of the label which read 'Daddy's Sauce'.

'Wonder how the hell he knew about that?' he mused.

Haley descended from the bridge slowly and wearily. By instinct his hands reached and found the various holds and finally he stood on deck, feet slightly apart, swaying, struggling to align several points which still hovered in his mind.

What he wanted to do was to get into his room, shut the door, and lie down on the settee. No more. Just lie down. Let his eyes close secure in the knowledge that he would not have to force them open, would not have to flog his brain into thinking of something more. .

Cox'n stood by him as he reached the deck.

'I'll get a couple of hands cleaning up the bridge, sir.'

'Very good, Cox'n.' That was something he should have remembered. Or was it Number One's job? But he had no Number One. Number One was in that ambulance. 'Very good, Cox'n.' Damn! He'd said that before. He turned and went into his room; lifting his feet over the high breakwater in the doorway was an effort and both feet scuttered as they touched it.

'Right! Now let me have a look at you.'

Haley jerked upright as the cool voice came to him. He forced his eyes open, saw a vague figure standing in front of him. He squeezed up his eyes for a moment and rubbed his face with the heel of his hand.

'Sit here, where I can have a look at you.' The voice was authoritative, and meekly Haley obeyed. Gradually it dawned on him that it was the doctor. A young, fresh-faced Lieutenant with the scarlet piping between his gold rings.

Haley allowed his head to slip back until it rested on the back of the settee. He closed his eyes, waited for the time when he would have to open them, waited for the moment when they would open protestingly and his brain would painfully whirl again as it was lashed into further activity. The moment came—and he kept his eyes closed. Wonderful! Tranquillity stole over him, and he felt it travelling from his head to his aching arms, reaching down to his legs.

The doctor looked at Haley, saw the thick vein swelling across the temple, studied the tightly clenched lips which cut across the face in a thin, straight line. At each end was a little shadow as tiny muscles fought and held off the droop. He opened his bag and shook into his hand two small tablets. These he dropped into a glass, topped them up with a small amount of water and stirred until they were dissolved.

'Don't move. I'm going to give you a quick once-over.' The doctor's voice was quiet, soothing. He put a finger-tip on Haley's lower eyelid and pulled it down. Gently he touched the thick vein on the temple, then dropped his hand.

'You been missing some sleep lately?'

Haley allowed the query to soak in. Missing sleep? Sleep? His head came up with a jerk and his eyes opened into a stare. Then he laughed, a harsh bark, one swift explosion of noise.

'Hah! Sleep? Sleep . . . what's that? I've forgotten. You don't sleep on this job.'

'Yes, yes, but don't get excited.' The doctor ran his hand round the back of Haley's neck and down between his shoulder-blades and clicked his lips once. 'Man, you're like granite down there. We'll have to soften you down a bit. Here, drink this.'

Haley took the glass, looked dully at it and sipped it. It was bitter.

'What's this?'

'If I told you it wouldn't help. It will get you nicely off to sleep and slackened down.'

'Slackened down! Good God, man, I've got a dozen things to do.' Haley tried to thrust the drink away but the doctor rescued it, and held Haley's hand. 'I've got defects

313

to report, I've got . . . Is he hurt badly?'

'They've both taken a nasty knock. You've done all you can for them.' The doctor became firm. 'Now drink it.'

'Booth—my Number One—his face . . . and hands . . .'

'It will all be taken care of. Drink this.' The voice was patient, like a grown-up's dealing with a child.

Haley shook his head. 'I've a lot of things to do. Leave it; I'll drink it later.' He caught the incisive look on the doctor's face. 'Good lord, man, I've been tired before. Once I've had a sleep I'll be all right. I'm in command here, you know.' He felt he had made an unassailable point there, but it glanced off the doctor, who chuckled.

'A little more and you'll be in command of a nice little white cot—bed-pan to match. Why try to push yourself over the edge?'

The impasse might have continued indefinitely but, after a sharp tap at the door Cutter came in. Ah! This was the man to convince the doctor that there were other things to do besides taking temperatures and feeling pulses. There were defects . . . other things . . . can't remember them just now, but with Cutter's help . . .

But Cutter sided with the enemy.

'Bad show about Booth, I mean. Engineers will be tackling your defects first thing tomorrow morning. Got a few new holes, I see.' Cutter was talking to Haley but he gave the doctor a shrewd glance. As Haley closed his eyes for a moment the doctor raised the glass and mutely shrugged.

Cutter took it, crossed to Haley and put it in his hand. 'Drink this, my boy. It will do you good.' The tones were soft, fatherly, and Haley drank it without demur.

'Fine,' the doctor said. 'A few hours and you'll be O.K.'

Haley woke a few hours afterwards feeling stiff and with a dull headache, but he could think clearly. After a bath he felt better and walked up to Base.

Mahoney listened to his report and for a time they discussed technicalities.

314

'I tried to find out something about your two lads,' Mahoney said. 'I had the usual reply: "As well as can be expected. Comfortable." I'll get hold of Surgeon Captain this evening and get the whole of the story. They'll be moved inland to hospital in a day or two, I've no doubt.' He looked shrewdly at Haley. 'It's going to take three days or so to fix your ship up. How would a nice little forty-eight hours suit you?'

Haley smiled. 'Always welcome, sir. But there's a tremendous lot to do....'

'Rubbish! Cutter will look after everything. That's what he is for. He'll be hanging around the ship until midnight, pestering the dockyard mateys.' Mahoney leaned back in his chair. 'With luck you can catch the late afternoon train and have Christmas dinner with your wife.'

'Christmas?' Haley sent the puzzled thought chasing through his mind. 'Christmas . . . of course . . . it's Christmas Day. Early this morning Number One said "Merry Christmas" . . .'

In less than an hour Haley was in the train, London bound. At various stops he was conscious of people getting in and out of the dimly-lit compartment, but he was content to rest his head against the padding and doze. Possibly he was still slightly under the effect of the draught the doctor had given him, because the train was pulling slowly into Charing Cross almost before he was aware of completion of the journey.

As he entered the main door of the block of flats he remembered he had no latchkey. It would be too funny if she were out and returned to find him sitting on her doorstep.

He ran up the stairs two at a time, along the short corridor and stopped outside the door. His hand remained poised then he knocked.

Tum-tiddy-ump-tump, tump-tump—partly with the knuckles, partly with the heel of his palm. The old knock he had always used even when he opened the door with a

315

key. He had always called out, 'Is there a man in the house?'

A quick scutter of footsteps preceded the click of the latch, the door swung open, she stood framed in the light behind.

'Is there a man . . .?'

'Bill!'

Somehow they got to the lounge and again he wrapped his arms round her. Over her shoulder he saw a small Christmas tree standing on a table, festooned with coloured lights. 'Nice tree,' he said into her hair.

She nodded. Without moving her head away from his shoulder she went on: 'I put your parcel for me on it last night, I played fair. I didn't open it until this morning. I . . . cried a little bit . . . and I wished . . . and my wish came true.'

She felt him stiffen against her.

'Let's have a drink,' she said quickly. As she poured them out she covertly studied him. Something was wrong. There were tight, straight lines on his face, a look of tense-ness about him.

A drink or two loosened the tightness slightly and eventually Haley volunteered a scrap of information.

'We had a bit of damage so Big Chief said why not slip home for Christmas night?'

'Lovely thought! Is your Number One, Booth, staying on board?'

His face tightened again.

'No, he's staying somewhere, with some other people.' He looked into space. 'He was hurt—rather badly. . . .'

She smoothed a place beside her on the settee and suddenly he found himself sitting there, telling her everything, of Booth's wounds, of the hours of darkness on the bridge . . . of *Solan* . . . and of Regan who came out of the darkness, across the minefields.

And when it was all over he felt exhausted, sat stretched out on the settee, something soothing was happening to him. After a while he identified it. Very gently her finger-tips were running to and fro on his temple. He snuggled up a little closer.

'Don't stop.'

The forty-eight hours went all too quickly and Haley found himself looking from the window of his train as it stopped on a bridge over a little stream. He watched the muddy brown water swirl down from a weir, sluice about the red-brown banks and rejoin the main stream. A sodden branch rolled and spun along, looking like something struggling, until eventually it, too, gave up the struggle and was swept along remorselessly but effortlessly.

Vaguely he detected a moral there.

Leave was what one made it; he went off at a tangent. A week could be too long, a fortnight could be too short. This one had been just right. It had everything. Surprise, tenderness, intoxicating roughness of passion . . . and forgetfulness.

'Our patient seems to be sitting up and taking some nourishment,' Mahoney said to his secretary, approval warming his voice, after Haley had reported back. 'That little bit of leave was a good investment.'

The Wren nodded agreement as she put a cup of tea on his desk.

'Tell me, sir,' she said, 'about one thing that has long puzzled me.'

Mahoney looked up. 'Speak on, scribette.'

'How do you manage to get your shirt on over the wings?'

Mahoney's eyebrows shot up. Then he threw back his head and laughed out loud. 'That's a good one! Must remember that for the missus. I have holes cut in the shirts.' He looked shrewdly at the girl. 'How's the sugar lasting out? Short? Um. I'll have to rearrange a couple of patrols.'

As she left the room she heard him chuckle, 'Wings under shirts . . . must remember that.'

14

Haley sat back with a sigh of triumph and laid down his pencil. Regan, busily engaged restoring the whipping on a delicate, spidery fly-rod, looked up, flexed the rod two or three times experimentally, and twisted his head in an attempt to decipher the mass of figures with which Haley had covered a sheet of paper.

'Two ones are two, two twos are four . . . you're learning to count correctly. It's not very hard, even when you get up to big numbers like ten tens.'

Haley looked at the Irishman and gave him an affectionate grin. For more than an hour they had been sitting in *Solan*'s little wardroom in complete silence each concentrating on his own task, each completely satisfied with the presence of the other.

Such is friendship.

'I've worked it out that in just over three years in command of *Arandite* I've steamed fifty-four thousand miles, disposed of two hundred and eleven mines. . . .'

'Also disposed of umpteen tons of ammunition, three First Lieutenants, and helped to produce one male child in inverse order of importance,' Regan chuckled. He looked at Haley, glanced down at the mass of figures once more and added, more seriously, 'That's a fair effort, I think.'

'Multiply that by the number of ships we have here and it comes to nearly half a million miles. . . .'

'I said you wouldn't find it too hard when you got to the bigger numbers. But why the mathematical mood tonight?'

Haley topped his glass up and did the same for Regan. He started a cigarette before answering and Regan recognised one of the pensive, analytical phases which he had come to know were part of his friend.

'I was thinking earlier today of the colossal waste of war; millions and millions of pounds being spent—for what? To get something we already had before we started. Peace. From that I began thinking of the effort and the pain involved in just keeping open that small Gap outside so that a few convoys could pass through in comparative safety each week.'

Regan laid the rod down carefully. Now, this wanted handling. A little more of this mood, two or three drinks, and he will be tearing the soul of him apart because he can't put the world right in five minutes.

' 'Tis a great idea, Bill. I suggest we contact the Hun and put it to him. We'll say, "Heinrich, why bother to lay mines? We'll only sweep them up. It will waste your time and if you try to stop us we'll jab you one. Heil Hitler." '

'Chump!'

'Why not? He could come over once a week on a token lay, and we could go out once a week on a token sweep, and arrive at just the spot we are now. The Gap would still be open.'

Haley thrust his hands into his pockets and stretched straight out. 'Maybe it hasn't been a big part of the war. Maybe in the whole scheme of things just keeping that hole open has been no more important than keeping the big brass knocker on the front door of the Admiralty bright and shining. But it has been done, and at what a cost.'

'Go on, me boy. Get it out of your system. If you don't, tomorrow you'll be walking about with shadows under your eyes the colour of Sean O'More's best funeral hat, and sleep a thousand miles away from the eyes of you.'

Haley touched his finger-tips. 'Pearl, Sheila, Red Wing, Honeybell and the Bible boats, Yoshmite, and Amalekite;

319

between us—we and the double LL's—we've taken quite a beating.'

Haley stared into space and Regan looked at him from under his lowered eyelids.

'. . . and that little Wren, Heather. . . .' He was whispering now.

'Do you ever hear from Booth now?'

'Occasionally. He's at St. Dunstan's, learning something or other.' Haley's mind slipped back to the time he went to hospital to visit the youngster. It was a few weeks after they had been shot up. He steeled himself and walked the length of the ward to a small room at the end. The smiling nurse beckoned him in; and his heart turned over. Gone was the fresh, smiling face with the deep, rich blue eyes. The whole of one side was a torn, serrated, livid scar, now healing. There was no semblance of shape about it. A tiny slit was where the eye had been. The other eye, although unmarked, had no gleam of life; it lacked lustre and was fixed ahead in a stony stare.

'He's looking fine, isn't he?' There was a smile in the voice of the nurse but her face was set in a hard warning look as she glanced fixedly at Haley.

'In good shape.' Haley forced the words from between his dry lips. 'But can I bribe you to keep him here a bit longer? I'm getting some peace and quietness without him about.'

'Make it worth our while and we'll try.' Approval shone from her face. 'But we have to label him "On the danger list". He wants to marry the entire staff of nurses.'

'He's got a string of wives from here to Aberdeen already. Don't trust him an inch.'

'Fifteen minutes,' she warned as she closed the door.

Haley stepped to the bed and touched Booth.

'Number One.' The twisted, distorted mouth worked and writhed, and down the torn, scarred cheeks tears started to roll. Booth gulped and a hoarse noise escaped him.

320

Haley stood in silence. What could he say? How do you do? How are you? It was Booth who broke the ice. 'How are things?' Just a simple question, just the phrase Haley had contemplated and rejected.

'Struggling along.' From then onwards it was a little easier. Haley lit a cigarette and passed it to Booth, lighting one for himself. They talked of ships and men, Haley earning one chuckle with an anecdote about Clay, another with a story of Regan. The nurse tapped the door. 'A couple of minutes more,' she said and gave Haley a penetrating look.

'That's the red-haired one,' Booth chipped in brightly. 'She's got a boy friend in the R.A.F. but I'm working away at her.'

'I'm getting weaker every day,' she laughed.

When the door had closed with a slight click they sat in silence for a short while.

'I'm glad you are so chipper, Number One,' Haley said at last.

'Number One. It's good to hear that once again,' Booth answered quietly. 'Number One . . . well, that's over.' He lifted up his poor scarred face and Haley saw the jaw jut out.

'I'm blind, you know.' It was said so simply, without a trace of bitterness or emotion, that for a moment the significance of the words escaped Haley. He sucked in his breath and Booth hurried on. 'Don't have to pretend, cap'n, sir, and boss.' The old humorous phrase—what Booth had used to call his 'all-embracing' title. It was a private little joke between them; he used to accompany it with an exaggerated half salute, half knuckle to forehead. 'And these . . .' He lifted up the still-bandaged arms. 'I don't know what's there.' He sat still, his head poised, as if listening acutely, listening for some sign of emotion from Haley. He dropped the bandaged arms but his chin was up and thrust out.

The door opened. 'Time to feed the animals,' the nurse said brightly. 'You must come again soon. We're glad to see somebody who can handle him. How do you do it?'

'Whips and hot iron bars,' Haley said.

She wheeled the little trolley to the bed. Haley moved towards Booth, rested his arm across the youngster's shoulders. 'See you again, Number One. Chin up!'

'Higher than a kite, sir, boss, and cap'n.'

Haley walked to the door. It opened with a click. Suddenly he remembered something and closed the door again. Click.

'Is he gone?' It came from Booth in a hoarse, half-strangled cry. Haley's half-opened mouth was checked by a gesture from the nurse.

'Yes.'

Booth's head dropped. Tears rolled slowly down his scarred cheeks; a heavy, shaking sob racked him. It was followed by others. Haley felt his eyes go hot, begin to burn. Something rose in his throat and threatened to choke him. He raised an arm.

'Mr. Booth, Mr. Booth!' Her voice was sternly reproving. 'Any more of that and I'll call him back. I will, you know.' She moved to the door and opened it. Click. Her head motioned to Haley and he slipped through. As it closed he heard her say: 'Now, let's battle this out together. We'll . . .'

And the door was closed.

Regan carefully poured out a drink for Haley. 'All right, me boy, I'll have you waking up come the morning with a head so size. You'll be unfit for human consumption, but it will be all out of your system.'

'How's the boy?' he inserted artfully.

'Full of beans! Eating crowbars and spitting nails.'

'And the mussus?'

'Perfect.'

Regan lifted his drink. 'In a few years, Bill, we'll have him casting as neat a fly as ever tempted a trout.' He replaced his glass and gave his friend a wary look. 'On a horse —or a pony maybe—with just a bit of wickedness in it, we'll put him at a hedge. None of your two-foot-high scrub things, but a real Irish jump. Over he'll go, off he'll come, and begob, I can see him now, cursing blue lights. He'll try again and him with his head and heart up and his feet and hands down. Up, change feet, over, and him still in the saddle. What a boy!'

'Sounds like a broadcast of the Grand National,' Haley chuckled.

'Aye, maybe that, too, and him in the lead on a jumper bred by me.'

'Outrageous, but it will serve. Come on, me boy, I've got you in the groove I want you to be in.'

Haley dealt faithfully with his drink without questioning the amount in it.

He still found it strange being a father. On leave it gave him a curious feeling to find that a sprawling, gurgling child shared his wife's attention, demanded much of her affection. He remembered the letter he wrote with his news:

Dear Madam,
    I beg to inform you that on and from this date you are now the spouse of Lieutenant-Commander (repeat) Lieutenant-Commander William Haley, R.N.V.R. So much brass around I don't know how to cope with it. . . .

And she had written back:

    I'm so delighted, Bill, And now, Dear Sir, I beg to inform you that some time in the near future, say September or October, Lieutenant-Commander Haley will become a father. It's true, Bill. I've just come from the doctor. I'm so glad . . .

Then the telegram, which Mahoney had opened and

323

translated into a biblical signal: 'Unto us a son is born.'

Haley smiled as he arrayed the thoughts pleasantly in his mind.

The smile disappeared as he recalled the occasion when his heart had stopped, jumped, and restarted with a thudding tempo which sent the blood pounding up behind his ears.

It was following one of the now occasional raids on London. *Arandite* had just tied up after a long, monotonous sweep and patrol in which the bitter wind and sapping cold had been the worst enemy.

A Welfare Officer, totally unsuited to his job but equally unsuited for any other naval job, came on board. His uniform was exquisite, a near copy of the American drape cut, with wide shoulders, the buttons grouped closely together.

The Welfare Officer, in addition to commanding sundry sporting gear, also dealt with the multitude of problems which occurred in the lives of the seamen on the sweepers. Anything, from a girl trying to contact the father of her child to coping with a stunned man whose family had been wiped out by a bomb.

His was a job which required tact, feeling, discretion, and experience of human beings, none of which he possessed.

He confronted a weary Haley with a neat array of problems. Haley's home had been bombed; it was understood that the family had been rescued and 'suitably dispersed'. Had Haley anybody to whom he could delegate the responsibility of caring for the 'salvaged chattels'. He talked like that. *Solan*'s irrepressible First Lieutenant once said, 'Additional dialogue by the Civil Service,' and it sounded so.

Haley could not get from him one single fact beyond his brief. A man's home had been bombed; he had the other details neatly pigeon-holed; all that was required was a series of equally neat answers.

It was Cutter who saved him from being taken by the

324

throat and shaken like a rat. Cutter sent Haley up to Mahoney with the problem and it became a problem no longer.

C.M.S.P. sat back in his chair talking quietly, partly to himself, partly to Haley, with his fingers touching and resting under his lips.

'They've been rescued, that's something. . . . Shouldn't be hard to find out where they are. . . . Let me see . . .' Suddenly Mahoney sat up. 'Damn me for a fool, and I've been married to the woman for more than thirty years. Give me the address, Haley, and go back on board and sleep. I'll keep you posted. Now, no arguments. If it is necessary I'll let you have twenty-four hours' leave.'

He stood up and walked to the door with his arm across Haley's shoulders. 'Sleep! That's an order. I can't afford to have my Commanding Officers cracking up.'

And Haley slept.

A few hours later a smiling Mahoney sat across the table and gave him what he most wanted to know. All the news.

'I remembered my missus was in London and I started her working. When she gets her teeth into something, then I sit back and wait for the results. We've got them. Now, your home was damaged, not demolished, by a bomb which hit across the road from you. Your wife is with friends'— he leaned forward to study a sheet of paper—'who live at Hampstead, Lulworth Gardens, name of Milton. Know them? Mrs. Mahoney has seen her, drunk tea with her and has duly admired young Haley—he's like you I'm told— and they are both in good hands. No damage, just slight shock.'

Haley felt like jumping round the room, so strong was his reaction.

'Regarding your furniture,' Mahoney went on, studying his sheet of paper again. 'Some of it was damaged but has been stored in a repository—it's going to cost you ten bob

325

a week, and you will have an approximate inventory in a few days.'

He sat back smiling again for a few seconds before crossing to his large wall map.

'You sail 2200 hours tonight, taking *Jacinth* with you, and I want you to concentrate on this area.' He covered one side of the Gap. 'Stick to it; there ARE mines there. I know it. They've been over a couple of times, shot up a convoy by night, and I'm convinced it was merely decoy work. They probably slipped in at the end of the convoy and put a couple of sticks of mines down. Clever people, these Chinese.'

After Haley had gone Mahoney's Wren secretary picked up her telephone and spoke softly into it.

'Sir, is the deputy Welfare Officer ready for a cup of tea?'

Mahoney chuckled. 'Bring it in. I've always held the view that the only way to run a war properly is to allow women to take a hand in it. How would you like to ship as First Lieutenant with Haley? Could you keep him in order?'

The girl did not answer until she arrived with the small tray. She placed the cup near Mahoney. 'I don't think so sir. I'm always seasick. Besides, I have a full-time job looking after one officer.'

'Who is that?' Mahoney's bland innocence made her laugh. 'Do I know him?'

'I sometimes wonder,' she countered.

He tasted the tea and pulled a wry face. 'You losing your grip?' he asked. 'Time *Solan* was in harbour. Only Irish people realise that tea should be strong with lots of sugar.'

Three separate statements which, severally or together, did not puzzle the girl for a second.

The reference to a First Lieutenant for Haley came from a more or less pressing problem of the moment. After Booth had been wounded Haley had been particularly unlucky with the officer appointed as his Number One. From a recollection of his talk with C.M.S.P., when his family affairs were so nicely settled, to another interview was but a short jump. Haley stirred in his chair, looked up and found Regan's blue eyes watching him quizzically. He grinned in answer.

'I seem to have drawn a winner in this new Number One,' he said. 'He's not brilliant, but he knows this job and can handle the men. When I think of the two others I start sweating again.'

Regan nodded sympathetically. He, too, realised the value of a good First Lieutenant. On such small ships as theirs, with only two officers, if a First Lieutenant was not up to his job it threw an enormous amount of extra work on the captain, which meant in effect that the strain was constant both at sea and in harbour.

Shortly after Booth had departed Haley was sitting in his room when he heard a sharp knock. Before he could turn a languid voice said, 'Are you the skipper?' And nothing annoyed Haley more than to be addressed as 'skipper'.

He turned to find a youthful Sub-lieutenant, R.N.V.R., framed in the doorway.

'I am the captain,' he answered tersely, taking an instant and instinctive dislike to the junior officer.

The Sub-lieutenant stepped into the room and held out his hand: 'I'm your new "Jimmy". I wanted Fleet Air Arm, but I've come down to this.' He vaguely waved his arm round the room.

Haley bit back a savage retort. He remembered his first reaction when posted to minesweeping. But as time progressed he and Passmore, the new officer, clashed time and again. To begin with, the Sub-lieutenant was lazy and inefficient but nearly successfully concealed both those bad faults behind a brisk front. It was over his treatment of, and his attitude towards, the crew that he and Haley joined issue stormily. The list of defaulters to come before Haley grew steadily. It worried him because he felt he ought to know his crew by heart, and this sudden and persistent outbreak puzzled him for a while. Technically, the offences were such that merited light punishments and on a larger ship the offenders would have received them dispassionately and fairly. But on smaller ships where the enforced degree of intimacy was inevitable, such as submarines and sweepers, more often than not a dressing down at the moment of the offence was sufficient.

Haley found the same sullen atmosphere creeping over the ship as he had found when he first took her over. It worried him quite an appreciable amount for two reasons. Despite changes in the personnel he felt that basically he had the same good crew that was there when he assumed command. He had always treated them fairly and never hesitated to call on them for the last ounce—and then more. He held the theory, and had proved it in practice, that a man with a grievance was only fifty per cent efficient. It mattered not so much in the day-to-day tasks, but a decrease in efficiency crept into look-out work and even gunnery. That could mean the difference between living and dying.

In one of his conversations with Passmore he tried, with a considerable amount of restraint, to make this point. Passmore's answer was typical of the man and was the rock upon which his career as *Arandite*'s First Lieutenant foundered.

'They are just cattle; crack a whip and they jump to it. Soon it is only necessary to shake the whip and you have them leaping all over the scene.'

Haley's eyes were like gimlets as he spoke to the Sublieutenant. 'You feel that there is no other way to handle men in an inferior position to you?'

Passmore smiled, a smirking, self-satisfied smile which infuriated Haley. 'It's the easiest way. Given time and patience, we can make monkeys do it.'

'You wouldn't call that bullying?' Haley fought back

328

his surging temper and a desire to rip into Passmore with a barbed tongue.

The supercilious answer did nothing to help to suppress that desire. 'Officers don't bully ratings. It is only bullying when a senior officer does it to me, or any other junior.' The smirk gained size.

Haley dropped the discussion as unprofitable, but the sullen atmosphere and recurring petty punishments continued. He felt the situation was becoming desperate.

'What can I do?' he appealed to Regan. 'I can't dry-nurse every man on the ship. Technically, he is quite in order. The little offences are occurring, and once the men are up before me formally I have to whack out the punishments. Booth's way was to cuss 'em good and hearty before making an official issue of it. If that didn't work—and it seldom failed—we would jam their tot, and that was murder.'

But Passmore brought about his own downfall. In rapid succession he committed sins of omission through sheer laziness, until in the end Haley had to take him before Regan as Senior Officer of the group.

Haley had seen Regan in many and varied moods. This was a new one. He was cold, formal and listened to the end of the recital by both men. Then he opened fire.

'I have watched *Arandite* slip back from being an efficient ship to become a slipshod, untrustworthy unit in my group,' he started coldly. 'I have wondered, because I have known her a long time. Now I know the reason.' His blue eyes were like twin bits of ice. 'What was your background before you came here? What class of ship were you on?'

'I was training for Fleet Air Arm.'

'Why were you rejected?' Regan put a wealth of stress on the last word.

Passmore shuffled and hesitated. Regan went on. 'Never mind, I can guess. Apparently the instructors had their own ideas about what constitutes a good pilot. We, too, have our

329

own ideas about what makes a good minesweeping officer.'

'I didn't want to go minesweeping,' Passmore interjected. 'When I was turned down I wanted ...'

'You are minesweeping,' Regan cut in bitingly. 'And whatever you may consider its social level, and presumably you consider that important, it's a full-sized man's job. You obviously don't measure up to my standard. Whatever the time of day or night, at sea or in harbour, I and your Commanding Officer are entitled to feel that we have behind us a junior officer we can trust. At the moment we haven't that feeling. Very well, I will take the matter up.'

Passmore returned on board *Arandite*. Haley stayed with Regan, who cocked one eyebrow. 'Sorry about the slipshod bit, Bill. I had to lay it on thick. It isn't true, but I can see that you are worried.'

And in the course of time Passmore went his way.

With his next officer Haley was equally unfortunate in a different way. The youngster was willing enough, but was completely incapable of any measure of command. Any order he had to pass to the crew became a diffident, halting request. The ratings, quick to react, took advantage of him when they found he could not enforce a command. To make matters worse, he was singularly helpless at sea in the dark hours. He could more easily lose all sense of direction and course than could a ten-year-old boy. He had one attribute. He had a mathematical mind. A problem of time, tide and angles was as simple as one-two-three for him.

'And that is how he passed out as an officer. That and a pleasing manner, plus a public school accent,' Regan suggested. 'He must have been the instructor's joy.'

Mahoney craftily put him forward for an Asdic course and once more Haley had the task of fitting a new officer into his small firm of Minesweeping, Limited. And the third officer fitted.

Bolt was older than any of the other First Lieutenants. He was nearly thirty. At first Haley thought he had drawn

330

another misfit. Bolt was quite disillusioned about the war. He was frank enough to say that he wanted no part of it, had viewed his call-up in his age group with distaste, but as there was a job to do—well, the best thing was to get on with it and get it over. He had sailed as a rating on larger fleet sweepers, but mainly on escort duties. Nevertheless he had the rudiments of minesweeping grounded in. He showed singularly little initiative, but when something had to be done he clarified an order, passed it, and it was done to his satisfaction, or done again.

'And not such a bad idea, really,' Haley submitted when discussing his latest arrival with Regan. 'And on one point we are in complete unanimity. He said the other night that he wanted only one thing out of the war. That was "to be alive when it finished". Fair enough, I thought.'

And Bolt stayed, earned Haley's trust and the respect of the crew. Once again the voice in the mess deck claiming that all officers were bastards was as a voice crying in the wilderness.

From the occasional snatches of conversation and the following long silences Regan had shrewdly followed the trend of Haley's thoughts, and knowing that if he could keep them on a more or less pleasant level there would be less chance of Haley spending a long, sleepless night tortured by extensive, introspective thought. From fragments of conversation spread over the three years and more of their friendship, he knew that Haley would lie in his bunk staring into the dark, reliving far too much of what had passed, living it over again vividly, feeling the pain and exhaustion. He was near the truth, too. Haley would occasionally do just that, and almost inevitably there would come a time in the darkness when he realised that all between him and the water outside was a steel plate little more than half an inch thick, a steel plate which could be twisted and riven into an ugly shape by a shattering explosion. He would thump the bulkhead with his clenched fist, get out and walk round the deck until the acute, torturing mood would be dispelled by the cold dawn of another day, or sheer weariness which made his eyes close, blotting out the thoughts.

'How are the notes on Great Oaks progressing?' Regan employed cunning and slipped the query in, at the same time topping up Haley's glass. Two more drinks, he figured, would set his friend glowing, would soften the harsh outlines of life for him, and would send him back to his ship to sleep, perchance to dream.

'I've got enough to write two books. What a wealth of material there is in that little village. Think of it! Four hundred years and more of history in miniature.'

Haley had started taking notes a d forming the rough outline of a book after one of his afternoon visits to Great Oaks. The many façades of life in the small village with its manor house fascinated him. He found the story growing in detail in his mind, with the planting of the successive oaks as the underlying theme.

The idea originated with Mrs. Lambert when she found that Haley wrote short stories. 'You'll find enough material here for a dozen,' she told him. And Haley started collecting data.

'You'll be telling the truth about that beast Cromwell,' Regan inserted artfully. 'Don't twist history to shelter the murdering cratur.'

Haley smiled. 'Apart from a mention, I'll dismiss him like that.' He clicked his fingers. 'Except as a prologue I think I'll confine myself to this century.' His eyes took on a faraway look. 'And that will be plenty for a long, long book. Two wars, two generations, each of which . . .'

'Bedamn, he's off again and me heading him for a sleep.' Regan looked at the clock on the bulkhead and stood up. 'G'wan, sailorman, go to your solitary couch, dream of another half-ring and you on foreign station with a dozen houris hopping round you. . . .'

'With saucepan lids,' grinned Haley, also standing up.

'How much drink has that crazy Irishman pumped into me? I don't recollect seeing the bottom of the glass.'

'With or without, to taste. One for the road?' Regan held the bottle invitingly.

'No, thanks; another and I'll be seeing three ships instead of one.'

'That's all right; take the middle one.'

They reached the deck, and the cool night air acting on the moderate amount of gin that Haley had taken made his head sing slightly. He breathed in deeply. As the Quartermaster shone a shaded torch on the ladder reaching to the top of the quay he heard the faint drone of an aircraft. Regan listened also. They turned their heads to one another in the darkness and Haley saw the flash of Regan's teeth.

'One of ours . . . we hope.'

The faint thump of a gun, the later clop of an exploding shell, and slowly climbing ribbons of tracer gave them the lie. To emphasise it the wail of the warning tore apart the peace of the night.

'There's something in your idea after all, Regan. If only we could persuade Heinrich to adopt it.'

'We'll try tomorrow after clearing up the lot he's putting down tonight. Sleep tight, and if a bomb falls down your ventilator . . .'

'I'll bring it along to you and you can lay it with a complaint on C.M.S.P.'s desk.'

'Good night.'

'Good night.'

Haley walked along the quay with a slightly exaggerated calmness. His solemn steps gave no indication that his heart was thumping, that there was a tightness in his chest, that he wanted to race along, throwing dignity to the wind, wanted to scrabble quickly down the ladder to his ship and hide away behind something, behind the half-inch-thick steel plate, or even behind the futile painted canvas round

333

the bridge—anything so long as it was something to crouch against.

The 'plane seemed to come no nearer and for a few moments he stood on the quay looking down on his command. Darkness hid many of the harsh details; starlight, diffused and charitable, was just enough to show him the mass.

'Well, there you are, all 140 feet of you. And God, how I disliked you when I first saw you! Not now, old girl; so much has gone into you. You've seen a lot and so have I. You've always done what I asked. There are worse ships, not many better. Hell, that crafty Irishman must have kept them rolling into me tonight . . . but we'll show him in the morning. Now, easy, old girl. Don't rear up and hit me; just lay nice and steady as I come on board. Easy, now . . . keep this damn' ladder still . . . bloody nonsense talking, at a ship, 140 feet, more'n 400 tons of ship, just steel and rivets and . . . and engines.'

The deck climbed surely to meet him and the Quartermaster stepped quietly from the shelter of a hatchway. Haley stood swaying slightly for a moment. His head was singing and things were going round, but he could think clearly. He watched the searching lights and listened to the drone of the 'plane. . . .

' *"Chaos of thought and passion, all confused;*
   Still by himself abused or disabused,
   Created lord of all things, yet a prey to all." '

He turned and saw the Quartermaster standing near him.

'Pope has us all neatly docketed, hasn't he, Quartermaster? Number One on board?'

'Yes, sir. He's turned in.' He allowed the light from his torch to drop dimly and diplomatically in Haley's path to his room.

'It goes on:

334

' "*Sole judge of truth, in endless error hurled
The glory, jest and riddle of the world.*" '

Haley had one foot inside his doorway. 'That's from his
Essay on Man. I forget the rest. Good night.'

A cantankerous Clay, called an hour later to take over
his watch, listened in jaundiced silence as the man he was to
relieve talked on.

'He rolls down on deck and starts reciting poetry at me
and hundreds of German 'planes dashing about overhead.
Then he says "That's what the Pope says of man." '

He dragged off his boots.

Clay looked at the dingy gunner's badge on the man's
sleeve and sneered openly.

'Do 'em as much harm as some shooting I've seen lately
round here.' He dragged on his duffle. 'Leave any coffee in
the galley?'

A little later he listened carefully outside an open port-
hole and nodded. Only one cup wanted tonight. Inside the
room a man slept.

15

Through the late autumn and early winter it became obvious that the build-up for invasion was gaining momentum. Almost nightly convoys of small landing craft and other unidentifiable objects were towed down-Channel with attendant escorts of destroyers and trawlers.

Some of the escorting ships were old friends of the small force operating from the Base. They had never seen them in daylight and intercourse had consisted of exchange of signals by dim light, but they were old friends on more than nodding terms, just as people who shut their front gates each morning and trek off to the station are old friends with the other people who converge there with them. From a brief greeting would grow an exchange of remarks about the weather, then to gardens and children and the problems of the office, until the man in the grey suit from up the road became as much part of life as the season ticket. And so would the man who always left his arrival until the train was actually steaming into the station.

So it was with the ships who passed through the Gap, the escorts and the escorted, and the ships which kept it open. Fragments of gossip would be tacked on to more formal signals as those gatherers-up of unconsidered trifles, the signalmen, gained material for a 'mess deck buzz'.

Haley, who could read signals as well as any Patrol Service bunting tosser, frequently intercepted these odd fragments. A formal signal would run like this: 'Straggler with engine trouble is eleven miles astern with M. L. escort, estimated speed four knots. A pause, then: 'Us for the beach this time. Seven days boiler clean.' Or: 'Floating mine sighted one mile north of Nine buoy'—pause—'Got a new Jimmy this trip.' *Arandite*'s signalman's lamp would flutter and the other ship would reply: 'Could be worse.'

On one occasion, after an exchange of complicated signals necessary because of the splitting of a convoy, Haley's signalman offered to the bridge at large: 'Her Bunts got married last week. Married a Chatham girl. The boys all went to the wedding.'

And all that was done with a faint blue light scarcely visible at five hundred yards.

It gave the monotonous patrolling a slight zest to guess at the identity of the escorting ships, to pick up and challenge first, then add a minute trifle to the growing mass of gossip.

As winter slipped in, heralded by a succession of severe gales, the work of the ships at the Base was suddenly increased.

With charts spread over his desk to amplify his larger scale chart on the wall Mahoney explained the problem.

'There is so much stuff going through now, particularly to the west, that it has become necessary to clear an alternative passage—a swept channel—for twenty miles down. In effect, it will be a sort of siding into which we can shunt an east-bound convoy as the west-bound passes. Is that clear? It will be an Oropesa sweep first to clear the way. We will search it for magnetics and acoustics, then give it a final thorough going over. After the first week it will be largely sweeping for the Mickeys, so the trawlers will do escort and anti-aircraft guard as they sweep.'

He looked round the room at his Commanding Officers and saw that one of them was paying for more attention to the trim figure of Mahoney's secretary as she leaned over the table adjusting charts. It was the Commanding Officer of one of the motor minesweepers, vulgarly called Mickey Mice, who was allowing his attention to wander.

'I would like ALL your attention, gentlemen,' he said severely. 'I want you to be all ears for a moment.' The Mickey captain had the grace to blush and Lister murmured, ' "To bury Caesar, not praise him." I must say she has nice lines.'

The work took longer than expected and by Christmastime officers and men were weary from endless nights at sea and only short intervals in port. The spells in harbour demanded a certain amount of work, so sleep was to a minimum and labour to the maximum.

Mahoney edged over from irritability to irascibility as the delays extended. Regan, who was Senior Officer at sea, carried the sweeps on into daylight hours in the mornings, when visibility was down enough to discourage shelling, taking a chance on any F.W. 190's being out on a hit-and-run raid.

But the work lagged also because of bad weather. A full night's work would be ruined if a ship put up a mine in a sweep and had to pull out of line. Filling the Gap was a simple matter in daylight, but at night-time it meant peering into the darkness for the other ships, jockeying and joggling for station, and precious hours slipped by before a satisfactory formation could be built up again. Or a convoy would trickle through with a long string of weather-battered stragglers behind it, causing infinite delay.

Regan and Haley, sharing the Senior Officer work, stepped over the thin line which bounds weariness and became automatons, deriving the maximum of benefit from a short rest and driving to the full when at sea.

With the week estimated for a preliminary Oropesa sweep dragging into three, a minor disaster reduced their already small force by one.

Almarina, getting in her sweep in the first pale threads of dawn, dragged a mine close under her stern. It was a typical piece of the carelessness which grows from that vigorous bloom, contempt rooted in familiarity. The rule, according

338

to the book, the *Minesweeping Manual*, more often honoured in the breach than in the observance, was to steam full ahead with the sweep close-hauled and sight the gear on the surface.

Almarina's First Lieutenant was wet, cold and tired. A sweep in and stowed meant relative comfort and shelter from the biting wind and lashing rain. As the dripping wire rolled in over the shining sheave he kept his finger moving in a circle above his head. 'Heave away.'

Suddenly the waters opened up under her stern. Those on the bridge felt a shattering jolt; the water cascaded down on the stern, a wet shroud for the man who had taken one too many chances, and sluicing the blood away from the other wounded men.

Lister, on *Jacinth*, cut his sweep and raced in to the rescue of his friend's ship. *Almarina* did not sink; low down in the water, her stern a gaping, ragged hole, she was slowly towed in by *Jacinth*.

'The Old Man touched lyrical qualities,' Regan told Haley during a spell in harbour for stores and bunkers. 'He didn't repeat himself once in ten minutes. *Almarina*'s poor Number One must have rolled over, although he is a fathom deep. But Lister came in for the real broadside.' Regan lit a cigarette. 'Lister started to talk of friendship, and of wanting to help, and Mahoney cut in telling him that friends count for nothing on the job. You know the drill. It was fierce.'

'And in the meantime we still have half the area to do, with gale warnings in the offing.'

Regan nodded. 'C.M.S.P. has bitten somebody's ear. We are having two ships on loan from round the corner somewhere. They can't arrive too soon for me.'

When they did arrive, two sturdy, battered craft, they had the shock of their naval lives.

Regan intercepted them on their passage down as the sun slipped quickly behind angry orange clouds, leaving the stage clear for a boisterous night.

Signal lamps started flashing.

'Advise me on state of your bunkers and readiness of sweeping gear,' he sent.

The senior ship of the two was smart. 'Bunkers low. Gear needs spares and calibrating,' she sent. The other replied: 'Topped up. Gear in order.'

To the first Regan flashed: 'Proceed into harbour.' The second received a signal: 'Take station at number four. Port sweep,' and a string of explanatory directions. An hour later it was sweeping astern of the fleet.

Saturn, the trawler which proceeded into harbour, had scarcely tied up before Cutter boarded her. 'How much bunkers do you want? Why is your sweep not calibrated?' The questions came thick and fast and the Lieutenant, R.N.V.R., in command, began regretting the move which had brought him from a nice out-in-the-morning-back-at-night job.

'What's the hurry, sir?' he asked. 'We haven't had a mine for two months. And why the sweeping to night?'

In a few terse sentences Cutter gave him the picture and in fairness to the officer he accepted its full value.

'Sounds tough,' he commented. 'I ought to point out that, apart from an odd search sweep at night, we've done little night stuff. It's been mainly anti-minelaying patrol.' He looked at Cutter for a moment. 'In fact, I understand that field sweeping cannot be done at night.'

Cutter smiled bleakly. 'I'd heard that, too.' He touched the officer on the shoulder. 'But we've been doing it for a couple of years.' He changed tone rapidly. 'Move over for bunkers at 6 a.m. tomorrow morning, proceed to sea at 8 a.m., calibrate sweeps, and join the group immediately afterwards. You'll have a confirming signal. Let me have your charts. I'll have 'em marked up with local data and delivered to you in the morning.'

When Cutter had bustled away the Commanding Officer

looked at his First Lieutenant and shrugged. 'What's cooking here? Everybody seems to be in a devil of a hurry.'

'Perhaps there's a war on, or something,' Number One offered.

'God forbid! Wars upset me.'

'Me, too, but I'd like to upset the nice little Wren driving that Lieutenant-Commander's truck. She . . .'

'Sex rearing its ugly head again? Keep your strength. You'll want it.'

So slowly but surely they swept the area. The sullen, thudding jolts became few and far between until one grey, cold windless dawn saw the four ships sweep the area without result.

Mahoney leaned back and sighed with satisfaction when the signal was placed on his desk. 'That will do for a start. Now we'll get the Mickeys moving. Get these signals off.' He dictated a string of signals to his Wren. When he had finished a reflective look stole into his eyes. 'D'you know what I've a mind to do?' he said.

She looked severely at him. 'Yes, and you'll be wet and cold and you'll catch pneumonia. Tea?' she queried at a tangent. 'I've plenty of sugar.'

He looked at the movements graph on his wall, ran his hand through his greying hair. 'I suppose you're right. I'd give a year's pay to be out there with them. *Solan* was in when? . . . two days ago. Make it two good spoonfuls.'

'Yes, sir.'

Even the elements came on their side for the latter part of the operation. The gales changed to bitterly cold weather with a moderate wind which helped the biting frost search out every nook and cranny of the bridge. But the sea was calm and the nights clear with a moon shedding a pale light over it all.

Regan looked back at the array of sweepers behind him. In half an hour or so it would be dawn. The moon had

341

dipped behind the horizon with a self-satisfied glow tingeing its face, conscious of a full night's assistance gladly given. Abeam of *Solan* was *Arandite* seeming scarcely to move; only the thin line of the wake extending astern showed that she was slipping through the water at six knots. Astern of the motor minesweepers was *Golfitt*, there in case any curious *E*-boat decided to investigate the extra amount of activity.

And this was the last run through the new channel. In an hour he could signal: 'Operation By-pass completed.'

For a little while Regan busied himself writing out some signals behind the curtained-off chart table. When he came out the first pink tinge of dawn was colouring the eastern sky, while the reluctant shadows of night were still hanging to their decreasing western empire.

'I'll bet Bing Crosby never saw it, but this is "the blue of the night meeting the gold of the day". It looks odd, doesn't it?' *Solan*'s Number One lifted his chin towards the sky.

'It does, but you try singing it at this time of the morning and I'll throw you over the bridge into the sea,' Regan growled.

'Wot, no keel-hauling? No flogging round the fleet? Getting soft in your old age, sir,' the First Lieutenant chuckled. 'Even I, bright soul that I am, could not muster a song at this time.'

'See if that is alive.' Regan nodded towards the curled-up ball at the back of the bridge which they both knew was the signalman snatching a quite legitimate doze. 'I've got some work for him.'

By the time the signalman had sent his messages ashore, reporting the new channel was clear, and had flashed others to weary-eyed reluctant opposites on the other ships, the tip of the sun was a red arc above the horizon.

' "Something attempted, something done," ' Regan quoted. He was watching the motor minesweepers rolling in

342

their long sweeping tails, more than five hundred yards of thick rubber-covered electric cable. 'Soon this place will look like Piccadilly for traffic.'

Number One was interested. 'With sweet damosels popping out of doorways saying "Hullo, dearie!" and American soldiers leaning against every buoy in the Channel?'

Regan looked sourly at him and slowly shook his head. 'I have often wondered how you spend your leaves. Have you no shame?'

'I was nicely brought up, sir. I'm always polite to them. I answer "Hullo, dearie!" and then I talk to the man as earnest seeker after knowledge.'

'To the American soldiers?'

'God forbid!'

Regan frowned, not at his Number One's levity, but at the fact that he was afraid he had stretched the final operation a shade too much into daylight; at least, this sort of daylight when the French coast was visible in the clear dawn, which meant that they, too, were to be seen from the other side.

'Why don't they get a move on? We'll be having all the bricks in the world chucked at us if we stay here much longer,' he snarled.

He walked about the bridge in growing irritation, watching the pennants slowly climb to the yard-arms of the stumpy masts on the motor sweepers as one after another completed getting in the sweep.

'That's better,' he growled as the last pennant soared up. 'Bunts, call up the Senior Officer of the Mickeys,' and for a few minutes the signalman earned his keep once more. The ships, trawlers, and motor minesweepers engaged in what looked like a complicated movement in a maritime set of lancers but finally evolved itself into a neat column of Mickeys in line ahead with *Solan* leading, *Arandite* along their beam and *Golfitt* bringing up the rear as whipper-in.

Four columns of water climbed skywards and the roars merged into one sullen wave of noise.

'Damn, they've opened up!' Regan said. 'Ahead and short. Now, will Heinrich keep the same line and lift his sights? Or will he . . . ?' It was a familiar problem. They had been shelled before and evasive action consisted of out-guessing the gunner the other side, trying to guess what his next correction would be. Regan altered course towards the disturbed water. The nearer to that the safer it would be until the next salvo gave him some indication of the corrections.

'Flash.' Number One, standing on the small searchlight platform above, reported the flash of the guns from Cap Griz Nez.

'. . . 39 . . . 40 . . . 41 . . . 42 . . . and . . . now.' Regan, counting the seconds off to himself, had timed the next explosions to within seconds. The usual estimate was from forty to forty-three seconds from flash to fall of shot. There was no warning whistle from the high velocity shells. They just arrived with a terrific bang in salvoes of four.

The four columns of water climbed like feathers ahead of him. 'Only lifting his sights, eh?' Regan chewed his bottom lip. He altered course to pass between the last fall of shot and the French coast, so that the next salvo, if straight, would be over.

'Flash.' Silently Regan ticked the seconds off. *Solan* jolted and heaved like a vehicle driving over a deeply ploughed field. The pale morning sunshine was blotted out. Three columns of water climbed upwards to port of her, another reached skywards to starboard, so close that the first scattering of spray slashed their faces, then tons of water crashed down on the deck and bridge. The First Lieutenant tumbled from the searchlight platform in a scrabbling movement and finished on his hands and knees. The signalman stood transfixed, arms held slightly from his side and rigid. He looked like somebody who had just emerged from an unexpected and extremely cold shower bath, which in fact he had.

Regan dashed the water from his eyes with the cuff of his duffle. His head was ringing from the explosions and he was soaking wet. For a second he stood still, felt the tremble of the engines transmitted to the bridge. Good! Still moving. He looked over the bridge front to the gun. The crew were just rising from a crouch and some hearty curses drifted aft. All right there.

'Straddled. As near as we want,' he rasped. 'Slip around lively, Number One. See if there is any damage, see that the engineers sound for leaks.' He felt himself go slightly rubbery at the back of his knees.

The signalman suddenly galvanised into action and grabbed his lamp.

'From *Arandite*, sir. "Are you O.K.?" '

'Answer: "Yes, a bit wet." '

On *Arandite* Haley blew sharply from his pursed lips. He had actually been watching *Solan* when the projectiles fell, had seen the columns of water rise round her and had breathed in sharply as she disappeared. The reaction when he saw her cocked up bow steam on through the descending water was terrific. A sudden empty feeling manifested itself in his stomach. He leaned against the front of the bridge, letting it take his weight until his legs stiffened again and his internal economy resumed its normal function.

He read *Solan*'s reply as it flickered across, and blew sharply again. No nearer than that, not a hairsbreadth, please.

Regan heard his First Lieutenant climb back to the bridge.

'No damage, no leaks. The Chief says he'll have to slow down some for about half an hour. Something about an oil feed fractured. To his large bottom, or something like that.'

'His bottom end, you buffoon! Is that the lot?'

Number One grinned wickedly. He was undergoing the same mental process in enlargement as a small boy who has escaped a clutching hand while raiding an orchard. He felt suddenly brave and had to show it. 'It gave her a wonderful wash down; saves getting the hoses out.'

Regan hunched his shoulders as another salvo crashed out. This time it was well over and abeam of *Golfitt*.

'Hold your face out to the next one which comes nearer. A wash will do it good,' Regan growled. 'Bunts, call *Arandite*. Tell her to take lead. I have to slow down with engine trouble. Suggest she makes a smoke-screen as she pulls ahead.' He turned to his Number One. 'We'll sidle along behind that until the Chief repairs his defect.'

Solan pulled out of line towards the shore, and the line of ships passed her, their crews peering at her curiously.

Arandite moved ahead, and from her stern a wisp of chemical smoke-screen twisted, writhed and settled down on the water, a grey-white protection. Haley called up *Golfitt* and ordered her to follow suit, and soon *Solan* was steaming along slowly behind a long line of smoke which clung to the water, writhing slowly to the height of her mast.

Regan felt better with the protective screen hiding him from the gunners the other side. 'Our Piccadilly is a bit foggy today, Number One. We won't have any *E*-boats bobbing through it. They're real night birds.'

Number One grinned. 'If one did . . . I say "if". We could always say "Hullo, dearie!" and shiggle our stern at him.'

Regan chuckled. 'When you run out of thoughts on sex what do you think of?'

Number One's reply was prompt. 'Women.'

Regan shook his head in mock dismay. 'Hopeless! Well, here's another line of country for you. Go down and stand over those engineers and whip them into a frenzy.'

Number One had almost disappeared down the bridge ladder when he looked up with an impudent grin. 'Yes, sir . . . dearie.'

Regan swung a wild kick at his head and laughed.

Haley watched *Solan* disappear into the grey blanket and replaced his binoculars on the ledge in front of the bridge.

'Right! This is the fastest trawler in the Base. Those Mickeys are always shooting a line about their speed. Now we'll see what they can do when they have to stand on the pedals.' He pressed the engine-room button, waited at the voice-tube.

'Engine-room.' The voice came up from a background of noise.

'Give her everything you've got, Chief.'

The Chief looked at his steam-gauge and smiled. There was a bit in hand. 'Aye, aye, sir.' His grease-blackened hand nudged a shining wheel; silently he counted the revolutions for half a minute, then he pressed a button and spoke up the tube.

'One three o revolutions, sir.'

'That's fine! Keep her at it.' Haley stretched up and smiled.

'Fine? That's five more than the makers said she could do.' The Chief talked to himself. 'An' I've a few more she can have gin ye want to risk breakin' somethin'.'

'Yes, Sparks?' Bolt put his face to the wireless office tube.

'Air-raid warning—Blue. Gate area, sir.'

Bolt repeated it to Haley, who clicked his fingers with a sudden violence.

Bolt intercepted his glance and nodded. 'All guns manned, sir.'

Haley knew they were. It was a formality. He knew that if an enemy 'plane came into range it would have to fly through a ripping barrage of tracer. He picked up his binoculars and tried to locate *Solan* but the smoke-screen from the two ships, scarcely disturbed by the light wind, lay like a bank of fog for several miles back. He shrugged.

Regan could look after himself. He leaned on the bridge front to steady his glasses and slowly searched the sky just above the horizon. F.W. 190's invariably flew low, kipper-kissing, to avoid the radar ashore for as long as possible. Twice he stopped in his slow search and concentrated on something, but continued after a second or two. Finally he picked them up as the sun glinted from one.

'Two of them,' he grunted. 'Green seven o, going down Channel. See them? Low on the water-line.'

'Yes, sir. Wonder if they'll be curious and look behind that smoke-screen?'

'Maybe. Their curiosity will be satisfied if they do.'

Bolt watched the aircraft intently. They were four or five miles away and flying on a reciprocal course to that of the ships.

Suddenly Bolt jerked upright. 'They're turning, sir. They're cutting in towards the smoke-screen.'

In silence Haley watched the two aircraft. They lifted slightly as they turned at right angles to their previous course, then slipped down low to the water again. That lift would show them *Solan* creeping along behind the smoke. *Solan*, alone, not such a formidable opposition as nine ships in close formation.

They reached the smoke-screen and screamed over it. As they did so tracer climbed upwards; there was a sudden jolt and a shell burst close to the first machine. It swung away, dipping one wing as it did so.

'*Solan* was waiting for them, all right. There they go, swinging away inshore.' Bolt kept them framed in the circle of his binoculars. 'They're turning for another go.'

Tracer from *Solan* still chased them as they banked in an acute turn. Two thuds sounded over the water and two puffs of smoke marked the circle as shells burst in their path. Then they straightened out for another shallow dive. Haley saw them grow wider apart. They were going to try a stern and bow attack simultaneously. As the two 'planes raced towards one another *Solan* steamed slowly through the smoke-screen in a wide arc. Her 12-pounder gun spoke once before she again disappeared into the grey blanket.

The 'planes roared in, each seeming to be hanging on the end of a red necklace of tracer. They swung away at right angles and a sudden, jolting explosion sent the mist twisting up as though climbing a darker column of water and smoke. Haley caught his breath, then breathed hard in through his nose. Tracer still climbed lazily after the 'planes.

Near miss. She was still shooting. He chewed his lips and his clenched fists moved as if he were crumpling something in them. Can these Mickeys look after themselves if I go back. There's enough of them, plus *Golfitt*, and only two F.W.s. But if more come over . . . ? This was a target such as the Hun had not had for many moons. Half a dozen enthusiastic pilots would nearly wipe out the little flotilla before it could reach harbour and the protection of the shore guns.

Again the 'planes shot in, disappeared behind the smoke. Bump! The sullen thump of the explosion came some time after they watched the climbing water and smoke. Both 'planes spiralled in a climbing turn.

There was no tracer following them.

'That kippered herring is always boasting of the damage he'd do if a 'plane attacked him.' Bolt was at his side, pointing vaguely towards a Mickey whose camouflage in stripes of grey and black did resemble the comic paper conception of a herring-boned skeleton. 'They've got *Golfitt* and a couple of guns apiece.'

'Shut up!'

One 'plane circled wide and high. The other slipped along the water, parallel with the smoke-screen. From the screen *Solan*'s bow poked out like a questing animal. Flash! Her bow gun spoke; twin ribbons of tracer curved up to meet the machine, which rolled away violently. *Solan* slowly slipped back behind the screen.

'The Mickeys are turning, sir.' The signalman's voice climbed upwards in surprise. Haley looked quickly. They were breaking formation, each turning sharply back to go to the rescue of *Solan.*

'Damn and blast them! We'll have half the German air force over us in a few minutes, besides more shelling,' Haley grated. He leaned forward to the voice-pipe. 'Hard a port.'

'Hard a port, sir.'

She swung in a quick half-circle back towards *Solan.*

'Get the Senior Officer of the Mickeys. Tell him to continue on in to port. Signal *Golfitt* to take the lead.'

Arandite throbbed and trembled as the Chief drove his engines almost to full capacity. As one and then the other motor minesweeper turned again *Arandite* swept past them. As she passed the senior ship it signalled, 'We'll stick around.'

Haley answered : 'Return to harbour all speed. We are likely to attract more shelling.'

To lend emphasis to his order there were four sudden jolts and four columns of water reached above the end of the smoke-screen. They were a mile or more away. The gunners were searching behind the screen, but the shells gave added weight to Haley's order.

As *Golfitt* passed they could see the smoke still pouring from the chemical containers on her stern, adding to the long, writhing cloud astern of her.

'Can you see the 'planes?'

'No, sir. But I can hear them. They're the other side of the smoke.'

Haley listened intently, then he, too, picked up the snarl of them.

'I'm going through the screen. Stand by to open fire as soon as we break through.'

He heard Number One transmit the order, saw Clay freeze to his sights and heard the signalman swing the drum

350

on the machine-gun behind him. He dropped his head to the level of the bridge, peering through the acrid cloud round them as they steamed through the screen. Now, where was *Solan*?

Four sullen roars merged into one as four shells burst somewhere, a fairly long way off, blindly searching the screen and hoping. But where are the 'planes?

The 12-pounder barked sharply. Haley felt the blast and the biting smoke made him cough. The bow gun, clear of the smoke before the bridge, had let fly immediately it was clear. It barked again and Haley, screwing up his eyes, saw the burst of the shell low down ahead. There was only one 'plane flying close to the water. *Solan* was about a mile away, skirting the smoke-screen. Tracer skimmed the sea from her but the 'plane flew on apparently unhurt. A short distance from *Solan* the water suddenly rippled into a long line of froth as the German's guns opened up. It stopped as it reached *Solan*'s side. The plane dipped lower, then swooped up and away in a climbing turn. Two short bursts of tracer followed it, then *Solan* disappeared into a rolling, heaving climbing mass of water.

'Got her!' Bolt jerked it out.

Haley shut his eyes. He opened them again to see *Solan*'s bow cutting through the descending water.

'No, near miss.'

Arandite surged on, the bridge shaking as the engineer risked breaking something for the few extra revolutions.

'She's stopping.' The small bow wave under *Solan*'s stem died away. With the little steering way she had left she moved into the protection of the smoke. Her outlines became blurred.

Haley swiftly worked out the tide, direction of the wind, almost subconsciously. He turned to Bolt.

'Drop two smoke containers over the side. They'll go

351

with the tide and help to thicken it up.'

Bolt leaned over the back end of the bridge and passed some orders, and two containers splashed into the water, rolled heavily a few times and settled down to add their quota to the thickening protection.

'*Solan* calling, sir.' The signalman peered at the fuzzy light coming from the screen. His lamp trigger clattered.

' "My engines are out of action entirely. Will you tow me?" '

'Will I tow you? Right through hell, if need be.'

'Tell him: "Stand by to take tow. I will come up close on your starboard side." '

The lamp clicked again.

As *Arandite* slowed down and crept through the shrouding smoke towards *Solan* Haley listened intently. 'Hear any 'planes, Bunts?'

'No, sir.'

'You, Bolt?'

'Not a sound, sir. I'll nip down and see to the tow.'

Solan was only ten yards away as Haley gave his ship a touch astern to slow her down.

'Jump to it with that tow. Wait.' Five yards, three . . . 'Get it over.' Heaving lines flew through the air.

'All fast aft.' The voice came faintly from the stern.

'Slow ahead.' A bell jangled down below. He heard the slow thump of the engines. As the two ships pulled apart Haley reached for the microphone of the loud hailer. He could see a shadowy figure on the bridge of *Solan*.

'Any other damage?' he called.

There was a pause, a hollow coughing noise from *Solan*'s loud hailer. 'Nothing much. A few holes.'

Haley cocked his head to one side. That was the First Lieutenant's voice. He swallowed. 'Any casualties?'

'Yes.' The voice quavered slightly. 'Several . . . including the Old . . the Captain.'

Including the Old Man.

'How badly is . . .' Haley searched for the simple word to finish the sentence. The voice from the other ship helped him.

'In the chest, one wound. He's . . . he's lying quiet up here. He's still breathing. One man is dead, I think.' The quaver was definite now. It sounded as if he was glad to have somebody to tell it all to. 'The C.O. got it in the first attack.'

So it was Number One, youthful, impudent, who had handled the ship in and out of the smoke-screen, taking avoiding action, keeping his guns going? Up there, and alone.

Haley spoke into the voice-pipe.

'Up 20 revolutions.' He picked up the mike again.

'Your guns all right?'

'Yes, sir.' No doubt about the confidence in that reply. 'We hit one about a bit.'

'Good man! We'll soon have you in.'

'Yes, sir.' The loud hailer coughed hoarsely once. It could almost have been a sniff. 'Sir?'

'Yes?'

'He said . . . the Captain . . . just before he went unconscious . . . "Don't worry, Haley'll be along soon." I was glad to see you, sir.'

Haley clicked the switch of his loud hailer over to 'off'.

'Engine-room. I've taken *Solan* in tow. Up 20 more revolutions.'

'Aye aye, sir.'

'Aft, keep your eye on that tow. Let me know if it goes bar tight. I'm going to tow as hard as I can.'

'Aye, aye, sir.'

Somewhere ahead four sullen thuds rolled along the water. 'Go ahead! Shell all you want. I've got her in tow and I'm going to take her in if you bring the bloody guns themselves over and drop them on us.'

'Engine-room? Give her another 20.'

353

He had said: 'Don't worry, Haley'll be along soon.'

They were out in the cold, pale morning sun again, the smoke-screen dispersed and harbour little more than two miles away.

Who is that hanging around outside? *Golfitt*. Good steady ship, *Golfitt*. No flashy trimmings, but does a job to its full value. There she is, waiting to be useful if needed.

Haley chuckled quietly. Bet the Mickeys were fed up at being herded into harbour like a lot of chickens. But orders were orders; better to lose one ship than half a dozen shot up and out of commission. Let Mahoney deal with them. He gave the orders. But there would be harsh words from the M.M.s. He smiled again as he remembered Booth's description of the first motor minesweeper they ever saw. It was grotesquely camouflaged in a pattern which accentuated its chunky, almost square outline.

'Strike a light!' Booth had jerked out. 'Here's a floating council house.' Such an opportunity had been too much for him and he had signalled: 'Who knitted that pattern?' The reply had been terse.

But they were hard-working, invaluable little craft. Wonder why the Admiralty always gave them numbers? Could a man develop an affection for a number? Suppose he could. But the ships' companies gave them unofficial names.

What was the name of that one which was always having trouble with her sweep, getting it wrapped round herself? What did her crew call her? Knotted Nora. That was it. Christened in affectionate exasperation. Lends itself to elaboration. Could be Tangled Teresa. Must point that out to her C.O. We'll have a party and invite them. Send a signal: 'R P C 1900 hours to stretcher time. Bring your own thirst.' Should meet them more socially, anyway. Apart from occasional mine-sweeping conferences, it's been only signals. As Regan said. . . . His mind slipped back from pleasant conjecture as he looked over the stern. *Solan* was coming along with a nice bone in her teeth. The tow was as

354

near bar tight as he could get it. He had nudged up his revolutions five at a time until it was like a bow-string, then dropped back a couple. With no sea running the strain was even. Five knots, fair towing speed. Less than half an hour and we'll have you in expert hands. He stood watching her for a while, his mind just meandering, but refusing to contemplate the damnable luck which threatened to part him and Regan after years of close friendship.

'Bunts, *Solan* is calling.'

Haley stood behind the signalman and read the message. A wide smile enveloped his face.

'From C.O. to C.O. Nice work, Bill.'

The signalman was astonished to receive a sound slap on the back from this cold, austere officer who seldom spoke to him except to talk of signals, or to correct him when he tried guessing at words.

'Good! Let's hear some more about this, Bunts. Ask her "How is C.O. now?"'

Back came the reply: 'Taking a little nourishment. I am taking the punishment. Bleeding stopped, tongue started.'

'That's Number One. I'll bet the back-chat on the bridge on *Solan* is wonderful to hear. Like some dialogue from Hemingway. Send: "What is the damage?"'

'Wound in the ribs and slight one in the head.'

Haley smiled again. 'Send him: "Head wound could not possibly hurt you." Then we'll give him a rest.'

Just over a mile to go, a mile of smooth, slick glistening water.

Bolt grunted. 'I wondered where they had got to. Gone back for a couple more bombs. Aircraft green nine o. See them?'

Haley saw them, low on the water a few miles away, and his mouth tightened. He looked at Bolt, who nodded. A glance aft showed him *Solan*'s gun-crews grouping round the 12-pounder.

'Right! Come on in! This is no helpless, lame duck.

We are wide awake and have a punch. Come the four corners of the Luftwaffe and we shall shock them.'

'Get a long-range shot away, 4,000 yards, right in their track. It won't hit them, but they'll know we are ready.'

Bolt spoke sharply over the bridge front. The 12-pounder cracked and a few seconds later they saw the shell burst well ahead of the 'planes but in line with them. They swerved and altered course, and only the thin line of their wings could be seen.

'That's serving notice,' Bolt said.

The faint drone became a snarl as the German 'planes, abandoning any hope of a down sun stalk, came racing in. *Solan*'s gun spoke once at 1,000 yards range; tracer started ripping across the water from her Oerlikons. Bolt, mouth to voice-tube, kept his eyes on Haley. Haley nodded.

'Open fire.'

By an odd chance both *Solan* and *Arandite* concentrated on the first 'plane, and a dozen lines of tracer converged to a point on it. It lurched, climbed upwards, and let its one bomb go. The water rose in a slow plume harmlessly five hundred yards away.

For a second or two there was a pause. The second 'plane roared in unattacked. The tracer streams dropped and searched for her as the gunners strove to get her in their sights. A 12-pounder shell burst just ahead, whipping a dark shadow over the water. A little line of froth started and fell short of *Solan*. The 'plane started to lift.

Haley saw the bomb leave, like a small part of the 'plane travelling at the same speed, dropping lower. He saw it strike the water close to *Solan*'s bow. The water climbed spectacularly upwards and the thudding jolt reached *Arandite*'s bridge. It was followed by a heavier, jarring, rolling explosion, and a billowing blossom of flame and black smoke climbed upwards through the descending water of the bomb burst.

Haley watched, his heart thudding, waiting for *Solan*'s

bow to thrust through the broad, rolling column. Come on! Come on! COME ON! He beat the bridge rail with his hands in time to his silent prayer. The smoke and water dissipated, thinned until he caught the glint of shining water through it. She wasn't coming through. He saw the tow dragging slackly. The smoke cleared. The water dropped back vaporously to the sea. Stark, twisted, writhing slowly as it disappeared, was the shattered remnant of *Solan*'s stern. It slipped under, there was one huge bubble and the sea closed over it. Only bits of wreckage remained.

Mahoney was filling his pipe when a Communications Wren dropped a signal in front of him. He glanced at it; the match burned his fingers and he shook them vigorously. He moved to the door. His secretary was sitting at her desk with her head down on her arms. Mahoney moved over to her.

She heard him approach and looked up. Her eyes were dry but her lips trembled as she looked at him. Without moving her gaze she pulled open a drawer and took out a small tin. On it was a printed slip. 'Operation S.'

She swallowed, bit her trembling lip for a second. The tin tilted and a few grains of sugar fell out. 'He always brought some ashore with him. It was our little secret,' she said. ' "Operation S." "S" for "Sugar", or "*Solan*".'

Her head dropped. Mahoney let his hand rest gently on her shoulder for a second.

"I want you for some dictation, when you are ready,' he said gruffly, and returned to his room.

In the mess deck Clay stood, with arms slightly bent, facing the small crew.

'The Old Man has given orders that he doesn't want to be disturbed. If one of you—one of you, mind—makes a noise outside his room, till he shows up I'll—I'll swing him round my head and throw him over the side.' The muscles rippled on his thick arms.

The signalman, a privileged character, shook his head as he watched Clay climb on deck.

'Beats me! There's our chummy ship blown up right under our arse. What does he say? Not a peep! "Hard a starboard. Men with heaving lines on the sides." Then: "Steer for the lighthouse." Not a bleedin' peep except for orders. "Signalman, send: 'F.O.I.C., C.M.S.P. *Solan* sunk by enemy aircraft. No survivors.' Just like saying: "Pint, please, with a dash of mild." He ain't human. Ain't he got ANY feelin's at all?'

A stoker stopped scratching himself. 'What did you want him to do? Start crying?'

'He could say he was sorry, or something, couldn't he?'

'Maybe he is. Pipe down—here's Clay. Don't start him off.'

'I can speak, can't I?'

The ripple of talk silenced the indignant signalman as Clay climbed down the ladder with some clean clothes on his arm.

'You for the beach, Guns?'

Clay nodded as he arranged his clean clothes on his bunk. 'I am. I'm going to get as drunk as six fiddlers' bitches. And if that pavement-pounding, white-gaitered bunch of bastards in the Picket say one word to me . . .' His bunched fist slapped into his curved palm.

And it had come to pass that the Picket spoke harsh words—and regretted them because Clay replied. Men work off the first flaying cut of their grief in varying ways.

16

Throughout the winter and spring the fist which had been remorselessly clenching tightened every sinew, hung poised in early June—then struck. The invasion started. All the weight and power, largely American sponsored, landed on one vital spot, a weak, comparatively unguarded spot farther west, drove inland for a finger-hold on the first few days—and the world knew that allied armies had invaded northern France and had invaded to stay, to spread over it, to liberate it and to carry that liberation to all Europe.

As the build-up for the striking of the clenched fist increased more ships arrived at Base. One morning Haley walked out on deck to see four more trawlers, strangers, moored alongside the short stone pier. Their decks were filled in every available space with smoke cans and boxes. Lying out at the buoys were several fleet sweepers, ships designed for fast sweeping in front of a fleet, if necessary. They were ships of more than 1,200 tons not unlike destroyers in appearance, and were Asdic-fitted for escort work. Most of the fleet sweepers had been so employed; quite seventy per cent of their time they had been escorting from Murmansk to Malta.

Haley had looked at them with interest. It was the first time he had seen their type at close range. A little smile crossed his face as he stood scrutinising them.

One little word had stood between him and command of such a ship. Shortly after *Solan* had disappeared in a flash from an exploding magazine Mahoney had sent for Haley.

'Sit down, Haley. I want you to wait a few minutes before you make up your mind. I have been asked to submit the names of two officers capable of command of large sweepers, fleet sweepers. They must have had long experience of sweeping, among other qualifications.' Mahoney toyed with an official-looking communication in front of him. 'A month ago I would not have hesitated. You and . . . and . . .' He stopped and started again. 'A month ago I had two officers tailor-made for just that job and I would not have hesitated in recommending them. Furthermore, they would have gone, and there would have been no arguments.' He looked up and smiled at Haley. 'You know—volunteers wanted for a job so one pace forward you, you and you.' They both smiled at the little Service joke.

'No, I gather from your remarks, sir, that it is only "You, one pace forward." '

Mahoney shook his head. 'There is no "must" about it. I won't even press you, I want you to make up your own mind. Although you didn't know it, I have been having innumerable fights with heavy brass elsewhere because I had two Lieutenant-Commanders in one group, both commanding trawlers, both decorated, both experienced. It offended a certain sense of proportion and dignity in the minds of various people, and they have been chewing my ears for months to toss you into their hands. There was something to be said for their point of view. On paper it seemed a wicked waste of experienced officers, but I wanted that wealth of experience here, so I persuaded them to seek elsewhere.'

The smile crept over Haley's face again. The slight stress and hesitation over the word 'persuaded' pointed to some strenuous correspondence and possibly heated telephone conversations.

'What do you advise me to do, sir?'

Mahoney shook his head. 'You make up your own mind,

my boy. How do you feel about a larger command, more responsibility, a wider field?'

'I don't think that enters into it, sir, so far as I am concerned. This is not my career. There are various reasons why I would like to finish the war here; they are purely sentimental, but real.'

'I know. There is another point.' Mahoney stood up and crossed to the shuttered window. He opened it and stepped out on to the little balcony. 'Your work here is virtually done. Look.'

It was a grey day, with occasional wisps of rain, visibility was down to about five or six miles. Haley looked out over the Base, beyond the stone piers, out to sea. With a destroyer in the lead a convoy of ships was steaming eastwards, brazenly, openly, some of them regardless of the smoke pouring from their funnels. Passing them down the other channel was a smaller convoy of tugs. Some had London barges in tow, others had mysterious, un-shiplike objects wallowing astern of them.

'Two convoys passing, in daylight, and each with an optional channel into which they can be diverted. And not a mine in the entire Swept Channel. At least, I hope not,' Mahoney added hastily.

Haley shook his head. 'Not one, sir. If there is I'll have it for lunch. Bit impudent, that, sir, isn't it?' He jerked his head seawards.

Mahoney shrugged. 'A reasonable risk. Necessary in view of the urgency of the invasion build-up, and possible because . . . because of the work done around here. And that is going on all round the country at this moment.'

They walked back to the table after Mahoney had fastened the window. C.M.S.P. opened a drawer and pulled out some strips of printed cardboard and placed them on the table.

'From our personal point of view the cost has been heavy. Because'—he leaned forward—'because we knew the men

361

and the ships intimately. Their loss was something personal. But in terms of men and ships—and that can be the only assessment in war—we have lost . . .' Mahoney lifted up the strips of cardboard and tossed them down on the table one by one like a player laying down a hand of cards . . . '*Bathdown* . . . *Pwlldu* . . . *Hartland Point* . . . before your time, I think . . . *Pearl* . . . *Sheila* . . . and'—he glanced at Haley —'*Regan*. A round total of nine or ten ships, about ninety men. I'm not counting the ships which were badly damaged and went elsewhere after repairs.' Mahoney sat down. 'In return for that I have never had to make the signal: 'Swept Channel closed by mines for an indefinite period.' Not once in nearly five years. Cold figures and cold comfort, probably, but there it is.' He shuffled the strips of cardboard between his fingers, then tossed them into an open drawer. 'In the overall picture of the war it might be a minute fragment, a tiny detail, but'—he tapped his table with a fingertip—'it was worth it. Think over that larger command offer, Haley. Let me know in the morning.'

'I can give you an answer now, sir, but I'll give it a night's thought.'

'Good!'

As he passed the Wren in the outer office he stopped at her desk, cocked an inquiring eye at her, then tilted a chin towards the drawer. She smiled, opened the drawer, pulled out a small tin and shook it speculatively.

'Another day, maybe' she said.

'Give.' Haley held out his hand. She placed in it the tin labelled 'Operation S'. He thrust it into his pocket. 'Back in the morning with "Operation S" completed,' he smiled. Not only 'Operation S' would be complete; 'Operation Promotion Refusal' would be delivered bound and sealed.

Haley walked through the small town and out into the country until he came to the gate against which he and Regan had leaned the first time he had been shown Great Oaks. Once again spring was delivering its message, thrusting irresistible evidence under the nose of decrepit winter to prove that his departure was over due.

A mental frieze of disconnected pictures passed through his mind, disconnected in the sense that they jumped long periods, were of different people and different ships, but a fine thread guided them along in a given direction. He had reached the point where he could think of the loss of *Solan* without the pain being acute. It had been that way after he had heard of *Culver*'s loss. The same for a little while after Booth went.

But Regan would never merge into the background in quite that way. Time would soften the savage, raw edges but so much would remain sharp, vivid.

He remembered the moments after he had seen *Solan*'s twisted stern slide under the water. Inside him there had been a boiling turmoil. He had wanted to scream, to beat the bridge with his hands, yell foul obscenities after the twisting, weaving 'plane disappearing low down over the sea. Again he heard a voice repeat an order up the voice-pipe.

'Hard to starboard.'

Another voice, Bolt's, had answered: 'Men on either side with heaving lines. Aye, aye, sir.'

Somebody had guided *Arandite* through the pitiful bits of wreckage floating aimlessly about, aimless and detached from the body of which they had been so long a part.

A small wooden raft, carefully painted in yellow. On one side of it *Solan*'s Number One had inscribed a large red 'L' on a white square and beneath it a red triangle with the letters 'F.W.B.'. It had been one of his many outlets for his bubbling humour. He had it in mind to add 'No right-hand signals' and had discussed it earnestly with Regan. Now it floated past, empty.

A deck-chair, its canvas repaired with naval sailcloth. Regan's Leading Hand had 'found it' one night and brought it on board to soften the blow inevitable for overstaying night leave.

A box, an empty drum, a line of washing still attached to a boat-hook, somebody's dhobi-ing sliding by half submerged, long pants, short flannel, a vest or two and a towel, trailing aimlessly through the water as if looking for the round, sturdy body to which they belonged. A cork fender, bobbing in the water, bringing a faint spark of hope because it looked like a head, but the spark had died as quickly as does that at the glowing end of a match.

Golfitt and *Arandite* had quartered every inch of the wreckage-cluttered spot. And returned to harbour.

The ship came alongside; somebody giving a series of terse orders; telegraphs ringing and mooring lines snaking up to the quay, and all the time Haley had wanted to scream and yell. The picture he had had clearly in his mind was the descending, thinning water, with the sun glistening through it, his tow dragging weightless in the sea. *Solan*'s bow was not coming through. He had striven to hold in his mind the picture at the point where the water was still climbing, mixing with the smoke. He had tried to hold it still, as a film projector can suddenly freeze and hold its actors motionless in a gesture. He had wanted to keep it like that until *Solan*'s bow came through it, glistening, water dripping from every plate and angle, rising and falling as it clove through the explosion-riven water. But the picture refused to stay frozen; the two WOULD come through dragging, attached to nothing astern of him. The sun WOULD glint through the descending vapour. *Solan*'s bow would NOT come through.

Haley recalled sitting on his settee for a few minutes until a knock at the door brought him jerking upwards.

'Ship all fast, sir. Leave to one watch from 1300 hours?'

Bolt, Number One, First Lieutenant. Stolid, unimaginative. If all Hell fell on him and the ship he would say afterwards: 'All Hell cleared away, sir. Leave to one watch 1300 hours?'

Haley had nodded as Bolt looked at his face, haggard,

364

eyes narrowed up to slits, mouth set in a fine, hard line forming a triangle with the two lines which ran from its corners up to the sides of the nose.

'Grant leave. I . . . I don't want to be disturbed for a while, Number One.'

'Very good, sir.'

Haley had slipped the brass catch on his door, standing, eyes closed, hands rigid to his sides. Then a hoarse, inarticulate noise had broken from his lips. In a scrambling, rushing dive he had flung himself on the settee and lain face down with his head rocking from side to side.

Haley found much comfort from his visits to Great Oaks during the succeeding weeks. Mrs. Lambert proved to be a woman of wisdom and understanding. With a great deal of subtlety she guided him into conversations in which he talked at length about his ship, about *Solan,* about Regan.

'I, too, know the grief that seems so heavy—too heavy —at times,' she told him once as they strolled between the rows of gnarled oaks. 'Twice have I had taken from me by war somebody I loved very much.' She stopped and a faraway look crept into her eyes. 'My husband . . . that was in the last war, brutal senseless war that it was. And now . . . I don't know where Alistair is. I merely keep hoping. Sometimes hope says: "I can't go on. I must have something to sustain me." ' She stopped by a tree and looked at Haley. 'When that happens I come out here and walk among the trees. When grief is too heavy to carry I lean against one and listen to the wind through the branches It says softly: "Keep faith. In time all things work out." ' She drew her light coat round her shoulders. 'I find it cold out here. You sailors are so hardy. Don't you hurry in. Tea will be ready in an hour.' Her hand rested lightly on his shoulder, then she turned and walked away. As she climbed the stone steps she looked back.

Haley was standing with his back against an oak tree. His

face was lifted up—as if he were listening.

But at times he missed Regan painfully, both at sea and in harbour. The pain would become severe after a period of introspection. He would be standing on the bridge during an operation, and when the necessity came for a decision the thought would flash into his mind : 'I wonder what Regan will say?' and then would come the stab of pain. Sometimes he would be stretched out in the deep arm-chair in the ward-room, with the fire glowing and only one light burning, leaving the corners in soft shadow. Something would occur to him and he would turn to the settee, which Regan always occupied when he came on board. An inarticulate, intro-ductory sound would escape from his lips as he started to say something to Regan who would be there, who SHOULD be there. The place would be empty. Again the stab of pain and a clenched fist ground into a palm.

On one occasion he was so shaken that he left a cinema queue and walked to the Officers' Club, a curious, weak feeling attacking him at the back of his knees. It was dark and the queue moved slowly towards the dimly lit vestibule. A girl's voice behind him said : 'What's on, anyway?'

'A musical,' a voice replied. 'But the second picture is a western. Posse riding and the sheriff saying : "They're gone thataway. We'll go thisaway," but 'tis the horses I'm liking.' The accent was richly Irish, the words almost pure Regan, as were the sentiments. Haley spun round with a gasp and peered at the speaker, a vague shadow behind him. So start-ling was the effect on him that he pushed his way roughly out of the queue. ' 'Tis the horses I'm liking. . . . We'll have him on a pony as soon as he walks, Bill, me bhoy, and him over a good Irish bank with a seat as safe as the Bank of Eire. . . . Him with the biggest trout ever caught in Tralee at the end of his line and me with a word of wisdom at his elbow . . . he's something to keep faith with, Bill. . . .'

Haley had strode into the Club and ordered a large whisky.

'You don't look too good, Haley. Anything wrong?' A Mickey captain was solicitous.

'No, just tired, but leave me by myself, old man, will you?'

But there was one moment when Regan's name was mentioned and it brought an inward glow to Haley. Shortly after the large fleets sweepers arrived in the Base he received a personal note from the Senior Officer on *Radstock* asking him if he could come on board that afternoon. Mahoney amplified it.

'They're here to do a big sweeping job. You know the waters here better than anybody. You'll find *Radstock* a cheery ship. A drifter will take you off at 1400.'

It was drizzling with rain when the drifter took him off and Haley wore a raincoat, a somewhat shabby and paint-dabbed veteran for which he had great affection.

'Haley, Commanding Officer *Arandite*. I believe your Commanding Officer is expecting me,' he told the young Sub-lieutenant who was Officer of the Day. As he walked along the steel deck he was struck at the similarity in lay-out to that of a destroyer. But for a firm 'no' he might have been in command of just such a ship.

'Skipper Haley from the trawler, sir.' The young Sub-lieutenant infused his announcement with a suggestion of superiority. Haley's lips twitched. He could imagine the youngster ushering a supplicant in to the manager of a bank. 'A man about an overdraft, sir.'

The officer on the settee, Commanding Officer of *Radstock* and Senior Officer of the flotilla, stood up and held out his hand. He was a youthful Commander, R.N.

'So glad you made it,' he said with a smile. 'Try a noggin?'

Haley declined.

'Commander Mahoney, whom God preserve until the sands of the desert grow cold, tells me you are the one man who can save my bright young things from putting half my

367

flotilla ashore on the banks outside. Grab a pew.'

Haley sat down. 'I can't subscribe to that entirely, but if I can help I will do so gladly.' He looked round him and went on: 'This brings back a few memories. Not unlike destroyers, are they not?'

'My spiritual home's destroyers. Do you ken the breed?'

They talked of ships and destroyers and swung back to Mahoney.

'I was a snottie with him when he was in command. What a lád, what a man!' The Commander looked curiously at Haley. 'We had him and his wife on board to dine last night. Interesting talker, isn't he? He kept us enthralled, yet didn't step outside the harbour once with his yarns.'

'You should meet Cutter, our Maintenance Commander. You'd be fascinated.'

'I must arrange it. Cigarette?' The Commander offered a light. 'You prefer trawlers?'

The query was casually put and for a moment its significance escaped Haley. But only for a moment. Easy, Bill, me boy! He's edging you towards the end of a plank and a slight push will put you off.

'It's scarcely a question of preference. I didn't want minesweeping in any shape or form, certainly not in trawlers. But now . . . well, after four years . . .' He finished with a gesture.

The Commander nodded. 'I know just what you mean.' He stood up. 'Not bad ships, these; fast enough for the job. We've been doing escort work mainly since commission. A couple of trips to Murmansk, Iceland—all cold stuff. I've just finished a flotilla work-up on sweeping. Hadn't seen some of the ships for months. They turned up from the four corners of the universe. You know—"Doctor Livingstone, I presume? I'm part of your flotilla, and what about some perishing leave?"'

'How did the work-up go?'

'For your information, Oxcar is now forty feet to the

368

east of its charted position. We towed it. We missed Inch-keith Island. It was dark.' The dry comment hid a wealth of bitter errors of omission and commission.

Haley laughed out loud. 'We all did it.'

'I assure you our early efforts were superlative. Instructors went white-haired overnight.'

The Commander pressed a button. 'Messenger, tell the Pilot I want him to bring the charts of this area down to the wardroom. Shall we get to business?' He turned to Haley.

Together they walked to the wardroom, and Haley felt a little catch in his throat. It was a typical wardroom with typical wardroom inhabitants. Five officers occupied chairs or settees and were engaged in the Service-wide occupation of baiting a midshipman.

'. . . *Voulez vous promenade avec moi* will get you into trouble, Mid. You stick to *au revoir.*'

The midshipman, reading a green-back book, *French for the Forces*, stood up as Haley and the Commander entered.

'Don't let them get you down, Mid,' the Commander said. 'I like the bit, *comme ci, comme ca*. It has a musical ring about it.' He turned to an officer who came through the door with a rolled-up chart under his arm. 'Ah, Pilot, spread it out. The Commanding Officer of *Arandite* is going to give us a tip or two. He knows these waters, actually swept over in front of Bill the Conqueror. Mason, take the Lieutenant-Commander's raincoat, will you?' The young officer who had greeted Haley at the gangway allowed his eyebrows to arch. Lieutenant-Commander, and he had called him skipper! Well, the raincoat looked frowsy, anyway.

Haley surrendered his coat to the young officer and caught him eyeing the blue-and-white ribbon of the D.S.C.

'This is the bit that has been worrying me.' The Commander covered an area with his hand. 'It looks confoundedly cramped, and look at the tides! You'll have to whip it in quick, Mason, or you'll have the sweep wrapped round the buoys in less time than that.'

'There have been illustrious precedents,' Haley said dryly. He leaned forward. 'It looks more alarming than it is. Actually, you will find that the tide kicks off that bank in reverse direction to the run and is a help. It used to be a bit tricky when the Swept Channel was only two cables wide, but now it's three times that you will have all the room in the world.'

'Still a bit naughty if visibility is down,' the Navigating Officer interjected thoughtfully.

'Extremely naughty on a dark night with a fresh wind loaded with rain.' The Commander looked at Haley from the corners of his eyes.

Sub-lieutenant Mason stood upright. 'We're not going to career about there in the dark, sir?' His voice climbed upwards incredulously.

'We are not, thank heaven. But it has been done, with the odd *E*-boat providing noises off.'

'But, sir . . .' The Commander held up his hand.

'Ask Haley; he's been doing it for years. It was all night Sweeping round here until recently, wasn't it?'

'Yes. What with shelling, aircraft and *E*-boats at night, it was . . .' Haley searched for a word.

'Distracting?' The Midshipman provided one.

Haley nodded.

The doubting Mason submitted his point. 'A quick dash-out, a swift search sweep, and nip in smartly before the Hun was awake, I take it.'

Haley looked at him solemnly. 'Young man, with little persuasion I could dislike you. A portion or two more of sweeping out there, and less of the *Manual of Minesweeping*, and you might be good enough for a Number One on the trawler you mention with such a wealth of comment.'

The First Lieutenant, a Lieutenant, R.N.V.R., stared coldly at Mason.

370

'Had you stayed on board last night and listened, instead of tearing off ashore on conquest bent, you would have heard something. The ships here did search and field sweeping by night—that means in the dark, Sub—in this area, which gives me a cold sweat at the thought of doing it in daylight.'

'I'd want survivor leave every time I came back into harbour,' the Midshipman chuckled.

Mason joined issue with him.

'You want leave any old time.'

Baiting midshipmen can be a painful game. They carry a sting in their tongues.

'Some people want it because a Dornier hits them with a snowball,' the Mid murmured. The laugh was all-embracing.

'I'd better explain,' the First Lieutenant said. 'We were off Iceland with a convoy and a Dornier dropped a bomb quite a way off. It dislodged an appreciable amount of hard snow in one foul swoop. And Mason got the lot. He thought we had been hit. . . .'

'And nattered about shattered nerves all the way home,' Pilot added.

Mason decided to make the best of it and grinned. 'It was damned cold, I assure you. And I had just come on watch.'

The Commander had been watching Haley's face all the time while listening to the back-chat. He broke into a smile as Haley turned to the midshipman and asked innocently: 'Have you by any chance any old copies of *Men Only*?'

'Yes, sir, lots. Do you want some? I'm afraid some of the best bits have been cut out.'

'That's what I thought. But you have them framed in your berth, of course?'

'Yes, sir, but how did you know?' Frank curiosity lit up his face.

'A little bird told me.'

'Run true to type, don't they?' the Commander chuckled. 'Now, tell me one thing more. Can I do a cross-tide sweep here?'

For the next hour or so the chart was well investigated and Haley thoroughly cross-examined. Finally the Pilot, Commander and First Lieutenant stood up. As the chart was rolled the Commander said: 'I feel a lot better about it now. I'm deeply grateful. Haley, dine with us tonight?'

The others added their pressure and Haley dined with them. As the evening progressed, and a few drinks thawed him out, he related amusing stories of trawler crews, about Noisy's unofficial gun, of Booth's drawings on the charts, and laughter was frequent and hearty.

As he stood finishing his last drink the First Lieutenant said: 'We heard a lot about an Irishman last night. At first we thought you were he today. But the C.O. told us he was . . . .' He trailed off.

Haley hesitated, the remnant of his drink hovering near his lips. He tossed it back and put his glass down. 'Yes,' he said.

The First Lieutenant smiled slightly. 'Quite a stout lad, wasn't he?'

'He was; "stout lad" is right. Come to think of it, there could be worse epitaphs. He would have enjoyed tonight. If he had gone perhaps we—he and I—would have been on just such ships as this, he and I. A last drink before turning in. If he hadn't gone. . . .'

Haley's smile was soft and reflective. 'You're right. Stout as they make them.'

As he stood on deck saying good night to the Commander and First Lieutenant, the Commander said: 'I wish you were coming out with us, Haley.'

Haley thought swiftly. Nothing was scheduled for the next day. Number One could run the ship for a day in harbour.

'Can do,' he replied.

'I mean in command of'—the officer's head moved slowly towards the dim bulk of the other fleet sweepers moored to buoys near—'one of them.'

The motor-boat slipped swiftly across the small harbour; a whistle cheeped and the boat slid alongside *Arandite*. Haley climbed on board, watched the motor-boat curve back to its parent. He rested his hand on the dented rail of the trawler as he heard the Quartermaster clatter out of the galley and along the deck. He patted the rail softly. 'It's been too long for a divorce now, old girl. Anyway, you haven't provided me with any grounds.' He swayed gently away from the rail.

' 'Evening, sir. Number One's on board and turned in.' Time-honoured question and answer. Number One's on board and turned in. God's in his Heaven and the world is all right.

'Like some coffee, sir?'

'I would.'

In his room he pulled his writing-pad towards him. Now was the time to write, when he was slackened down, when nervous tension was not battling for the right things to say.

'Mother of His Royal Fatness and H.R.F. himself. Darling,' he started. The first page or so was a letter from a man to his wife, then he went on:

Any time now the balloon will go up. Somehow I feel that I will come through it all. I have a hunch that my allotted task is practically done. All I have to do is to taper it off and come home. I've been out tonight and dined with a nice lot of fellows. One of them voiced the perfect epitaph for Regan. 'He was a stout lad.' Couldn't improve on that. This is a strict order to His Regal Tubbiness. Tell him to hold you tightly until I arrive to take over. . . .

It was the sort of letter a woman reads, keeps in an apron

373

pocket and reads again, and little damp stains on it makes the ink run.

A few weeks later Mahoney sent for him. To say goodbye. On his sleeves he had four gold rings.

'They've found me out, Haley. Some hush-hush job for the invasion. I'll have to work for a living. Look after yourself. We'll meet again, I've no doubt.'

As Haley walked slowly back on board the last words ran over and over in his mind. 'We'll meet again . . . we'll meet again . . . we'll meet again . . . we'll meet again.' Sickly, sentimental words to a sickly, sentimental tune, yet they had the depth of a heartfelt prayer. 'We'll meet again, don't know where, don't know when . . . but we'll meet again some sunny day.'

Mahoney's successor viewed trawlers as carriers and fetchers and maids-of-all-work. They did no sweeping. Some were utilised for smoking convoys through. Others departed, unsung, to other ports.

The invasion came and went. The first breathless excitement died away, and it was realised that the event was the beginning of a long slugging match. Up the coast careered the troops. Keeping pace with them went ships. Port after port fell. The big guns the other side blazed off all their ammunition before tamely surrendering.

The intimate touch of war passed Haley by.

He stood outside Base office a few months after the invasion had been launched and watched the sentry spring to salute. So much had happened since the day he first saw a sentry there. Haley shrugged and went in.

'Oh, Haley, I have orders for you. You are to take four other trawlers with you and sail for this port.' The new C.M.S.P. named a port in northern France. 'I don't know what the job is. I gather you will not be coming back here. Sail 0900 tomorrow morning.'

Just that. Nearly five years and 'Sail 0900 . . . you will not be coming back here.' Not coming back to a place which at times he had salted with bitter tears.

The challenge from the pier-head in the French port was prompt. After a short delay a signal followed. 'Enter harbour. Senior Officer to report to S.N.O.M.S.N.E. forthwith.'

'Do we say that, sing it, or write it on the wall?' Bolt asked.

'Don't ask me! The world is full of puzzling fractions of the alphabet.'

Haley walked ashore looking curiously about him. These were the ports from which his old friends, the E-boats, had sailed. Their crews had walked these very streets, boasting of the mines they had laid, bragging of the trawlers they had shot up. 'And bemoaning their dead, too,' he finished grimly.

He reached the building from which flew a White Ensign. He entered, passed through various rooms until a Wren officer looked at him inquiringly.

'Lieutenant-Commander Haley?'

Haley nodded.

'This way, please.'

She tapped at a door, opened it and spoke round it. 'Lieutenant-Commander Haley to see you, sir.' She stepped to one side and held the door wide open. Haley gave her a passing smile as he went in and faced the table.

Sitting the other side of it was Captain Mahoney.

'Got you! Thought you'd seen the last of the old slave-master, eh?' Mahoney's hand was outstretched. 'And not before time. The tea is horrible. No sugar. Haven't had a decent cup for weeks. How are you, Haley?'

17

Mahoney spread a large chart over a trestle table. As he placed two books to hold down the curling edges he smiled at Haley. 'Like old times, this, isn't it?' The refractory chart finally reacted to treatment and they both leaned over it. 'Now, this is the job.' Mahoney rested his elbows on the chart and ran his hands along the coast. 'The invasion has gone quicker than we planned, at least in one respect. We thought the Hun would put up more resistance in these important ports.' He touched Dieppe, Fécamp, Boulogne and Calais. 'But he hasn't. The only place where he has stuck his toes in is Dunkirk. I can't make out why, but he has.' He stood up, turned his back to the table and leaned against it. 'So minesweeping has been strictly utilitarian. We have cleared channels into the harbours, two-cable channels leading from the main QZ, and swept the harbours. I want the edges trimmed both sides until they are at least six cables wide, and in some cases I want a sort of fan-shaped approach swept clear, plus an anchorage area outside the harbours. Can do?'

Haley looked at the chart, then met Mahoney's eyes. 'Daylight work, sir?'

Mahoney nodded. Haley stepped back.

'Sorry, sir, I can't do it. My Union strictly forbids me to do any sweeping after sunrise. My last employer will tell you that I'm clean about the house, have no followers, but I'm only good at night sweeping.'

Mahoney chuckled. 'Your last employer could say a lot

more, too. He regrets that he cannot occasionally arrange a couple of *E*-boats to keep you on your toes. I'll promise you the next best thing. The Hun has introduced a one-man submarine. Heard about them? They have a big nuisance-value and, make no mistake, those boys would consider a minesweeping trawler a first-class prize.'

Cigarette-ends accumulated in the ashtray and others burned away on its edge as they discussed the project.

'Well, there it is. I've collected a mixed bag of ships. You brought . . . er . . . four, with an M.L., a drifter and with an old yacht which—shall we say?—came my way we have a sort of Harry Tate's outfit. You will be directly under me and I will now and then come to sea with you. We have no permanent home. We shift up the coast and take our bag and baggage on the yacht.'

Haley clicked his fingers. 'This formidable array of initials. S.N.O. something or other?'

'Senior Naval Officer Minesweeping in Northern Europe. Quite a mouthful, isn't it?'

Haley returned on board with his feet walking on air. He attempted no analysis of the feeling of exhilaration. It was just there. The fact that shortly he would be sweeping mines again, with a reasonable prospect of more explosions far too frequent and far too close, he thrust well to the back of his mind. Lying astern of *Arandite* was an old clipper-bowed steam yacht, graceful in every line, defying even the Admiralty grey paint to conceal her beauty. So that was Mahoney's flagship?

'Number One,' he said briskly as soon as he was on board, 'come down the wardroom. I have a lot to talk about.'

The ears of the group of seamen standing near pricked up and Clay whispered: 'Tell that flunkey to get cracking. Get some coffee down to the wardroom, and tell him to keep his big lugs open.'

'About leave, sir. Any chance of one watch having a

377

couple of hours before we sail?' Bolt looked inquiringly at Haley.

'Certainly. Leave to 2300. Find out what money the men have and how much they want in casual payments, then go to the Base and collect it in francs.' He lifted his voice slightly for the benefit of the seamen. 'We are going to live here for a while.'

Down in the wardroom he gave Bolt all the details he had and then outlined what they would want in the way of gear. Their wants were simple except for a new contraption Mahoney had described. It was a long tube down which a succession of Mills hand grenades were thrust. As they emerged the lever was released and the grenades exploded six seconds after entering the water, the intervals of explosion being decided by the speed at which they were released from the tube.

'A new type of mine and all they know is that it gives a measure of immunity. See that you have a couple of ratings instructed in it. Oh, by the way, the Hun has a new submarine. A one-man job which feeds on trawlers. That yacht astern is Asdic-fitted and she will have to spot them for us.'

The steward discreetly climbed the companionway. 'We're going to carry a lot of small bombs to fight one-man submarines. Us and the yacht astern. The Boss ashore here is our old Boss. The Old Man has a smile like a cat wot's drunk all the milk.' His audience listened intently. 'This is our new Base for keeps—until we move up the coast, the Old Man says.'

A stoker joined the small group. 'I thought you said these kids spoke foreign,' he said.

'So they do.'

'Well, the couple I was talking to on the quay knows plenty of English. They asked me for chocolates and cigarettes. When I said "No" they called me something shocking.'

378

sheet. As if they were saying: 'Tear and rend yourselves as much as you like. Rip your ships apart, break your men into many hideous pieces, but when I take them and close over them nobody sees anything afterwards.'

It was about here that Booth . . . Haley shrugged vigorously once. He turned and looked shorewards. Just inside, a couple of hundred yards, Regan had come through the murk of a winter's morning, had come out of the dark when fear shared the bridge, when things were going bomp in the night. Go on, look out over there, farther west! That was where he waited, that is where he lies, just where that big-bellied tramp is rolling along. Maybe her screws are beating his requiem.

'Maybe you will die, maybe I will, and a lot more of us besides, but that ingrained faith will live . . . faith to plant acorns.' Haley spun swiftly. Only Bolt and the signalman were on the bridge with him. 'That's the BIG THING—FAITH . . . we'll have him casting a fly . . . or on a pony, maybe, and him with head and heart up . . . He said: "Don't worry; Halcy will be along soon." . . .'

Haley felt his throat go tight; his eyes burned and the little muscles in the corners of his mouth bunched.

He heard the clatter of the signalman's lamp behind him. 'Worry away, ocean-going corvette, worry away! You afraid you'll have to come back to pick up survivors? Nobody comes back until they've finished the job around here, but I can't tell you that.'

'Corvette says, sir, "Those waters have not been fully swept." '

'As if I didn't know that, corvette! But where you are has been swept, time and time again; it was never closed up. We saw to that. Any day, any night, you could have sailed through there because we kept it open. We, *Sheila, Morning Star, Solan* . . . Five long years.'

'Answer: "Thanks." ' Clatter-clatter.

'Answer made, sir.'

Haley leaned forward to the wheel voice-pipe.

'Hard a-port. Full ahead.'

Arandite began to tremble as her screw bit into the waters. Her bow swung round and the boil of water under her stern lengthened into a wake.

'Steady... Steer N 65 E.'

'Corvette is calling again, sir.' The signalman sounded peeved. Why didn't the Old Man choke him off?

'From the corvette, sir. "Where are you going?" '

A smile stole over Haley's face; he clicked his finger towards the signalman. 'Give me the lamp.' He rested it on his forearm with the V-sight framing the corvette and the trigger clattered.

'Home to plant acorns.'

He leaned forward and pressed the engine-room button. A voice spoke dimly from a background of noise. 'Engine-room.' Haley put his mouth to the voice-piece. 'Whack her up—full revolutions! We're going home.'